Hear No Evil

GEORGIE HALE

Hear No Evil

Hodder & Stoughton

First published in Great Britain in 2004 by Hodder and Stoughton
A division of Hodder Headline

All characters in this publication are fictitious
and any resemblance to real persons, living or dead,
is purely coincidental.

A CIP catalogue record for this title
is available from the British Library

ISBN 0 340 81835 2

Typeset in Plantin by Hewer Text Ltd, Edinburgh
Printed and bound by Mackays of Chatham Ltd, Chatham, Kent

Hodder and Stoughton
A division of Hodder Headline
338 Euston Road
London NW1 3BH

For the small hands in mine that make me strong

Nicola Smith turned the key in the lock and stepped quietly into the apartment. She stood quite still for a moment, breathing in the clean, welcoming smell of fresh paint, then walked down the hall, feeling her way in the darkness, visualising the layout from the plans she had seen so many times. Her spiky heels clacked on the hardwood floor. But that was all right. There was no one to hear. She'd arrived early enough to be sure of that.

She pushed the door open into the living-room. Not so dark in here; the streetlights below streamed in through the thin voile curtains on the huge patio window that took up the whole of the far wall. The unmistakable, expensive scent of new leather mingled with the paint smell. She ran her hand lovingly over the arm of one of the low sofas that flanked the marble fireplace. Soon, this luxury would be hers. Not here, of course. Not in Coventry. That would be indiscreet, and discretion was something to which Nicola Smith had become very accustomed. But somewhere. Soon.

She crossed the room and held back the curtain to survey the scene below her. In the distance, she could see the snake of the ring road. Closer to, the ghostly blue light of the West Orchard shopping centre dome illuminated the darkening sky. Cranes spiked up from the bottom of Hertford Street and the new buildings going up there. The Phoenix Initiative, the council called it; Coventry rising from the ashes. Nicola's mouth twisted.

Pretentious crap. But the place was finally on the up, no doubt about it; reinventing itself as Cardiff and Liverpool and Manchester had done before it. Even the concrete wasteland of its traffic-free centre was at last beginning to come to life, dilapidated factories transforming themselves into luxury city-living apartments, run-down shops into trendy bars and restaurants. Under different circumstances, she might even have been tempted to stick around. But she couldn't wait to get away from this city where she'd been born and bred. From the dump of a terraced house in Earlsdon with the pigsty students one side and the family of screaming kids the other. From the mind-numbing boredom of the office. Most of all, from the moron she'd been stupid enough to marry. The man – if you could call him a man – at whom she looked every morning, and couldn't remember a single reason why she'd ever fancied him. Everything about him bored her. Even down to the sur-name he'd lumbered her with. Smith. What sort of a bloody name was that? The sour grimace distorting Nicola's small, regular features eased into a smile of triumph. She wouldn't be looking at him much longer. And she wouldn't be using his name, that was for sure. No more plain Nicola Smith for her.

She slipped the catch on the patio window and stepped out onto the tiny balcony, shivering slightly in the chilly evening air. In the distance, a siren wailed. She could see the counterpoint of blue lights flashing their way along the ring road. Some pathetic little crook robbing a second-hand car, or making off with a few hundred quid from a post office somewhere. She despised the unambitious. Soon, she'd have her own pent-house miles away from here; take up her place in the kind of life she'd craved for so long. The kind of life she deserved.

She took a compact from her bag, flipped open the mirror, touched up her scarlet lipstick. It was important she looked her best, although he wouldn't be here for a while yet. She'd wanted some time on her own first. Just to savour the moment, to take in the full luxury of the realisation that this was to be the very last time. That from now on there would be no more subterfuge, no more clandestine meetings. Maybe she'd even miss the excitement of it all. But not that much.

She examined the face her mother had always said would be her fortune. The silly bitch had never taken it on board that if a woman wanted to get on in this world, brains mattered as much as beauty. And if you had both, so much the better. Nicola Smith allowed herself a small, complacent smile.

She was concentrating too hard on her young, pretty reflection in the little gilt mirror to hear the muffled click of the latch, the soft pad of stockinged feet along the hallway, too intent on the perfection of her curving scarlet smile to see the figure that paused for a moment in the dimness of the living-room to observe her.

The face that had been predicted to be Nicola Smith's fortune was about to become her very literal downfall.

It wasn't until she caught a second reflection in the mirror that she realised she wasn't alone on the balcony. And by then, of course, it was too late.

Maybe if her heels had been less spindly, she could have maintained her balance. Maybe if she had been less rigid in her dieting over the years, she would have had sufficient bulk to put up some kind of a fight. But as it was, it took only the minimum of effort for her neat little frame to be pitched over the balcony of the penthouse flat.

Nicola Smith's scarlet mouth opened wide, screaming a name into the cool evening air as she flailed her final, helpless journey to the newly paved communal patio forty feet below.

But that was all right. There was no one to hear.

2

Blood.

Diane Middleton recognised the warm stickiness without having to see it; recognised the dull drag of the stomachache that had woken her. And the sharper pain of loss.

She pulled herself up in bed and looked at the alarm clock. Four forty-five. Sunlight already streamed through the crack in the curtains. Beside her, her husband stirred and muttered, then rolled onto his side, the pattern of his gentle, regular snoring disturbed for no more than a couple of seconds.

Diane wondered whether to wake him. It would be good to have his arms around her, let his comforting words wash over her. She laid her hand on his shoulder, but he frowned, muttering in his sleep as he moved away from her touch. Carefully, she withdrew her hand, eased herself out of the bed and went through to the bathroom. Better to let him sleep.

Not looking in the mirror, she stripped off, and put her nightdress to soak in the basin. She turned the shower to full power, gasping as the hot needles of water battered her upturned face, and tried to empty her mind. She forced herself to focus on the list of things she had to do that day. Malcolm was playing golf and having lunch at the club, so she wouldn't have to bother preparing anything. She'd said she'd be at Ian's around nine, and that would probably take some time. Maybe she could get to the studio for a couple of hours first, make a start on sorting out the stuff for the exhibition. Better that way round. She'd need her wits about her to decide how to go about choosing the right pieces, and she was bound to have more energy first thing than when she got back from Ian's, and the chaos of the children.

The children. A sudden wave of despair reared up to engulf her. Stepping quickly from the shower, she opened the window, welcoming the coldness of the breeze against her wet skin as she sucked in gulps of the sharp morning air. She'd only been a few days late. It had been stupid to imagine, to hope . . .

She grabbed a towel and rubbed briskly at her skin. Concentrate on the plans for Agnes's surprise birthday celebration. She and Ian needed to finalise the arrangements, get everything booked. They'd been talking about it on and off for weeks, trying to come to some sort of decision; their mother wasn't the easiest person to please. Diane grimaced as she dragged a comb through her dripping hair, her thoughts temporarily diverted from everything but the impending party. Maybe she could talk Ian out of his latest hare-brained scheme. Much better to invite only adults, somewhere civilised. A few of Agnes's closest friends, instead of practically everyone she'd ever met. Ian's idea had disaster written all over it. What if it rained, for one thing? There was no guarantee the present spell of lovely spring weather would last. There was no guarantee that anything lasted.

Abruptly, Diane dropped the comb. Just face it. Face the disappointment, the same as she had done every month for the last fifteen years. She rubbed an impatient hand across her eyes. Face it and move on. Focus on all that was good in her life – her satisfying career, her comfortable marriage, the beauty of this glorious spring day. She rested her head against the window frame. The sun was already beginning to warm the wood. She tried to view the garden outside as if it were a prospective painting, concentrating on the clarity of the early-morning colours, the pleasing form of the weeping larch, the mass of pansies in the Dutch wall, their small, perfect faces turned up towards her like an expectant audience. The sky was a flawless blue, the air thick with quintessentially English birdsong. How would she go about trying to capture that on canvas? Think. A starling darted into the cherry tree, its beak stuffed with dried grass. Busy nest building . . .

Diane put her head in her hands and very quietly, so as not to disturb Malcolm, began to weep.

The solitude of the cottage that Diane used as her studio was not what she needed, she decided. She wasted as much time as she could over breakfast and the previous day's crossword. She took Malcolm a cup of tea in bed, half tempted to get back into bed herself. She kissed the top of his head as she put the cup down beside him, but he didn't stir. Even the sunlight that streamed onto his face as she opened the curtains had no more effect than to send him burrowing further into the bedclothes. Chas and Lorraine Newbould's silver wedding party the previous evening had been a boozy affair. Diane had volunteered to drive; sticking to orange juice for the sake of the non-existent baby. She suppressed another wave of despair. Malcolm would probably wake up with a monumental hangover. She'd tell him later, she decided.

Diane took the country route to the large, isolated farmhouse near Stratford-on-Avon where her brother and his family lived, but it was still ridiculously early when she arrived at the end of the narrow, rutted lane that led up to the house. The villages she'd driven through had been all but deserted. She stopped, letting the engine idle, wishing she'd thought to bring her mobile so she could check it was OK to turn up at such an uncivilised hour. But Ian wouldn't mind. Weekend or no weekend, the family would already be up and running. Or most of it, at any rate.

She put the car back into gear and made her way up the sweeping driveway that led to Arden Hall, the house Ian had renovated for his American bride some two years earlier. Half-timbered, latticed windows, barley-twist chimneys, even a huge, gnarled wisteria snaking up and over the gabled porch, it all but personified the Stratford-on-Avon of the travel brochures. Almost too good to be true, Diane thought sourly as she glanced up at the still-closed curtains of the master bedroom.

'Bloody hell, you're up and about early.' Ian Somerford, still in his dressing-gown, picked his way across the jumble of Lego, crayons and assorted toys that cluttered the spacious oak-beamed hallway. 'Was it a good do last night?'

'Lively.'

Ian grunted. 'I can imagine. I wasn't expecting you to surface for hours yet.'

'You don't mind, do you?'

The deafening blare of gunfire came from the playroom. Diane stuck her head round the door. The two children, still in pyjamas, were sitting inches from the huge wide-screen television that had been Dominica's Christmas present, watching a video. Diane bellowed a greeting, which they both ignored.

Ian shrugged expressively. 'Not at all. We were up anyway, as you can see.'

'Chas and Lorraine were disappointed you couldn't make it.' She couldn't resist the snipe as she closed the door on the racket, although she knew it would only upset him.

'I was hoping I might be able to pop in for a while after the meal, but Angelika came back from her yoga with a headache, so it didn't seem fair to leave her on her own to settle Thomas.'

Diane heard and regretted the defensiveness in his tone. Why couldn't she just let things be? He was a grown man, for God's sake; his marriage was his own business.

'Isn't Thomas well?' she asked.

'Only teething. But he was up and down all night, and as we're between au pairs at the moment . . .' Ian shrugged again. 'Anyway, come through. He's in the kitchen. I was just giving him his breakfast.'

Diane followed her brother into the kitchen, biting her lip on any number of comments that sprang to mind. Angelika got through au pairs the way most people got through disposable contact lenses. And as for her needing the relaxation of yoga classes when she did bugger all the rest of the time . . . Diane struggled unsuccessfully to suppress a great surge of anger at the sheer injustice of it all. If she were able to have a baby, it would be everything to her; she wouldn't leave it with anyone else for five minutes. Yet Angelika, who could pop them out like shelling peas, didn't seem to have the time of day for any of them.

Her face softened as she caught sight of her ten-month-old nephew, strapped into his highchair and covered in porridge, his upturned cereal bowl like a blue plastic skullcap over his blond curls.

'Oh, bloody hell, Thomas,' Ian grabbed a tea towel and dabbed ineffectually at the mess. Thomas twisted his face away and issued a roar of protest. Ian's mobile, on the table beside the highchair and liberally smeared with oatmeal, immediately set up in competition.

Diane's mood had lifted, as it always did, in Thomas's

presence. 'That'll be Mum,' she grinned. Agnes was a notoriously early riser. 'You get it. I'll see to this little monster.' She bent down to the baby, and was rewarded with a wide, four-toothed grin.

'Work.' Ian barely put his ear to the receiver before switching the phone off.

She frowned. 'At this time of the morning?'

'Not all of us can work a nine-to-five shift.' Ian's tone was uncharacteristically irritable.

Diane looked up at him in surprise. She wondered if the comment could be a dig at Malcolm. 'Not all of us run the business,' she said mildly.

'Sorry.' Ian gave her a tight smile. 'Lack of sleep. Your fault, monkey.' He pushed the phone into the pocket of his dressing-gown and tousled the baby's porridgy hair.

Diane refrained from the obvious comment. 'That's why I hate those things,' she said as she lifted Thomas out of the highchair. 'They make everyone too damned accessible.'

Ian grunted.

'So is there a problem? At the site, I mean?'

'No. Not really. We're just a bit behind schedule. Careful, you'll get yourself covered.'

'I don't mind.' Diane held the soft, squirming little body against her own and planted a kiss on Thomas's sticky cheek. 'A bit of porridge never hurt anyone, did it, baby?' She glanced across the blond, downy head with concern. Despite the smile, Ian looked exhausted. 'You work too hard, Ian.'

'Tell me about it.'

'Look, you go and have a shower. I'll get Thomas dressed and keep an eye on him till you're ready.'

Ian rubbed his hands across his stubbled cheeks and gave her a rueful grin. 'That would be great. If you wouldn't mind.'

'Mind?' she laughed, relieved to have said the right thing at last. 'I'd be delighted.'

She was on her hands and knees stacking a tower of plastic bricks for Thomas to knock down for the hundredth time when the doorbell rang. She went to pull herself up, then heard the tread of Ian's feet coming down the stairs.

'OK, buster. Over to you.' She sat back on her heels and watched as Thomas whacked at the bricks with his chubby fists, squealing in delight.

The doorbell rang again.

'What's your daddy up to?' she muttered as she got to her feet.

Thomas's face crumpled.

'I'll only be a minute, silly sausage,' she laughed.

Thomas held his arms up to her and began to cry.

'All right. You win.' She bent down to pick him up, secretly delighted.

By the time she reached the front door, it was already ajar. She could hear raised voices; Ian's and another man's. Against the heavy purple fretwork of the wisteria, she caught a brief glimpse of a tall, silhouetted figure, vaguely familiar, before Ian glanced round and then pulled the door shut to block her view. Diane quelled a stab of childish resentment. It wasn't a deliberate snub; Ian was entitled to his privacy. It was just that she could remember the time when the two of them had shared everything.

'Let's go and make Daddy a cup of tea,' she whispered to Thomas. Ian wasn't her little brother any more, she told herself. She pushed open the door to the playroom, where the older children were still glued to the television, then, holding the baby under one arm, went back into the kitchen and turned on the radio to a volume that excluded other sounds. She filled the kettle, found a clean mug, and put Thomas down on the floor, surrounded by his toys.

'Let's tidy up a bit as well, shall we?' she murmured as she glanced round at the chaos of wrappers and the half-eaten remains of last night's take-away pizzas. The big, farmhouse kitchen had been totally gutted when Ian had bought the place. Every conceivable gadget had been incorporated. To the best of Diane's knowledge, Angelika had never so much as boiled an egg.

She set about loading the dishwasher while Thomas concentrated happily on attempting to cram one of the plastic bricks inside his mouth. By the time Ian came back in, the tea was stone cold.

'Everything OK?' she asked lightly.

'Fine.' Ian bent down and ruffled Thomas's hair, his back to his sister.

Diane didn't speak. She poured the tea down the sink and flicked the switch on the kettle. From the corner of her eye she watched her brother as he sat on his haunches, apparently absorbed in helping Thomas, who had tired of the bricks, slot coloured wooden rings onto a cone.

After a moment, he straightened up and flexed his shoulders. 'Do you mind?' He gestured to the radio.

'Of course not.' Quickly, Diane turned it off. 'I just didn't want you to think I was eavesdropping . . .'

Her words were cut short as Dominica cannoned into the room and, ignoring both the adults, yanked open a cupboard and grabbed a handful of chocolate bars. Thomas, unbalanced by the sudden movement, toppled forwards and landed face down on the quarry tiles.

'For goodness sake, Dominica!' Diane snatched up the

screaming baby and examined him for damage. 'Can't you be more careful?'

The girl glared at her with undisguised hostility.

'And don't you think you should ask before you take those?' Diane wished she could find it in her heart to like Ian's stepchildren, but she couldn't. She'd tried; she resolved before each visit to make allowances, be more tolerant. And each visit her fingers itched, as they were itching now.

Dominica held her gaze. Very deliberately, she unwrapped one of the chocolate bars, took a bite, and dropped the paper on the floor. 'What's it to you?'

'Dominica! That's no way to talk to your aunt.' As always, Ian's remonstrance was irritatingly mild as he bent to pick up the wrapper.

'She's not my aunt,' Dominica said coolly. 'And you're not my father. If I want a chocolate bar I can have one.' Her lip curled into a sneer of contempt that was an exact replica of her mother's. 'This is supposed to be my home, isn't it?'

'Leave her.' Ian caught Diane's arm as she went to follow the child out of the kitchen.

'Ian! You can't just let her . . .'

He shook his head. 'Just leave her.'

There were dark shadows beneath his eyes. Diane had arrived with the intention of pouring out her woes to him, she realised guiltily. As if he didn't have enough on his plate already. It couldn't be easy trying to bring up an eight-year-old and a ten-year-old who were not your own. Particularly an eight-year-old and a ten-year-old as unpleasant as Marshall and Dominica. Not for the first time, Diane wondered what had possessed Ian to take them on – what, for that matter, had persuaded him to take on a selfish, demanding bitch like Angelika. It had been obvious from day one that the relationship would be a disaster. It took more than a perfect figure and big blue eyes to make a marriage, as everyone but Ian had been able to see. She'd tried hard to tell herself it was none of her business. But she knew in her heart of hearts that Ian's unhappiness would always be her business.

Dominica flounced back into the playroom, shutting the door with a defiant slam. Diane raised an eyebrow, but said nothing, knowing that any comment she had to offer could only serve to make things worse. Instead, she made fresh tea then sat down, Thomas on her lap. She patted the chair next to her and asked, 'So what's the problem?'

'Who knows?' Ian shrugged. 'Probably fallen out with one of her friends again. You know what girls are like.'

'I didn't mean with Dominica.' Diane had always been able to read her brother like a book; she realised he was being deliberately evasive. 'Outside. I thought I was going to have to call the riot police any minute!'

'You could hear what was going on?'

She'd made the comment jokingly, with the intention of lightening the situation, but Ian looked appalled as he glanced towards the stairs.

'Of course not.' She reached across and touched his hand. 'Look, what's wrong?'

'I don't know what you mean.'

'Ian . . .'

'It's nothing.' He bent to pick up Thomas's teddy bear and ran his hand over its silky fur. 'A storm in a teacup, as Mum would say.' He placed the bear carefully on the table, then said with studied cheerfulness, 'Talking of whom, we'd better get down to business.'

Diane knew from experience that good-natured as her brother was, he was also as obstinate as a mule. Pushing him would get her nowhere. And his early-morning visitor had probably been no one more sinister than one of the villagers complaining about Dominica or Marshall again, she told herself. Only the previous week, the postmistress had arrived on the doorstep threatening to call the police after she'd spotted Marshall stoning cygnets on the river, little charmer that he was.

'OK,' she sighed. 'So about this tent . . .'

It appeared that Ian had it all planned. Caterers would provide the food, his wine merchant the champagne. He fetched a brochure, the page folded back to display the interior of a large marquee, set out with spindly gilt tables and elaborately swagged in pink satin. Dominica and Marshall would have a field day amongst that lot, Diane thought gloomily as she gazed down at the picture. But it would be churlish of her to say so, when Ian had clearly put so much effort into the project. And Mum would be in her element.

'It looks fantastic.' She shifted Thomas on her lap, grimacing slightly at the dull ache in her stomach and back.

'You OK? Do you want me to take him for a bit?'

Diane shook her head. She gave a shrug, her lips compressed into a tight smile. 'Time of the month.'

'Damn.'

They were both silent for a moment. Diane knew Ian was searching for the right words; knew there weren't any. She prayed that he wouldn't fall back on the hollow words of consolation she had been offered by one specialist after another over the years. Just a matter of time. She was nearly forty-two, for God's sake. How much time did she have?

'Well, you two sure look like you're having fun.' Angelika stood in the doorway.

She was tall – an inch or so taller than Ian – and big boned, her pale colouring hinting at her Scandinavian roots. Even with her long mane of white-blonde hair still tousled and her blue eyes bloodshot and smudged with last night's mascara, she still managed to look devastatingly attractive, Diane thought with more than a tinge of envy.

Ian jumped to his feet. 'Sit down, darling. I'll get you something to eat.'

Diane bit her lip. The idiot would be rolling over so that Angelika could tickle his tummy next. How was it some women managed that, without putting the slightest effort into a relationship?

'Just coffee. Hi, sweetie.' Angelika wiggled her fingers towards Thomas, then wrinkled her nose in exaggerated distaste at the comfortable dungarees Diane had chosen for him in preference to the more elaborate outfits in his wardrobe. 'And who got *you* dressed this morning?'

'Someone had to.'

'Well thank you, Diane.' Angelika's smile could have taken the limescale off taps. 'Maybe I can do the same for you, one day.'

Diane could feel the colour flood into her face. She would not rise to the bait, she told herself. She registered Ian's anxious glance as he returned with a steaming mug of black coffee, and was glad she'd managed not to bite back; he could do without the two of them bickering with each other.

'We were talking about the party,' he said as he handed the coffee to his wife. 'I was just showing Diane . . .'

Angelika yawned, displaying perfect white teeth. 'In that case, I think I'll go take a shower.' She nodded towards Thomas as she drifted from the kitchen, mug in hand. 'His nappy needs changing. He stinks.'

Diane could contain herself no longer. 'God Almighty,' she exploded as soon as Angelika was out of earshot, 'how can you just sit there and let her . . . ?'

'I'll see to him.' Ian picked up his son.

'She walks all over you, Ian. Can't you see . . . ?'

'Don't.' The single word was spoken so sharply that Thomas's bottom lip started to tremble. Ian held the baby into his chest and closed his eyes. 'Don't,' he repeated quietly.

Diane touched his arm. 'Is there anything at all that I can do?'

It was a moment before Ian spoke. Then he passed Thomas over to her and said with a smile so false it broke her heart, 'You can change your nephew's nappy, if you like.'

There wasn't really the need to give Thomas a bath; Diane could have cleaned him up perfectly well with wipes. But she ran one anyway, in the en suite adjoining the nursery, with lots of bubbles and all his toys, allowing herself the malicious hope that she'd interrupted the water flow to Angelika's shower. She felt her anxiety subside as she watched him play, delighting in his own delight as he kicked and splashed. He was a beautiful child, with the same blond hair and wide, startlingly blue eyes as his mother. But his sweet, placid temperament was all Ian's. If nothing else could be said for the union, it had at least resulted in Thomas, Diane thought as she wound up his plastic dolphin and sent it ploughing through the water.

It was only when the doorbell rang again that she glanced at her watch and realised they had been up there together for the best part of an hour.

'Come on, you.' She scooped the baby out and wrapped him in a towel. 'We're supposed to be planning your grandma's birthday party this morning, not having a water fight. Daddy will be wondering where we've got to.'

The bell rang again, more insistently.

Diane felt a flicker of unease. 'Do you want me to get it?' she called down the stairs.

No reply.

Marshall appeared from the playroom, his face flushed with excitement. 'Cool! It's the cops. There's a patrol car and everything.'

By the time Diane had run down the stairs, he'd already pulled the door open. A uniformed police officer was standing on the step.

Diane pushed Marshall aside. 'Can I help?'

'Mrs Somerford?' The policeman flashed an ID card. A trifle self-consciously, Diane thought; he looked about fifteen.

'No.' She glanced towards the kitchen. 'My brother . . .'

'He's in the garden.' Dominica had sidled out to join Marshall in the hall. 'I'll go get him.' She shot out through the kitchen.

Diane glared after her, then down at Marshall, who was gazing up at the policeman, the picture of innocence. What on earth could they have been up to this time?

After a moment, Ian appeared, looking worried. Dominica rejoined her brother, looking pretty rattled herself.

'Mr Somerford?' The policeman stepped into the hall.

'That's correct.' Ian glanced at the children and cleared his throat. 'How can I help you?'

'You are the managing director of Somerford Construction, I believe, sir?'

'I am.'

Dominica was looking less wary. She caught Diane's glance, and stared her out. Nothing to do with us, her expression said.

'What the hell is going on down there?' Angelika, draped in a towel, had appeared at the top of the stairs.

'Nothing, darling. I can handle it.' Ian turned his attention back to the policeman. 'Could I ask what all this is about, officer?'

'Your company owns the Trinity Walks development, I understand.'

Angelika rolled her eyes. 'More fucking vandalism. Jesus wept! I keep telling you to relocate, Ian. You try to build quality places in a dump like Coventry, what do you expect?'

The policeman coughed and produced his pocket book. 'There appears to have been an incident . . .'

'So what have the bastards done this time?'

'We haven't accessed the site yet, madam.' The man flushed as he dragged his gaze from Angelika to Ian. 'I understand you have a set of keys, sir . . .'

'Oh great!' Angelika snorted. 'Every crackhead in the area can find a way in, but the boys in blue need the fucking keys!' She flounced off to the bedroom, slamming the door behind her.

The policeman was beginning to look flustered. 'We've received a report from a member of the public of what appears to be a body . . .'

A million times in the weeks that were to follow, Diane would try to analyse the expression that flashed across her brother's face. An expression that came and went so fleetingly that she alone seemed to register it. An expression that filled her with unease.

'A body?' Marshall's eyes lit up. 'Wow! You mean someone's been murdered?'

'Go back in the playroom. Both of you.' Ian's voice was so uncharacteristically fierce that, for once, both children did as they were told.

'It's most probably just another hoax,' the policeman said hastily. 'We've had a lot the last couple of weeks, what with the

Easter holidays and the kids being off. We had a display dummy in the canal, yesterday. Gave the old girl who found it a right scare.' He gave a nervous smile to which Ian didn't respond, then coloured faintly and went on in a more formal tone, 'The officers on patrol couldn't see anything amiss from the street. They didn't want to force entry to the premises only to find it was a false alarm.' He paused and looked expectantly at Ian. 'So if you wouldn't mind coming down to the site with me, sir . . .'

'I . . .' Ian rubbed his hand across his face. 'Yes, of course. If you could just wait here for a moment . . .' He headed towards the study.

Diane shivered involuntarily. 'A body?' she echoed, holding Thomas more closely to her.

'As I say, madam, it's probably just a hoax.' The man smiled at the baby, who grinned back and reached forward to make a grab at the notebook. 'The call was anonymous. But we have to check it out, just in case.'

Ian reappeared, a large bunch of keys in his hand.

'Do you want me to come?' Diane asked, without quite knowing why.

Ian glanced quickly at her. 'If you've got the time . . .'

The policeman looked dubious. 'And you are . . . ?'

'Diane Middleton. Mr Somerford's sister,' Diane said with as much authority as she could muster. If Ian wanted her there, some teenager wasn't going to stop her, uniform or no uniform. 'My husband is the sales director,' she added in a tone that she hoped didn't invite argument.

She was equally brisk with Angelika, when the other woman demanded to know what in hell was going on. Nothing important, she said as she plonked the naked and still-damp Thomas on her sister-in-law's bed. They just had to go and check the site. Angelika would simply have to hold the fort with the children on her own for an hour or so.

The centre of Coventry was all but deserted, the Broadgate shopfronts unlit. Diane checked her watch and was surprised to see that it was not yet eight o'clock. The day somehow seemed much older.

The patrol car parked on double yellow lines in front of Holy Trinity Church. A high hoarding marked the boundary of the building site: '*This site acquired by Somerford Construction. Twenty-five luxury apartments . . .*'

In several places, attempts had been made to prise the painted boards apart, but the padlock that secured the metal gates was intact.

Ian fiddled with the keys.

'Let me, sir.' The policeman took them from him. He slipped off the padlock and pushed the gates open.

Diane could see the progress that had been made since Malcolm had taken her round the site some weeks before; the area was all but cleared of equipment, a row of saplings marked out what was to be the communal garden, and the sign to the penthouse show flat was already in place. The pathway round to the front of the apartments was gravelled. Like walking on a shingle beach, Diane thought inconsequentially as they crunched across it. The air was warm now. One of the saplings was bent almost double under the weight of a plump pigeon that cooed contentedly to itself in the sunshine, entirely oblivious to their presence. Diane smiled despite herself as she glanced at the policeman's purposeful back, his close-shaved neck as slender as the sapling beneath his slightly oversized hat. The scene had a slightly surreal quality to it, to which a tailor's dummy would add a fitting finishing touch.

The policeman rounded the corner of the building, then stopped so suddenly that Diane all but walked into him. She felt, as well as heard, the sharp intake of his breath, and stepped sideways to peer around his shoulder. Her hand flew to her mouth at the sight that greeted her, and she gagged on the acrid bile that welled up to scald her throat.

'Oh, Jesus.' Ian was beside her. As the policeman pulled out his radio and began to speak rapidly into it, he darted forward. 'Oh, Sweet Jesus, no.'

'Don't go any closer, sir,' the policeman shouted, making a grab for his arm. But he needn't have bothered; abruptly, Ian's knees buckled under him.

He looked up at Diane, his face sheet-white, his eyes wide with horror. 'It's Nicki,' he whispered, before he fainted.

3

'She'd been Ian's secretary for about six months, I suppose.'
Malcolm Middleton took another sip of Ian's malt whisky.
'I still can't believe it. She was the last person on earth I'd have
expected to . . .' He shook his head.

'How can anyone tell?' Diane rested her head against the
back of the chair and closed her eyes. She was exhausted.

It was nearly midnight, and they were sitting in Ian and
Angelika's living-room. The day seemed to have gone on for
ever. First the anxiety of the seemingly endless wait in the
accident and emergency unit at the nearby Walsgrave hospital; the strain of attempting to calm Agnes, who had arrived
by taxi from Leamington Spa within half an hour of hearing
of Ian's collapse. Then the interview with the police. Then the
drive back to Leamington with the still-fretful Agnes. It had
been decided to keep Ian in hospital overnight. Although the
heart attack the doctors had originally suspected had been
ruled out, he was still in a deep state of shock.

Angelika had refused point blank to go to the hospital,
claiming – to Agnes's outrage – that she'd find the experience
too upsetting. Her response to the crisis had apparently been
to pour herself a large gin, pop a sleeping tablet and take
herself off to bed; by the time Malcolm had driven over to
Arden Hall to collect her, she was fast asleep and the children
were running riot. He'd had to hold the fort for the rest of the

day. Diane glanced over at him with gratitude. He looked exhausted too, the small tic beneath his eye telling its own story of how stressful his day had been.

'I can't remember her, you know.' Diane knew it was morbid to keep returning to the subject, but she couldn't stop herself. Nicola Smith's car had apparently been found parked in the apartments' garage block, well hidden from sight. From the kind of questions the police had been asking, it seemed clear they suspected suicide. The thought of such a young woman having nothing to live for was appalling.

'Pretty little thing. Mid-twenties, at a guess. Very vivacious.' Malcolm stared into his whisky, then looked up. 'She was at the Christmas do.'

Diane frowned, trying to conjure up a mental image that might tally with the broken body lying beneath the apartments. 'What was she wearing?'

'Oh God, I don't know.' Malcolm tempered the sharpness of his tone with the ghost of a smile; his utter lack of fashion sense was a standing joke between the two of them.

'And she was married, you say. Christ, how must the poor husband be feeling?' Diane murmured, trying and failing to imagine what it must be like to lose a partner in such hideous circumstances. She glanced again at Malcolm. Not to be allowed to share the despair of someone so dear to you; it must seem the ultimate betrayal, the greatest failure.

'There's not much point in trying to speculate, is there? It won't help the poor woman now.' It was clear Malcolm didn't want to discuss it further.

A typically male reaction, Diane thought; there was nothing he could do to alter the situation, so why keep going over and over the same ground?

He swallowed the last of the whisky. 'Come on. Time we

were in bed. No doubt we'll be in for an early start in the morning.'

Diane nodded. 'I'll make up one of the spare beds.' There had been no question of going home and leaving Angelika to cope overnight.

Malcolm reached across and touched her cheek. 'Are you all right, love? In yourself, I mean.'

She enclosed his fingers in her own. She knew exactly what he meant. She'd been almost a week late this time; they'd both been beginning to get their hopes up. With everything else that had happened, she hadn't got round to telling him how the day had started.

'Just a bit of a stomachache,' she said quietly.

It was Malcolm who represented the company at the inquest into Nicola Smith's death. Ian had taken a couple of weeks off work once he was discharged from hospital and had given his statement to the police. Angelika had booked the family into a luxury hotel in deepest Cornwall. Diane couldn't help thinking he would probably have been more relaxed at work.

'You'll call me when it's over?' She brushed anxiously at a speck of dust from Malcolm's shoulder on the morning of the hearing. 'I'll be at the studio.'

Malcolm nodded. 'I know. You've told me a dozen times already.' He bent and kissed her lightly on the cheek. 'There's nothing to worry about. It wasn't as if the balcony gave way on her; it was as solid as a rock. She must have deliberately climbed over it.' He put his fingers to Diane's lips as she began to speak. 'What happened was terrible, but it wasn't our fault. The site was properly secured. I've already spoken to the Health and Safety people. The company's in the clear.' He turned as he reached the door, and grinned. 'Don't forget to take your mobile. And try to remember to turn the damned thing on, this time.'

Despite his reassurance, Diane found it impossible to concentrate on her work when she arrived at the tiny, secluded cottage near Corley Moor that she used as a studio. Malcolm had bought it for her as a fortieth birthday present – a place where she could make as much mess as she needed to, where she could block out the demands of everyday life. The extravagant gift had seemed all the more special because she knew Malcolm had never completely understood her need to paint. Once, when they'd first been married, she'd got bogged down with a particularly trying commission; a portrait that just wouldn't come right. Malcolm had only been half joking when he'd asked in exasperation why the subject couldn't just settle for a decent photograph instead.

Usually, Diane could feel her spirits lift as she drove off the ring road, through Keresley and then out onto the Tamworth road and away from Coventry towards the open farmland and wooded copses that lay beyond the city's northern boundary; her ideas would begin to race as she shut the heavy five-barred gate that divided her from civilisation. Almost as if she were driving to meet a lover, she'd teased Malcolm. But that morning, as she climbed the stairs and wandered around the light, airy space into which the architect had so cleverly transformed the entire upper floor of the cottage, her creativity had deserted her utterly. All she could think of was Nicola Smith's crumpled body; the young life snuffed out so needlessly.

She went back downstairs and made herself a coffee. The original cramped interior had been redesigned into a small, functional kitchen and an open-plan living area with an old table, a couple of mismatched dining chairs and a shabby sofa that could double up as a bed if the need arose. The stone floor was bare but for an ancient, fraying rug. The elderly, faded velvet curtains had fulfilled the role of dustsheets for years until Diane had salvaged and re-hung them. No television. No telephone. The place was very different from the stylish comfort of her home, and she loved it with a passion she found hard to explain, even to herself. Maybe it was that it reminded her of when she'd been a student, her life still filled with endless possibilities.

She took the coffee up to the studio, checked for the hundredth time that her mobile was on, and spent the best part of half an hour staring without inspiration at the big, half-finished canvas in front of her before deciding she was wasting her time. It was a portrait of Ian. She'd started it several years earlier, before he was married and unable to find the time to sit for her. She'd gone back to it in recent weeks, working from photographs of him in the vague hope of completing it before Agnes's birthday, but even without the distraction of Nicola Smith's death, she knew it wasn't going to happen. Working from photographs just wasn't her style. She needed the physical presence of a subject to breathe life into her work.

She allowed her gaze to travel towards the stack of canvases and sketches piled accusingly in the far corner of the studio. They'd been there for weeks. She sighed heavily. No more excuses. She would set about selecting pictures for the annual nightmare of The Show.

What had started as a one-off several years earlier had become a traditional end-of-year event with her students at the various art classes she taught. It was only held in the foyer of one of the local FE colleges; at best, it might attract a couple of dozen visitors and a paragraph or two in the *Coventry Evening Telegraph*. But each year it seemed to engender more disappointment, more backbiting and acrimony than the Royal Academy's summer exhibition.

If talent were the sole criterion, choosing the exhibits would be easy, she thought as she picked up a painting by one of her younger pupils. It depicted a landscape of looming stone monument and tortured, gale-tossed trees. The fierce energy of the piece wasn't something that could be taught, any more than was the clever symbolism of the menacing sky and the scattered blossom strewn beneath the trees. The subject she'd suggested was the War Memorial park, a large open area to the south of the city centre in which a cenotaph had been built and trees planted in memory of those who had died in combat. The class had met there one Sunday afternoon the previous summer to make some preliminary sketches. It had begun to rain heavily before they left. Most of her students – mainly elderly housewives and voluble, retired self-styled captains of industry – had produced, with greater or lesser success, scenes of disrupted family picnics, disgruntled dog walkers, cricket players running for cover. They'd seen what was there, and nothing more. Only Lee had acknowledged the symbolism of the place; the resonance between the sudden, disrupting storm and the violence of war; the individual loss, the sheer waste of life, that each scattered, oil-daubed blossom seemed to re-present. Lee was good, very good indeed. He'd been coming to her classes for more than a year, and had the intensity of one who treated art as more than a passing hobby. Diane would have liked to fill every wall with his paintings, give him the recognition he deserved, but she knew from past experience that that wasn't how it worked. Everyone, including those who couldn't draw a straight line, would expect their work to have pride of place. She'd tried, tactfully, to intimate as much to Lee before the Easter break, and feared he might have taken offence; classes had resumed the previous week, but he had failed to put in an appearance.

Well, he'd need to develop a thicker skin than that if he wanted to get anywhere, she told herself briskly as she put the painting aside and turned her attention to the rest of the stack.

She worked systematically, sorting the pictures according to their merit, then readjusting her selection on the basis of equality. It wasn't an easy task, but at least it occupied her mind. She was pulling a face at a particularly garish oil painting submitted by an irredeemably untalented retired dentist when her mobile rang. She glanced at her watch, amazed to realise that it was already mid-afternoon.

'George!' She was alarmed to hear the voice of George Bonham, the family solicitor, on the other end of the phone. 'What's happened?'

She could hear the laugh in his voice. 'Malcolm said you'd panic if I rang, but he had to rush off for a site meeting, so I said I'd fill you in.'

'I'm sorry, I just hadn't realised he'd asked you to be there.' Malcolm must really have been playing things down, not to have told her.

'He didn't. I was between cases in the Magistrates' Court, so I thought I'd pop across to see how things were going. I caught them just coming out.'

'So what happened?'

'All done and dusted. The coroner brought in an open verdict because the woman hadn't left a note, but it seems pretty clear it was suicide. There was apparently no way she could have fallen accidentally, and the post mortem showed no signs of a struggle.'

'A struggle?' Diane echoed. She felt herself go cold; it had

28

never even occurred to her that anyone else might have been involved.

'The police always have to cover every possibility,' George said reassuringly.

'Did Malcolm have to answer many questions?'

'Not at all. Just confirming what he said to the police about the keys that had gone missing from the office, as I understand it. The police apparently found them on her body. From what Malcolm said, it sounded as if she had the whole thing horribly well organised, poor woman.'

'That's awful.' Diane closed her eyes, trying to imagine what must have gone through Nicola Smith's head as she'd fastened that padlock behind her and made her way up to what she knew was going to be her death. 'I wonder why she chose to do it there?'

'No chance of being stopped, presumably.' George's voice was sober. 'Once the site was locked up for the night, the place would have been completely deserted, wouldn't it? The security cameras had evidently been vandalised the week before, so she'd have known she was unlikely to be found until the next morning, even if she survived the fall. Which apparently she didn't, thank goodness. Not that she'd have been likely to, from that height.'

'Dear God.' Diane shivered.

'Quite.' George was silent for a moment. 'Anyway,' he went on in a more businesslike tone, 'I must let you get on. Malcolm said not to bother with supper. He thought you might like go out somewhere, which sounds like an excellent idea to me. I suspect the inquest has been more of an ordeal for him than he's letting on. Ian might have been the woman's direct boss, but her death, particularly in such circumstances, must have been a hell of a shock to everyone at Somerford's.'

'Has anyone rung Ian yet?'

'I spoke to him a few moments ago, as a matter of fact.'

'How did he sound?'

'Pretty strung out, I thought. I'd have expected him to attend the inquest himself, to be honest. He seems to have taken the whole thing pretty badly.'

'That's hardly surprising, is it?' Diane thought she could sense a trace of criticism in George's voice.

On the other end of the phone, her old friend chuckled.

'What?'

'Nothing.' He chuckled again. 'It's just that I had this vivid mental picture of you and Ian when you were little. I seem to remember you used to beat the lights out of anyone who dared so much as look at him sideways in the playground. You were the most ferocious older sister in the school!'

'Yes,' Diane grinned suddenly, a hundred different memories flooding her head. 'Yes, I guess I was,' she said softly.

4

The funeral took place the following week. Diane volunteered to accompany Malcolm to the crematorium. To the best of her knowledge, she had never met Nicola Smith in life, but being present when the body was discovered made her feel an obscure bond to the woman in death. She was also more than a little irritated that Ian seemed so reluctant to attend the service himself. She might brook no criticism of her brother from others, but that didn't stop her giving him a few home truths herself occasionally. Nicola Smith had been his secretary. Not to pay his last respects by going to the funeral, however distressing he might find it, would be to appear a wimp. Sending a wreath, no matter how expensive, was not enough, and Diane had told him so in no uncertain terms. She half expected to see his car when she and Malcolm drove into the carpark at the crematorium, but there was no sign of it. The modest collection of vehicles parked up in front of the bleak, brick-built chapel comprised mainly small family cars, the majority of them elderly. Malcolm's BMW looked out of place enough; Ian's sleek Mercedes would have stood out even more.

She glanced around at the people gathered in the small courtyard in front of the entrance to the chapel. There appeared to be two distinct contingents, one much larger than the other. Even from a distance, the hostility between the two factions was palpable.

'Nicola's family and the husband's, I imagine,' Malcolm murmured. 'I recognise some of them from the court.'

Other, smaller groups stood around. Diane recognised one knot of women as typists from the office, which had been closed for the morning as a mark of respect. She nodded at them, her lips compressing as she wondered crossly what they would make of Ian's absence. She was surprised to notice the young constable who had discovered Nicola's body. He was standing on his own, slightly away from the rest of the mourners, contriving somehow to look more conspicuous in plain clothes than he would have been in uniform. He half smiled at Diane as she made eye contact with him. Was it standard practice, she wondered, for him to be there, or had he just come along out of curiosity? She glanced back towards the two main groups. Judging by the atmosphere between them, he might be needed before the end of the service.

An elderly man smiled grimly at her and broke away from the smaller contingent. He came over and introduced himself as the grandfather of Nicola's husband. He'd seen Malcolm at the Coroner's Court, he said.

'Not the sort of publicity you needed, eh? Don't suppose it'll have done your house sales much good?'

Malcolm blinked. 'Sorry?'

'Her throwing herself off your roof.' The man shook his head. 'Always struck me as a bit unstable, right from when she was a little lass. Terrible temper on her. Family didn't help, of course, forever sticking their beaks in and causing trouble. Couldn't even agree on what flowers were going on the coffin. God knows what they'd have come up with if our lad hadn't put his foot down.' He raised his voice and shot a venomous glare at the other group, to Malcolm's visible discomfort. 'Always did have ideas above their station, that lot.'

A large, peroxide blonde turned and stared him up and down.

The man upped the volume even further. 'Thought he wasn't good enough for her, because she'd got a couple of A levels.'

Malcolm cleared his throat and murmured, 'If you'll excuse us . . .' He put his hand under Diane's elbow and steered her into the chapel, where they were ushered to seats much nearer the front than she would have chosen. He raised an eloquent eyebrow before bending his head in the pretence of prayer.

The chapel began to fill up. Whoever had shown them to their seats must have seen Diane and Malcolm in conversation with the old man; they found themselves on the husband's side. Lifting his head, Malcolm glanced around him, caught Diane's eye and shrugged helplessly. 'If they start throwing the hymn-books, we'll make a run for it,' he muttered.

Diane suppressed a giggle; the whole thing was descending into farce.

The moment of levity lasted only a second. The muted babble of whispers hushed suddenly as those at the back of the chapel got to their feet. Those further forward turned and craned to get their first glimpse of the coffin. Diane stared down at her feet, abruptly overwhelmed by the memory of Nicola Smith's mangled body as, on the other side of the aisle, a woman began to weep. There was nothing remotely funny about the situation.

She glanced at the coffin as it passed. She'd expected it to be loaded down with flowers, but it was bare but for a single red rose, poignant in its simplicity. Her gaze travelled to the young man who walked behind the coffin, his head bowed. She let out a small gasp of shock. The man looked up, and for a second their eyes locked before he moved forward.

Malcolm turned his head towards her, his expression questioning.

She shook her head slightly and attempted to regroup her thoughts. It wasn't until the organ struck up for the first hymn that she leant towards him and whispered, 'It's Lee.'

Malcolm looked blank.

'From my art class. He must be Nicola's husband.'

Diane sang the familiar hymn automatically. No wonder the poor kid hadn't turned up the last couple of weeks. She'd been on the point of writing to explain to him again why she'd had to leave some of his work out of the exhibition. She could only thank God she hadn't got round to it.

Lee Smith . . . She ran the name around her head. She must have taken it down when he first registered, but she tended not to use surnames, except with the most formal of her older students. And even if she had, Smith was such a common one that she'd never have made the connection. She stared at the back of the tousled dark head just a few rows in front of her, and tried to readjust her image of him. Lee was much younger than the others, handsome in a dark, rather Byronic fashion. If pushed, she'd have guessed he might be a university student; she tended to keep conversation to a minimum in her classes and, as a consequence, knew little of her pupils' backgrounds, nor they hers. But she had sometimes wondered what inner turmoil had driven Lee to produce his dark, turbulent paintings. Now, perhaps, she knew.

As the hymn finished, she heard the door at the back of the chapel open and close, the muffled echo of footsteps.

Malcolm turned his head and nodded in acknowledgement. 'He must have changed his mind,' he murmured. 'Good.'

She glanced around to see Ian slide into the seat next to the aisle in the back row. His face was taut. She smiled at him encouragingly. She'd always known he would come.

Proceedings were brief; the obvious hymns, a short, impersonal sermon. As the curtains closed around the coffin, the peroxide blonde began to sob volubly, but Diane's eyes were on Lee. His shoulders slumped, his head down as the final prayers were intoned; he had to be helped to his feet as the piped organ music signalled the end of the service. The minister stepped forward and murmured something to him before leading the way back up the aisle. Lee followed, his eyes downcast, his mouth working as he fought back tears.

Diane turned to watch his shuffling progress towards the back of the chapel, and felt her heart go out to him. He looked so young, so utterly alone. She experienced an unaccustomed stab of antipathy as her eyes strayed to Ian, who was on his knees, his head buried in his hands. He'd never been a religious man, she thought irritably; so why this sudden display of piety?

The rest of the congregation began to surge out of the pews, the two warring factions jostling for position. As he reached the door, Lee stopped, so suddenly that the peroxide blonde, who had elbowed her way to the front of the queue, cannoned into his back. Lee did not appear to notice. To Diane's horror, he reached down and dragged Ian to his feet.

'This is all your fucking fault!' The young man's voice scythed across the muted hum of conversation. Only the reedy strains of *Jesu, Joy of Man's Desiring* broke the sudden silence.

Ian took a step backwards. His face was ashen. 'I don't know what . . .'

Lee made to swing a punch at him. 'We were happy, before you . . .'

35

'Let's calm it down, shall we, sir?' The constable's voice was reassuring as he stepped forward and took hold of Lee's arm. Lee tried to shake him off, but the man's grip was firm. 'I don't think this is going to help, do you?'

'We were happy . . .' Lee turned towards the policeman, his face collapsing abruptly as he began to cry, great wrenching sobs that shook his tall frame.

'Let's talk about it outside, shall we?' The policeman steered him towards the door.

Diane noticed that Ian's hands were shaking as he straightened his lapels. Without a glance in her direction, he shouldered his way through the bottleneck of mourners, most of whom were staring at him with unconcealed curiosity.

'What the hell was all that about?' Malcolm hissed over the growing babble of sound.

Diane shook her head uneasily. It had only been because of her badgering that Ian had shown up at all. Could he have had some inkling that something like this was going to happen?

There was no sign of him by the time they had got out of the building. Diane caught a glimpse of his black Mercedes, already speeding towards the exit from the crematorium.

'Right.' Malcolm's mouth hardened as he looked around. 'I'm going to find out exactly . . .'

'Not here.' Diane put a restraining hand on his arm. She glanced around and lowered her voice. 'Not in front of all these people.'

A few of the mourners were already heading for their cars, but most were still milling around, chattering animatedly as they made a show of examining the neat row of floral tributes that now lined two walls of the small courtyard. Lee was standing some distance from the chapel, deep in conversation with the police officer, and very much the object of everyone's covert attention as his grandfather hovered nearby.

'No.' Malcolm sounded reluctant. 'No, you're right.' He frowned as he followed her gaze. 'Ian hasn't said anything to you?'

'About what?' Diane looked at her husband sharply, wondering if he knew something she didn't.

'God knows.' Malcolm held up his hands as if in self-defence. 'I haven't got the first bloody idea what's going on. Maybe the guy thinks Ian was putting her under too much pressure. She had been working some long hours lately.' He took Diane's hand and squeezed it. 'Don't look so worried. It can't be anything that important, can it? Ian would have told you.'

'Yes,' she murmured. She glanced back towards Lee, her certainty growing that his was the silhouetted figure she had seen in Ian's porch on the day Nicola Smith's body was discovered. She knew it was herself she was trying to reassure as much as Malcolm, as she added firmly, 'Yes, of course he would.'

5

The last person Diane had expected to see at her art class that evening was Lee Smith.

She had rung Ian when she got back from the funeral, determined to find out just what was going on. He was in an important meeting, the temp who had replaced Nicola Smith informed her somewhat obstructively. Diane had told the girl to ask him to ring her back as soon as he was free. It had been after six thirty when she'd left the house to drive to the community college, and there had still been no word from him.

She glanced at the mobile on the seat next to her. Ian had bought it for her not long after his marriage, although it was a standing joke that she detested the things and rarely even remembered to turn it on. 'I'm an artist,' she'd say loftily when teased. 'I don't do technology.' She'd had it switched on all day; had even remembered to charge the battery. She checked it again, just in case, but there were no messages.

The weather had broken during the afternoon, and it was pouring with rain. Every set of traffic lights seemed to be against her. By the time she reached the ring road, she was in a thoroughly bad temper. She hated the frantic lottery of the entry slip roads, and slowed to a crawl as she attempted to force her way into the stream of cars. The visibility was poor, the traffic still heavy, and she had to swerve to avoid a black cab that cut in front of her. A lorry honked and flashed its lights as it braked hard behind her then overtook her in a wall of spray, the driver gesturing obscenely. To her intense irritation, Diane felt the hot prickle of tears.

'Pull yourself together, you silly cow,' she muttered as a sudden volley of hailstones tattooed against the windscreen.

She wished Malcolm hadn't had to go up to Manchester. Usually, she was quite content with her own company, almost relished the thought of an early night watching TV in bed, but that evening she felt anxious, unsettled. She dreaded the prospect of rattling around in their big house, alone.

She rubbed an angry hand across her eyes as she accelerated hard. She knew perfectly well that it wasn't the thought of being alone in the house that was unsettling her. She and Ian never kept things from each other. Right from when they were small, if he had ever been in any sort of trouble, it had been her to whom he'd turned for help. Fresh tears welled in her eyes as she remembered how he used to write her name on birthday cards and the like: the 'D' and the 'E' embellished to enfold the three middle letters.

'I'll always stay at the heart of you, won't I?' he'd asked, the day she'd left home for art college. An awkward, gangling sixteen-year-old, the words had been spoken jokingly, but she'd recognised the earnestness beneath the mock melo-drama. And in the intervening years that had seen them both marry and make their careers he had, in a strange, special way, stayed at the heart of her.

Now, for the first time she could remember, he was blanking her out. And she didn't understand why.

The carpark was practically deserted when Diane pulled into the college. She glanced at her watch. It was barely ten past

39

seven. Evening classes started at seven thirty. Even given the lousy driving conditions, she'd allowed herself far longer for the journey than was necessary; more than partly in the perverse hope that Ian would ring and find her not at home. Resolutely, she pushed her various worries to the back of her mind as she yanked the box of her materials from the back of the car and made a dash for the entrance. Any poor devil who did make the effort to get there on such a foul evening deserved her full attention.

Lee was already in the art room when she got there. He was standing by the window, staring out at the rain-lashed football pitches beyond, apparently unaware of Diane's arrival. She paused in the doorway, both taken aback and slightly alarmed by his presence. His jeans and teeshirt were soaked through, she noticed; as if he'd left home on the spur of the moment, oblivious to the weather. Had he come to cause trouble? For the second time that day, she found herself gazing at the back of his dark head and wondering what was going on inside it. Unsure of how to react, she opted for the professional approach. She dumped the box on the table, flicked the light switch and said brightly, 'Goodness, it's dark in here.'

Lee turned. In the harsh flicker of the fluorescent lights, his face was grey; an old man's face, haggard and thin. 'I didn't know whether to come. I haven't done any painting for a bit.' He glanced at Diane and away again, then said softly, 'Thanks for turning up this morning. I appreciate it.'

Diane flushed, embarrassed. She had absolutely no idea what to say.

'I'm sorry about the scene.' He glanced at her again with an awkward attempt at a smile. 'I made a right fool of myself, didn't I? I bet you wondered what the hell was going on.'

It occurred to her that he might not realise her connection to his late wife; that he might think she'd been at the crematorium on his behalf. She hesitated, wondering how to respond.

Lee's face darkened. 'I can't believe that bastard turned up.' He bit his lip. 'Even so, I shouldn't have . . .'

'You were upset,' Diane said quickly. Now wasn't the time; not with the class about to start, she told herself, feeling slightly dishonest. She looked at the easels, already arranged in a semicircle; a job she normally did herself. 'Thanks for . . .'

He nodded. 'I was here early.' For the first time, he looked her full in the face. 'I wanted to explain.'

'Lee, you don't have to . . .'

'It's important.' He hesitated then added quietly, 'There's not many I can talk to.'

Diane didn't reply. The intensity of Lee's gaze embarrassed her. She was relieved to hear the clatter of approaching foot-steps in the corridor outside.

The door flew open and Sidney Cunningham strode in, flapping his umbrella and showering them both with droplets of water.

'What a bloody awful night!' Sidney threw his dripping overcoat across the back of a chair. 'I shall expect preferential treatment at the exhibition for turning out in weather like this, you know!' He was the extrovert of the group; Diane couldn't have wished for anyone better to have interrupted the con-versation.

'No favouritism in my classes, Sidney,' she said with mock severity, grateful for the opportunity to lighten the mood. 'You should know that by now.'

'Hear that?' He raised a bushy eyebrow in Lee's direction. 'She's a hard woman, you know. I hope you didn't help her put out those damned easels. Complete waste of time, old boy. You won't get round her that easily!'

Diane was surprised at how many of her students braved the weather; the class was almost full. She found it difficult to concentrate as she set up the evening's subject and got them started. She'd have to let Lee know Ian was her brother; she should have done so already. But something was going on between the two men. Maybe, if she kept quiet, she could find out what it was. It wasn't as if she were trying to extract the information from Lee, she told herself by way of justification; he seemed to want to confide in her. She found herself ridiculously flattered that he did.

The room was silent but for the faint scratch of pencil on paper and the steady drumming of the rain against the windows. She glanced across at Lee, cursing herself for her choice of the evening's subject. She'd set up a still life: a bottle of wine and two half-empty glasses, one smudged with lipstick. It had struck her as an ideal subject when she'd planned it at the beginning of the term; not too daunting for the less talented in the group to take at face value, but with any number of suggested possibilities for those able enough to pick up on them. Most of the group were still studying it, a few making hesitant preliminary sketches. Lee was already bent towards his easel, his face a mask of concentration, his pencil moving quickly, savagely.

After a while, Diane circled the group, answering queries, making suggestions, now and then adding a few pencil strokes of her own. Some of her pupils were more demanding than others; a few seemed to expect her undivided attention. She left Lee until last, as she often did. The two-hour session was nearly over before she got round to him.

She stood behind him, surveying his work, forcing herself to concentrate. To describe his sketch as 'still life' was to do it an injustice. The pencil lines were bold, heavy. He'd deliberately skewed the perspective, so that the bottle looked as if it were about to topple forward, an offensive weapon. The glasses tilted on a dangerous collision course towards each other. He'd used red ink for the lipstick. It seemed to ooze from the glass like blood. It was all that Diane could do to stop herself from shuddering.

Lee leant his head back to look at her, his hair brushing against the bare skin of her forearm.

'It's good.' She felt the sudden prickle of goose bumps, and folded her arms across her waist. She cleared her throat and tried to refocus on her role as tutor, formulate some sort of constructive criticism. He didn't come to the classes to be told what he must surely already know. She looked away from the scrutiny of his gaze. 'Very good,' she added feebly. It was all she could think of to say.

The group broke up quickly. There was less to clear up than normal, as they'd been working in pencil, but Diane wondered if Lee's presence might also have something to do with the speed with which coats were put on and goodbyes said; Nicola's death had been well documented in the local paper, and the others might have been better at connecting Lee to the deceased woman than Diane herself had been. Loss had that effect, she'd noticed; it isolated its victims, because those around were too embarrassed to know what to say. Within a couple of minutes, only she and Lee remained.

'It was a good class.' He was standing by the door, his head bent as he slowly folded one of the easels. 'I'm glad I came.'

'Can I give you a lift somewhere?' The words were out of

Diane's mouth before she could think about them. She felt the colour rise in her face as she gestured at his teeshirt, still damp from when he'd arrived. 'You'll get soaked again . . .'

'Couldn't get my motorbike to start.' Diane had never seen so sad a smile as he added, 'Just not my day, I guess.'

The silence between them seemed heavy with unspoken words as Diane pulled out of the carpark.

'Where do you live?' she asked, in an effort to fill it.

'Earlsdon.'

Diane knew the area well. Despite its proximity to the city, it had managed to retain something of its original 'village' feel; an eclectic mix of large Victorian and Edwardian villas and terraces of more modest two-up-two-downs, with a thriving centre of shops, restaurants and bars. Lee gave her his address: a street in the less-fashionable sprawl that fanned away from the central part of Earlsdon towards Hearsall Common. It was an area popular with students. Diane nearly told him that she and Malcolm owned and leased out several properties to the nearby University of Warwick, but somehow it didn't seem appropriate.

'This is kind of you.' Lee shot her a sideways glance.

'It's no trouble.' It was still raining hard. Diane kept her eyes on the road and told herself it was no more than she'd do for any one of her students. 'It's not even out of my way.'

Another silence.

'So where do you live, then?'

Diane hesitated. She loved the house, but it was also a source of some discomfort to her. 'On the Kenilworth Road.' It was one of the smartest roads in Coventry; imposing, substantial properties standing in their own grounds and concealed by long, tree-lined drives. Potential buyers would be pushed to find anything for sale under three-quarters of a million. The address signified serious money.

Lee pulled a face. 'Posh.'

'It belonged to my parents.' As always, she felt compelled to explain. 'It was too big for my mother after my father died and my brother got married, so my husband and I took it over.' She winced mentally. *My husband and I.* It made her sound like the queen.

'Nice.' Lee glanced at her again. 'You got kids?'

Diane shook her head. They had reached their exit on the ring road. A car behind her flashed its lights as she changed lanes. She forced a laugh and said, 'This wretched road gets worse, doesn't it?'

Lee didn't appear to have heard her. 'Nor me,' he said. Diane heard the wistfulness in his voice as he added, 'I always wanted kids.'

'I'm so sorry about your wife.' The words were hideously inadequate, but they were all she had.

'Nicki didn't want them anyway. Not lately, at any rate. Not since that bastard . . .'

Diane's hands tightened on the steering wheel. She should say something. She tried to imagine Lee's embarrassment when he discovered who she was.

He turned his head away from her to stare out of the windscreen, mistaking her silence for indifference. 'Sorry,' he muttered. 'Not your problem.'

She wanted to reassure him, but she didn't know what to say. She was desperate to find out what it was this boy had against her brother. And she was honest enough to acknowledge to herself that that wasn't the only reason she'd offered Lee Smith a lift home. She'd ignored her own interdiction and left the mobile on throughout the class, but it hadn't rung. The

Kenilworth Road house awaited her, dark and silent. Sterile. She very much wanted the warmth of human contact.

They were in Earlsdon now. She turned left into Albany Road by the old Technical College, then right towards Hearsall Common. The silence between the two of them lengthened as she turned right, then right again into the street where Lee lived and pulled up outside the house he indicated. She turned off the ignition.

Lee made no move to get out of the car. He was still staring straight ahead of him.

Diane could hear the rain battering against the windscreen. The sound of his breathing. What she was about to do was unforgivable.

'I could come in for a coffee, if you like,' she said quietly. 'And you could tell me about it.'

6

It explained everything. And it was so obvious that Diane couldn't believe she'd needed to be told.

Ian and his secretary had been having an affair.

Diane sat in Lee's living-room while he went through to the kitchen to make coffee, the guilt of her own deception temporarily overcome by curiosity as she looked around her.

The room didn't tell her much. It was sparsely furnished: cheap black leatherette sofas, pale laminate flooring, a *faux* fur rug. On the mantelpiece three identical small vases each bore a single, artificial lily; *Ideal Home* meets MFI, impersonally stylish but for the overlay of several weeks' neglect and muddle. What had Nicola Smith been like, to have tempted Ian into infidelity? Had Ian been infatuated with the woman, or had it been no more than a casual fling?

Diane attempted to see the situation as Lee must be seeing it: rich middle-aged man – thirty-eight would seem middle-aged to someone as young as Lee – seducing vulnerable young employee. The sheer banality of it would have been laughable, had the outcome not been so tragic. No wonder Ian was so anxious to keep on the right side of Angelika. Had she found out? Issued Ian with an ultimatum to ditch his mistress, maybe? Could that have been what had driven Nicola Smith to suicide? Small wonder he'd been in such a state the past few weeks.

'You're a fool, Ian,' she muttered.

'Did you say something?' Lee appeared from the kitchen, carrying two mugs of coffee. He handed her one of the mugs and slumped down next to her on the sofa.

'No.' Diane could feel herself blushing. 'Sorry. I was just . . .' She glanced round again and added feebly, 'Nice room.'

Lee followed her gaze. 'She had good taste, Nicki. Watched all the design programmes on the telly. She always . . . she always did know what she wanted.' Suddenly, his hands were trembling so much that Diane had to take his coffee from him to prevent it spilling. 'Daft, isn't it? You'd think I'd be getting used to it by now.' He scanned her face as if expecting to find some sort of an answer there.

She shook her head, moved almost to tears by the pain in his dark eyes. 'It isn't daft.'

'Maybe if I'd just let her get it out of her system. Let her have her taste of the high life . . .'

'None of this is your fault, Lee.' Diane put an awkward arm around his shoulders and asked herself uneasily what the hell she was doing here, offering consolation to the husband of her brother's mistress.

'Sorry.' Lee pulled a grubby handkerchief from his pocket and blew his nose. 'You don't want to be hearing all this.'

'You're not the one who needs to apologise,' Diane said with such vehemence that he looked up, puzzled. She felt an unaccustomed surge of real anger towards Ian. All right, so he couldn't have foreseen the devastating repercussions of the affair, but had he given any thought at all to the havoc he might be wreaking? Did he really care, even now? Nicola's death had obviously affected him deeply, but was his current erratic behaviour a function of grief, guilt, or the simple fear of having the affair made public? The clear picture of Lee, silhouetted in the porch of Ian's house, came back to her again. She moderated her tone and asked cautiously, 'Had you known for long? That she'd been having an affair?'

Lee looked past her, seemingly lost in thought. 'She'd changed,' he said finally. 'Right from when she first got that new job, she was . . . different.'

'In what way?'

'We were going to start trying for a family, but she kept saying the money was too good to give up.' Lee shook his head. 'But it's kids that make a marriage, isn't it?'

Diane felt her heart contract. It was only with effort that she asked, 'Had you been married long?'

'Yeah. We met at school. I'd fancied her for ages before I screwed up the courage to ask her out. She was dead bright. Dead popular, you know, like some people are. Couldn't believe it when she said yes. Fifteen, we were. I left at sixteen. Got a job at the Dunlop, where my dad works.' He shrugged. 'I was never that good at school, apart from art. Nicki stayed on in the sixth form. I was sure she'd dump me, but she didn't. Her family weren't too chuffed. They've always thought I was beneath her. But Nicki wasn't one to be told what to do.' He smiled, diverted for a moment. 'We got married the summer she left school. By the time we were twenty-one, we'd put enough together to buy this place.' He looked around the poky room with heartbreaking pride.

'You must have worked hard,' Diane murmured, embarrassed to think of the number of houses she and Malcolm had bought outright, as an investment.

Lee nodded. 'Nicki was earning good money. She'd gone to the Dunlop too, after school. As a typist. I got myself a job labouring at weekends. Didn't want her to think I wasn't pulling my weight. Got taken on by Somerford's.'

'You worked at Somerford's?' Diane tried to keep her voice impassive; the name had jolted her like an electric shock.

Lee smiled bleakly. 'Ironic, when you think about it. Nicki'd probably never have gone for the job there if she hadn't heard of the place through me. It was OK at first, while she was working in the office.' His face clouded abruptly. 'Then she got the promotion, and everything changed. It was "Ian" this, "Ian" that. She didn't want me working there any more. Said it wasn't good for her image.' He snorted. 'Thought I might hear some gossip on the grapevine, more like. She started working late, staying away overnight. Reckoned she had to go to meetings with him out of town. And I was stupid enough to believe her. I mean, I knew things weren't right between us.' He hesitated. 'Not . . . physically, like.'

'Look, I don't want to pry,' Diane said quickly. To be here at all was an enormous dishonesty. To allow him to confide the intimate details of his marriage was inexcusable.

'You're not. You don't know how good it is to be able to talk to someone who isn't going to slag Nicki off. Or call me a useless prick.' He gave a mirthless laugh. 'If you'll excuse the pun. I thought we were just going through a bad patch. She was always finding fault with everything, reckoning the house was too small, saying I wasn't ambitious enough. She never rated my painting, of course.' He glanced at Diane sideways. 'You don't know how good it was to hear you say I'd got a bit of talent.'

'More than a bit,' Diane murmured. 'You know that.'

'She thought it was just a waste of time. She was always on. Always wanting things.' Lee's mouth twisted into a sneer. 'And getting them.'

Diane shifted uncomfortably, wondering what he meant.

She had no need to ask; once Lee had started talking, he didn't seem to want to stop.

'We hadn't bothered with a car since the last one packed up. It wasn't like we really needed one. I've got the motorbike, and she used to get the bus to work. But she went on and on. I was going to try and get a loan off the bank. But suddenly she'd bought one. And not an old banger like the last one; a brand-new VW Golf. Said she'd saved up for it out of her salary. But she wasn't earning that kind of money. Not as a secretary, at any rate. First thing I did when the police let me have it back was get rid of the bloody thing.'

Diane breathed in hard. More than a passing fling, then. What the hell had Ian been thinking about, to imagine something like a new car would go unnoticed by his mistress's husband? 'So you confronted her?' she asked warily.

He shook his head and gave a slight shrug. 'You'd be amazed how long you can go on fooling yourself if you try hard enough. No, things didn't come to a head till that last night. The night before she . . .' He bit his lip.

Diane nodded wordlessly.

'The daft thing was, she'd actually seemed more herself those last few days than she had been in ages. Less dissatisfied, somehow. Singing around the place like she did when we were first married. I thought maybe . . .' He shrugged again. 'Anyway, I was due to go down to the pub with some of the lads from work like I usually did of a Friday night. I said why didn't she come down with me, but she said no, she'd got a headache. Well, I wasn't bothered, so I said I'd stay with her. But she reckoned she fancied a bath and an early night. So off I went. But I decided I'd call in at the shops first, get her some chocolate and a couple of magazines, seeing as she was going to be stuck in on her own. That's how much of a muppet I was.' The bleak smile faded as quickly as it had come. 'By the time I got back to the house, there she was, all done up like a dog's dinner and just on her way out. Make-up, perfume, the lot. Even I couldn't go on hiding my head in the sand, then.'

'And that's when she admitted she'd been seeing . . .' Diane stopped herself just in time from saying Ian's name '. . . this other man?'

'She said he'd rung and asked her to pick up some typing.' Lee shook his head slowly, as if in remembered disbelief. 'Even then, she thought I was stupid enough to fall for it. But not that time.' He stared down at his hands and said in a low voice, 'We had a row. I said some terrible things. Terrible. I was just, like . . . lashing out. I told her it was over between us, that I'd never really loved her in the first place. She just laughed in my face. Said it was just as well, because she was leaving me anyway. And then I . . . I hit her. The last time I touched Nicki was to hit her. I never saw her again.' An expression of such unbearable grief contorted his features that Diane had to look away. 'Not alive, at any rate.'

He bent forward and took a shaky sip of his coffee. After a while, he went on in a flat voice, 'After she'd gone, I went out and got pissed. I mean really, out-of-my-face pissed. Didn't give up until I got thrown out of the last nightclub. It was nearly morning by the time I'd found my way back here. I wondered if she might have come home, but she hadn't. Well, she wouldn't have, would she?' Lee's fists clenched. 'She was already dead by then.'

Diane swallowed hard. 'What did you do?'

'I found the bastard's number in her address book and rang him up. Demanded to know where she was. He put the phone down on me. So I rang again. And again. And then I went over to his fancy great house near Stratford. He was shit-scared I'd turned up, I could see that much. Didn't want his precious family to find out what he'd been up to.' Lee snorted. 'He must have been wetting himself when Nicki told him she'd left me for him. As far as he was concerned, she was just a perk of the job.'

'Did you say any of this to the police?' Diane asked carefully. A tiny part of her almost hoped he had; it would be no more than Ian deserved.

'There's no law against what he did, is there? Christ! Half the bosses in England would be banged up, if there was. And anyway, once she was dead . . .' Lee studied Diane's face in silence for a moment before he went on. 'I could try to make out I kept quiet because I didn't want to crap on her grave. But the truth is, I just didn't want everyone at the inquest knowing I wasn't even man enough to keep my own wife satisfied.'

'But at the crematorium . . .'

'I couldn't believe he'd had the fucking nerve to turn up.' Suddenly, Lee was sobbing uncontrollably. 'I just keep thinking of him, standing there in front of his flashy house that morning, telling me I was mad, looking at me like I was something he'd trod in. And all the time, Nicki was lying there. Dead.'

'Don't cry.' Diane didn't know what else to say. Ian's words echoed in her head. *Nothing. A storm in a teacup.* She put her arms around Lee, rocked him against her as if he were a child. She could feel the warmth of his shuddering breath, the fluttering of his wet lashes against the bare skin of her neck. Her own eyes filled with tears as she kissed his hair. 'Please, don't cry.'

They sat there, locked together, as gradually his sobs

subsided. Outside, the rain had stopped. Through the un-curtained window, Diane noticed the stars that had appeared from behind the scudding clouds and realised how late it must be.

'I should be going.' She brushed a stray strand of hair from Lee's eyes.

'Not yet.' He spoke into her shoulder.

'I must.' She tried to ease herself away from him. She was acutely aware of the warm weight of him against her, the faint smell of his sweat that should have been unpleasant but was oddly arousing. Malcolm always smelt of soap and deodorant and clean laundry.

'Don't go.'

'It's late. I've got to . . .' Go back to an empty, unlit house?

'Stay with me. Just for a while.' He lifted his head, his eyes half closed as his lips sought hers.

'No, Lee. This isn't . . .' The rest of her words were drowned in the urgency of his kiss.

His hand was fumbling for the opening of her blouse. Why didn't she stop him? Push him away from her? She shivered as his fingers slid inside her bra. It was all wrong. For a hundred different reasons, it was wrong. A thousand. She was a happily married woman. Somehow, she was lying back on the sofa, Lee's weight on top of her, his palm rough against the hardness of her nipple as his other hand forced itself up her skirt and searched the soft flesh at the top of her thighs.

Her knees slackened. She mustn't let this happen. She had to stop him. She gasped as his probing fingers found their mark, and arched herself against him, matching his urgency as she pulled at his jeans, dug her nails into the firmness of his buttocks.

Her legs splayed wide as he entered her. She heard a cry of

ecstasy that could only have been her own. She mustn't let it happen.

And then she was falling, drowning, the last vestiges of sensible thought shattering into the whirling kaleidoscope of her orgasm.

7

Diane was only grateful that Malcolm was away. He would have known, just by looking at her.

She pulled up at the traffic lights at Hearsall Common as they turned to red, and stared at herself in the rear-view mirror. Her face was still flushed; not just with shame, but with the exhilaration of a sexual satisfaction she had never before experienced. Malcolm was a gentle, considerate partner; their lovemaking unspontaneous, for years governed more by temperature charts than physical passion. There had been nothing gentle or considerate in what she and Lee had done. It had been quick; almost brutal in its intensity. They had torn at each other. Not an act of love. A fuck. The flush grew deeper as she recalled her total lack of inhibition. Whatever had possessed her?

God alone knew what Lee must have thought of her. She hadn't stayed long enough to find out.

The closer she got to home, the more ridiculous she felt. She should never have allowed it to happen. Lee Smith was young enough to be her son, for Christ's sake. Not to mention the added complications Ian brought to the equation. Her sudden laugh was on the edge of hysteria. People in glass houses . . . One minute she'd been condemning her brother for his unfaithfulness, the next she'd been flat on her back with her knickers off and her legs wide open to some boy she hardly knew. At least Ian had the excuse that he was married to Angelika. Her hands gripped the steering wheel. She'd never once been unfaithful to Malcolm; hadn't even considered the possibility. How could she ever look him in the eye again?

She made a conscious effort to calm herself as she turned right from Earlsdon Avenue and onto the Kenilworth Road. The important thing was to keep it in perspective, she told herself. See it for what it was: a temporary aberration, rather than an act of infidelity. It was on an entirely different scale to what Ian had been up to. After months of impotence with his faithless wife, Lee had been desperate for the comfort of sexual gratification; she had been feeling lonely, a bit low, and had simply been reckless enough to allow herself to respond to that need. That was all there was to it. A moment of madness. She grimaced at the cliché as she pulled the car into the winding drive that led to the house. But it was true; madness was exactly what it had been. A long bath, a good night's sleep and the entire incident would seem no more than some brief, erotic dream. There was no reason for Malcolm ever to know.

She was disconcerted to see Ian's Mercedes parked outside the house. He'd kept his front-door key when their mother had moved out. It had never before struck Diane as intrusive that he still occasionally let himself in if there was no one around, but she felt a surge of resentment as she noticed that the hall light was on and the living-room curtains drawn. She glanced quickly in the mirror and ran a hand through her hair to smooth it. If anyone could read her, Ian could. And when it came to illicit sex, he was apparently the expert.

Her earlier anger returned full force as she searched in her bag for her compact and reapplied her lipstick. If it hadn't been for Ian and his bloody affair, she'd never have offered Lee a lift in the first place.

He must have heard the car draw up; when she looked up, he was standing in the porch. She threw the compact back in her bag, wondering how long he had been watching her. Half shadowed in the overhead light, his skin looked pale; like ash.

'Where have you been? I was getting worried.' His smile wasn't entirely convincing as he held the car door open for her.

She reached into the back for her box of materials. 'You're not the only one who works.'

He picked up on the sarcasm. 'I'm sorry I didn't return your call. I was in a meeting. We've got some tricky planning applications coming up and I want to make sure they're as watertight as we can make them.'

Diane knew he was playing for time, waiting for her to make the first move. Well, he could damned well wait. She dumped the box in the hall and yawned ostentatiously. 'If it's Malcolm you've come to see, he's gone up to Manchester, I'm afraid.'

'I know.' There was an edge of irritation in Ian's voice. 'I sent him.'

Still she didn't help him out; if anything, the implied rank-pulling just annoyed her further. With a bright smile, she said, 'So what can I do for you?'

'For God's sake, Diane!'

She looked him full in the face then; saw the real anguish in his bloodshot eyes and felt a stab of guilt. Maybe it had been more than an affair; maybe, despite what Lee thought, Ian had felt real love for Nicola Smith.

In a quieter voice, Ian said, 'You know why I'm here.'

'Yes.' Suddenly, she was bone tired; wanted nothing more than to burrow down into her bed and pretend the day hadn't happened. 'Yes,' she repeated heavily as she sat down in Malcolm's armchair, felt the dent in his cushion enfold her. 'I know exactly why you're here.'

Ian sat down opposite her. 'I want to explain.'

Lee's words, she thought.

Ian closed his eyes briefly and massaged his temples as if he had a headache. Then he leant forward and said earnestly, 'Look, about what happened this morning. Nicki's husband . . . It's all some kind of crazy misunderstanding.'

'Please don't do this, Ian.'

'Do what?' Ian sat back in the chair. He looked puzzled. But then he would; he didn't realise she already knew the truth.

Diane shook her head, not trusting herself to speak.

'He seems to have got it into his head that Nicki and I were having some sort of affair!' Ian's attempt at an incredulous laugh made Diane want to slap him. 'You remember when you came to the house? To plan Mum's party? And someone kept phoning? Well that was him! Do you understand what I'm saying?' Ian was clearly unnerved by her lack of response. 'And when I wouldn't speak to him, he turned up on the bloody doorstep, ranting and raving that Nicki had left him, and threatening to kill himself. Christ, when the police arrived I thought at first it might be his body they'd found. The guy's a total nutter!'

'Lee Smith.' Diane heard the coldness in her own voice. 'He does have a name.'

'Well of course he has a name,' Ian looked bewildered. 'And I realise he must be feeling pretty bloody terrible about what's happened, which is why I didn't mention anything about it to the police. But that doesn't give him the right . . .'

'Oh, come off it, Ian!' Diane stood up, unable to listen to any more of it. It should have been the infidelity itself that appalled her the most, but it wasn't. How dare he try to lie to her? What kind of a fool did he take her for? Her throat was so constricted with anger that she could barely spit out the words. 'You didn't say anything to the police because you didn't want Angelika to find out you were screwing your secretary. At least be honest with me!'

Ian stared up at her, his face a mask of astonishment. 'What the hell are you talking about? I told you, the guy's a complete . . .'

'I know all about it. The late evenings, the nights away, the stuff you bought her. A new car, for Christ's sake? Didn't it dawn on you that people might talk? That sooner or later someone would tip Lee off, if he was too blind or too terrified of losing his wife to see for himself what was . . . ?'

'Lee?' Ian cut across her. 'What's all this "Lee" stuff? Are you telling me you *know* this man?'

'Yes, I know him. He's a student at one of my classes.' Even as she said the words, Diane could feel herself flush with embarrassment. Who was she to be damning anyone for deceit?

'Oh well, that's just bloody great, isn't it?' Ian jumped to his feet. 'The guy can hold a paintbrush, so you choose to believe him over your own brother! Thanks a lot, Diane. I was stupid enough to think I could count on your support.'

'Oh, for God's sake, grow up!' Diane called after him as he strode from the room. Why the hell had she allowed herself to get involved in any of this? She'd tried to help, and had ended up making everything infinitely worse. She followed him out into the hall. 'Look, of course you can count on my support. Just don't lie to me.'

Ian's face was stiff with fury. 'I've never lied to you in my life. I thought you understood me well enough to know that. Apparently, I was wrong.' He pulled open the front door.

'Where are you going?' Diane went to grab his arm. They hardly ever rowed; always resolved any disagreements before they parted. She felt the beginnings of something approaching panic. 'Look, come back inside and we'll try to talk things . . .'

'No thanks.' Ian shook himself free. 'I'd better get back to Angelika, before she starts to get suspicious, as it appears to be common knowledge that I've been playing away from home. Unless you've filled her in already, that is.'

Diane had never seen him so angry. 'Don't be so ridiculous!' she laughed incredulously. 'As if I'd ever . . .'

But Ian wasn't listening. Without another word, he left the house, slamming the door shut behind him.

Diane tossed and turned her way through an entirely sleepless night. It was true. Ian had always been a hopeless liar; not just to her, but to anyone. Even when they were children, it had been he who would give the game away when they'd been caught in some misdemeanour or other. Could he really have changed so much? Become so accomplished at deceit without her noticing?

But Lee had seemed so certain, so sure that Nicola and Ian had been lovers. Could it be that Nicola had been having an affair with someone else? Telling Lee she was working late with Ian as an excuse? Diane sat up in bed and turned on the light. Why hadn't she thought of that in the first place? She ran her fingers over her breasts, still tender from the work of Lee's hands and tongue. She knew the answer without having to ask the question. Because she'd been too swept along by lust, or whatever it was that had driven her to such unbelievable folly, to challenge his assumptions. Even if that made her own brother a cheat and a liar.

Hot with shame, she turned the light off and tried to sleep, but her brain went round in circles. She tried to make herself consider the situation logically. The obvious thing was to speak to Lee, find out what exactly had made him so certain it was Ian his wife had been seeing. Convince him he was wrong, before he let fly again and caused even more trouble. But she knew that she mustn't allow herself to be with him. Not alone. Even after the bath she'd taken before getting into bed, she could still smell him. She could feel the throb of him between her legs. She squeezed her eyes tightly shut, but she couldn't block out the shameful images that were imprinted inside her lids.

No. Not even to help Ian would she see Lee Smith again.

8

Diane smiled at the elderly man who was weeding the already immaculate flower-bed in front of Somerford Construction. The office block was still locked; she'd got up early to come and make her peace. She searched in her wallet for the security card she so rarely used and pushed it into the slot by the side of the door, then made her way through the plush reception area and along the deserted corridor that led to Ian's office.

She glanced in at the airy room adjoining his own. Until a few weeks ago, this was where Nicola Smith had spent every working day; the surroundings as familiar to her as the little house in Earlsdon. Diane looked at the cluttered desk. The temp had already begun to make it her own. A framed photograph of a smiling couple, their arms entwined, stood beside the computer monitor. She shivered slightly. Had Lee's picture once stood there?

The door to Ian's office was shut. Diane paused to examine the brass name-plate and asked herself if she would ever get used to the paradox. Ian Somerford, Managing Director. Her kid brother.

She had just sat down in his big leather swivel chair when the door was tapped and a young girl walked in. Diane recognised her from the photograph in the adjoining office.

'Oh.' The girl looked at her uncertainly.

Diane stood up and held out her hand. 'Hi. I'm Diane Middleton.'

The girl's expression remained blank.

'Malcolm Middleton's wife?'

The name clearly didn't ring any bells. 'Mr Somerford's expecting you, is he?'

'Yes,' Diane lied.

'Oh,' the girl said again.

'So I'll just wait here for him, shall I?' Diane resumed Ian's seat with a confidence she hoped was justified. She hadn't forgotten the expression on her brother's face when he had left the previous evening.

'Dunno.' The girl lifted her shoulders slightly. 'I suppose so.'

It was evident that Nicola's replacement had not been chosen on the strength of her social skills. Or maybe the poor kid was just nervous. Diane smiled at her. 'What's your name?'

'Samantha.' Her voice was sullen.

'Have you been working here long, Samantha?'

'No.'

Diane wondered how a single syllable could convey such truculence. 'Well, I mustn't keep you from your work,' she said pleasantly.

Samantha made no move to go.

'A coffee would be nice,' Diane prompted.

The girl rolled her eyes.

'Bring a pot.' Diane's patience was ebbing. She disliked pulling rank, but the girl's insolence was intolerable. 'And an extra cup for when my brother arrives,' she added crisply.

She had expected Samantha to be fazed, but the girl merely tossed back her mane of hair and said, 'I didn't know who you were, did I?'

64

'You do now,' Diane snapped. 'And don't forget the coffee,' she called after her as the girl flounced off, shutting the door behind her with more than necessary force.

'Well, that went well,' Diane murmured as she heard the resentful clatter of crockery from down the corridor. What on earth had possessed Ian to employ the girl, apart from the fact that she had long blonde hair, and even longer legs? Diane suppressed the unworthy thought that her brother might have jumped out of Nicola Smith's frying pan and into the fire. She mustn't allow her mind to go in that direction, she told herself firmly. It was reconciliation she'd come here for, not further recrimination.

Some minutes passed. The girl returned with a tray of coffee which she dumped on the desk without further comment. Diane drank two cups. She changed the date on Ian's calendar and aligned the heavy crystal paperweight with the leather blotter that had been their father's.

Maybe he'd been delayed. She stood up and walked to the window to look down on the carpark, which was filling rapidly. The drive to Somerford's from Arden Hall was an arduous one; sometimes the traffic was backed up for miles at the Longbridge roundabout, the point where the Warwick bypass crossed the M40. Not an ideal way to start each working day. It had only been Angelika's absolute refusal to live in the Kenilworth Road house, or indeed anywhere near Coventry, that had persuaded Ian to move to such an inconvenient location.

Diane was always galled by her sister-in-law's condemnation of the city that provided the family's comfortable lifestyle. Coventry might not possess the social cachet of some of its neighbours, but it retained a dogged sense of community born of the terrible devastation it had suffered in the Blitz and the even greater damage of the collapse of the motor industry on which its wealth had been built; a community that in more recent years had happily adopted the vibrant multiculturalism that Diane loved. Warwick might be chocolate-box pretty with its almost self-consciously half-timbered frontages, but Coventry had its own architectural jewels, the more precious for having to be sought out amidst bleak acres of post-war concrete. Stratford-on-Avon might have any number of the prissy boutiques Angelika adored, but Diane preferred to shop in Coventry's famous circular market, where apples, cabbages and carrots could be found cheek by jowl with an eclectic mix of plantain and mango, okra and coriander. Or in the Foleshill district of the city, with its dazzling array of rich, embroidered Asian fabrics and pungently spicy aromas. Not that any of that would impress Angelika, who couldn't sew on a button, and whose idea of arranging a dinner party was to ring the nearest restaurant for a reservation.

Diane checked herself. Criticising Ian's wife would be no way to endear herself to him either. She glanced at her watch, feeling increasingly foolish. Five past nine. For all she knew, Ian might have an appointment elsewhere. Having claimed she was expected, she was hardly in any position to ask the obstreperous Samantha to check his diary. She'd give him another five minutes, she decided, relief warring with disappointment that the confrontation might have to be postponed.

It was just before a quarter to ten when she saw the Mercedes swing into the carpark and draw up next to her car.

'She said you were expecting her.' Samantha's voice floated after him as Ian entered the room.

Diane's face was already arranged into a conciliatory smile which Ian didn't return. His voice was cool as he nodded to the adjoining office. 'Work experience. She hasn't got two brain cells to rub together, but the Personnel Office thought it would be a good way to strengthen our links with the local community college, as there's a tender coming up with the Education Department. And before you ask, no, I'm not screwing her either.'

Diane flushed at the accuracy with which he'd read her mind. 'I've come here to apologise,' she said quickly. 'I was completely out of line last night, and you had every right to be offended. I'm truly, truly sorry.' She took a step forward, hoping she hadn't imagined the slight relaxation of his shoulders. 'I don't know what else to say.' She risked a hesitant smile. 'Am I forgiven?'

Ian stood quite still for a moment. Diane tried to read his expression. She felt an instant of real fear. What if her apology wasn't enough? Where else could she go from there? She couldn't bear the prospect of the sort of long-term feud that other families seemed to uphold.

Abruptly, Ian sank down into his chair, his head bent forward and murmured, 'Thank God.'

Diane felt as if a huge weight had been lifted from her. There was a catch in her voice as she said, 'I hate it when we fall out.'

Ian looked up. She was surprised to see tears in his eyes as he reached out for her hand and whispered, 'I knew it couldn't have been you.'

'What couldn't have been me?' Diane gazed at him, nonplussed, her relief dissipating rapidly into confusion as she registered his expression. 'What are you talking about?'

'It was ridiculous to have thought . . .' He shook his head. 'I know you'd never do anything like that. But you seemed so strange last night . . .'

'What couldn't have been me?'

Ian took off his glasses and pressed his fingers against the bridge of his nose before he answered. 'A note came this morning. Addressed to Angelika.' He exhaled slowly. 'You can imagine its contents.'

'And you thought . . . ?' Diane was almost too stunned to speak; astounded that he could for one moment have suspected her of such malice.

'No. No, of course not. It's just that you seemed so hostile last night . . .' He glanced up at her. 'I'm sorry. I just wasn't thinking straight.'

She couldn't have begun to tell him how much the suggestion had hurt her. But now wasn't the time; he needed her help, not her recriminations. 'So has Angelika seen this note?' she asked.

'Oh yes.' Ian gave a thin smile. 'It was she who found it.'

Diane sank down into a chair. 'How did she take it?'

'How do you think? That's why I'm so late in.'

Diane could envisage all too clearly what Angelika's reaction had been. 'So how is she now?' she ventured.

'I think I managed to calm her down.' Ian didn't sound too certain. He put his head between his hands. 'It was Nicki's bloody husband again, wasn't it?'

Diane could feel the colour creep across her face.

Ian was looking at her closely. 'Look, I know you feel sorry for the guy, but if he doesn't stop harassing me, I'm going to have to go to the police.'

'No!' She tried to steady her voice. If he went to the police it would all come out; it would be bound to. 'Please, Ian, don't do that. I know all this must be irritating for you, but don't you think it'll just make things worse if you . . . ?'

'Irritating? Christ Almighty, Diane! You should have been in my shoes this morning!'

'You can't even be sure it was him,' she said weakly.

'It can't go on. He's going to wreck my bloody marriage!' Ian was on his feet again. 'What is it about this guy, Diane? Just what's so special about him that you'd put his interests above your own family?'

'Nothing!' Her cheeks were on fire. 'I wouldn't! I just don't want . . .'

'Or maybe you still think he's got every reason to try to wreck my marriage.'

'Of course I don't!' She closed her eyes to shut out her brother's angry gaze. 'Sit down, Ian. Please. The last thing either of us needs is another row.'

She heard the slow exhalation of his breath, the creak of his chair.

'I haven't lied to you, Diane,' he said more quietly. 'You do know that, don't you?'

'Yes.' Reluctantly she opened her eyes. Ian held her gaze until she looked away. She hadn't lied to him either, she told herself. Not exactly. It just felt that way. 'Yes, of course I do.' It wasn't enough. She hesitated then said quickly, 'Look, do you want me to have a word with him? Try to convince him he's got it all wrong?'

Ian snorted. 'You think he'd listen?'

'He might.' She looked down. 'I'm not sure.' That much, at least, was true.

'He can't keep doing these things, Diane.'

'I know. Just let me try, before you take matters any further. It's only going to get messy, if you involve the police.'

'It's messy already.'

'Not as messy as it could be.'

'Meaning what?'

'Nothing,' she said quickly. Too quickly?

'OK.' Ian's voice had cooled again. 'Although I can assure you I have absolutely nothing to hide.'

'Of course not. Anyway,' Diane forced a smile as she stood up, suddenly anxious to bring the conversation to an end, 'I mustn't keep you. You've got work to do. And so have I.'

'Mum's party.' Ian gave a hollow laugh. 'Thanks for reminding me.'

'Will Angelika be . . . all right?'

'Let's hope so.' He held the door open for her. Usually, he kissed her when they parted. 'Just try to make sure your little friend doesn't pull any more stunts in the meantime, will you?' he said unsmilingly.

She drove straight from the office to the house in Earlsdon, aware that if she didn't make arrangements to speak to Lee right away, she would lose her nerve. She guessed he would be at work, but didn't ring the bell to find out. Instead, she pulled a sheet from the sketchpad she always kept with her and scribbled the note she'd been composing on the journey. She needed to speak to him about his entries for the exhibition. Could they meet up for a drink that evening? She chose a big, impersonal pub in the city centre, all beech and chrome and loud music; where she prayed there would be no one she knew. She doubted he'd be taken in for one moment by the lame excuse of the exhibition, but what else could she put?

At least she wouldn't have to lie to Malcolm as to her whereabouts, she thought with guilty relief; he'd already rung to say he would be taking some clients out to dinner in Manchester, and wouldn't be back until late. She wondered how she should sign the note. She settled on 'D.', then added the rest of her name in case the initial alone suggested too great an intimacy. She folded the paper and, biting her lip, pushed it through the letterbox. She heard the faint plop as it hit the floor and knew there was no going back. She had no doubt that Lee would turn up. In less than nine hours they would be together again. She didn't care to analyse how she felt about that.

9

Most of the mundane chores leading up to Agnes's party had, inevitably, fallen to Diane. There were several elderly friends to be picked up at various times from the train and bus stations and installed in one of the small country hotels near Stratford-on-Avon; the possibility of them being put up at Ian's home hadn't even been considered, which was perhaps fortunate in the circumstances. There was a visit to the florist to check the table decorations and a final meeting with the caterers. There was the diamond brooch that Diane had designed to be collected from the jewellery quarter in Birmingham. Diane had felt mildly resentful when she and Ian had gone through the checklist and she had agreed to spend the day running backwards and forwards. Why was it she was always assumed to have more time, fewer commitments, than anyone else in the family? But in the event, she was grateful for the distraction. At least the tasks filled the crawling minutes and hours. It was after six by the time she had fought her way back home through the clogged M6 traffic. Less than an hour to go until she saw Lee.

She forced herself to scramble an egg and eat it. Malcolm phoned, and she took longer than normal asking about his day and telling him about hers. She watched the beginning of the Midlands news on the television, one eye on the clock, until it was time to leave. She got into the car at ten to seven. She'd managed not to shower, change, or freshen up her make-up. Why should she? It wasn't a date she was going on.

The pub was already full of office workers when she got there; young men in Next suits, ties already loosened; girls with glossy hair and glossier smiles. The air was heavy with smoke, chatter and loud, end-of-the-week laughter. Diane stood in the doorway, feeling middle-aged and dowdy. She spotted Lee sitting at the bar, his back to the door. He looked almost as out of place as she did herself, with his untidy tangle of curly hair and his faded jeans. Diane paused, disconcerted by the fluttering in the pit of her stomach as she gazed at the angular shoulders, the tanned, sinewy forearms, the strong fingers that gripped his glass. Fingers that less than twenty-four hours earlier had travelled every intimate, yielding inch of her . . .

She breathed in sharply as, with a lazy smile, Lee got to his feet and turned around. He'd been watching her in the mirror behind the bar, she realised. She made her way across to him and prayed her face hadn't betrayed her thoughts.

'Sorry, this was all I could get.' He bent forward to kiss Diane's cheek.

'This is fine.' She was relieved to see that all the tables were taken; there was less room for intimacy at the long, harshly lit bar. She ordered orange juice, refusing Lee's suggestion of wine.

'So.' Lee trailed a finger against her hair. 'How are you?'

She moved her head away. 'Lee, this isn't the place to . . .'

'We could always go back to mine.'

'No!' She said the word so sharply that a girl in a skimpy skirt and impossibly high heels turned to give them a covert glance. Diane lowered her voice. 'That wasn't why I wanted to see you.'

'What was it then?' She could hear the beginnings of

resentment in Lee's tone as he added, 'And don't say to talk about paintings. I'm not that stupid.'

'Look.' She took a shaky sip of her orange juice and wondered where to start. 'What happened last night was a mistake. I should never have . . .'

'A mistake.' His voice was dangerously quiet. 'Just a bit of a fling, was it? A quick bit of rough before you skipped back up the Kenilworth Road to your rich old man?'

She glanced quickly around and hissed, 'For God's sake!' The girl on the next stool was now staring with unconcealed curiosity.

Lee was picking angrily at a piece of loose skin by his fingernail, his head turned away from her.

She attempted to steady her voice; take control of the situation before it got entirely out of hand. 'We can't talk here.'

'What's to say?' Lee swallowed the rest of his beer. 'Don't worry, I won't tell him, if that's what you've come here about. I know how it feels to get crapped on from a great height, remember?'

'Please, Lee. I really do need to speak to you.' She rested her hand on his arm, trying not to register the warmth of his skin, the coarseness of the strong dark hairs that curled around his watch strap. 'It's important. My car's only in the Barracks.'

He gazed down at her hand. Then he scanned her face, his expression a mixture of anger, bewilderment and naked longing.

'Please.'

'OK.' His eyes belied the nonchalance of his shrug.

They walked in silence past the deserted shops in the Bull Yard and towards the Barracks carpark, jackets drawn around them against the unseasonably biting wind, careful not to touch each other. Diane caught a glimpse of them both in one of the darkened windows. Lee was walking slightly behind her, head down, hands stuffed in his pockets. If the scene were freeze-framed, he could be a mugger about to attack her. Or a rapist. She imagined a blurred still from a CCTV camera, the sort shown on *Crimewatch* appeals, then told herself impatiently to get a grip. She was the one who had set this up, not Lee.

They walked up the echoing concrete steps of the multi-storey. Only the odd car remained parked on each dimly lit level, and the place was eerily quiet. Diane's hands trembled slightly as she fumbled for her keys. Lee stood close behind her as she unlocked the car; she could feel the warmth of his breath on her neck. Desperately, she tried to marshal her scattering thoughts. She'd planned exactly what she was going to say; she couldn't remember a single word. She needed to get to the point, and quickly. Before Lee got the wrong idea. There couldn't be many reasons why a woman would invite a man back to her car in such a deserted setting.

She turned to face him and said in as formal a tone as she could manage, 'Listen to me, Lee. There's something I want to say to you.' She tried to avoid the devouring intensity of his gaze. She could feel her nipples hardening against the thin fabric of her blouse. 'As a friend.'

'You're cold.' He drew the lapels of her jacket together, but not before he'd let his eyes travel down to her breasts. He smiled his slow smile. 'It'd be warmer inside the car.'

She cleared her throat, knowing that she was beginning to blush. 'It won't take long.'

'Well, that all depends, doesn't it?'

His face was close to hers. She couldn't step back from him; she was pressed up against the side of the car. She knew that once inside, she would be even more acutely aware of his proximity. But what else could she do?

He slid into the passenger seat. There was a glint of humour in his eyes as he turned to her and said, 'So, tell me what this is all about. Friend.'

'What you were saying last night.' The words came out in a rush. 'About that man at the crematorium . . .'

'What about him?'

'Forget him.'

'I already have.' Lee pushed a stray strand of her hair behind her ear.

'I'm serious.'

'So am I.' He caught her hand. 'I don't care about him any more. If it hadn't been him, it would have been some other bastard.' Suddenly, his other hand was gripping the back of her neck. 'It's you I want, Diane.' He pulled her towards him. 'Last night was the best thing . . .'

She tried to struggle free. This wasn't the way the conversation was meant to be going. She attempted to visualise Malcolm's trusting face. 'Lee. I'm married. Middle-aged. You can do better than that. Find a girl your own age . . .'

'I don't want a girl my own age. I want you.' He dragged her towards him and kissed her hard; painfully hard, so that his teeth were bruising her mouth. For a moment she resisted. But only for a moment. Then her lips parted to his urgent tongue and they were dissolving into one another. After an eternity, Lee pulled back from her, breathing heavily. His eyes were bright in the semi-darkness as his fingers explored her. 'And whatever you try to make out, you want me too,' he whispered triumphantly.

Diane was in bed by the time Malcolm got back from Manchester. Feigning sleep, she listened as he moved stealthily around the bedroom, feeling his way in the dark rather than risk waking her. He was such a nice man, such a good husband, and she had let him down in the worst possible way. She could no longer pretend that Lee Smith meant nothing to her, that Ian was the sole cause of their involvement with each other. She'd been away from him for no more than a couple of hours, and already she craved him like a drug, panicked at the prospect of the void that stretched out in front of her until she could see him again after the weekend. Like an addict, she was frightened by what was happening to her. But she was powerless to stop it.

She tensed as Malcolm slid into the bed beside her, praying that he wouldn't reach out for her, forcing herself not to flinch as he laid his hand briefly on her shoulder. But he was too considerate a man to disturb her rest. Cautiously, he turned over onto his side. Within minutes his deep, regular breathing told Diane he was asleep. The sleep of the just.

She stared hot-eyed into the darkness, wide awake. Until yesterday, she'd thought of herself as an honest person.

She got up as soon as it was light, almost mad with the need to stretch her limbs after a sleepless night lying stock-still so as not to wake Malcolm. She dressed quickly and went downstairs. Her outfit for the party was hanging on the back of the kitchen door; the plan was that she would drive straight from the hairdresser to Arden Hall, to help with the last-minute organisation. She glanced without enthusiasm at the silk trouser suit she'd thought so smart when she'd chosen it; in the hard light of morning it looked frumpy and too formal.

The cat wove itself between her ankles mewing plaintively. Diane bent to stroke its velvety ear, but it ducked away from her, single-minded in its quest for food. Diane opened a tin of tuna and put some down. The cat crouched over its bowl, its back to her, and began to eat, dismissing her utterly. Diane envied it its contented egocentricity.

She made herself a coffee and sat at the kitchen table, staring into space. She thought of Lee, alone in the shabby little house in Earlsdon. Was he awake too? For the first time in her life, she wished she smoked. The digital clock on the microwave told her it was four thirty-five. She had nearly five hours to kill before her hair appointment.

She gazed around the immaculate kitchen, attempting to analyse what she felt for Lee. It could only be infatuation; what else? She knew next to nothing about him. So how could she even think of risking her relationship with Malcolm, about whom she knew everything? How he liked his eggs cooked, which page of the paper he read first, which pieces of music could move him to tears, which television programmes irritated him to distraction. She could have taken a PhD in the trivia of their everyday existence; the small domestic details that had taken fifteen years to acquire, that made them as comfortable together as a pair of well-worn shoes. The things that made them a couple. Was she really prepared to throw it all away for a man she barely knew; a man young enough to be her son?

Maybe that was it; maybe she was just a sad, childless middle-aged woman looking to fill the emptiness in her over-privileged life. That was how she would be judged by the outside world. But the outside world would be wrong. What she felt for Lee could not be explained away with middle-class psychobabble. Maybe it was a meeting of minds, then; two creative people drawn to each other by their passion for art. Except that only happened in books. She stood up and examined her reflection dispassionately in the shining glass door of the cooker. Maybe it was one last, frantic grab at life before she was too old. Or maybe it was simply lust, no more, no less. She found the notion oddly exhilarating. Lust. Exciting. Overwhelming. Unstoppable.

She went to the door, hesitated, then scribbled a note on the memo board by the fridge. '*Gone to the hairdresser's.*' It was true. Almost true. She'd be there eventually. She added a couple of kisses. Then she picked up her bag and let herself quietly out of the house.

It was nine forty-five by the time Diane got to the salon, breathless with apology.

The receptionist didn't exactly tut her disapproval, but it was close. 'Tristan has started on his next lady.' The woman's tortured vowels didn't conceal her Coventry accent any better than her over-glossed smile concealed her disdain for Diane's dishevelled appearance. 'You might have to wait.'

Diane was shampooed and shown to a chair. She caught her reflection in one of the ornate gilt mirrors. She wore no make-up and her hair was all over the place, but even to her own critical eye, she looked younger, more . . . alive. She took her mobile from the silly little embroidered bag that matched the trouser suit, then remembered that she didn't have Lee's number. She knew every intimate inch of his body, and he hers, and she didn't even know his telephone number. She smiled to herself as she pushed the phone back into her bag. A junior brought coffee and magazines. Still smiling, Diane closed her eyes, glad of a few moments to compose herself.

Lee had said nothing. He had simply held the door open for her, as if it were the most natural thing in the world to have her turn up on his doorstep at quarter to five in the morning. They hadn't even made it up to the bedroom. She blushed at the memory of the things he'd done to her. The things she'd done

79

to him. She could still feel the rasp of his stubbled cheeks against the tender skin of her breasts, her belly, her thighs. She'd never have believed herself capable of such wantonness. Her entire body was sore and burning with the pleasure of it. They'd arranged to meet at the cottage after the weekend. He'd come straight from work. She'd say she was working on the exhibition. She was already counting the hours until they could do it again. And again. And again.

'Penny for them!'

Diane opened her eyes abruptly, wondering how long Tristan had been standing behind her. Flushing, she stammered apologies for her lateness; the eyes of the outrageously camp stylist were every bit as sharp as his scissors, and he adored nothing more than a good gossip.

Tristan waved her apologies aside. 'So what are we doing today?'

'Just a quick trim, please.' Diane kept her eyes fixed on the magazine she'd opened at random. 'I'm in a bit of a rush, actually.'

'Going somewhere nice?' Tristan picked up his scissors.

'Family party.'

'Go on! From that smug little grin on your face, I thought you were going to say something much more exciting!' Head on one side, scissors poised, Tristan examined her in the mirror. 'You look absolutely fantastic, this morning, Mrs M!' He giggled as he tapped the side of his nose. 'Just like the cat that swallowed the cream!'

10

'ADULTERER!'

Diane swerved the car to a halt and stared up in horror at the banner that flapped lazily from the branch of an oak tree.

Ian was striding down the drive towards her. He followed her gaze, reached up and ripped the banner from its moorings then yanked open the car door.

'Thank you. I must have missed one.' The words were spoken between clenched teeth. 'I take it you didn't get round to talking to your friend yesterday.'

'I . . .' Diane got out of the car, her heart pounding. 'When did . . . ?'

'The florist was kind enough to point them out when she arrived first thing. Dominica and Marshall thought it was highly amusing.'

Diane closed her eyes. 'Oh, Jesus. Has Angelika . . . ?'

'Angelika has locked herself in the bedroom.' Ian jabbed a finger at her. 'This is all your fault, Diane. I shall be on the phone to the police immediately after the party. You're not going to talk me out of it this time. I should never have listened . . .'

'The party?' she echoed stupidly.

'Well, we can hardly cancel the fucking thing now, can we?' Ian snapped. 'I did try to ring you earlier, but Malcolm said you were at the hairdresser's.'

'Sorry. I . . .'

'You could try switching your bloody mobile on now and again. It's not much use doing it now, is it?' he went on angrily as she fumbled with her bag. 'I'll just have to say Angelika isn't well.' He crushed the banner in his fist. 'I'm telling you, Diane, if I could get my hands on that . . .'

'What . . . what time did the florist get here?' Diane forced her brain into gear.

'About eight thirty. For Christ's sake! Does it really matter?'

'But Lee . . .' She checked herself. What had she been about to say? That at eight thirty, and for several hours before that, Lee had been otherwise engaged?

Ian was already striding back towards the house. 'I don't want to hear that bastard's name,' he shouted. 'As soon as this fiasco's over, I'm calling the police, and that's the end of it.'

'Are you sure you're OK, darling?' Malcolm reached across the table and took Diane's hand.

'What?' Diane stared at him blankly.

The party was in full swing. Agnes Somerford had been duly surprised to find all her friends in attendance, suitably impressed with the marquee, and fulsome in her thanks to Ian for all his hard work. The buffet lunch had gone without a hitch, apart from the ice bucket that Dominica had sent flying in temper when told she wasn't allowed wine, and the entire chocolate gateau that Marshall had consumed whilst the first course was being served. He had at least made it out onto the lawn before vomiting copiously – at which point he had been taken back to the house by Claudine, the latest au pair – so things could have been much worse. Angelika had not put in an appearance, for one thing. Agnes, who abhorred her

American daughter-in-law, had seemed more than content to accept Ian's explanation of a sudden migraine.

A small part of Diane's brain had registered all those things. But only a very small part.

Lee had spent the time between their two meetings last night decorating Ian's garden with those poisonous banners – had been planning his vindictive little trip to Arden Hall even as he'd been fucking her in the back of her car. Had no doubt been gloating over the petty act of revenge as, later, he'd fucked her again on his cheap hall carpet. While, at home, Malcolm slept on, blissfully unaware of her betrayal. Those were the thoughts occupying Diane's conscious mind as the party went on around her.

Anger. Humiliation. Most of all, remorse.

'You know she's never very demonstrative with you.' Malcolm squeezed her hand. 'I'm sure she's thrilled with the brooch, really.'

Diane dragged her attention back to what her husband was saying. She followed his gaze to Agnes, who was sitting with Doris Crombie, her best friend from the bridge club, and a gaggle of their elderly cronies. Her face was flushed with pleasure and too much champagne, Thomas firmly secured on her lap. The pearl necklace Ian had given her was around her neck. The brooch Diane had designed for her was no-where in evidence.

'Mothers, eh?' Chas Newbould, a property developer and the money behind the Trinity Walks development, pushed his plate away from him and belched sympathetically. 'Who'd have them?'

He was a heavy man with a round, florid face, a drinker's nose and the small, inquisitive eyes of a rodent; a man whose proudest boast was that his considerable fortune had been accrued by cunning, rather than education. His big body never seemed entirely at home in its designer cladding; he had already tossed his jacket over the back of his chair and loosened his silk tie. He held up an empty bottle of wine to a passing waiter and revealed a dark semicircle of sweat in the armpit of his Yves Saint Laurent shirt.

'How would you know?' Lorraine Newbould, as thin as her husband was corpulent, held out her glass as the bottle was replaced. 'His is in a home in Solihull. He owns the bloody place, and still never gives the old bat the time of day. I'm the only one who goes to see her.'

'Lorraine's all heart.' Chas stuffed another after-dinner mint into his mouth and talked through it. 'What she doesn't tell you is that she always manages to combine the visits with a hefty dollop of retail therapy.'

'Might as well make the trip over there worthwhile, mightn't I?' She took a swig of wine and winked at him. 'Everyone knows I only married you for your money. Let's face it, why else would anyone put up with a tight-arsed old bastard like you?'

Lorraine and Chas Newbould had developed bickering to something approaching an art form. Diane smiled automatically. She found the couple wearing at the best of times.

'Hi, Lorraine! Enjoying yourself?' Ian had joined them at the table. 'Nice dress.'

'Bloody well ought to be nice,' Chas grumbled. 'Cost me a fucking arm and a leg.'

'Poor Angelika.' There was a glint of malice in Lorraine's eye. 'She must be ever so disappointed to be missing the party.'

'Yes.' Ian turned quickly to Diane. 'I think it's time to cut the cake, don't you?'

He'd made a good effort at playing the convivial host; even Agnes, who'd fussed over him since the day he was born, appeared not to have noticed the strain behind his expansive smile, the anxiety in his eyes when he glanced back towards the house, as he was doing now.

'I'll tell the caterers.' Diane forced herself to concentrate on the matter in hand. The quicker they could get the proceedings over with and everyone out of the way, the better. What happened after that, she'd face later. She looked down at Malcolm's strong hand, still resting on hers, and felt sick with shame and self-disgust. What had she done?

His fingers still lingered against her own as she got to her feet. 'Anything I can do?' he asked.

'Don't worry.' She stretched her lips into the semblance of a smile. 'Everything's under control.'

'Good party, Diane.' George Bonham looked up from his latest attack on the buffet as she made her way across the marquee. 'Brownie points all round, I'd say.'

'Let's hope so.' Under normal circumstances, Diane would have welcomed George's company; their friendship was casual, but had endured since primary school. Now, she found herself wondering whom he would represent in the divorce settlement, if Malcolm were to discover what she'd done.

'Not an easy task, pleasing your dear mother.' George helped himself to the last of the prawn vol-au-vents. His nonchalant tone didn't match the acuity of the glance he shot Diane as he added, 'You and Ian are both looking a little frayed around the edges, if you don't mind my saying so.'

'As you say, not an easy task.' She attempted a laugh, doubting he would be so easily fooled. Despite the carefully cultivated impression of a large, slightly shabby teddy bear, George Bonham possessed a sharp brain, as countless legal adversaries had discovered to their cost. Not meeting his eye she added brightly, 'Can't stop now, George. Cake and speeches to come yet, so keep your fingers crossed!'

There was a flurry of activity as plates were cleared and champagne glasses charged. A gasp of admiration went up from the assembled company as a trolley was pushed through the opening of the marquee, bearing a huge, pink-iced cake on which flickered seventy candles. Agnes's flush of pleasure deepened as Ian led the chorus of *Happy Birthday*. Dominica rolled her eyes and slumped further down in her chair. Everyone else clapped as Agnes blew out the candles, the wide-eyed Thomas still clasped to her bosom.

'To Mum.' Ian raised his glass. 'The bedrock of our family.'

It was at that precise moment, whether by chance or by a flawless sense of dramatic timing, that Angelika chose to make her entrance. She wove her way unsteadily towards her husband, her lipstick slightly smudged around the edges of her dazzling smile and called out, 'To Agnes.'

The glass she was clutching had clearly already seen plenty of action. She held it up in mocking salute and drained its contents before turning to Ian. 'Sorry to break up the party, honey. But there are a couple of cops in the hallway. They seem to want a word with you.'

Diane felt herself go cold. What was Ian playing at? Why the hell hadn't he waited until after the party as he'd promised? Surely he didn't intend to lay out the family's dirty linen for all to see? But Ian seemed as shocked as she. He looked across at her with a small shake of the head.

Angelika beamed around at the nonplussed guests. 'It shouldn't take too long. They probably just want to ask him a few more questions about the secretary he's been screwing. Threw herself off a high building a few weeks back.'

She shook her head with exaggerated care. 'Jeez, I wouldn't have said he was *that* bad in bed.'

Lorraine Newbould, her hand pressed to her mouth, let out a delighted giggle. The only other sound was a blackbird singing with glorious unconcern somewhere in the garden outside.

'You're drunk,' Agnes hissed.

Angelika rounded on her. 'And your precious son's in deep shit. But like the man said, come morning, I'll be sober.'

Agnes's expression remained unchanged. 'I haven't the faintest idea . . .'

'Damned right you haven't, you self-satisfied old crow! No fucking idea at all.' Angelika turned her attention back to her husband. 'What if I were to tell your doting mother you've been . . . ?'

'Angelika. Please.' Ian's face was ashen. 'This isn't the time or the . . .'

'Why not? Where better than in the bosom of your loving family? Don't you want to share it with the group, honey?'

Ian's eyes darted to his mother before he said weakly, 'It's her *birthday*, for Christ's sake.'

'Why, so it is! In all the excitement, I almost forgot.'

Diane's hands flew to her mouth as Angelika grabbed the knife that was lying beside the cake. There was a collective gasp of horror as those guests nearest to her scrambled to their feet.

'My, what a bunch of scaredy-cats you Brits are!' Angelika looked around the marquee and gave a high, brittle laugh. 'I only want to cut the cake! You don't mind, do you Agnes? Seeing as I missed out on the rest of the celebrations?' Not waiting for a reply, she plunged the knife into it, hacking it in two before turning back to her husband with a look of pure

87

venom. 'There, that seems about fair, doesn't it? Half for you and half for me.'

Ian stared at her in stunned silence.

She looked him up and down. 'What's the matter? Cat got your tongue? Well, let me start the ball rolling.' Teetering slightly, she pushed past him and snatched Thomas from Agnes's arms. 'Mine, I believe.'

The baby let out a startled wail at the abruptness of the action and tried to struggle free of his mother's grip.

'It's OK, sweetie.' Angelika grabbed a handful of cake and rammed it into his mouth. 'There, that's better, isn't it?'

Thomas spluttered and began to cough.

'Angelika . . .' Ian said helplessly. 'Don't. He doesn't want . . .'

Diane could contain herself no longer. As Angelika picked up another chunk of cake, she rushed forward and shouted, 'Stop it, you drunken bitch! You're choking him!'

'And you'd be the expert on babies, of course.' Angelika sneered. She pressed her face close to Thomas and whispered, 'Sorry, sweetie. Aunty Di says no more cake. And we all have to do what Aunty Di says, don't we?' She cradled the struggling child to her, her eyes still on Diane. 'Never mind, Tommy. You can eat as much cake as you like when we get you back to the States.'

'Angelika!' Ian tried to take hold of her arm. 'You don't know what you're saying!'

'I know exactly what I'm saying, you prick!' she yelled over Thomas's escalating screams. 'How dare you cheat on me?' Flecks of spittle had gathered at the corners of her scarlet mouth, tears of rage turned her mascara into sooty rivulets. 'Christ! You couldn't fuck your way out of a wet paper bag and you have the nerve to . . .'

'I think that's enough, don't you?' It was Malcolm who took control of the situation. Ian stood back as the other man strode forward and gripped Angelika firmly by the wrist. 'Give Thomas to me. You're frightening him.'

'And just who the fuck do you think you are, to be telling me what to do with my own baby?'

Malcolm's voice was like ice. 'Be quiet, you stupid woman. You're making an exhibition of yourself.'

For a moment, Angelika looked as if she was going to face up to him. Her mouth worked angrily and she tried to pull herself free of his grip.

Malcolm's face remained stony. 'Give him to me, before you do any more damage.'

Angelika stared at him hard; it couldn't have been often that a man had spoken to her so dismissively. Then she tossed back her hair, bundled Thomas into his arms and muttered, 'Whatever.'

Malcolm exhaled slowly. He nodded towards Dominica, who had been watching the unfolding spectacle in open-mouthed amazement. 'Help me get your mother back to the house. She's not feeling well.'

For a moment, Dominica looked as if she might be about to argue. Then, with an elaborate shrug, she shuffled forward, her face burning.

On impulse, Diane reached out to touch the girl's arm as she passed, and whispered, 'Are you all right?' She couldn't begin to imagine how Dominica must be feeling to have witnessed such a spectacle; despite her precocious ways, she was still only a child. And Angelika was her mother.

Dominica shot her a venomous stare and pulled back from her as if she had been scalded.

A muted, hesitant hum of conversation started up around

the tables. Thomas's screams had subsided to a snuffling whimper. Malcolm kissed the top of his head then handed him to Diane. She held the baby's hot little cheek against hers, her emotions churning, and murmured, 'Do you want me to come with you?'

'We'll manage.' Malcolm and Dominica hauled Angelika to her feet. He turned to Ian, who was still standing next to Agnes, sheet-white and silent from his wife's onslaught, and said curtly, 'You'd better go and see what the police want before they come down here looking for you. I think we've provided everyone with enough to gossip about as it is.'

'Yes.' Ian ran his hand through his hair. 'Yes,' he repeated, not moving. He caught the eye of one of the catering staff and waved an ineffectual hand towards his guests, most of whom were trying resolutely to act as if nothing had happened. 'Maybe some tea . . .'

Diane fought to suppress a laugh of pure hysteria at the very Britishness of the suggestion. His life was crashing down about his ears, and Ian was suggesting tea.

'I'll come with you.' George Bonham had moved discreetly to join them.

'No. I . . .' Ian gazed at the other man for a moment, then, making a visible effort to pull himself together, said firmly, 'Thanks, George, but I don't need a solicitor.'

George gave a small smile. 'I think I'm possibly the better judge of that.'

'But I haven't done anything.'

'Let's not be naïve, old chap.' George took Ian's arm and steered him towards the entrance of the marquee. 'You can fill me in on the way back to the house.'

Agnes stood by the entrance to the marquee, her mouth set in a thin line of disapproval as she watched the small party straggle back towards the house, Malcolm and Dominica supporting Angelika's weight, George and Ian some distance behind them, deep in conversation.

'I suppose I should be grateful that one of you at least managed to choose a sensible partner,' she observed in what was the closest thing to a compliment Diane had received from her in years.

Diane felt an unaccustomed wave of sympathy towards her mother. Appearance was everything to the older woman; for Angelika's exhibition to have taken place in front of all her friends would have been her worst nightmare.

'Let's have a walk round the garden,' she suggested. 'Try and clear our heads a bit.'

To her surprise, Agnes nodded.

They walked slowly and in silence towards the paddocks at the far end of the garden. Thomas, a hand in each of theirs, staggered happily between them, practising his new-found talent. One of the ponies ambled across to greet them as they reached the fence. Agnes hoisted Thomas up onto her hip and guided his hand to stroke the animal's head.

'Don't be frightened,' she said fiercely as Thomas flinched away from the pony's inquisitive muzzle. She placed his hand against its dusty neck. Hesitantly, Thomas patted it. The pony whickered softly and pressed itself closer to the fence.

'There. Show it you're not afraid and it won't hurt you.' It wasn't the pony she was talking about. Diane could see her mother was trying hard not to cry.

'What Angelika said about Ian,' she said gently, wishing they were closer; that she could have put her arms around her mother and given her a hug. 'It wasn't true, you know.'

'What a ridiculous thing to say. Of course it wasn't true!' Agnes gathered Thomas into her arms. 'And if that American trollop imagines she's going to take my grandson away from me, she's got a fight on her hands.' She took a lace handkerchief from her handbag, spat on it, and began to scrub angrily at his cake-smeared mouth. Then she straightened her shoulders and said briskly, 'Right. It's time I was getting back to the marquee.' She lowered Thomas to the ground, then blotted the corners of her eyes with the handkerchief, patted her hair and rearranged her features into a determined smile. 'I have my guests to attend to.'

The party had already started to break up. The caterers circulated with champagne and slices of salvaged cake, but no one's heart was in it, and those of Agnes's friends with their own transport sloped off as quickly as they decently could. Agnes was air-kissed and thanked for a wonderful day. No one mentioned Angelika's outburst. The fat-chewing would come later, Diane suspected.

Malcolm returned to report that Angelika had been put to bed without further incident and Dominica and Marshall were watching a video with Claudine.

'How's Ian?' Diane asked anxiously.

Malcolm glanced over at his mother-in-law, who was facing it out with a group of friends from her bridge club. 'He's been taken in for questioning.'

'Questioning?' Diane stared at him, aghast. 'What about?'

'Nicola Smith, presumably. Just routine, George said. Thank God he was here.'

'Why the hell didn't you come and get me? Someone should have gone with him . . .'

'George has gone with him.' Malcolm put his hand on her shoulder. 'I did offer, but there's nothing either of us could have done anyway. We wouldn't have been allowed to see him once he'd got to the police station.' He glanced around the marquee and lowered his voice even further. 'I thought it was best to play it down until we'd got rid of this lot.'

Diane nodded abstractedly. 'But why would the police want to . . . ?'

Malcolm gave a snort of mirthless laughter. 'You'd need to ask your friend Lee Smith about that, I imagine.'

Suddenly, it was all too much: the lies, the deceit. Malcolm was going to find out soon enough; better it was from her own mouth. Diane could feel tears welling in her eyes. 'He's not my friend. He's . . .'

'I'm sorry. I shouldn't have said that,' Malcolm said quickly. His expression softened. 'Try not to worry.' He slipped his arm around her shoulder.

'Why are you so good to me?' she whispered.

Malcolm smiled at her. 'Silly girl.' He held her to him. 'Everything will turn out OK. You'll see.' An expression she couldn't quite read crossed his face as he added, 'It's not as if Ian's done anything illegal, is it?'

The words jarred. Diane wondered what Malcolm had meant by them, but before she could ask he shook his head slightly, his eyes signalling the need for caution. A second later, Chas Newbould clapped his meaty hand on her shoulder.

'Everything OK?' Chas's shrewd eyes darted from one of them to the other.

'Fine, thanks.'

'Ian got things sorted then, has he?'

'Yes. He's inside with Angelika.' Diane could see Chas's curiosity was far from satisfied. She looked the man in the eye. 'He sends his apologies for not being here to see everyone off.'

'Right. Well, we'd better be going then. Thanks for the party.' Chas's voice was uncharacteristically subdued.

She managed a tight smile. 'It's Mum you should be thanking. It's her party.'

'What a performance, eh?' Lorraine bustled across, her face still alight with excitement as she air-kissed Diane. 'I'd never have thought Ian had it in him!'

'Had what?' Diane asked coldly.

'Don't you go making things worse than they already are, you silly bitch,' Chas grumbled. 'Trap the size of the Mersey tunnel, she's got. Take no notice of her, luv.' He turned back to Malcolm. 'You still on for tomorrow afternoon, Malc?'

Malcolm blinked, clearly as stunned by the man's insensitivity as Diane.

'A round of golf's just what you need. Do you good to blow a few cobwebs away after all this malarkey.'

Malcolm glanced towards Diane. 'Maybe I'd better give you a ring in the morning, Chas.'

'You don't mind, do you, luv? I expect you'll be off having a bit of retail therapy somewhere anyway.' Chas winked ponderously. 'That's what you ladies always do when you've had a bit of an upset, isn't it?'

Diane kept her mouth clamped tightly shut.

'We'll take that as a pass-out then, shall we?' Chas grinned at Malcolm. 'See you tomorrow afternoon.'

Malcolm's face was still set in a smile as Chas strode off across the lawn, leaving Lorraine to totter after him in her Jimmy Choos. He didn't allow his facial muscles to relax until the couple disappeared out of view. 'I'd like to have slapped the pair of them too,' he muttered, 'but Somerford's can't afford to get on the wrong side of the bloody man, I'm afraid. We'd feel the draught without his backing, and he knows it.'

'Lorraine will be dining out on it all for weeks as it is.' Diane glanced across at Agnes, who was waving off the last of her guests and still making a supreme effort to pretend everything was as it should be. She felt her heart sink as she thought despondently of how much more scandal was still to come. 'All of them will.'

'Well, Ian said he wanted to give her a birthday to remember.' Malcolm's face was grim. 'And it looks like he's managed it in spades.'

11

'Well, that's that, I suppose.'

Agnes turned from waving off the last of the guests. Her face sagged as she allowed her cheek muscles to relax. Despite the careful make-up, she looked every one of her seventy years. The woman who had ruled them with her steely, velvet-gloved hand for as long as either of them could remember was getting old, Diane realised with a small shock. It was hard to imagine her mother's strength diminishing, her grip failing; she could be irritatingly snobbish, exasperatingly domineering, but Agnes was also the centre of the family.

'Maybe you should get home too. It's been a long day for you,' Diane said quickly as Agnes turned back towards the house; she could only imagine the uproar that would ensue when her mother discovered Ian wasn't there.

'What nonsense!' Agnes batted her daughter's hand away. 'I'm not going anywhere until I've spoken to Ian. And someone needs to keep an eye on the caterers,' she added acerbically as Diane attempted to interrupt. 'Otherwise they'll be walking off with the rest of the champagne. You have to watch them, you know.'

Diane grabbed the chance to get her out of the way. 'Why don't you go and supervise them?'

'I want to check on Thomas first.'

'I can do that.' Diane steered her back towards the garden.

'You see to the caterers. You're much better at dealing with them than I am.'

'I should be, with all the parties I've thrown over the years. We weren't always off out to restaurants, like you young ones.'

Diane watched with relief as her mother strode off down the garden, then made her way back into the house. The playroom was empty; from the window, she could see that Claudine had taken Dominica and Marshall back into the garden and was attempting to keep them occupied as far away from the marquee as possible.

She went up to the nursery and checked on Thomas, who had been put down for a nap. He was fast asleep, his breathing so quiet she had to strain to hear it. Claudine had changed him from the elaborate outfit he'd been wearing earlier into his pyjamas, and freed his feet from the ludicrous black patent shoes they'd been laced into. He looked utterly comfortable and at peace, his chubby legs splayed out like a little frog, his hands behind his head. Diane reached into the cot, then checked herself. She felt too grubby to touch him.

The door to Angelika's bedroom was ajar. Cautiously, Diane stuck her head around it. The curtains were undrawn and sunlight streamed in on Angelika's recumbent form. She was sprawled across the bed, fully dressed. A thin trail of saliva dribbled from the side of her mouth, and she was snoring. Diane felt a brief surge of malice as she viewed the unattractive spectacle, before her eyes travelled to the bedside table, on which stood a nearly empty bottle of vodka, and next to it an open box of tablets.

'Oh, Jesus,' she muttered under her breath.

Moving quickly into the room, she snatched up the box. Mogadon. She was relieved to see that only a couple of the foil

97

compartments had been broken. Not some kind of dramatic gesture, then. Just a short-cut to help the vodka along.

Angelika stirred, letting out a gentle fart as she flopped over onto her side. Diane stared down at her for a moment in disgust before stuffing the tablets into her bag. As she did so a sudden, incongruous cheer drifted up from the back garden. She went over to the window to shut it, although she doubted a brass band would have disturbed Angelika in her present condition.

She paused to observe the scene below. Malcolm had the children engaged in a game of French cricket. Diane was amazed to see Dominica's face transformed from its habitual expression of sulky boredom by a wide grin. She was waving the ball she had evidently just caught, as Malcolm laughed good-naturedly and handed over the bat before turning to salute Marshall, the triumphant bowler. They switched places, and Malcolm made an exaggerated run-up before pitching the ball at the centre of the bat, allowing Dominica to whack it the length of the lawn. The girl's face was flushed with pleasure as he applauded. Diane turned away from the window, her eyes stinging. He would have made such a good father.

As she tiptoed out of the bedroom and stepped onto the landing, she heard the sound of the front door closing. Ian and George were standing together in the hall. Ian looked up at the sound of her footsteps, his face haggard. She hurried down the stairs, her heart hammering. 'What happened?'

George glanced at Ian queryingly. 'Just a few routine questions,' he said, when Ian didn't reply.

Diane felt an intense urge to slap him. It was like a ward sister saying the patient was as comfortable as could be expected. 'What did they say to you, Ian?' she demanded.

Ian jerked his head towards the study. 'Let's go in here.' He turned to the other man as he went to follow them in. 'Would you mind, George?'

George hesitated, glancing from Diane to Ian. 'No. No, of course not.'

Ian shut the door firmly behind them. 'Sit down.'

Wordlessly, Diane did as she was bidden. She needed no other indication than her brother's expression to confirm that George had been trying to make light of the situation.

'The police wanted to know where I was on the night of Nicki's death,' Ian said without preamble.

'But why?' Diane demanded, her other worries temporarily forgotten. 'She killed herself. The coroner . . .'

'Pronounced an open verdict. And now the police have "received additional information".' Ian's mouth twisted into a sneer. 'No guesses where that came from.'

Diane could feel the treacherous colour rising in her cheeks. 'What sort of additional information?'

'It seems someone has sent an anonymous letter to the Chief Constable. The bastard obviously didn't think it was enough, just writing to Angelika. Anyway, it seems to have set the police sniffing around. A lot of money was deposited in Nicki's bank account in the weeks before she died. So they've put two and two together and made five. I'm her boss, so therefore I'm her lover. I get tired of shelling out on her, therefore I push her over the balcony. Simple, isn't it? And thanks to her bloody husband, the more I deny I had any connection with her outside work, the more they think I'm lying.'

'But that's ludicrous!' Diane stared at him in horror.

'It's ludicrous to you, it's ludicrous to me.' Ian poured himself a large Scotch and held up the bottle, to which she shook her head impatiently. 'To the police it appears to make perfect bloody sense.'

'Well . . .' She ran her hands through her hair and tried to think. 'You must have some kind of alibi for the night she died, surely? Just tell them where you were . . .'

'I was here.' He took a sip of the Scotch. 'It was the night of Chas Newbould's party, if you recall. Angelika had gone to her bloody yoga class and I was baby-sitting.'

'So where's the problem?'

Ian gave a derisive snort. 'Well, quite apart from the fact that in her present frame of mind I doubt Angelika is likely to substantiate anything I say, how am I supposed to prove I actually stayed here?' He drained the glass in one long swig and poured himself another. 'I don't think the evidence of two sleeping children and a teething baby is going to get me very far, do you?'

'But you'd never leave them on their own . . .'

'Try telling that to the police.'

'Are you saying they didn't believe you?'

Ian rubbed his hand across his eyes. He sank down into a chair beside the desk. 'I've no bloody idea what they believe, to be honest.'

She wanted to shake him. 'So how was it left?'

'They thanked me politely for my time and asked me to make myself available for further questioning.' He gave her a thin smile. 'I think it rather caught them on the hop that I'd taken my solicitor with me.'

'Did you mention anything about . . . ?' Diane hesitated, despising the instinct for self-preservation that forced her to ask the question. 'Did you tell them about the other stuff?'

'Of course I did. And I think I know his game, as well. I was checking some old payroll stuff and I realised he worked for us, a couple of years ago. Just casual stuff. He got the sack for giving the foreman too much mouth. It must have really pissed him off that Nicki was doing so well with us. I told the police I reckon he's got some kind of twisted grudge against the company, and that's what all this is about.' He shrugged. 'Not that they seemed very interested.'

Diane's brain was racing. Concentrate on what was happening to Ian, she urged herself. She could hear the tremor in her voice as she asked, 'What did George say?'

'George thought I'd have been wiser not to volunteer any information they hadn't directly asked for. Reckoned rubbishing the grieving husband hadn't done me any favours. George doesn't believe I wasn't screwing Nicola, of course.'

Before Diane could respond, the door was tapped hesitantly and Malcolm stuck his head into the room. He scanned Ian's face and said, 'How did it go?'

Diane glanced past him and said in a low voice, 'Is Mum around? Or the children?'

'She's in the kitchen making tea. The kids are still in the garden.' Malcolm's frown deepened. 'Why?'

Diane looked at Ian, who merely shook his head and poured himself another Scotch. As briefly as she could, she filled Malcolm in.

'Jesus.' Malcolm gazed at them both in disbelief. 'The whole thing's . . .'

'Ludicrous?' Ian gave a low, bitter laugh. 'Damned right it is. But you try proving it, when even your own damned solicitor doesn't believe you.' He pulled himself to his feet. 'Still, no good sitting around here. I'd better go and get packed.'

Diane looked at him in alarm. 'What on earth do you mean?'

'I don't think Angelika's going to want me here when she comes round, do you?' Ian's voice snagged on the words. His shoulders drooped suddenly and he shook his head. 'Christ, what a bloody mess, eh?'

'You've got to be joking!' Diane jumped up, filled with sudden irritation at her brother's utter lack of fight. 'For God's sake, Ian, pull yourself together! You can't leave the children with her in the state she's in.'

'Claudine will be here.' He walked unsteadily to the filing cabinet and began rummaging through his papers.

Malcolm glanced across at Diane and cleared his throat. 'What are you doing, Ian?'

'Getting our passports.' Ian produced a fat brown envelope which he stuffed into his pocket. 'I can at least stop her taking off back to the States with the kids.'

'Don't be ridiculous!' Diane felt a small, cold flutter of fear in the pit of her stomach. 'Angelika would never actually . . .'

'Why not? You saw her this afternoon.' Ian threw back his head and gave a harsh laugh. 'Christ, she doesn't even know the half of it yet, does she?'

Nobody knew the half of it. Diane forced herself to concentrate on the matter in hand. 'But she can't just take them! There are procedures . . .' She turned to Malcolm who shrugged helplessly. 'There's no way any court in the world would think Angelika was a fit mother! Only five minutes ago, I found a packet of sleeping tablets on her bedside table where any one of the children could have got hold of them and thought they were sweets. That's how good a parent she is!' She turned back to Ian. 'This is your home! Why should you be driven out of it when you haven't done anything wrong?'

'And since when has that been of any relevance?'

'Ian may have a point, you know,' Malcolm said cautiously. 'It might be better if he stayed out of Angelika's way for a few days. Until he's got everything sorted out with the police, at least.'

Diane scanned her husband's face. It wasn't only George Bonham who doubted Ian's fidelity, she realised with a shock.

She turned back to Ian and said urgently, 'At least come and stay with us.'

'I'd rather be on my own.' He gave her the ghost of a smile. 'I need some space to get my head round all of this. I'll find a hotel.'

'We wouldn't hear of it!' It was suddenly imperative that he knew they were behind him. Both of them. 'Would we, Malcolm?'

Malcolm's expression gave nothing away. 'If Ian feels he'd rather . . .'

'He can have the cottage then.' Not waiting for a reply, Diane took her keys from her handbag and held them out. 'Here. Take them. At least you'll be somewhere familiar. The last thing you need is to be stuck in some miserable hotel room at a time like this.'

Ian hesitated.

'Take them. I insist.'

'Are you sure that's OK?' It was to Malcolm that the words were addressed.

Malcolm held Ian's gaze for a long moment. Then he took the keys from Diane and pressed them into his hand. 'Of course we're sure.' Diane hoped she was alone in registering the effort in her husband's smile as he added firmly, 'What are families for?'

Agnes was outraged.

'I've never heard such a ridiculous idea,' she snapped when Ian went through to the kitchen where she and George were drinking tea in an atmosphere of palpable hostility. 'Why should you be forced from your own home on the whim of that . . . woman?' The venom she packed into so apparently neutral a word was remarkable. 'And as for letting her . . .'

'The arrangement's only temporary, Mrs Somerford.' George Bonham's voice was soothing. 'It's simply a matter of . . .'

Agnes rounded on him. 'A fine solicitor you've turned out to be, letting the police trump up such filthy allegations against a good, decent family man like my Ian. You should be suing them for wrongful arrest, instead of sitting here talking about . . .'

'No one's been arrested, Agnes,' Malcolm murmured.

'No thanks to him.' Agnes glared at George. 'And what about the welfare of those poor children? You can't leave Thomas in the hands of some drink-sodden . . .'

'Claudine will look after the children.' Diane glanced anxiously in Ian's direction as Agnes opened her mouth in dissent. He had yet to join in the discussion, but she could sense his tension; his knuckles were white around the mug he was gripping, his face stony as their mother continued her list of objections.

'She'll never manage all three of them. I'll take Thomas home with me. I can pack up his things in no time and . . .'

'No.' Ian stared into his mug.

'I absolutely insist. No grandchild of mine is going to be . . .'

'I said no.'

The harshness of his tone silenced even Agnes, if only momentarily. She pursed her mouth into the expression of injured disapproval more usually reserved for Diane. 'Well, if you'd rather have some foreigner looking after your only son than your own mother, I suppose that's your business.' She gave Ian a long look, then, goaded by his lack of response, went on, 'But if you ask me . . .'

'I didn't ask you!' Ian slammed the mug down so hard that it shattered against the worktop.

There was a moment of absolute silence, broken as George Bonham cleared his throat and murmured, 'I should be off.' He held out his hand to Ian, who was staring fixedly at the tea as it spilled over the edge of the worktop and dripped into a growing puddle on the floor beneath. 'Right, then.' George withdrew the hand. 'Give me a ring after the weekend, and we'll talk things through.' He glanced warily at Agnes, then ducked his head towards Malcolm and Diane in valediction. 'I'll see myself out.'

Agnes picked up her handbag and turned to Diane. 'I'd like to go home.' She shot Ian a glare. 'Seeing as I'm obviously not welcome here.'

'I'm sorry,' Ian said in a low voice, his eyes still on the puddle.

Agnes bridled. 'And so you should be, speaking to your own mother as if . . .'

'For Christ's sake! I've said I'm sorry, haven't I?' Ian's eyes were blazing. 'What more do you want?'

'It's been a long day,' Diane said quickly, anxious to stop him saying something he might later regret. His anger had shocked her; she'd never heard him raise his voice to Agnes in his life. 'We're all a bit overwrought, that's all.'

Two bright spots of colour burned in Agnes's cheeks. 'Just take me home, please.'

'I'll go and get the car,' Malcolm muttered, clearly embarrassed.

'Don't let the day end like this.' Diane looked from one of them to the other. 'Remember what you used to tell us, Mum?'

she cajoled. 'Never let the sun go down on a quarrel? Especially this day.'

Agnes's lip trembled but she didn't speak.

Briefly, Ian closed his eyes. Then he said quietly, 'I'm sorry, Mum. I shouldn't have shouted at you.'

Agnes sniffed.

It was with visible effort that he reached for his mother's hand. But Agnes was not yet ready for reconciliation. She stood ramrod-stiff as he put his arm around her. She returned his kiss with only the most perfunctory and grudging of pecks; an act of petulance she would come to regret for the rest of her life.

12

'You don't believe him, do you?'

Diane and Malcolm were sitting at the dining-room table the following day, surrounded by their largely uneaten Sunday lunch. Until that moment, they had both studiously avoided talking about Ian. Malcolm had shut himself in his study when they'd finally got home the previous evening. Ian was hardly going to be in a fit state to handle the business, he'd pointed out; someone was going to have to hold the fort. He'd been up before she was awake, and had spent much of the morning on the phone before going out into the garden and tackling the high laurel hedges that bounded the plot; a job he detested but, involving as it did a tall ladder and a noisy electric hedge cutter, one that successfully precluded any communication. For Diane, the absence of conversation had been a relief. The need to unburden herself was almost overwhelming; how could they hope to tackle Ian's problems with the huge wedge of her deceit between them? But could she seriously choose this moment to throw another potentially explosive factor into the equation? She didn't need to ask the question; her own squalid little secret was going to have to wait.

She'd rung Ian as soon as she'd woken. He'd been distant; had made no secret of the fact she'd got him out of bed. She'd tried again later in the morning, but he hadn't answered. The third time she'd tried, his phone had been switched off. Maybe he thought she didn't believe him either.

Conversation over lunch had comprised a series of stilted non sequiturs: the weather, the need to find another gardener, the 'For Sale' notice that had gone up outside the house of one of their neighbours. But now, as the meal came to an end, Diane felt compelled to return to the events of the previous day, like a moth heading relentlessly towards a flame. Malcolm had retreated behind his paper as soon as he'd swallowed his last mouthful of rhubarb crumble. Diane pushed her own uneaten dessert aside and glared with unreasonable irritation at the unmoving barrier of newsprint between them. She knew he'd heard her. She also knew picking a fight with him wasn't going to help anyone. But she did it anyway.

'Do you?'

Malcolm lowered the paper with an air of resignation. 'If you're asking if I think Ian had anything to do with Nicola Smith's death, then no, of course I don't.'

Her own guilt made her snappy. 'You know that's not what I mean.'

Malcolm took an apple from the fruit bowl and peeled it with unnecessary care before replying. 'Then the answer is that I honestly don't know.'

'But he swore to me . . .'

Diane registered the faint flicker of annoyance that crossed her husband's face as he quartered the apple. 'Then my opinion doesn't really matter, does it?'

'Of course it matters.' She paused, knowing how much wiser, for so many reasons, it would be to let the matter drop. 'What makes you think he was having an affair with her, anyway?'

'I didn't say I thought he was having an affair. I just said . . .'

Malcolm sighed heavily. 'There's been the odd bit of gossip at work, that's all.'

'What sort of gossip?'

'Oh, I don't know.' He put down the apple. 'I don't think Nicola made any secret of the fact she didn't have much time for her husband, for one thing. And then there was the incident at her funeral, of course. That did nothing to dampen down the speculation. I suppose we can only thank God the bloody banners went up at Arden Hall, and not outside the office.' He reached across and took Diane's hand. 'Look, love, I know Ian's your brother and you don't want to think badly of him, but I have to say he and Nicola did seem pretty . . . close. And then there's that money that had been deposited in her bank account.' He paused. 'Ian's sold a number of his letting properties in the last couple of months. He told me Angelika had run up some debts that needed settling, but with hindsight . . .'

Diane snorted, glad to find a target for her anger. 'There's hardly anything new about Angelika spending Ian's money for him.'

'That's as maybe. But when you add Lee Smith's behaviour into the equation . . . No, just try to look at it rationally,' he cut across her. 'Would anyone really go to all the trouble of writing anonymous letters – painting banners, for God's sake – unless he was pretty bloody sure of his ground?'

Diane swallowed hard. Lee Smith was the last person she wanted to be talking about. 'Ian reckons he might have some kind of a grudge against the company. He was a labourer there, for a while.'

Malcolm pulled a face. 'Sounds a bit far-fetched to me. You know the bloke better than I do. Does he seem like that much of a nutter to you?'

'Forget it.' She jumped to her feet and began clattering the plates together, praying that Malcolm wouldn't notice the colour that had flooded her cheeks. Why the hell had she brought up the subject of infidelity, when it could only ever lead back to herself? 'Just forget I ever said anything.'

'I didn't mean to upset you,' he said stiffly. 'You asked me the question. I was just trying to answer it.'

The phone began to ring in the hall.

'I'll get it.' Diane fled the kitchen. She snatched up the phone. 'Yes?'

'I called earlier on but your old man answered, so I said I was selling double-glazing.'

She felt her knees buckle. 'How the hell did you get this number?' she hissed.

'How many Middletons do you think live on the Kenilworth Road?' Lee chuckled. 'Is it safe to talk?'

'No.' She slammed down the receiver, her heart pounding.

'Who was that?' Malcolm was frowning as he followed her into the hall.

'Nobody.' She pressed her hands to her sides to stop them trembling. 'Someone selling double-glazing.'

'I had the same thing this morning.' He sounded irritable. 'I thought you said you'd phoned somewhere and got those bloody calls stopped.'

She had, weeks ago. 'I forgot.'

'Well maybe you could get it sorted. I object to having my weekends disturbed by morons trying to sell me things I already have. I get enough of that at work.' He picked up his clubs. 'Anyway, I'd better get off. I'm supposed to be meeting Chas at two.'

Diane bit her lip. 'Do you have to go?'

'Someone's got to keep Chas Newbould sweet. I don't

suppose he was too impressed by yesterday's performance.'

She fought to suppress the absurd conviction that if he went, he might never come back. If they could just be here, together. Spend the Sunday afternoon as they had spent so many comfortable Sunday afternoons; pretend everything was as it had always been . . . She put her hand out to him. 'Listen, I'm sorry I snapped. It's just that . . .'

'It's just that you can't face the fact that Saint Ian the Divine might possibly be less than perfect.' Malcolm swung the clubs over his shoulder and headed for the front door. 'Well, don't take it out on me because he's turned out to have feet of clay.'

Diane was stunned by the bitterness in his voice. 'That isn't fair! He's my brother. Of course I'm going to . . .'

'Yes. And I'm your husband.' Malcolm slammed the door behind him.

She pulled it open and ran after him. 'Malcolm, wait . . .'

He threw the clubs into the boot and banged it shut without looking at her.

'What time will you be back?'

'Who knows?' he shouted over his shoulder as he got into the car. 'I expect you'll be over at the cottage holding Ian's hand anyway, so it doesn't really matter, does it?'

'You managed to get away, then.' Lee's face lit up as he held the door open. 'Come in.' He was barefoot and wearing only a pair of crumpled jeans that sat low on his hips. A line of dark hair snaked down his flat, muscled belly and disappeared below the open top button of his fly.

Diane stayed where she was, her arms folded defensively in front of her. 'We need to talk.'

Lee grinned. 'Is this how we've got to start every time?'

'What the hell are you trying to do to us all, you bastard?'

She'd come to the house with no clear idea of how she was going to handle the confrontation, but Lee's evident amusement stung her into immediate attack.

He put up his hands in mock surrender. 'OK, so I shouldn't have rung you when your old man was there. There's no need to . . .'

'Christ, you must have been laughing your head off! All that crap I was giving you about letting it go, and you'd already got your next move planned. *"Fuck the silly bitch. That'll keep her quiet."* Is that what you were thinking while you were screwing me in the back of my car?'

Lee rocked back slightly on his heels. Genuine surprise? Or parody? 'Just calm down, for Christ's sake! What the hell's going on?'

'You know damned well what's going on! Well you've achieved what you set out to do. Wrecked his marriage, for what that was worth. Most likely lost him his son. Oh, and the police have been questioning him too, so he'll probably get arrested next. And for what? You were all over me like a rash the night of your precious wife's funeral, so it was hardly Romeo and Juliet, was it?'

Diane knew she was being irrational, and she didn't care. She knew she was standing in the middle of the street and shouting like a fishwife for all to hear, and she didn't care. While Lee had been making love to her, his head had been full of revenge. The adultery that had seemed so momentous to her, that now threatened the very fabric of her existence, had meant nothing to him; a quick fix for his sexual frustration. Somewhere, deep in her heart of hearts, she acknowledged that at least part of her fury was fuelled by that humiliating knowledge.

'What's the matter with you?' Lee grabbed her wrist and

pulled her inside the house, slamming the door behind her. 'I don't know what the fuck you're on about.'

'Or maybe Ian's got the right idea.' She could feel the heat from his body, smell the sharply erotic tang of his sweat. She concentrated on her anger. 'Maybe you're just trying to get back at him because Nicola was a success and you couldn't even hold down a job carrying bricks, or whatever it was you . . .'

'Ian?'

'Yes, Eeyun.' Savagely, she mimicked Lee's strong Coventry accent. 'Ian Somerford. How many other men are you accusing of sleeping with your wife?'

He took a step back from her, looked her up and down before saying slowly, 'So how come you know so much about what's going on in that bastard's life?'

'Because he's my brother, you stupid prick. That's how.' Diane turned away from him and fumbled with the door catch, desperate to be away before she gave way to the tears that were suddenly constricting her throat.

Lee's hand shot up over her head and shoved the door shut again as she opened it. 'You're telling me you're Ian Somerford's *sister*? Why the fuck didn't you say so from the start?'

Diane felt a prickle of fear. 'Let me out.'

'It never occurred to you to say? Just slipped your mind, like?'

'I said, let me out.' She tugged ineffectually at the door catch, but Lee's weight remained against the door.

'So did he send you here, or what?' His voice was dangerously controlled.

'No, of course he didn't!' She turned to face him, seriously frightened now. 'He doesn't know anything about us.'

'So what was it made you offer me a lift home that night?

Idle curiosity?' Lee made a sudden lunge for her, slamming her head back against the door. 'Or did it just seem like a good laugh to shaft me, same as he'd been shafting my wife?'

'Let go of me!' Diane brought her knee up hard. But not hard enough; the blow caught Lee off balance, but he was back at her before she had time to get the door open.

'You bitch!' He hit her, hard, across the face.

She dropped to her knees, her head exploding into stars. She'd never been struck in her life; the tears that sprang to her eyes came as much from shock as from the searing pain. She could feel the sticky warmth of blood, taste its saltiness as it filled her mouth. She tried to curl herself into a ball, arms raised instinctively to protect herself from the foot or fist that would surely follow.

Lee dragged her to her feet and pinned her back against the door, his hand around her throat so she could barely breathe. 'So what was the plan? Flash your cunt so I'd forget what he'd done to my wife?'

She tried to shake her head, too terrified to speak.

'Bet he doesn't know what a goer you are though, does he?' Lee pushed his face close to hers, his breath hot and sour against her cheek. 'Does he know I can get you to open your legs for me just by looking at you?' He shoved his other hand up her skirt and slid it deftly inside her knickers, kneading her and laughing as she tried to fight him off. 'Don't try to pretend you don't want it.' He rammed his fingers inside her and she let out a strangled cry of pain. 'See? I know how to get you going. What would your precious brother think if he could see you now, eh? Moaning for it like a whore.'

'Get off me.' Sobbing for breath, she tried to struggle free as he released his grip on her neck and reached down to unbutton his fly. But he only thrust his fingers deeper into her, leaning his whole weight against her as he jammed his knee between her legs.

'Like it a bit rough, don't you? A bit kinky?' He tried to kiss her but she twisted her head away. 'Bet your brother never got Nicki doing half the stuff we've done. It was only his wallet she was after, the bitch. I don't have to pay you though, do I?' He forced Diane's hand down to his erect penis. 'This is what you want.'

'No!' Frantic, she tried to pull her hand away, but his grip only tightened.

'You're gagging for it.' His voice thickened as he rubbed himself against her. 'You know you are.'

It was only sheer terror that lent Diane the courage to dig her nails into him as hard as she could. Terror that gave her the strength to shove him full force in the chest as he screamed out in agony, and send him crashing backwards away from her. Terror that got her out of the house and back to the car. She fumbled her key into the ignition, stamped her foot onto the accelerator and hurtled away from the house, not daring to look in the mirror.

It wasn't until she was nearly home that she began to cry.

13

Diane could hear the phone ringing as she pulled up outside the house. She sat in the car, still shaking uncontrollably. Lee Smith knew where she lived. Even as she sat here, he might be on his way to finish what he had started. She slammed the car into reverse. Home wasn't a safe place to be any more.

She glanced at her reflection in the rear-view mirror as she headed on up the Kenilworth Road and out of Coventry. Her mouth had stopped bleeding, but her lip was split and swollen, one cheekbone already showing the beginnings of an angry bruise. She raised her fingers to her reddened throat and winced. She realised she'd been heading automatically towards Leamington and her mother. She shook her head slightly, blinking back tears as the pain flowered again. The habits of childhood must die harder than she'd thought; it had been a very long time since she'd run to her mother for comfort. But she couldn't run there now, any more than she could run to the cottage, and Ian. She couldn't face the thought of trying to explain her injuries. Not yet. She didn't have the energy left for that. She longed for Malcolm's solid dependability; his warm arm around her shoulder, his dear face smiling at her, telling her that everything would be all right. Except that once he knew what she'd done, nothing would be all right ever again.

She passed Crackley Woods, and slowed the car. Maybe

she could hide herself away here, find solace in the secret glades where she and Ian had played as children. In front of her, a four-by-four was disgorging its cargo of children and excitedly barking dogs. A golden Labrador grinned at her, wagging its happy tail as she drew to a halt. Normal people doing normal, Sunday-afternoon things. Maybe here she would be safe.

But what if Lee were following her? She heard the distant roar of a motorbike; froze, her hands rigid on the steering wheel as it swooped over the crest of the hill behind her; almost fainted with relief as it zoomed past, its anonymous, helmeted rider crouched over the handlebars, oblivious to her existence. The father from the four-by-four gazed at her quizzically through the windscreen. Diane stared straight ahead of her, refusing to meet his eye. Then she pulled the car round in a U-turn and headed back towards the centre of Coventry.

The shops were still busy. Head down, hand shielding her face, Diane hurried through the West Orchard shopping precinct. Even if Lee were behind her somewhere, surely he couldn't attack her here, amongst all these people? It had always struck her as ludicrous when, in films, the villain's prey headed unerringly towards the back alley, the deserted building, rather than the protection of the crowd. Here, in the city centre, she must be safe.

As her panic subsided, she began to think more clearly. This wasn't a film, it was real life. Lee Smith was a violent, abusive yob, but he was far more likely to be in a pub somewhere boasting of his sexual conquests than stalking her round the centre of Coventry. Diane shuddered with appalled disbelief at her own stupidity. To have betrayed Malcolm at all was bad enough; to have done so for such a sordid, trivial affair . . . no, not even an affair; a series of brief, animal-like couplings.

What the hell could she have been thinking about? It was as if she had been struck down by some temporary insanity which now, just as abruptly, had deserted her.

She went into Marks and Spencer and headed for the cosmetic department, where, studiously ignoring the assistant's inquisitive stare, she bought a tube of concealer. She grabbed a polo-necked jumper at random in the womenswear department; new autumn stock that was already nudging the racks of teeshirts and swimming costumes, although the summer was barely under way. She headed for the cloakroom – mercifully empty – and changed out of her blood-spotted blouse, which she stuffed into her bag. The jumper was a hideous colour and far too hot, but at least it hid her throat.

Almost revelling in the pain that was no more than she deserved, she splashed water onto her face and scrubbed the encrusted blood from around her mouth with a paper towel. Once cleaned up, the damage didn't look quite so dramatic. Gingerly, she patted the concealer onto her throbbing cheekbone and examined the effect. Apart from a striking resemblance to Mick Jagger, she didn't look too bad at all. Maybe she could say she'd walked into a door, or tripped down the stairs. She'd once had a woman at one of her classes who'd turned up claiming a similar accident. It had only been after the third or fourth that people had stopped believing her.

Diane nodded at her reflection as her brain marshalled straws for her to clutch. Maybe Malcolm didn't have to know. She'd never see Lee Smith again; surely he'd be as anxious as she to pretend nothing had happened. Maybe he was frightened she'd report him to the police. She'd lay odds he hadn't told anyone he'd hit Nicola the night before her death. The last thing he'd want was to have his violent temper exposed. If the police knew what he was really like, behind the façade of grieving husband . . .

She gripped suddenly at the basin as the thought hit her. What if Lee Smith had done more than just hit his wife, that last night? The police seemed less than satisfied, suddenly, that Nicola had committed suicide. What if he'd been so eaten up with jealousy that he'd followed her and . . . ?

She splashed more water on her face, washing off the make-up she'd so carefully applied. The idea was utterly ridiculous. There was a world of difference between slapping a woman around and throwing her off a balcony. She pulled out another paper towel and dabbed her ruined face. Until an hour ago, the suggestion would have seemed madness. But having experienced at first hand what an animal the bastard could be . . .

Maybe she should go to the police, report him; he was a far more plausible suspect than Ian would ever be. She sank down onto the plastic chair next to the basin. But that would mean admitting to the world what she and Lee Smith had done. Detailing the ferocity of their sexual encounters. She closed her eyes, nauseated by the images that flooded her brain. She heard the young constable from the crematorium, sniggering with his mates: '*I might have been in there myself, if I'd played my cards right. The bloke says she was gagging for it . . .*'

'Are you all right, my dear?' An elderly woman was staring down at her in concern. 'Would you like me to get a member of staff?'

Diane shook her head and got to her feet, trying to shield her face with her hand. 'Just a bit faint,' she mumbled.

'Are you sure? You look as if you've . . .'

'I'll be OK.' She forced the approximation of a smile. 'I just need some fresh air.'

She hurried outside, grateful for the light breeze that ruffled the trees lining the wide, traffic-free square, and sat down on a concrete wall beside the fountain that divided the Upper and Lower Precincts. She stared at a polystyrene container bobbing in the scummy foam and tried to clear her aching head. It wasn't easy. The pain of her injuries collided with her fragmented ideas, making her lose her train of thought.

She glanced at her watch. Almost four o'clock. The shops would be shutting soon. Maybe she should go home, think things over properly before she rushed into something she might regret for the rest of her life. She couldn't just march into the police station and accuse Lee Smith of murder; they'd think she was mad. She hadn't a single shred of proof, for one thing. And even if they did take her seriously, what then? She needed to come clean with Malcolm, and with Ian too, before she set God alone knew what chain of events into motion. She visualised the disgust on Malcolm's face, felt the panic rise within her. He'd never forgive her. Why should he?

She needed to speak to Ian, ask him what she should do. If she could just explain to him why she'd gone to Lee Smith in the first place, maybe she could make him see, and he could help Malcolm to understand. She reached into her handbag for her mobile, but it wasn't there. A cloud scudded across the sun and she shivered, touched by an irrational sense of foreboding. She got up and walked quickly to the nearby row of phone boxes, suddenly desperate for the sound of his voice. She took out a handful of change and dialled his mobile. The person she was calling was unavailable, she was told. She wondered whether she should simply drive over to Corley Moor, pour her heart out to him and throw herself on his mercy. But after his coolness earlier, she had absolutely no idea how he might react. It made her realise just how very much their relationship had changed since Nicola Smith's death.

The shopping precinct was all but deserted now, the shops already shuttered. Unwilling to return to the emptiness of the house, Diane walked through the Upper Precinct to Broadgate. She cut down past Holy Trinity Church, sixties concrete instantly replaced by ancient sandstone; wide sunny squares by narrow, cobbled streets. A different world. And in front of her, the ultimate juxtaposition: the new cathedral, growing like a grafted branch from the war-ruined remains of the old. Tempted by the promise of its cool, echoing stillness, Diane headed towards it.

A young Japanese couple, hand in hand, were gazing up at the etiolated angels engraved on the great west window. They turned and bowed solemnly to her as she entered the nave, and she bowed back with a sense of almost proprietorial pride. An elderly man, his hands clasped behind his back in rapt attention, stood dwarfed before the gigantic Sutherland tapestry of Christ in Majesty. Even as a child, Diane had been overwhelmed by the sheer, awe-inspiring scale of the dramatic backdrop to the high altar; had defended it fiercely against those, like her mother, who maintained that Christ looked as if he were wearing a nightdress.

She sat down at the back of the church, studiously ignoring the hovering figure of the verger who had followed her, collection plate in hand. She concentrated on the tapestry, gazing at the tiny, life-sized human figure that stood between Christ's bare feet. How good it must be to have faith. To be able to dump one's sins at the feet of that vast, all-knowing deity and receive forgiveness. She closed her eyes and attempted to allow the atmosphere of the place to wash over her, but the throbbing of her mouth and cheek kept her thoughts firmly rooted.

She looked up and found herself staring into Christ's eyes.

Christ stared back at her with an intensity that forced her own eyes quickly away again. A half-remembered line of poetry came back to her: '*Love bade me welcome: yet my soul drew back/ Guilty of dust . . .*' She looked up again into the tapestry gaze, then got to her feet, suddenly uncomfortable. Her soul was guilty of a great deal more than dust. She fumbled in her purse and found a twenty-pound note which she shoved onto the verger's plate as, head down, she passed him. She might live locally, but spiritually she was as casual as any other visitor.

Without allowing herself time for further thought, she walked briskly out of the west doors. As she made her way down the wide flight of stone steps that led away from the cathedral, she was confronted by Jacob Epstein's massive bronze of Saint Michael, spear raised as he stood astride the cowering Devil. The triumph of good over evil. If only real life were that simple; made up of such clear-cut, black-and-white choices.

Or maybe it was.

She turned her back on the statue and cut down past the Tourist Information Centre and the Herbert Art Gallery, and back into the High Street. From there, it only took her another couple of minutes to reach the police station.

14

Little Park Street Police Station was a modern, brick-built building in the centre of Coventry, flanked on one side by the ring road and on the other by the Magistrates' Court and Council Offices. Diane had passed it a thousand times on her way into town without giving it a second glance; a place where one went to seek information, or to report a crime – at worst to hand in a driving licence, as Malcolm had had to do once when he'd been caught speeding. Just another part of the bureaucracy that kept the city ticking over.

She wasn't sure what she expected as she entered the building, but it wasn't a crowded reception area lined with chairs that looked more like a doctor's waiting-room and smelt strongly of unwashed bodies. Several people queued in front of the desk. More sat slumped on the chairs, gazing morosely into space or talking in hushed, urgent tones into mobile phones. No one seemed interested in the hugely pregnant woman who sat in the corner, crying noisily. Diane joined the queue, feeling utterly out of place.

It was some minutes before she reached the front; the young woman who was holding the fort disappeared frequently into the back office to answer the phone or to use the tannoy. Her resolve was beginning to desert her. The overheard complaints of the people in front of her had sounded so concrete, so banal: an elderly man reporting the loss of his moped from the multi-storey, a woman giving a description of a missing dog, a spiky-haired youth enquiring truculently as to the where-abouts of his girlfriend. In comparison, her own story sounded ridiculously far-fetched.

'Can I help you?' The young woman reappeared from the back office.

'I . . .' Diane swallowed and glanced around. A uniformed officer appeared from the security-coded door at the back of the reception area. He was wearing a padded vest, his belt weighted down by truncheon, radio and keys. His face un-smiling, the officer called out a name and the pregnant woman lumbered to her feet and followed him out. The door swung shut behind her with a thud as they were swallowed into the darkened corridor beyond.

'Yes?'

Diane turned back. The woman gazed at her patiently, pen poised.

'I . . .' Once she was summoned beyond that heavy wooden door, she knew there would be no turning back; her life would be changed for ever. 'I wonder if you could direct me to the cathedral?' she stammered, adding cowardice to her catalogue of sins.

She walked slowly, aimlessly, back to the car and sat inside it, her hands on the steering wheel, the engine off. The clock on the dashboard told her it was five fifteen. She gazed vacantly at it and attempted to make up her mind what to do next as the digital display slid to sixteen, seventeen, eighteen. Come clean? Bury her head in the sand and hope everything would go away? All she knew was that she had to sort out her head before she faced Malcolm.

It was as if the car had made its own way towards the

cottage; she was almost at Corley before she asked herself what she thought she was doing. She didn't know what she would say to Ian, even if he was prepared to talk to her. She couldn't expect him to take on her problems as well as his own. She'd never felt so utterly incapable of making a decision; she even wondered fleetingly if the blow to her head could have caused concussion. She pulled into a lay-by and sat there for a while, window down, letting the birdsong and the late-afternoon sun wash over her. Then she turned the car round and headed back towards Coventry.

She'd have been insane to throw away everything that mattered to her, she reasoned with herself as she drove back up the Tamworth Road. Lee Smith wasn't the mad axeman, for Christ's sake; accusing him of murder would only compound the damage she'd already done to those around her. She focused on the road ahead of her and attempted to strengthen her resolve. More than anything, she needed to keep her nerve. If she kept quiet, waited for the storm to blow over, everything might yet be all right; there was no reason why Malcolm need ever know. By the time she finally pulled into the drive, she'd almost managed to convince herself that she'd made the right decision.

There were fifteen messages on the answering machine. Ian, was her first instinct. She pressed the replay button, cursing the self-preoccupation that had made her turn the car round.

'What the fuck are you trying to do to me, you vindictive . . . ?'

The sound of Lee Smith's voice was like a hammer blow. Diane's heart felt as if it were about to jump out of her chest as she silenced him with the delete button and went to the next message.

'I know you're there, you bitch. Just pick up the fucking . . .'

And the next.

'I'll get you for this, you . . .'

She stabbed the 'delete all calls' button and stood quite still in the cool hall as she struggled to calm herself. What if Malcolm had come home first? If it hadn't been for their row earlier, he might well have done. The very thought made her go cold. A jumble of emotions had swept over her as Lee Smith's voice had invaded her home. Fury was coming out on top. She would not be a victim; she would not allow him to persecute her and wreck everything she held dear. Just who did the bastard think he was?

Cursing, she pulled the telephone directory from the desk. Why did he have to be called Smith? At last she found his number, and punched it into the phone, her hands trembling with rage.

There was no reply. She slammed down the receiver; she'd had no idea what she'd intended to say to him, but not being able to say anything at all only served to fuel her anger.

'Bastard!' she yelled. The word reverberated round the empty house. She punched the wall, bruising her knuckles. 'Bastard!'

She glanced at the grandfather clock that stood on the turn of the stairs. Ten past six. Malcolm could be home at any time. She switched off the answering machine, then went through to the kitchen and pulled the blood-spattered blouse from her bag. She'd never wear it again, she knew. She went into the kitchen and stuffed it in the bin, then hesitated. What if Malcolm saw it? How could she explain it away? She wondered if she should burn it, but even in her present state, the notion seemed ridiculously melodramatic. She retrieved it, went upstairs and threw it in the laundry basket. She'd wash it and then quietly take it down to the charity shop.

She ran a bath; scrubbed at herself until she was red-raw. Wrapped in a towel, she sat down at her dressing-table, shocked afresh as she caught sight of her battered face in the mirror. There was no way Malcolm wouldn't notice. Maybe she could tell him she'd tripped in the garden. Perhaps she should go out and bag up some of the laurel cuttings, so she could make him think . . .

The phone rang. For a moment, she stared at the handset beside the bed as if it were a deadly snake. But then her anger returned full force. She was damned if she was going to allow herself to be intimidated in her own house. She'd call the bastard's bluff; threaten to report him for attempted rape, if he didn't leave her alone. She snatched up the phone, holding it slightly away from her, unable to bear even that much contact with him. She didn't speak. Let him make the first move.

'Diane? Are you there?' It was Malcolm's perplexed voice that filled the silence.

'Malcolm!' Her heart swooped. She pressed the receiver closer to her ear and smiled nervously as if, even at the other end of the phone, he might read her guilt. 'Sorry. I was in the bath . . .' She should be saving the lies for when they mattered. Or maybe it was better to get the practice, she thought bitterly.

'I've been trying all afternoon. Didn't you get my message?'

Her cheeks burned. 'I think the answering machine might be on the blink. Is everything all right?'

'Fine. Had to let Chas win the golf, of course. I think it's the only reason the old sod keeps asking me for a game.' His laugh sounded strained. 'So how's Ian?'

'I haven't seen him.' Instantly, she was on the alert. 'Why?'

'I just thought as you weren't in you might have . . .'

'I . . . I had to go into town for a few things.' Would there ever be a time in the future when she'd be able to answer a simple question truthfully, without even having to think? 'I've been in the garden since I got back,' she added, laying her plans.

'Oh, right.' Malcolm paused. 'Listen, love, I'm sorry I snapped at you earlier. I hate it when we part on bad terms like that.'

'I do, too.' Her eyes filled with tears. He was such a kind man. And she had betrayed him utterly. Betrayed everyone. How could she hope to unburden herself to him and receive his forgiveness, after what she'd done? 'It was my fault,' she added shakily.

'Well let's split it down the middle, shall we?' He sounded relieved. 'Listen, I thought I might pop over to the cottage later. Check Ian's OK. I'm going over with Chas to look at some new site he's got his eye on near Bedworth, so it's practically on my way home.'

Diane bit her lip; she recognised the unsubtle olive branch. 'I do love you, Malcolm. You know that, don't you?'

He'd heard the catch in her voice. 'Are you sure you're all right? I could come straight home if you'd rather . . .'

'No. I'm fine.' She prayed she sounded more convincing to Malcolm than she did to herself. 'Honestly.'

'I won't be late back.' Another pause. 'I'll give Ian your love, shall I?'

Diane's intention, when she'd gone out into the garden, had been to do just enough to make her story of a fall plausible, but she soon became absorbed in the task of bagging up the laurel cuttings. She set herself targets – just down to the laburnum tree, just the next clump of delphiniums – relishing the small sense of achievement as she completed each task. At one point, the cat stalked down to join her, its tail erect, demanding to be fed; Diane all but tripped over it as she stepped back from the border. She smiled grimly at the irony as she bent down to stroke it.

She worked methodically, filling bag after bag, her mind blessedly free from thought as the colours sharpened and the light began to fade. The garden filled with the rising cacophony of birdsong. By the time she'd finished, it was so dark she could barely see. She peered at her watch. Nine o'clock. There was a concert Malcolm had wanted to listen to on the radio, she remembered. She'd record it for him. Her back was aching, as she straightened up and gazed with satisfaction at the order she'd restored to the chaos of Malcolm's pruning, but her mind felt clearer than it had all day. It might not be much by way of reparation, but it was a start.

The phone rang again as soon as she turned the handle on the back door. Almost as if someone had been watching, waiting for her to come in. She flicked on the light and bent down to pull off her gardening shoes, attempting to dismiss the notion.

One ring.

Two.

Half a dozen.

A dozen.

Steeling herself, she went through to the hall, trying to rekindle some of her earlier rage. Her new-found optimism was already beginning to evaporate. If it weren't Lee Smith now, it would be sooner or later. She glanced at the grandfather clock. Three minutes past nine. The concert would already have started, she thought inconsequentially as she picked up the receiver.

'I'm at the cottage.' Malcolm's tone drove every other thought from her head.

'What's happened?'

'Now don't start to panic. It's just that . . .'

'Panic?' Diane's voice rose. No one ever told you not to panic unless you should be doing just that. 'What do you mean?'

'Ian isn't here.'

Which could have meant he'd gone for a walk, decided to drive down to the local . . . Except she knew from Malcolm's voice that none of those things had happened.

'The place is a bit of a mess . . .'

'What sort of mess? What are you talking about?'

'Stuff overturned. Crockery smashed.'

She tried to think logically. 'There could have been a break-in. Have you called the police?'

'No. Not yet. I . . .' Malcolm paused. 'I think he's been drinking. There's an empty whisky bottle on the table.'

'Is his car there?'

'No.'

'Shit. Have you tried his mobile?'

'It's switched off. Look, maybe I should call George Bonham.'

'George won't be able to do anything. Not if the idiot's caught drink-driving . . .'

'It isn't that.' Malcolm cleared his throat. 'I'm just worried he might have . . .'

'Might have what?'

Another pause.

'What?' Diane tried to quell her rising panic, keep her voice level.

'That painting you were doing. He's destroyed it. Slashed it to shreds.' The words came out in a rush, as if Malcolm had been struggling to hold them back. 'Listen. I'm going to drive over to Arden Hall. Just to check everything's OK over there.'

Diane felt an icy trickle of dread. 'What do you mean?'

'It's just that I've rung and there's no reply. Now, look. Try not to worry. I'm sure there's some perfectly simple . . .'

But Diane wasn't listening. Leaving the phone dangling from its hook, she was already halfway down the stairs. Behind her, she could hear Malcolm's faint voice echoing, 'Diane? Diane, are you there?'

15

Diane would never be able to remember how she got to Arden Hall; had no knowledge of whether she'd broken speed limits, crossed red lights, caused other cars to swerve. All she would recall was her absolute certainty that Ian was in some desperate sort of trouble, and that she was the only one who could help him.

The house looked much as it always did as she screeched to a halt in front of it. The lamps were on in the living-room, cutting a swathe of light through the half-drawn curtains. Angelika's Range Rover was parked in front of the old stables that ran at right angles to the house. A curtain flapped lazily from an open bedroom window. The babble of a television floated out from somewhere inside. Yet the house felt oddly empty.

She tried the heavy oak front door. It creaked as it slid open to her touch. Fearfully, she stepped into the darkened hall.

'Ian?'

No reply.

'Angelika?'

Nothing.

Diane's palms were sweating, her knees shaking. Scenes from every horror film she'd ever watched flooded her imagination. She took a deep breath, forcing herself to get a grip, and switched on the overhead light.

Everything was in order.

She scanned the doors that led from the wide, oak-beamed hall: kitchen, study, living-room, playroom, snug. All closed. She took a step towards the living-room then changed her mind and ran up the stairs to check on the children. The night-light was on in the nursery. She could make out the small hump of Thomas's frame beneath the Tank Engine quilt she'd bought him a few weeks earlier; just his blond curls visible, and one small, bare foot that dangled through the bars of the cot. She tiptoed out, and stuck her head cautiously into Dominica's and Marshall's bedrooms. They too were sleeping peacefully beneath their quilts. Slowly, Diane let out her breath as she felt her taut muscles begin to relax. There was no way Ian would have left the children here, alone, if anything had happened to Angelika.

She checked the other bedrooms – all empty – and went back down the stairs. There was probably some perfectly rational explanation for all of this. Ian could have simply taken himself off to the local pub. The cottage could have been vandalised in his absence. And as for the front door being open when she'd arrived . . . Ian had told her only a couple of months earlier that Marshall had started walking in his sleep; on one occasion the child had been discovered wandering down the lane in his pyjamas. Maybe he'd been off on another of his nocturnal jaunts, and found his own way back to bed.

Diane stood at the bottom of the stairs, beginning to feel slightly foolish. She wondered what to do next. The sound of the television was coming from the snug at the back of the house, loud enough to have drowned out both Marshall's comings and goings and Malcolm's call. Diane visualised Angelika and Claudine, glued to the screen quite unaware of the panic they'd caused.

She was tempted to sneak out of the front door and leave them to it. She hovered by the phone; she ought at least to ring Malcolm to tell him everything was OK. But how on earth could she explain her presence not only in the house but on the telephone, if Angelika should happen to come out? She'd look completely unhinged. Or, more probably, Angelika would assume she'd been snooping around to check up on her, and there would be another scene.

She took a step towards the snug. She was just going to have to brazen it out. Surely there wasn't anything so very unusual in a sister-in-law visiting to check that all was well? Maybe, if Angelika were in the right frame of mind, she might even be persuaded to listen to Ian's side of the story.

Resolutely, Diane pushed open the door to the snug. Sure enough, Angelika was sprawled on the sofa, her head turned towards the television. A glass and an empty wine bottle stood on the table beside her, banishing any hope of civilised dis-cussion. Diane felt a flicker of anger as she thought of the three sleeping children upstairs. Too pissed to have heard, more like. What if it had been a burglar creeping around upstairs, instead of a concerned relative? What if there had been a fire? But throwing such recriminations at Angelika wouldn't help anyone, least of all Ian.

'Hi. I let myself in,' Diane said brightly.

Angelika didn't move.

'I just wanted to make sure . . .' Diane's planned explana-tion petered into silence. There was something odd about the angle of Angelika's head. Something too still about the hand that trailed limply against the carpet.

'Angelika?' she whispered, knowing she would get no reply.

She stood stock-still in the doorway, devoid of any sensible thought. This was just some hideous nightmare, her mind assured her. Any minute now, she'd wake up and find . . .

She shook her head, the residual pain of her own injuries helping to clear it. Adrenalin kicked in, clicking her brain into gear, forcing her legs into action. She ran back into the hall. Malcolm. She must ring Malcolm. She stabbed randomly at the buttons on the phone, her whole body shaking uncontrollably. She sank down onto the bottom step of the stairs, desperately trying to concentrate on the practicalities, not allowing her mind to glimpse the bigger picture, as she attempted to dial the number again.

'Madame Middleton?'

The phone clattered uselessly from her hands. She looked up to see Claudine standing in the doorway.

'Where were you?' Diane screamed. 'You were supposed to have been here. You were supposed to . . .' She buried her head in her hands, sobbing.

'What has happened?' Claudine knelt beside her, prising Diane's hands away from her face.

The walls seemed to be closing in around her, the air being sucked out of her lungs. Surely she must wake up soon? She felt her shoulders being violently shaken. Claudine's face floated into her line of vision.

'Where is Madame Somerford?'

Diane glanced back fearfully towards the snug. 'I . . . I must call the police.' She managed to dial 999, but still the sense of unreality persisted. The tremulous voice giving the details to the operator wasn't hers; she was observing the scene from elsewhere, directing the action as if she were in a play: *A little louder, please; the audience won't hear you . . .*

Claudine had disappeared.

As she put down the receiver, Diane heard a small cry. A burst of tinny canned laughter erupted from the television in the snug and was abruptly silenced. The girl's face was ashen as she came out, slamming the door behind her.

'*Les enfants*,' she cried, as she headed for the stairs.

'They're safe.' Diane dragged herself to her feet. 'Don't wake them. Not yet.' There would be wakefulness enough for them soon. 'Please! Let them sleep . . .'

But Claudine was already racing across the landing. Diane heard a second, louder, cry. Her legs seemed to have lost the ability to obey instructions, but somehow, she stumbled up the stairs. The door to Marshall's room was wide open. Claudine was sitting on the bed, the little boy's head cradled in her lap. She looked up at Diane, her face a mask of horror, and whispered, '*Qu'est-ce que vous avez fait?*'

Diane didn't bother to respond. She threw open Dominica's door and flung back the duvet. The child was lying flat on her back, her hands arranged across her chest as if in prayer, her blonde hair spreading out across the pillow. Her face, emptied of its habitual scowl, was quiet and very beautiful. It was without hope that Diane reached out her hand to feel for a pulse, but still her fingers recoiled from the little girl's already-stiffening wrist.

She sank down onto the bed. Across the landing, the door to the nursery was ajar as she had left it.

Claudine appeared in the doorway, her hands pressed against her mouth, her eyes blank as she stared into Dominica's room. Slowly, she turned her head to follow Diane's gaze. A low moan escaped from between her clamped fingers. She took a step towards the nursery, but Diane got there first.

'No!' she hissed, blocking the doorway. 'Don't touch him. Don't you dare touch him.'

'*Vous êtes folle!*' Claudine tried to push past her, but again Diane was too quick. She shoved the girl's shoulder as hard as she could, catching her off balance and sending her crashing against the banister. Not pausing to see what damage she'd done, she entered the room, slammed the door shut behind her and slipped the catch.

She rested her forehead against the cool wood for a moment, drank in the sweet, familiar baby smells of the silent room. Then she turned to face the cot, her heart contracting at the sight of the one tiny foot protruding from the covers. So many times she'd wondered where those feet would take him as he grew from baby to man. She clutched her arms around her and rocked backwards and forwards, winded by grief. He'd never taken an unaided step. He never would. All gone, now.

She forced herself to approach the cot. What was there to be afraid of? It was only Thomas.

'Hello, little one,' she whispered. 'It's Aunty Di.'

She bent to touch the soft curls then hesitated, desperate to hang on, just for one more second, to the illusion that he might still be warm.

A sudden flash of blue light pierced the patterned curtains and arced the ceiling. She heard the slam of doors, the sound of voices, calling. They were here. Thomas would be taken away from her.

'Don't worry, my darling. Aunty Di will look after you.'

She lowered the side of the cot. Willed herself to touch him, before it was too late. Would his small limbs already be stiff?

She could hear Claudine's hysterical shrieks, the pounding of feet on the stairs, hands rattling at the doorknob.

Clenching her jaw, Diane pulled back the quilt and bent to gather the little body into her arms one last time.

The door crashed open. A bulky figure blocked the doorway.

Diane snatched Thomas up.

A voice bellowed, too late, 'Police! Stay where you are!'

She turned towards it, tears streaming down her cheeks, Thomas clutched to her.

'He's still alive,' she whispered. 'Oh, thank God. He's alive.'

She didn't want the policeman to take Thomas from her.

She didn't want to let him go.

But she couldn't keep him.

It wasn't safe.

He was holding out his arms towards her, but he was already beginning to dissolve and float away as the darkness enveloped her.

The roar of blood inside her head was so loud that she only just heard his sleepy whimper.

A voice shouted, 'She's going!'

And then there was only silence.

16

Diane tried to focus on the little sprig of lavender beside her face. She didn't have any pillowslips with sprigs of lavender embroidered on them.

She attempted to lift her head to get a better look, but as soon as she moved, the purple flowers began to dance. She was floating. She closed her eyes, then snapped them open again as memory swept into her brain, grabbing at her consciousness and sucking her down.

She struggled up in the bed, realising she was in one of Ian's spare bedrooms. A uniformed policewoman stood at the end of the bed. She gazed at Diane, her eyes expressionless, then opened the door a fraction and murmured something to someone outside. The house was filled with noise; the crackle of radios, the muted babble of voices, the tread of many pairs of feet.

The door opened wider and two men came in, one young, sharp-suited, the other older, dressed in slacks and polo shirt and carrying a worn leather bag. Beyond them, Diane glimpsed a green-gowned paramedic crouched over the bed in Marshall's room. The younger man turned to follow her gaze before shutting the door.

She tried to get out of bed, but the other man put his hand on her shoulder and shook his head.

'I'd like to have a quick look at you first.' Even before he clicked open the bag, his smooth, reassuring tone told Diane he was a doctor.

She snatched back her wrist as he went to take her pulse. 'Where's Thomas? Is he all right?'

The man didn't answer. He took out a small torch and shone it in her eyes.

'Is he hurt?' Diane twisted her head away. 'Tell me.'

'The baby's fine.' It was the younger man who answered.

'Where is he? Can I see him?'

The doctor straightened up. He turned and murmured something to the younger man, then shut his case and left the room.

Diane pulled herself out of bed. She swayed and reached out for the bedside chair to steady herself. 'I want to see him.'

'Not yet.' The man's voice was pleasant. He was wearing too much after-shave. The musky smell of it made Diane feel sick. He perched himself on the edge of the bed and indicated the chair. 'I'm Detective Sergeant Phillips. I'd like to ask you a few questions.'

'Yes.' Diane swallowed hard. Tried to think straight. 'Yes, of course.'

Shakily, she gave her details and explained her relationship to Angelika and the children.

'So your visit here this evening was a social one, Mrs Middleton?'

Diane hesitated.

'Mrs Somerford was expecting you?'

'Well, no.' To explain the reason for the visit would be to condemn Ian with her own lips. It was something Diane couldn't bring herself to do. 'You see, my husband rang from the cottage to say Ian wasn't there. He'd called in on his way back from Bedworth and the place was a mess. So I drove over here to make sure everything was all right, and then . . .' She clamped her lips together, realising she was babbling.

'Ian?' Phillips looked at her questioningly.

'Ian Somerford. My brother.' She swallowed. 'Angelika's husband.'

Phillips nodded. 'So you were concerned for your sister-in-law's welfare?'

'Yes.' Diane rubbed her hands across her face, confused. 'No. That is . . .' She winced involuntarily as her fingers brushed her damaged cheekbone.

'Nasty bruise. What happened?'

'I tripped. In the garden.' She stared at Phillips, stricken; she'd practised the lie so well it had slipped out before she'd had time to think about it.

'Today, was that?'

Why was he asking her about a stupid bruise, when beyond the door, Angelika, Dominica and Marshall lay dead?

'So what time did you . . . ?' Phillips was halted mid-sentence by a sudden commotion downstairs. They both turned towards the door. Diane heard raised voices. The thud of feet on the stairs. A second later the door burst open and Malcolm strode into the room, followed by a uniformed officer.

'Sorry, guv. I tried to . . .'

'Too bloody late now, isn't it?' Phillips silenced the man with an impatient wave of the hand. He turned his attention to Malcolm. 'And you are?'

'Malcolm Middleton.'

'You realise this is a crime scene and you could be contaminating vital evidence, Mr Middleton?'

Malcolm barely gave the man a glance. He bent down over Diane. 'Are you all right, my darling?'

Diane began to tremble. Seeing his dear, familiar face

somehow brought home the reality of what had happened as nothing else had done.

Malcolm turned to Phillips. 'What the hell's going on? Where are Angelika and the children?'

Diane looked up at him and shook her head, unable to speak.

Phillips looked from one to the other. Then he said, 'I think you'd better sit down, sir.'

Diane couldn't see Malcolm's face as Phillips broke the news; after the first few words, he covered it with his hands. She was glad. To see her own pain reflected in his eyes was more than she could have borne.

'Dear God,' he whispered at last. 'Why the children? Why did he have to . . . ?'

'Who, Mr Middleton?'

Malcolm looked up from between his fingers. His face was haggard. 'Ian.' He glanced at Diane and then away again. 'My brother-in-law.'

'No!' Diane jumped up. 'You don't know that! Ian would never . . .'

'Oh, Diane. Diane.' Malcolm gazed at her. His eyes were filled with pity. 'Who else?'

He turned back to the detective and hesitantly, reluctantly, repeated what he had told her earlier. Diane stared down at her hands, numb. The evidence against Ian as Malcolm had reported it could hardly have been more damning.

Phillips scribbled notes, fired questions. His back turned to them, he spoke rapidly into his radio, ordering an immediate search of the cottage and its surroundings. Then, switching his attention back to Malcolm, he asked, 'So it was you who suggested your wife check up on Mrs Somerford and her children?'

Malcolm closed his eyes. 'I just wish to God I hadn't rung her. At least she'd have been spared . . .'

'And at what time would that conversation have taken place?'

'Nine.' Diane's tongue felt too big for her mouth; even to say the single word took an immense effort of will.

Phillips switched his attention from Malcolm. 'You'd been in the garden, you say, Mrs Middleton?'

She nodded.

'And how long did you spend there, would you say?' He waited expectantly. 'All afternoon?'

'Why are you asking my wife these questions?' Malcolm demanded.

Phillips dragged his eyes from Diane's face. 'Your wife was the first on the scene, sir,' he said pleasantly. 'I just need to establish a sequence of events.' He turned back to Diane. 'Had you received any phone calls apart from the one from your husband?'

Diane shook her head.

'No messages?'

She remembered the other twelve calls, the ones she had deleted, and began to sob, despairingly.

'The answering machine's not working,' Malcolm snapped. 'For goodness' sake! You can see for yourself what a state she's in. Can't it wait?'

Phillips seemed to be considering the point. He flicked back through his notes then looked up with a smile. 'That will be all for tonight, Mrs Middleton. I take it you'll be at the address you've given me, if we need to speak to you?'

Malcolm took her hand. 'Can we see our nephew now?'

'That won't be possible, I'm afraid, sir. He'll be kept in hospital overnight. Just as a precaution,' Phillips added, evidently anticipating Malcolm's reaction. 'The police surgeon checked him out and he seems fine.'

'Which hospital?'

'Warwick, I believe. But you won't be able to see him at this time of night.'

'But that's ridiculous! Surely, under the circumstances . . .'

'As you say, your wife's probably had enough for now. Why don't you just take her home?'

'What about . . . ?' Diane was still trying to gather her thoughts. 'What about Ian?'

'We'll keep you informed of any developments, Mrs Middleton. You can be sure of that.' Phillips turned back to Malcolm. 'Would you be able to come to the mortuary tomorrow morning, sir? To formally identify the bodies?'

Malcolm cleared his throat, but when he spoke his voice was still hoarse. 'I don't know where the mortuary . . .'

Phillips nodded. 'I'll arrange for someone to pick you up.'

The bodies.

Even as Diane registered the words, she retained the sensation that they were all actors in a play. She felt suddenly, overwhelmingly exhausted. She wanted to go home. Crawl into her bed and sleep. So that when she woke up in the morning, refreshed, the nightmare would be behind her.

17

The following morning, Diane was dragged back to consciousness from a sleep so deep it might have been drug-induced, to find Malcolm standing over her with a cup of tea, his face grave.

'Have they found . . . ?' She struggled to sit up as reality hit her like a wave of icy water.

Malcolm shook his head. 'They're still searching.' He sat down on the bed and took her hand. 'Someone should tell Agnes.'

'Oh God,' Diane mumbled. She hadn't so much as given her mother a thought.

'Do you want me to go? I could drive over there now and fetch her back.'

Her head was made of concrete, her lids so heavy she could barely keep them open.

'Diane?' The pressure of Malcolm's hand increased. 'There was something on the seven o'clock news . . . No names, yet. The police are trying to find out if Angelika had any relatives in the States before they give out any details. But it's not going to take anyone long to realise . . .'

She pulled herself to her feet. How could she have gone to bed, when Ian was out there somewhere? How could she have slept? 'We must go back to the house. We've got to help look for him.' She put her hands to her head as the room started to spin.

Malcolm pushed her gently back down onto the bed. 'We'd only be in the way. I've already spoken to the police. They're doing everything they can. They'll let us know when there's any news.'

Diane shook her head, too tired to argue.

Malcolm took her face between his hands. 'We'll get through this, love. Somehow we'll get through it together.' Briefly, he held her to him. 'Try to rest. I'll go over to Leamington and get your mother.'

It was as if Diane were on automatic pilot. She showered, pulled clothes from the wardrobe, dressed. She'd seen women at press conferences, women who had lost a husband, a child, and had wondered how they'd managed to look even barely presentable. Now she knew. One's body just got on with the things it had always done. Rather in the same way a decapitated chicken would continue to run, brain and sinew no longer connected.

She made up a bed for her mother in one of the spare rooms. She went down to the kitchen and set the table for breakfast. She put coffee on to brew. Agnes enjoyed fresh coffee. She fed the cat. She thought she heard the sound of Malcolm's car, but when she hurried to the front door, there was no one there. She glanced at the clock. How could it have been his car? He'd been gone less than a quarter of an hour; he'd just be getting to Agnes's now. Just breaking the news.

She went out into the garden. Picked up some stray laurel cuttings. Dead-headed some pansies. She should have gone with him. Agnes was her mother, not his. She threw the flowerheads down on the path. What the hell did she think she was doing, dead-heading pansies? She went inside and poured herself a glass of water, more for something to do than because she was thirsty. The inactivity was unbearable; there must surely be something she should be doing? Maybe she should drive over to Arden Hall despite what Malcolm had said. Was that where the police were searching? She picked up her car keys, then put them down again. Someone needed to stay here. She shouldn't even have gone out into the garden. What if the police had been trying to get in touch? Or Ian? She ran through to the hall and checked the phone for messages, but the answering machine was still switched off. She stabbed the button, cursing herself. How could she have left it switched off?

She went upstairs and bundled the laundry together. The sight of the blouse made her feel so sick she could barely bring herself to touch it. Another suffocating wave of self-loathing engulfed her. Carrying it at arm's length, she took it down to the kitchen, fetched a pair of scissors and hacked it to shreds. It didn't make her feel any better; it just made a mess. She picked up the scraps of material and stuffed them into a carrier bag, which she pushed into the bin beneath the sink. The rest of the laundry she crammed into the washing machine. As she straightened up, the corner of her eye caught a dark shape in the doorway. She spun round, her heart hammering.

'Want to be more careful, leaving your back door open like that. Anyone could get in.' Lee Smith took a step into the kitchen. 'You nearly castrated me, you vicious bitch. I think I'm owed an apology.'

'My husband's here.' Diane glanced towards the hall. 'He'll . . .'

'I'm not that bloody stupid. I saw him leave ten minutes ago.'

'He'll be back any minute.' Even to her own ears, it sounded feeble. She tried to hide the fear in her voice; inject some conviction into it as she added, 'And so will the police.'

In one quick movement, he was across the kitchen, the sneer dropping from his face. He grabbed her arm, twisting it painfully behind her back. 'What the fuck do you think you're trying to do to me? You're trying to stitch me up, aren't you?'

'I don't know what you're talking about.' Diane tried to keep her voice calm.

'I'm talking about the pack of lies you've been feeding the coppers about me and your bastard brother.'

The washing machine's mechanism gave a loud click, and water gushed into it. Momentarily distracted by the sudden noise, Lee turned his head, his grip slackening. Diane seized her chance. She pulled herself free and made a dash for the hall, slamming the door shut between them. Swearing, Lee threw it open and made a lunge at her as she tried to pick up the phone. She grabbed at the banister, determined not to fall. The hall table toppled over and the heavy glass vase that stood on it crashed to the ground. The handset skittered across the polished wooden floor. Diane made a dive for it. But Lee was quicker.

'Go on then.' He held it out to her.

Breathing heavily, Diane just stared. What was his game?

'Go on. Report me. And while you're at it, you can tell them it wasn't me sent those fucking letters.'

Dumbly, she shook her head.

He shoved the receiver into her face. His hand was trembling. Sweat glistened on his forehead. 'There's no way I'm getting dragged into all that shit. Tell them, you cow. Or I'll stay here and fill your old man in on a few things.'

She would have expected to feel fear, but all she felt was rage. The bastard was in a blind panic; he must have been listening to the radio, and heard about the murders. He was as guilty as anyone for what had happened, and now he was trying to deny any part in it.

'Do you think I care about that any more, you stupid prick?' she shouted. 'I'll ring the police all right. To tell them how you beat me up. And how you beat up your wife just before she died. I'm not the only one who's going to put two and two together. They're going to be a damned sight more interested in how you use your fists every time a woman stands up to you than in your pathetic bloody letters.'

Diane could see she'd hit a nerve; Lee took a step back from her, the colour draining abruptly from his face. 'I never. I didn't beat her up. I only . . .'

'You just couldn't bear the thought of anyone else satisfying her when you couldn't do it yourself, could you? Is that why you threw her off that balcony? And then picked on the first poor sod who fitted the bill and tried to frame him?'

'Threw her off the balcony?' Lee wiped his mouth with the back of his hand. 'What the fuck are you on about?'

'I could kill you for what you've done to my brother and his family.' Before he could stop her, she darted down and snatched up a long shard of glass. Tears of fury and despair streamed down her cheeks, all but blinding her. 'Perhaps I will kill you, you bastard. What have I got to lose, any more?'

'You're mad, you know that?' He backed away from her. 'You're fucking mad.'

'Come near me again and I'll do it.' She hurled the spear of glass after him as he fled. It landed harmlessly against the door and shattered into a thousand useless splinters. 'I swear I will.'

By the time she got back into the kitchen, he'd gone. Sobbing, she ran to the back door and locked it. She leant against it, trying to compose herself. Malcolm would be back soon, with her mother. She couldn't let them find the place in the state it was in. She hurried back into the hall and bent down to gather up the fragments of the broken vase. It was one Malcolm had bought some years before, when they had spent an anniversary in Venice. She pressed the back of her hand across her eyes as fresh tears came. This time yesterday, the prospect of having her squalid little affair discovered had seemed like the end of the world.

She began shakily to restore some semblance of order, righting the hall table and collecting what she could of the glass. Concentrate on the trivia. Don't risk a glimpse at the bigger picture. She fetched a dustpan and brush from the cupboard and began to sweep up the remaining fragments.

The doorbell made her all but jump out of her skin. Trembling, she pressed herself against the wall.

It rang again. To her horror, Diane saw the letterbox being pushed open. Images of house fires flashed into her mind; paraffin-soaked rags being pushed through people's doors.

'Mrs Middleton?' said a female voice.

Diane hesitated, then slipped the latch. A young woman stood on the step, a large, battered briefcase in her hand. She was tall and angular, with prominent teeth that looked too big for her narrow face. Her frizzy ginger hair was pulled back into an untidy ponytail.

'Mrs Middleton?' she repeated in a tone of mild apology, as if she might be trying to sell something.

'Whatever it is, I don't want it, so just . . .' The words died on Diane's lips as she noticed the warrant card in the woman's hand.

'Detective Constable Tracey Collingwood, Little Park Street.' She held up the card for inspection. 'I'm here to help.'

'Help?' Diane stared at her stupidly.

'I've been appointed Family Liaison Officer.' The woman

smiled and gestured to the man who was standing some yards behind her, scanning the front of the house with the critical air of an estate agent. 'My colleague, Detective Inspector Baker.'

'Good morning, Mrs Middleton.' Baker smiled, but only with his mouth. He was stocky, with close-cropped blond hair and a bristling, nicotine-stained moustache. His pale blue eyes were already taking in every detail of the hall as he stepped forward and flashed his warrant card. Diane found herself wishing she'd had time to tidy up, empty the dustpan of the broken glass.

'Is there any news of . . . ?'

For a moment, Baker observed her with the same unnerving attention that he'd bestowed on her surroundings. Then he said, 'Maybe we could come inside.'

Diane gripped at the edge of the table. She thought she might faint. Her voice seemed to be coming from somewhere a long way off as she said, 'Have you found him?'

'Not Mr Somerford.' Baker stepped into the house. 'His car. It was parked up in one of the outbuildings behind the house. Do you happen to know if he usually keeps it there?'

She shook her head, trying to make some sense of the information. Why would Ian have tried to hide the car?

'Mrs Middleton?' Tracey Collingwood touched Diane's arm, her expression sympathetic. 'DI Baker asked if your husband was here.'

'Oh. No.' She tried to collect her thoughts. 'No, he's gone over to Leamington. To collect my mother.'

'It must be a very difficult time for you all.' The words were spoken automatically. Baker wasn't even looking at her; his eyes were on a shard of glass she'd missed. She wondered if she should offer some kind of explanation, but he didn't comment on it. Instead, he said, 'I'm afraid I need to ask you a few more questions. Maybe we could go somewhere more comfortable?'

She showed them through to the living-room. Baker took a chair and indicated for her to do the same. Obediently, she perched herself on the sofa.

'Would you like me to make you a cup of tea, Mrs Middleton?' Tracey Collingwood offered.

Diane nodded, grateful for the small show of kindness, although she had no desire for the tea. She started to get to her feet. 'I'll show you where . . .'

'Don't worry.' Collingwood smiled. 'I can find my way round.'

'Right.' Baker took a notebook from his briefcase. 'I wonder if we could start by just going back over the information you gave to DS Phillips last . . .'

'What do you think's happened to Ian? Do you . . . do you think he's still alive?'

'I'm afraid I don't deal in speculation, Mrs Middleton.' The man's expression was neutral. Diane tried to dismiss the notion that he disliked her. Surely he should be showing more sympathy? Offering some reassurance? Or maybe distancing himself was the only way he could handle the horrors of his job.

'He's devoted to his family,' she whispered.

Baker nodded briefly. 'If you could start with your husband's phone call, please.'

Diane did as she was bidden. She answered Baker's questions as he took her back over the previous evening's events as accurately and unemotionally as she was able, without making any further attempt to get through to him. She was surprised how painless it was. Like having a filling, once the dentist's injection had kicked in; you knew it was happening, but you couldn't feel anything.

'And can you remember what time your husband rang you?'

She nodded. 'Three minutes past nine.'

Baker looked up questioningly from his notes.

'I remember looking at the clock in the hall.'

'That was very efficient of you.'

'I thought it might have been . . .' Her voice trailed off.

'Might have been who, Mrs Middleton?' Baker looked at her expectantly.

She shook her head. 'No one.'

It was a while before his eyes left her face. 'OK. Now then . . .' He flicked through the pages of his notebook as if looking for something.

Collingwood reappeared with a tray and three mismatched mugs of tea, one of which she handed to Diane. It was sweet and too milky.

Baker reached forward and picked up one of the other mugs. 'Your facial injuries. DS Phillips's notes mention something about a fall.' The pale eyes came up and met her own. 'Can you tell me what happened, please?'

Diane felt the heat of the blood that suffused her cheeks. 'Actually, that isn't quite true.'

'Oh?'

'I was . . .' She hesitated. Once the words were out, she'd never be able to take them back. 'Someone hit me.'

She'd expected Baker to look shocked, but he just jotted something down and said conversationally, 'And who was that?'

Maybe middle-aged women announcing they'd been assaulted was something he came across all the time.

'It's . . .' Diane studied her hands. They were shaking, she noticed dispassionately. 'It's a bit complicated. Look.' She got to her feet. 'My husband will be back with my mother very shortly. Is there somewhere else . . . ?'

For a moment, Baker didn't speak. Then he said in the same conversational tone, 'Are you asking to come back to the station with us, Mrs Middleton?'

Diane took a deep breath. 'Yes,' she said quietly. 'Yes, I suppose I am.'

18

It wasn't until DI Baker punched in some numbers, drove into the carpark and the barrier came down behind them, that the incongruity hit Diane. She might not know much about the way the system operated, but she was aware that Coventry fell within the West Midlands police force, and Stratford didn't. She frowned and turned to DC Collingwood, who was sitting beside her in the back of the car. 'Why are we at Little Park Street? Shouldn't it be Warwickshire police who are . . . ?'

She saw Collingwood and Baker exchange glances in the driving mirror. It was Baker who cut the question off. 'ACPO guidelines provide a protocol for incidents that involve more than one force. In this instance . . .'

'ACPO?' She suspected he was being deliberately abstruse.

Baker got out of the car and held the door open for her before he answered. 'The Association of Chief Police Officers. The SIO,' he inclined his head as Diane started to speak again, 'the Senior Investigating Officer has decided that as the West Midlands force was already involved with inquiries into the death of Nicola Smith . . .'

'I know you think Ian might have had something to do with it, but that's what I want to speak to you about,' she interrupted. 'You see, I think I may know who did kill her.'

Again, Baker seemed less interested than she would have expected. He merely turned to her as he showed her into the building and said, 'Let's wait until we can do this properly, shall we, Mrs Middleton?'

He showed her to his office; a small, cluttered room lined with bookcases, each filled with textbooks and procedure manuals. Tables of crime figures for each operational area of the city, together with targets for detection rates, were Blu-Tacked to the wall above his desk. It made Diane, whose knowledge of such things was based on TV drama series, realise that in real life there must be a great deal more to solving crime than staring moodily out of windows and waiting for inspiration. Or for members of the public to walk in off the street to share their hunches. Momentarily, she felt her resolve weaken. But only momentarily. She'd already come too far to turn back. She focused on the photograph of two grinning, gap-toothed children that stood on the grey metal filing cabinet. It made DI Baker seem just a bit more human.

'So.' He pulled out a chair for her and sat himself down behind the desk. 'What was it you wanted to tell me?'

Diane hesitated, unsure of where to start.

'Someone hit you, you said.' Baker prompted. 'When was this?'

'Yesterday afternoon.'

'And was the assailant known to you?'

'Yes.'

Baker looked up expectantly.

'Lee Smith.'

'I'm sorry?'

She cleared her throat and said in a firmer voice, 'Lee Smith. Nicola Smith's husband. I went round to see him yesterday afternoon. I told him he'd got to stop.'

'Stop what?'

'He's been making Ian's life a misery. Letters, banners . . .

That's why Angelika was threatening to take the children back to the States. It wasn't even as if he had any proof. Just because they worked late together. It could have been anyone. But that didn't put him off. Nothing was going to put him off.' Once the bitter torrent of words had started, they wouldn't stop. 'And Angelika played right into his hands, of course, reacting the way she did, and right in the middle of Mum's party, too, with everyone there to see. He even sent a letter to the police, and got Ian dragged in for . . .' She broke off, realising how little sense she must be making. Baker was regarding her inscrutably from the other side of the desk; he probably thought she was deranged. In a more moderate tone, she went on, 'Of course, you already know. It was probably you who questioned him.' She leant across the desk, desperate to make him understand. 'You know Lee Smith had been harassing him – Ian told you that himself. Ian didn't have an affair with Nicola. Lee was just trying to frame him, and I think I know why. What if . . . ?'

'If we could return to the alleged assault,' Baker said calmly.

'There's nothing alleged about it!' Exasperated, Diane pointed to her cheek. 'You can see for yourself what the bastard did to me. Anyway, it's all tied in together. It isn't only me he's beaten up. He told me he'd hit his wife on the night she died. He's a thug. He's got no control over his temper. What if he . . . ?'

Baker held up his hand. 'One thing at a time, Mrs Middleton. You say you went to see Mr Smith yesterday. Did you know him prior to that?'

She clenched her hands together in her lap. 'Yes.'

'In what capacity?'

'I'm an artist. I run some local authority evening classes. He's . . . he was one of my students.'

'One of your students,' Baker repeated, writing something down. Diane thought she detected the merest twitch of his mouth. They'd questioned Lee already, she realised; why else would he have arrived on her doorstep in such a state? He'd told them all about the affair.

'Until yesterday, he was also my lover.' She could feel herself colouring, but when Baker looked up again, she forced herself to hold his pale gaze. 'Which is why I didn't want to talk to you at the house. My husband doesn't know anything about it, yet.'

'I see.' Baker's tone was neutral.

'Look, I know this must all sound ridiculous.' It was clear he'd got her down as an hysteric, probably a nymphomaniac as well. 'Let me try to explain.'

'That would be very helpful.'

Diane curbed her instinct, which was to reach across the desk and slap the man's impassive face. 'I was at Nicola's funeral. She was Ian's secretary.' She shook her head impatiently. 'Well, you know that already. I hadn't realised until that point that Lee was her husband. We tend not to use second names, and even if we had, with a name like Smith, I doubt I'd have . . .' She was rambling. Baker wasn't even bothering to write any of it down. 'I wanted to find out why he'd attacked Ian after the service. He turned up at the class that night. I offered him a lift home.'

'You weren't worried that his animosity towards your brother might be directed at you?'

'He . . .' Diane cleared her throat. 'I didn't tell him I was Ian's sister.'

'I see.' Baker picked up his pen again and made some notes. 'So you offered Mr Smith a lift home. And?'

'He asked me in for a coffee.'

'Which you accepted?'

'Yes.'

'Because you were hoping to get information out of him about the relationship between his wife and your brother?'

'There wasn't a relationship. Not an improper one.' The man seemed deliberately to be trying to twist what she was saying.

'But you still wanted to speak to Mr Smith about it. Without him knowing you were related to Mr Somerford.'

'I didn't exactly have to force the information out of him,' she said defensively. 'He was more than willing to talk about her. I felt sorry for him. And that was when things got a bit . . . out of hand.'

'You felt sorry for him,' Baker repeated.

'I did then, yes. It was only later that it dawned on me that . . .'

'And when did this first . . . liaison take place?'

'I've just told you. The day of his wife's funeral.' She leant forward. 'Don't you see? That's just my point. He tries to make out he's devastated by her death, yet the very day . . .'

'And that was . . .' Baker cut her off. He flicked back through his notes, 'Last Thursday?'

She stared at him, nonplussed, unable for a second to believe that a mere four days earlier she'd been a dutiful wife, with nothing more to occupy her thoughts than her mother's birthday party and whether Angelika and the children would manage to behave themselves. And now they were dead. Ian was missing. She was an adulteress . . . She made a supreme effort to pull herself together. 'Thursday. Yes.'

'So your relationship with Mr Smith was not exactly a long-established one.'

Again, Diane was certain she could detect a hint of mockery behind the pale, deadpan eyes.

'That's not the point,' she snapped. 'The point is, he's trying to make out he's some heartbroken widower, yet he was making a pass at another woman within hours of . . .'

'So you'd describe what happened last Thursday night as Mr Smith making a pass at you?'

Diane hesitated. 'Yes.'

'And did you resist his overtures?'

'Yes. No. I mean . . .' She was beginning to feel flustered. 'Look, does it matter? I'm not trying to absolve myself from blame. I allowed it to happen.' She blinked back the tears that were prickling her eyes. She was not going to let herself cry in front of Baker. 'My behaviour was unforgivable. But that doesn't give Lee Smith the right to beat me up and try to rape me.'

'You're saying the assault was also sexual?' Baker raised an eyebrow. 'These are extremely serious allegations you're making, Mrs Middleton.'

'It was an extremely unpleasant experience,' she snapped.

Baker nodded. 'Of course.' He scribbled rapidly on the pad of paper in front of him for some moments before looking up and asking, 'And at what time yesterday do you say this incident took place?'

Diane could see instantly what he was getting at. 'I didn't report him straight away because I lost my nerve. I didn't want my husband to find out what had happened. He's . . .' The tears threatened again. She pressed her fingers under her eyes and struggled to control her voice. 'My husband's a good man, Inspector. I'm well aware that I've let him down dreadfully. Which is why I can assure you I wouldn't be telling you any of this unless it were absolutely true.'

'So what changed your mind between yesterday and today? About reporting Mr Smith?'

'I'd have thought that was obvious! You're assuming Ian murdered Nicola Smith, aren't you?'

'Why would I assume that, Mrs Middleton?' Baker was watching her closely.

'Well, you obviously don't think she killed herself, or you wouldn't have taken him in for questioning. And then the very next day his family are murdered, he disappears, and . . .' She clamped her lips together. She was just making things worse.

Baker ran his thumbnail thoughtfully across the gingery bristles of his moustache and continued to gaze at her.

'The very fact that I'm here, not at Stratford, means you think he did it. Doesn't it?'

Baker didn't respond.

'Well, you're wrong. If anyone killed her, it was Lee Smith. Who then systematically hounded my brother to divert attention from himself.'

'And what makes you think Mr Smith would have any reason to murder his wife?' Baker spoke patiently, as if he were addressing a child.

'Because she'd been having an affair, of course! He couldn't bear the thought of her . . .' Diane broke off, almost crying with frustration. She wasn't making any sense, and they both knew it. If Nicola hadn't been having an affair, why murder her at all? 'She must have been seeing someone, I suppose. But it wasn't Ian,' she added fiercely.

Baker sighed. He opened one of the desk drawers and pulled out a sheaf of papers. 'Do you wish to make a formal complaint against Lee Smith?'

'After what he's done to my brother? You bet your life I do.'

'I'm talking about the alleged assault against yourself, Mrs Middleton.'

'Yes, I do. But I also want to make it clear that in my opinion, Lee Smith is also responsible for what happened at Arden Hall.'

'Let me make sure I've got this straight.' Baker put down his pen and made a careful steeple of his stubby fingers. 'You're now also accusing Mr Smith of the murders of Angelika, Dominica and Marshall Somerford.'

'No, of course I'm not,' she snapped. 'I know you think I'm just some hysterical, middle-aged woman, but I'm not. I just want . . .' She tried and failed to swallow down the sobs that were closing her throat. What did she want? If she blamed Lee Smith for driving Ian to kill his family, then she was accepting Ian's guilt. Is that what she believed? The sobs bubbled up to choke her. What other possible explanation was there?

'Let's just deal with your allegations of assault for the moment, shall we?' Baker said quietly. 'Are you prepared to make a formal statement?'

Diane put her head between her hands. She'd been so focused, so fired up with the simple desire to bring Lee Smith to justice. But here, in the harsh fluorescent light of Baker's office, those certainties had blurred. Would bringing everything out into the open make things better for Ian, or worse? Formal charges would mean a court case. She visualised Lee Smith in the witness box, laying bare every last sordid detail of their liaison. Would people simply conclude she and Ian were tarred with the same brush, as Agnes would say? Agnes. Diane closed her eyes. Would her mother be able to bear the shame of it, on top of everything else? Would Malcolm?

'I don't know,' she whispered.

Baker got to his feet. 'Maybe you'd be as well to go home

and think about it for a while. Talk it over with your husband, perhaps.' His voice was cool. 'I'll arrange for DC Collingwood to drive you home.'

'Ian didn't kill her.' Abruptly, the tears were pouring down Diane's face. 'Somebody's set him up. He didn't kill any of them. You don't know him. He wouldn't . . .'

Baker looked up. His pale eyes gave nothing away. 'Go home, Mrs Middleton,' he said.

19

It was David Fawcett, the family GP, who answered the door to Diane when she got back to the house.

'Malcolm's just left for the mortuary,' he said, his glance darting questioningly towards Collingwood, who had followed Diane in. The woman introduced herself and he nodded, his expression clearing somewhat. 'He wondered where you were,' he said, turning back to Diane. 'I said I'd wait until you got back.'

'There were a few questions . . .' She should have left a note for Malcolm, she thought guiltily; she'd been so fired up, she hadn't given a thought to the fact he would be worried.

'Of course,' Fawcett murmured. 'Well, now you're back, I'd better get on my way. Your mother's in bed.'

Diane glanced up the stairs and lowered her voice. 'How is she?'

'I've given her a fairly strong sedative. I'd expect her to sleep for several hours yet.' He took Diane's hand. 'I can't tell you how terribly sorry I am about all of this. To tell you the truth, it hasn't sunk in yet.'

Diane nodded, not trusting her voice.

'I'm only on the other end of the phone, if there's anything you need.' He turned to Collingwood. 'Will you be staying with her until . . . ?'

'I'll be here most of the time, sir,' she said.

'Do take care of yourself, my dear.' With a squeeze, he released Diane's hand. She gave an automatic half-smile, more at the absurdity of the injunction she'd used so many times herself than at the man himself.

She gazed around the hall when she'd let him out. The dustpan and brush were on the floor beside the table, where she'd left them. 'Look. You see?' She picked up the dustpan and thrust it at Collingwood. 'Lee Smith tried to push me over, when he forced his way in this morning. This vase fell off the table. I know Inspector Baker thought I was making it up. No, please, I'm not stupid,' she shook her head impatiently as Collingwood began to speak. 'But this is proof, isn't it?'

'I'll make certain it's documented.' Collingwood's voice was reassuring as she took the dustpan. 'I'll empty it for you, shall I?'

'Shouldn't you be keeping it? As evidence?'

'Did Mr Smith come into contact with any of it?'

Diane shook her head.

Collingwood smiled. 'I think it'll be OK to throw it away, then.'

Diane followed her into the kitchen. The washing machine was coming to the end of its last, noisy spin. 'Stupid, isn't it?' she muttered. 'Doing stuff like that, when your whole life's . . .' Abruptly, her legs no longer felt up to the task of supporting her. She sat down at the kitchen table. 'What are we going to do?' she whispered. 'What in the name of God are we all going to do?'

Tracey Collingwood laid her hand on Diane's shoulder. 'I'll make us both some coffee, shall I?'

She placed a mug in front of Diane, then wrapped the shards of glass in an old newspaper. 'Where's your waste bin?'

'Under the sink.' Diane was relieved that Collingwood

hadn't tried to offer any words of consolation. There was something oddly soothing about the woman's easy domesticity. She wondered inconsequentially what had made such an ordinary, homely person want to join the police.

Collingwood opened the cupboard door. She paused, then put the newspaper parcel on the floor and pulled out the carrier bag containing the shredded blouse. 'What's this?'

'It's the top I was wearing yesterday. When Lee Smith tried to . . .' Diane shuddered. 'It made me feel ill just to look at it.'

Collingwood nodded. Taking the carrier with her, she walked quickly from the kitchen.

Diane followed her out. 'What are you doing?' she asked, as the other woman took an evidence bag from her case and emptied the shreds of material into it, looking suddenly very professional.

'Forensic.' She didn't look up. She labelled the bag, then went back to the kitchen and, to Diane's intense surprise, started to pull the washing from the machine. 'This yours?' she asked, holding up the skirt Diane had been wearing the day before.

Diane nodded.

'Why were you washing it?'

'I don't know. Because Lee Smith had had his hands all over it, I suppose. I'm sorry. It never occurred to me you might need it for tests. Do you think it might have helped prove . . . ?' She broke off at the sound of Malcolm's key in the lock.

'Diane? Are you there?'

'In the kitchen,' she shouted, then lowered her voice. 'Look, he doesn't know anything about this. Could you at least let me break it to him on my own? Please?'

Collingwood looked at her appraisingly for a moment, then nodded. 'I need to make some calls. Perhaps I could go up into one of the bedrooms? I won't disturb your mother.'

'Where have you been? I was . . . Who are you?' Malcolm stared at Collingwood as he came into the kitchen.

'I was at the police station,' Diane said.

'God, can't you people leave us in peace for five minutes?' he said wearily as Collingwood produced her warrant card. 'Don't you think my wife's been through enough already, without dragging her off to . . .'

'DC Collingwood's been appointed Family Liaison Officer. She's here to help us.'

'Oh.' Malcolm turned back to the woman, his expression hostile. 'Well, in that case, perhaps you can tell us what's going on regarding our nephew.'

'Thomas?' Diane was instantly on the alert. 'What do you mean?'

'I rang the hospital to see what time we could go over to visit him. They said he'd already been discharged.'

'Discharged? Who to?'

Tracey Collingwood looked faintly embarrassed. 'Thomas is in local authority care for the time being.'

'*What?*'

'In the circumstances, it was felt more appropriate . . .'

'Circumstances?' Malcolm snapped. 'What fucking circumstances?'

Diane glanced towards him, then whispered fearfully, 'Is it because of what I . . . ?'

Quickly, Collingwood shook her head. There was compassion in her expression as she said, 'An application was made last night for an emergency protection order.'

'*Protection?*' Malcolm shouted. 'From his own family?'

167

'He needs to be here, with people he knows.' Diane tried to sound calmer than she felt.

She could hear that Malcolm, too, was trying to control his emotions as he asked, 'Can't we at least see him?'

'Not for the moment, I'm afraid.'

'But why not, for God's sake?'

'I'm sorry, sir, but until Mr Somerford is located, it's been decided it's in Thomas's best interests not to reveal his where-abouts.' Collingwood paused. 'Not even to his remaining family.'

'I don't believe this!' Malcolm exploded. 'Which idiot came to that conclusion? Some fool at Social Services, I suppose?'

'The application was granted by a magistrate. There will be the opportunity in due course for you to . . .'

'We'll see about that,' he snapped, already on his way out of the kitchen. 'I'm going to ring my solicitor and see what he's got to say about due bloody course.'

'Not yet, Malcolm,' Diane said quietly. 'There's something we need to talk about, first.'

Collingwood cleared her throat. 'I'll leave you to it. I need to ring in to the station.'

'You do that,' Malcolm called after her. 'And you can tell them we shall be fighting this lunacy every inch of the way. Jesus,' he slumped down onto a chair. 'What else can happen to this bloody family?'

'Are you OK?' Diane scanned his face. He looked old; older than she'd ever seen him. Ashamed, she realised that she hadn't given a single thought to what he must have gone through at the mortuary, but his face told its own story. 'It must have been a nightmare for you.'

'It wasn't the best.' Malcolm compressed his lips. 'So what is it you want to tell me? Has there been some news?'

'I'll get you a coffee.' Diane couldn't look at him. The timing of what she was about to do to him couldn't possibly be worse. She tried to concentrate on pouring milk into his cup, but still she managed to slop the last of the carton onto the draining board. She watched the white rivulet trickle slowly into the sink.

'What is it?' he said. 'Is it something about Ian?'

She turned on the tap, and the circlet of milk around the plughole bubbled up, then disappeared cloudily down the drain.

'Diane?'

'No, not Ian.' She looked round to meet his worried gaze. 'It's something about me. And you're going to hate me for it.'

Malcolm heard her out in silence. He stood by the kitchen window, his back towards her, the whiteness of his knuckles against the sill the only indication of what might be going on inside his head.

'I'm so sorry,' she whispered when at last the whole sordid tale was out. 'I don't know what made me . . . I've never done anything like that before. Never.' She stared at her husband's unmoving backview. 'I love you, Malcolm. I've only ever loved you.'

Nothing but the slightest tensing of his shoulders suggested he had even heard her. For what seemed like an eternity, he remained quite still. When he turned towards her, his eyes were filled with disgust. 'How could you? With Lee Smith of all people. How could you, Diane?'

'I'm sorry!' Her head felt as if at any minute it might explode. She gripped her skull in an attempt to stop everything colliding inside it. She rocked back and forth, heard her voice screech in her ears, louder and louder as it rose towards hysteria. 'I'm sorry, I'm sorry, I'm . . .'

'Stop it!' Malcolm's fingers dug hard into her shoulders. 'Pull yourself together!' He shook her hard, snapping her head back on her neck, shocking her into silence. 'Who knows about this?'

She stared at him, dazed.

'You haven't told that bloody policewoman, have you?'

'I had to. Don't you understand? If I'm right, and he's been trying to frame Ian . . .'

'Jesus Christ!' Malcolm slammed his hand down on the table. 'Do you have any idea what you've done?'

She began to weep again; quietly now, despairingly.

'Not only do you betray me, betray everything I thought we stood for,' Malcolm's voice shook with emotion, 'you then broadcast the fact to the entire world. And for what? You really think all this rubbish about Lee Smith setting Ian up is going to change one solitary bloody thing? Do you? Angelika and the children are *dead*, for Christ's sake! Ian's *murdered* them. What the hell does it matter if . . . ?'

'No!' Sobbing, she put her hands over her ears to shut out his relentless voice. 'You don't know that.'

'Who the fuck else do you think killed them? Do I have to spell it out to you? Ian's questioned by the police about his lover's death, and the following day his family are wiped out. That's a fairly bloody huge coincidence, wouldn't you say? Even ignoring the fact he's now disappeared into thin air.'

'I won't listen to this! I won't. He's my *brother*.' She screamed the word at the top of her lungs. It reverberated around the kitchen in the small silence that followed.

'And he's my friend.' Abruptly, Malcolm sat down. 'Don't you think I'd like to bury my head in the sand, too? But if we've got any hope of surviving this at all, we've got to face reality. Both of us. Christ alone knows what must have been going on in his mind, but you have to accept the fact that Ian went back to Arden Hall some time yesterday afternoon and killed Angelika and the children. Who else do you think would have left Thomas alive? Who else . . . ?' He broke off, and buried his head in his arms. When he looked up again, his eyes were blazing with rage. 'And because of what you've done, because of your squalid little fling, the only one of them we've still got is going to be taken away from us as well. Christ! I could forgive you most things, Diane. But I'll never, *never* forgive you that.'

'I don't know what you mean,' she whimpered.

He met her uncomprehending gaze with contempt. 'Do you really imagine we'll have a chance in hell of getting Thomas back, once Social Services find out you've been having an affair with some . . . some fist-happy lout young enough to be your son? Let alone the husband of your brother's murdered lover.' He gave a bitter, humourless laugh. 'Oh yes, I can see magistrates queuing down the road to let us take charge of his welfare!'

'I didn't mean it to happen,' she moaned. 'I thought if I got close to Lee . . .'

'Well you certainly achieved that, by the sound of things.'

'Please, Malcolm. I'm trying to explain. I thought if I could gain his confidence, I might be able to . . .'

'Sidetrack him from Ian?'

'No! I just wanted to . . .'

'That's how it's going to look.' He jabbed a finger at her. 'That's what the police are going to think, you stupid . . .' He brought his fist down again on the table. 'What in hell possessed you to tell them?'

'I had to! He hit me. Beat me up. What did you expect me to . . . ?'

'Shall I tell you something, Diane?' Malcolm's voice cut icily over hers. 'I really don't care if Lee Smith hit you.' He got up and walked to the door. 'In fact, I think I'm quite glad he did.'

Tracey Collingwood was coming down the stairs as he left the kitchen. Diane wondered how much of the conversation she'd heard. It was a moment before she noticed that the other woman was carrying a couple of small plastic bags. One of them contained Diane's mobile phone.

'What are you doing with that?' She'd forgotten all about it; it must still have been in the silly little embroidered purse she'd taken with her to the party. Her heart lurched. 'Is there something from Ian on it? Let me see.'

'You can't have it, I'm afraid.' Collingwood slipped it into her case. 'It's evidence.'

'Evidence of what?' It was Malcolm who spoke.

'There is, isn't there?' Diane's hand flew to her throat. 'He was trying to get in touch with me, wasn't he? Oh, God!' Wide-eyed, she stared at Malcolm. 'Why didn't I take the bloody thing out of that other bag? Why didn't I think to check it? Please,' she grabbed the woman's arm, 'you've got to tell me what he said. Please. Just tell me if there's been anything from him since . . .'

'I can't discuss that, I'm afraid.'

'Do you have any right to confiscate my wife's personal possessions in this way?' Malcolm demanded.

'Yes, sir,' she said politely. 'I do.'

He glanced over to Diane. 'But surely, for God's sake, you could just tell her . . . ?'

'I'm sorry, sir.'

'I thought you were here to help us,' Diane pleaded.

'I am.' Collingwood gave her the ghost of a smile. 'I'm also a police officer.'

'Please.' Diane clutched her hand. 'Just tell us if he's still alive.'

Collingwood paused. She searched Diane's face, then said quietly, 'I'll be back soon.'

Her hand clamped to her mouth, Diane watched the woman make her way back to the waiting police car. She felt the hesitant touch of Malcolm's hand on her shoulder.

'I'll phone George. See if there's any way he can find out what's going on.'

Diane turned round, hardly daring to look into his face.

Malcolm's hands dropped to his sides. He leant his head back against the wall and closed his eyes in a gesture of sheer, hopeless exhaustion. 'Christ, what a bloody mess.'

'I never meant to hurt you,' she whispered. She didn't know what else to say.

His eyes snapped open again. 'No, I don't suppose you did.' His voice was cold. The tiny moment when she'd thought she might reach him had vanished. 'I don't suppose Ian meant to hurt anyone when he started screwing your lover's wife, either.'

20

George Bonham was with them within the hour. He shook Malcolm's hand, kissed Diane on the cheek and murmured his condolences.

'Terrible business. Unbelievable,' he repeated as he followed them back through to the living-room. 'Why on earth didn't you ring me last night, Malcolm?'

'I'm sorry. I thought maybe the police . . .'

'I rang Inspector Baker as soon as I got off the phone to you, to see what I could find out. Which wasn't much. As you know, they've discovered Ian's car . . .'

'No.' Malcolm glanced at Diane. 'I didn't know that.'

'I . . . I'm sorry. I forgot to say, with everything else . . .' Diane didn't meet his eyes. 'It was parked in one of the outbuildings.'

'Oh, shit.' Malcolm rubbed his hands across his face.

George took a seat. It wasn't until he'd taken some papers from his briefcase and shuffled them that he said carefully, 'The perpetrators of family mass murders tend to commit suicide within the first few hours, usually somewhere in the immediate vicinity. The police have found no trace of Ian. They seem to think it's more likely he's made a run for it.'

'But the car . . .'

'Could have been parked in the outbuildings before he made his way to the house, so that Angelika wouldn't be alerted to

174

his presence.' George turned to Diane, his face full of concern. 'It appears Angelika's passport and the children's were at the cottage, but the police can find no trace of Ian's.'

Malcolm cleared his throat. 'He took them with him on Saturday evening. He said . . .'

'He just didn't want Angelika to take off with the children,' Diane snapped. 'You know that as well as I do.'

'Well, the police have instigated all the necessary procedures, notified the ports and suchlike, so let's just hope they find him quickly.' George gazed down at his papers. 'There's a warrant out for his arrest, of course.'

'Something's happened to him. It must have,' Diane said desperately. 'If he'd been trying to get away, why wouldn't he take the car? It doesn't make sense.'

'Too easy to trace.' It was Malcolm who answered.

'So what do you think he did? Called a bloody taxi?'

George looked at both of them in turn. 'Malcolm's right. The first thing the police would have done is to feed the details into the PNC. And Arden Hall's only a mile or so from the junction with the Longbridge roundabout, remember. Ian could easily have hitched a lift onto the M40, and then . . .'

'It sounds like you've got it all worked out, between you.' Diane, who had sat down on the sofa beside George, jumped to her feet. 'Maybe you'd be better acting for the bloody prosecution, instead of trying to pretend you're Ian's solicitor.'

'Diane's finding it rather difficult to face facts,' Malcolm said tersely.

'Well, of course. She must be. God knows, it was enough of a shock to me, and I'm not even family.' George held out his hand to her. 'But you're absolutely right, we shouldn't be trying to speculate. None of us knows exactly what happened yet. In some ways, that's the hardest part.' Again, his eyes strayed from Diane to Malcolm and back again. 'This must be appallingly difficult for you both.'

Malcolm breathed in sharply as, for the first time, he looked directly at Diane. 'Are you going to tell him, or am I?'

'Tell me what?' George looked alarmed.

Diane swallowed hard. 'I will,' she said.

Malcolm got to his feet and stood in front of the fireplace, his back to them, as once again Diane repeated the whole, humiliating story. George didn't try to stem the flood of words. He sat quite still until she'd finished. Then he took off his glasses, pinched the bridge of his nose and murmured, 'Oh dear.'

Malcolm spun round. ' "*Oh dear?*" Is that all you've got to say?'

'What would you like me to say? That I'm sorry? Of course I am. That I think Diane's theories concerning Lee Smith have any validity whatsoever?' George glanced across at her, his eyes showing more sympathy than she knew she deserved. 'No, I'm afraid I don't. That I think she did the right thing in going to the police?' He talked over her as she started to speak. 'Yes, I do. Absolutely the right thing.'

Malcolm snorted. 'That's easy enough for you to say, isn't it? It's not your dirty linen that's been hung out for all to see.'

Diane looked down at her clenched hands and subsided into silence.

'Listen to me, Malcolm.' George's voice was patient. 'It appears that, for whatever reason, the police are interested in how Diane came by the bruises to her face. They are also bound to want to know where she was yesterday, as they will undoubtedly want to know where you were, in due course.

And any other interested parties, for that matter. Are you seriously suggesting she should have lied to them?'

The look Malcolm shot her was the nearest to pure hatred she had ever seen on his face. 'If that was the only alternative to losing custody of Thomas, then yes, I am.'

'Oh.' George exhaled slowly. 'I see.'

'Well thank God for that.' Malcolm's voice was heavy with sarcasm. He brought his fist down on the mantelpiece. 'He's in care, for God's sake!'

'So I understand. But that's only as a precautionary measure until . . .'

'It might be precautionary now. But I don't see the courts rushing to give us custody now Diane's seen fit to broadcast to all and sundry what's she's been up to behind my back. Not exactly happy families, is it?'

'She'd have done even less for your chances of being granted residence by getting herself imprisoned for perverting the course of justice,' George answered with some acerbity. He turned to Diane. 'Have you pressed charges against Lee Smith?'

Her gaze still firmly fixed on her handkerchief, she shook her head.

'Do you intend to?'

'Yes, I do.'

'What's the bloody point?' Malcolm snapped. 'It can only cause even more damage, if that's possible.'

Diane's head came up. 'I'm damned if I'm going to let him get away scot-free for what he's done, that's for sure.'

'If I got my hands on the bastard, I'd break his bloody neck.'

George ignored the comment. His attention was on Diane as he asked, 'Do you mean for what Lee Smith has done to you, or for what you perceive he's done to Ian?'

'I don't care what he did to me. It's no more than I deserve, is it?' She shot a look at Malcolm. 'But if it's the only way I can make him pay for the way he hounded Ian . . .'

'It sounds from what you've told me that he has a case to answer, although I should warn you these things do tend to get pretty unpleasant once they get as far as the courts. It's a decision you're going to have to make for yourself.' George glanced again from one of them to the other. 'Preferably in consultation with Malcolm. And I can assure you, before Malcolm asks, that if you do go ahead, it will have no bearing whatsoever on your chances concerning Thomas. However, I would advise you very strongly, both as a solicitor and as a friend, to examine your motivation carefully, whatever you decide. Because if you are pursuing Lee Smith through some misguided sense of loyalty towards Ian, it will become apparent in no time. And in the current situation, you could well end up doing both yourself and Ian nothing but further harm. You made the first approach to this man, remember. With the admitted intention of finding out what it was he had against Ian. What do you think any half-decent defence barrister is going to make of that, if the matter comes to court?'

'My point precisely,' Malcolm muttered.

'You would say that, wouldn't you?' Diane retorted. 'All you're interested in is trying to sweep everything under the carpet.'

'Under the carpet? Jesus Christ! Isn't it enough that your brother's massacred almost his entire family, and most probably the tart he was shagging as well, without you giving the papers something else to throw at us all? Just how much fucking publicity do you think we need?'

'You bastard!' She leapt up again. 'If that's the way you

were intending to bring Thomas up to think about his father, it's probably just as well . . .'

'Stop this, both of you!' It was the uncharacteristic anger in George's voice that silenced her. She compressed her lips and gazed down at the small fleur-de-lis pattern on the carpet as he went on. 'For one thing, it's somewhat premature to be arguing about Thomas's future before we even know what's happened to Ian. And for another, if it does come to a question of deciding residency, behave like that in court and I can tell you now that neither of you is going to be allowed within a mile of him. So just sit down, the pair of you, and let's at least attempt to discuss this like adults.'

'I'm sorry,' Malcolm muttered. 'I hadn't intended you to get involved in . . .'

'You're in an unbearably painful situation.' George looked up at Diane. 'Both of you. Tearing at each other's throats isn't going to help.'

Diane nodded and resumed her seat. Malcolm took a chair on the other side of the fireplace, as far away from her as possible. The hostility was coming off him in waves.

'Do you think Ian's still alive?' Diane searched her friend's face for any sign of hope, but all she could read there was compassion.

George sighed. 'I can't answer that, can I? I can't begin to imagine what must have been going through Ian's head. I don't think any of us can.'

'But you do believe he killed them?'

'I find it almost impossible to believe. I've known you and Ian most of my life. But I simply don't see any other explanation.' A look of real anguish crossed his face. 'Dear God, if I'd had any idea of just how much of a mess he was in . . .'

'What do you mean?'

It was a moment before George replied. 'I don't know how much Ian told you of what happened at the police station on Saturday afternoon.' He paused, his gaze switching between them. 'The police have discovered that substantial sums of money had been paid into Nicola Smith's bank account in the weeks before . . .'

'He said that,' Diane cut him off impatiently. 'All that proves is . . .'

'Did he also say that their investigation of his own finances had shown that corresponding amounts had been withdrawn from his accounts?'

'Oh Jesus,' Malcolm breathed. 'The idiot. The bloody idiot.'

George gave him a tight smile. 'I suppose he thought he'd covered his tracks sufficiently by spreading the withdrawals across a number of different bank and building society accounts and by using cash dispensers rather than writing cheques, but once the police started looking into things. . . .'

'Someone could have stolen his cards,' Diane countered. 'He's always been careless with money, you know that. He might not have realised . . .'

Malcolm exhaled sharply.

George said gently, 'We're talking of sums in the region of several thousand pounds a week, Diane. Over the course of nearly three months. Do you really think Ian wouldn't have noticed?' Wearily, he shook his head. 'The ridiculous thing is that if he'd just admitted to having an affair with Nicola Smith, that they'd been stashing a bit away to buy a love-nest together, or whatever, the police would probably have been prepared to leave it there. There's no law against extramarital flings.' He flushed, as Malcolm shifted in his seat. 'I'm sorry. That was thoughtless. But what I'm trying to say is that I advised him that, by continuing to deny any involvement with the woman in the face of such conclusive evidence, he was simply going to make the police suspect him of a great deal more than infidelity. At the time, I thought he was just frightened of what Angelika was likely to do to him,' he added soberly.

'And now?' Malcolm asked. 'Do you think he was responsible for Nicola Smith's death?'

George spread his hands out in front of him and examined them before replying, 'I don't know. To be frank, I think there's a strong possibility we shall never know.'

For a moment, no one spoke.

'What is going to happen to Thomas?' Diane whispered at last.

'Well,' George looked relieved to be back on more certain territory, 'the EPO – Emergency Protection Order – runs for seventy-two hours in the first instance, and then it will have to come back before a full bench of magistrates sitting in the Family Court. It will only be an interim hearing; no long-term decisions are ever made until all the necessary reports have been undertaken, and this is going to be a particularly complicated case, given that Ian's whereabouts are unknown. Clearly, the application from Social Services will be for Thomas to remain where he is for the time being. And that has nothing to do with anything Diane may or may not have done,' he said firmly in response to Malcolm's derisive snort. 'Now, my suggestion is that you ask the court for leave to apply.'

'Apply for what, for God's sake? You've just said . . .'

'You and Diane are not Thomas's parents, Malcolm. You have no automatic right to have any say at all in what happens to him. You have to apply to be a party to the hearing.'

'I've never heard such a load of bureaucratic crap . . .'

'You're entitled to your own opinions.' George was beginning to sound irritated. 'The fact remains that it's the way the system works. The aim being to ensure the best interests of the child, not your convenience.'

'What would happen then, George? If the application was successful?' Diane was anxious not to alienate him further.

'I can see no reason at all why you shouldn't be able to see Thomas, as long as the meeting were to take place at a neutral location. The contact centre would be the usual venue. I'll have a word with our family law expert as soon as I get back to the office. He can find out when the hearing's scheduled. He can even appear on your behalf, if necessary. I imagine the next few days will be fraught enough for you, without the stress of a court appearance.' George snapped his briefcase shut and got to his feet. 'I don't think there's a great deal else I can tell you for the time being.' He kissed Diane on the cheek, then held out his hand to Malcolm. 'Above all, the court will be looking for a stable, happy environment for Thomas. Only the two of you can decide if you're able to provide that for him.' He risked a small smile, which wasn't returned as he squeezed Malcolm's hand and added, 'If granting residence depended on the absolute chastity of the applicants, the care system would grind to a halt in about five minutes.'

Diane watched George's car disappear down the drive. She remained on the step for several minutes after the sound of the car engine had dwindled into silence. It was only with a huge effort of will that she made herself go back into the house.

Malcolm was in the kitchen. She heard him running water into the kettle. It was such an ordinary, domesticated sound that it made her want to weep.

'There's no milk,' he said tonelessly as she went through.

Even in the midst of disaster, the mundane business of life still went on. Their family had been torn apart, their marriage hung by a thread; every certainty of their comfortable, un-eventful lives had been destroyed. And there was no milk. Diane felt paralysed at the thought of going to the super-market; coming into contact with ordinary people going about their ordinary lives. How could she ever do anything ordinary again?

'I'll go and get some.' Malcolm didn't look at her.

'No, I'll do it.' The kitchen clock told her it was almost one; they'd eaten nothing since the day before. 'I'll pick something up for lunch,' she added tentatively. The least she could do was feed him. Or maybe the most.

'I'll go.' He picked up his car keys, his face stony. 'I need to get out of the house.'

21

Malcolm had put Agnes in the little single bedroom at the top of the stairs; the one that had been Diane's when it had been the family home. They'd only recently got round to taking down the faded pop posters and gymkhana rosettes; there was still a faint smell of paint.

Diane watched the split second of confusion in her mother's face as she opened her eyes and gazed around her unfamiliar surroundings, followed almost immediately by the horror of recollection.

'I've brought you a cup of tea. There's no milk, I'm afraid. Malcolm's just gone out to . . .'

Agnes pulled herself up in the bed. Her carefully permed grey hair was awry, the prissy bow at the neck of her blouse unknotted to reveal the fragile, wrinkled skin beneath. Without her false teeth, her face seemed to have collapsed. Diane's heart went out to the older woman; she'd never seen her look more vulnerable.

As if sensing her daughter's pity, Agnes grabbed the dentures from the bedside table and rammed them back in her mouth. Then, swinging her sturdy legs over the side of the bed, she said fiercely, 'I've a good mind to report that doctor of yours, giving me an injection when I didn't want one.' She swayed slightly as she stood up. 'Lying about in bed. What good is that going to do anyone?' Her lips were trembling so much that the words were barely audible.

'Oh, Mum.' Diane held her arms out to her. For a long moment, they clung together.

'I wished Angelika dead, you know,' Agnes said, her voice muffled against Diane's shoulder. She pulled herself away, her face stricken. 'God help me, when I went to bed the night of the party, I prayed for it. And now they're all dead.'

'You can't blame yourself, Mum.'

'I didn't even kiss him goodbye.' A single tear rolled down her cheek, unheeded.

'The police will find Ian.' Diane heard the quaver in her own voice.

Agnes shook her head. 'Hope is the hardest thing of all to bear, isn't it?' she said quietly.

Diane gazed at her, mute, and acknowledged to herself her absolute certainty that her mother was right. It was as if a great rock were crushing her chest. She had to fight to get the words out at all. 'What do you think happened?'

'I don't know. But I know Ian didn't kill himself, or his family. We both know that.'

Diane envied her mother's certainty. 'I can't imagine Ian hurting anyone. I can't imagine him being unfaithful.' But then, until a week ago, she couldn't have imagined herself being unfaithful, either. Wearily, she shook her head. 'There just seems to be so much evidence . . .'

'The only evidence I need comes from thirty-nine years of knowing my own son.'

'Oh, Mum . . .'

'I'm not a fool, Diane.' Agnes looked hard into her face. 'I don't think Ian was without his faults. I can accept that he might have had a mistress, although I find it hard to believe. I can even accept that he could have lost control of himself enough to kill Angelika. But I will never, never believe that my son cold-bloodedly took the lives of those two children. You look me in the eye and tell me you think he did.'

This was Ian they were talking about. Ian who, as a child, had been inconsolable for weeks when a neighbour had drowned an unwanted litter of kittens. Ian who, even as an adult, would spend minutes at a time wafting a wasp out of the window, rather than swat it.

'You can't,' Agnes said briskly. 'And if we're not able to make the police see sense, we're just going to have to find a way of proving your brother's innocence ourselves.' She sat down at the dressing-table, straightened her hair and retied the bow on her blouse with a vicious tug. Only by looking very carefully could Diane detect the tremor of her mother's capable, liver-spotted hands. 'So you'd better tell me exactly what you've found out so far.'

'Yes,' Diane said heavily. She was filled with dread, both at the prospect of cataloguing the seemingly irrefutable list of evidence against Ian, and of admitting her own shameful part in the tangled chain of events. This new, fragile bond of complicity with her mother was all she had left. And she was about to shatter that, too.

She went over the events that led up to the discovery of Angelika's and the children's bodies. Agnes sat bolt upright, her face grim, her hands clenched together in her lap. Diane could see that her mother was deeply shaken by the details of Ian's financial involvement with Nicola Smith, and of Malcolm's phone call on the night of the murders. Finally, haltingly, she described the scene at Arden Hall and then petered into silence.

Agnes closed her eyes and pressed her lips bloodlessly together. For a long moment, the only sound was the faint ticking of the bedside clock. Then she opened her eyes and said, 'There's more, isn't there?'

Now that the moment had come, Diane had lost her nerve. She glanced at the china cup and saucer next to the clock and said quickly, 'Look. You haven't even drunk your tea.'

'I'm not senile, Diane.' Agnes bent forward, took Diane's hand and said more gently, 'Don't you think I have a right to know whatever it is you're keeping from me?'

So, sitting on the bed in the newly decorated spare room, Diane told her mother everything there was to tell about Lee Smith. She did so as truthfully and dispassionately as she was able, not attempting to justify herself or to minimise her guilt. At no point did Agnes's grip falter. All she said, when Diane at last fell silent, was, 'Poor Malcolm.'

Diane nodded. She felt hollow, as if her insides had been scooped out, and all that was left was grief.

'You embarked on this silliness because you thought you were helping your brother? You're telling me the truth?' Agnes gave her the look she'd given them when they were small; when a vase got broken, or some change went missing. Diane could no more have lied to her now than then.

'Yes. It was stupid. Just a stupid . . .' Diane's eyes filled with tears.

'Poor girl.' She touched the bruise on Diane's cheek.

'Serves me right.'

'No, it doesn't.' Agnes patted her hand, almost absently. 'He'll forgive you, you know. Malcolm. Given time.'

Her mother's kindness was almost harder to bear than the recriminations Diane had been expecting. 'No, he won't. Why should he?'

'Because you have a sound marriage.'

'Not any more.'

'Malcolm won't leave you. He won't forget, but he'll forgive. For little Thomas's sake, if for no other reason.' Agnes smiled faintly. 'The same as I forgave your father.'

Diane gazed at her, wondering if she could have misheard.

'Oh, I know you thought I was the one always wanting to better us, but that was just your dad's way of trying to make amends.' Agnes looked round at the room, as if seeing it for the first time. 'Even this house. He bought it because he thought it would make me happy, when all I really wanted was him, the silly man.'

'But you never said . . .' Diane mumbled stupidly. She thought she'd known everything there was to know about her parents; her mother's snobbishness and social climbing, her father's quiet charm. And she'd known nothing. She shivered slightly, and wrapped her arms round herself for warmth. She tried to push from her head the small voice that asked if she could have been equally wrong about her brother.

'Would you have wanted to know?' Agnes stared down at her hand, still clasping Diane's. 'You and Tom were always like two peas in a pod.'

'When did it . . .?'

Agnes shook her head. 'You were just a baby. I think maybe I blamed you. Just a bit. That's why I was sometimes a bit resentful that you always loved him so much more than you loved me.' She looked up, her own eyes bright with tears. 'And why I've perhaps favoured your brother.'

'Oh, Mum . . .'

'Anyway, that's all in the past.' She dodged Diane, who had reached out her arms to her. Getting to her feet, she blew her nose briskly, shooed Diane off the bed and straightened the covers, the old Agnes again. 'We're not going to help anyone by sitting here wallowing together.' She cocked her head at the sound of the front door being opened and closed. 'It sounds as if Malcolm's back with the milk, so you can start by making me a drinkable cup of tea.'

Malcolm was in the kitchen, bending down to put the milk in the fridge.

'How's your mother?' he said, not looking round.

'Not too bad.' Diane poured the cold tea down the sink and put the kettle on. 'Can I get you a drink?'

'No, thank you.' He folded the plastic carrier with care. 'I bought some more bread for lunch. They only had wholemeal. I hope that's all right.'

'Fine. Thanks.' She cleared her throat. 'Malcolm, I . . .'

The doorbell rang.

'I'll go.' He pushed past her without looking at her.

Diane leant against the work surface and closed her eyes. It was like talking to a polite stranger; his anger had been easier.

He returned, bearing a huge bunch of lilies. For an absurd second, her heart soared, until she looked at his face.

'From Chas and Lorraine.' He held out the typed florist's card that offered their deepest sympathy. 'I rang Chas earlier. I didn't want him hearing it on the news.'

Diane nodded. She went to get the vase from the hall then remembered it was broken.

Agnes came in. She looked at the flowers, then from Diane to Malcolm. 'I'll make the tea, shall I?' she said. 'And then I'd like one of you to take me home.'

'No, you must stay here with us.' Diane realised how much she didn't want to be on her own with him.

'And I would like to go via Arden Hall to see for myself how this investigation is being handled.'

Malcolm sighed. 'There's no point, Agnes. I told you, the police said . . .'

Agnes made a derisive noise in her throat. 'I've no intention of being told what to do by the police, Malcolm. If neither of you will take me, I'm sure I can call on one of my friends.'

'It's not just going to be the police there, you know. The place is going to be crawling with the press by now.' Diane could tell from Malcolm's voice that he was making a supreme effort to be tolerant. She felt a wave of gratitude towards him for not venting his hostility on his mother-in-law as he might have done. He added patiently, 'You're only going to upset yourself.'

'I think I can be the judge of that.'

'I can't bear the thought of you in the flat on your own, Mum,' Diane said. 'Please, stay with us.'

Agnes shook her head.

'At least have some lunch.'

She patted Diane's hand. 'You don't need me here. Anyway,' she added firmly, 'if we're going to set about proving Ian's innocence, I've got things to do.'

'Nothing you can do is going to change anything, Agnes.' Malcolm sounded infinitely weary. 'You do know that?'

Diane looked into his face and said pleadingly, 'Until we find Ian, we don't really know anything, do we?'

Malcolm held her gaze. It was she who looked away first. She heard his slow exhalation of breath.

'I'll drive you over there,' he said.

It was as Malcolm had predicted, only worse. Cars were parked crazily up the steep verges of the lane that led to the isolated farmhouse. As he slowed to nose his way between them, they were met with a battalion of flashlights.

A police van blocked the entrance to the driveway itself.

'Stay here,' Malcolm ordered as he brought the car to a halt in front of it.

Agnes went to open the car door. A young man darted forward and pushed a microphone against the window.

'I said, stay here,' Malcolm snapped, reaching into the back to slam the door shut. He shouldered his way past the reporter and went to speak to the uniformed officer on guard.

Fluttering blue-and-white tape cordoned off the front of the house. Through the living-room window, Diane could glimpse shadowy figures moving backwards and forwards. It didn't seem like Ian's house any more.

The reporter rapped his knuckles against the windscreen. Diane covered her face with her hand and turned her head away from him. She glanced at Agnes, who was sitting in the back, her hands clenched in her lap, her gaze fixed straight ahead of her.

Malcolm was back within seconds. 'Let's go,' he said as he slammed the car into reverse.

Agnes didn't argue. 'Can we go to see the cottage?' she said instead, as they sped away from Stratford.

Malcolm's hands tensed on the wheel.

Diane twisted round to look at her mother. She looked awful; as if every ounce of fight had been drained from her by the reality that the scene at Arden Hall had brought home to her.

'I know it won't do any good,' Agnes said simply. 'I just think I might feel closer to him there.'

After the scrum at Arden Hall, the cottage was oddly peaceful. Apart from the inevitable tape, a single constable barred their entry and, for the moment at least, there was no sign of the press. The constable was polite, but unmoved; the cottage was a crime scene and no one without authority was to enter. Both the front door and the faded velvet curtains were shut on whatever scene of destruction lay behind them. Diane felt obscurely cheated that she'd been denied even that much of Ian.

From somewhere deep in the trees, the cuckoo that had delighted her the previous week still chimed its monotonous call. The hawthorn hedge was the same froth of creamy flowers she'd been trying to capture in watercolour. The convolvulus she'd meant to pull out still snaked up the tender birch sapling by the gate to strangle it. All unaltered. All utterly different. Everything had changed. Permanently. And no amount of effort by any of them could alter that.

'There must be something we can do.' Agnes's subdued voice echoed Diane's thoughts as Malcolm started the engine.

'Wait.' Malcolm gave a tight smile as he turned back towards Leamington. 'That's all we can do. And pray, I suppose.'

At least he hadn't said he'd told them so.

The phone was ringing as they got back after dropping Agnes at the flat. They looked at each other for a moment, then Malcolm darted forward to answer it. Her heart hammering, Diane watched his mouth tighten as he listened to what was being said, then banged the receiver down without speaking.

'Press,' he snapped. He went through to the study and came back carrying his briefcase. 'Just say, "No comment," if they ring back. You'd better not leave the phone off the hook in case the police try to get in touch.'

'Where are you going?'

'Work. I've got a meeting with Chas at the bank.'

'Can't it wait? Surely even Chas isn't going to expect you to . . .'

'Someone's got to keep the business going.' He turned at the door, his face expressionless. 'Can you think of any better way for me to be filling my time?'

Oppressed by the silence of the empty house, Diane went out into the garden. The pansy heads lay in a small, withering pile at the side of the path. She stared at them stupidly, wondering how the crumpled petals could still retain some vestiges of colour, until she realised she'd picked them only a few hours before. Time seemed to have been suspended. Less than two days ago, they'd been singing *Happy Birthday* to her mother.

She bent to gather the petals up. As she did so, she heard a slight movement. She felt a prickling sensation at the base of her spine. Someone else was in the garden.

'Ian?' she breathed.

A robin rustled out from behind a clump of lupins, and hopped towards her.

How could it have been Ian? Ian was dead.

The robin darted forward, grabbed a worm. It was so close Diane could have reached out her hand and touched it. She found its presence obscurely comforting. Carefully, lest she startle it, she went to pull up another weed. The robin observed her for a moment, its head on one side, its eyes bright, then hopped forward again.

Another weed, another worm. Another. Just focus on the robin. Another. How did it get so many in its beak at once? Did the writhing worms realise what was happening to them? Feel panic as they were ripped from the earth?

A sudden shadow fell across the path. The robin flew high into the laurel hedge, dropping its prey as it set up its high-pitched call of warning.

Diane froze.

Someone was behind her.

'Ian?' For a split second, her heart soared, before she looked up to see Inspector Baker staring down at her, DC Collingwood at his side.

'Now, why would you think I was Ian, Mrs Middleton?' he asked.

'I didn't. I just . . .' Flushing, she scrambled to her feet and wiped her hands down the front of her jeans.

'We let ourselves in round the side. We did try the front door. Sorry if I made you jump.' Baker's expression belied the apology; Diane suspected he was all too pleased to have caught her unawares.

She looked past him, to Collingwood. 'My mobile. Was there something from Ian on it?'

'Oh, I think you already know what was on your mobile, don't you, Mrs Middleton?' Baker said.

'No.' She shook her head, mystified. 'I've already said. It was in a different bag. I'd forgotten all about it. Please. Just tell me.'

Baker fingered his moustache and observed her in silence for a moment. Then, stepping forward and firmly gripping her upper arm, he said, 'Diane Middleton, I'm arresting you for the murders of Angelika, Dominica and Marshall Somerford. You do not have to say anything, but . . .'

Diane stared at him, too stunned to speak, as he continued the caution. For a wild moment, she wondered if it could be some terrible, sick joke he was playing on her. She felt the gentle pressure of Tracey Collingwood's hand in the small of her back.

'You must come with us, now, Diane,' she said.

Above them, the robin flew away, up into the flawless blue sky, until it was nothing more than a tiny, indistinguishable dot.

22

The door that led to the custody suite at Little Park Street Police Station bore a large sign: PRISONERS ONLY. It was as if Diane had crossed an invisible line that divided her from the rest of society.

The room beyond the door was hot, crowded and noisy. The strong smell of disinfectant didn't quite manage to disguise the underlying stench of tobacco, sweat and stale urine. A young Asian girl, her face streaked with mascara, was swearing and crying as she struggled to free herself from the grip of the bulky, impassive uniformed officer who held her arm. At the desk, another officer was attempting to take the details of the elderly man who was slumped against the counter, clearly drunk. Two youths lounged against the grey gloss-painted wall, looking profoundly bored. One of them, a heavily built West Indian wearing a hooded top and wide, baggy trousers, glanced at Diane without interest, then returned to scuffing the cracked linoleum with the toe of his trainer. Had Diane met him in the street, she would probably have tightened her grip on her handbag.

In one corner of the area was a holding cell, to which Diane was steered.

'I'm sorry.' Collingwood didn't meet her eye. 'I'm going to have to search you. Standard procedure,' she added with a small shrug.

Diane stood motionless. She felt more assaulted by Collingwood's efficient, impersonal touch than she had been by Lee Smith's fists. Her bag was taken from her, and her keys and purse removed. Collingwood said something to her, but the words were drowned out by the racket from the Asian girl, who was being dragged, kicking and screaming, to the corridor of cells beyond.

'I need to take your belt, too,' Collingwood repeated. She held out her hand and, for the first time, met Diane's gaze. 'Just in case.'

'This is totally ridiculous. You do realise that?' Diane prayed she sounded more confident than she felt.

Collingwood gave her a brief smile as she took the belt, and said nothing.

The drunk had been led obediently to the cells. Diane took his place before the custody sergeant, a bald, paunchy man who barely lifted his eyes from his paperwork as he took Diane's details, made an inventory of her possessions and handed her a small booklet: *People in Custody – Your Rights and Entitlements*. That's what she'd become, Diane thought as she took it from him – a person in custody. The same as the drunk, the foul-mouthed girl, and the scary-looking thug in the hooded top.

She was allowed to make two phone calls. George was in court, she was told when she rang his office. His secretary promised to get a message to him. Malcolm's mobile was switched off, so she had to leave a message for him too, speaking as quietly as she could into the public telephone that hung on the wall of the reception area. She tried to sound calm, so as not to alarm him. She wondered what his reaction would be when he received the message, and realised she had no idea.

She was escorted into a tiny office, where her fingerprints were taken, and the inside of her cheek swabbed to collect a DNA sample, then she was led along the corridor to a cell; a cheerless room painted the colour of over-boiled cabbage and furnished with just a bench covered with a thin blue plastic mattress. A recessed cubicle held a stainless steel lavatory and washbasin. The walls were covered with graffiti. The heavy clang as the door was pulled shut was almost melodramatically loud.

She was brought a cup of tea, which she didn't drink. On one side of her, the Asian girl was still bellowing a non-stop stream of obscenities. From the other came the sound of regular, stentorian snoring. It seemed an eternity before the custody sergeant poked his head round the door and said, 'Your solicitor's here, luv.'

Diane got to her feet, more relieved than she would have thought possible at the prospect of George's familiar, reassuring presence. But it was a young woman who followed the officer into the cell.

'Winifred Keilly.' The woman held out a well-manicured hand. She smiled, displaying large, perfectly white teeth. 'George Bonham asked me to come and see you.' Her accent still bore a faint trace of her Caribbean origins. Diane stared at her in dismay before recovering herself sufficiently to return the handshake as the custody sergeant closed the door on them.

Winifred Keilly perched herself on the bench and took a notepad and pen from her immaculate briefcase. Diane remained standing. The woman looked up at her. 'I know. I'm black, I'm a woman, and I'm not George Bonham. But I am very good at my job.'

'I'm sorry.' Diane fought to stifle the twin prejudices that had taken her so completely, shamefully, by surprise. She was a woman herself, for God's sake. And she'd always despised any sort of racism. 'It's just that George is a friend, and . . .'

'I know. He told me, and he's distraught that he can't represent you himself. But as he's been acting for your brother . . .' The woman gave an eloquent shrug. 'Conflict of interests. A legal no-no, which is why he contacted me instead.' She grinned suddenly. 'If it's any consolation, I'm known in the trade as Win, because I generally do.'

Win Keilly's casual friendliness disappeared as soon as she got down to business; it was as if she had flicked some internal switch. She listened to everything Diane had to say, making notes but few comments. She offered no sympathy or reassurance. When Diane had told her everything there was to tell, she glanced through her notes then got briskly to her feet and said, 'OK. Let's see what Baker's got to say for himself.' She left the room without a backward glance.

Diane heard the woman's high heels clack away down the corridor, her confident voice as she announced she was ready to speak to Bill Baker. The use of his first name wasn't lost on Diane; it was as if all of them were in some kind of private club from which she herself was excluded. She tried to focus her thoughts, but her brain felt as if it had been turned to treacle. She had the distinct impression that Win Keilly didn't believe her any more than Baker had, and tried to imagine the conversation that was taking place at that moment in Baker's poky office. She stared at the graffiti: '*Leanne woz here . . . Mel 4 Leroy . . . Fuck the Pigs . . .*' She tried to imagine the former occupants of the cell. She wished she could speak to Malcolm. She'd never felt so utterly isolated in her life.

After a few minutes, Win Keilly swept in again, overlaying the stench of disinfectant with a brief whiff of Rive Gauche.

'Things aren't as bad as they seem,' she said breezily, as she sat down on the bench and patted the space next to her.

Diane remained standing. 'Would you mind telling me how it could be any worse?'

'Trust me. Just try not to . . .'

'Lose my cool.' Diane finished the sentence for her. 'I know. You said.' She gazed down at the other woman. 'This is just another job to you, but it's my *life*, do you understand that? How the hell do you expect me to stay calm, when no one will believe a word I say?' She banged her fist against the wall, suddenly furious. 'Lee Smith's the one who should be in this cell. He's behind all this, I know he is. Ian would never . . .'

'No.' Win's voice was sharp. 'You've got to stop all that and stop it now. You've absolutely no proof Lee Smith was involved in his wife's death, far less any of the others. Do you have any idea how vindictive and hysterical these entirely groundless accusations make you sound?'

'If that's how you think, maybe I should find myself another solicitor.'

'Grow up, Diane. Do you want to get out of here or don't you?'

It wasn't the response Diane had been expecting. She glared at the other woman. Win's face remained perfectly composed. Abruptly, Diane sat down next to her on the unyielding bench and buried her head in her hands. 'Of course I do.'

'Good. That's a start. Now, most of what Baker has got against you is circumstantial, at best. There's nothing he'd get past the CPS in a million years, and he knows it.'

'Great. So I'll just get up and walk out, shall I?'

'I'm on your side, Diane.'

'Are you?'

'Yes, I am. Now do you want to hear what I've got out of Baker or not?'

'I'm sorry.' Diane massaged her temples. 'It's just . . .'

'I know.' Win laid her hand briefly on Diane's. 'We can get this sorted, I promise you. But only if we work together.'

Diane nodded.

'So let's go through it from the top, and see whether we've got anything that will corroborate your story. These bruises of yours, for a start . . .'

'Why does everyone keep asking about that?' Diane's hand went defensively to her face. 'I don't see . . .'

'Angelika had bruising to her face too.'

It took Diane a moment to realise the implications of the statement. 'They think Angelika and I . . .?' she started incredulously.

'Look, Diane. Let's get things straight. The police find you at the scene of three murders, with facial injuries that match those of one of the victims. What conclusion do you expect them to jump to? It's up to us to show them they're wrong.'

'But I've already told them. Lee Smith . . .'

'Smith has apparently denied all knowledge of any assault.' Win raised her shoulders. 'Which is pretty much what you would expect. In fact, he's denying any involvement with you at all.'

Diane closed her eyes. 'The bastard.'

Win gave a slight smile. 'There are plenty of them around. So what time did the assault take place?'

'I went round after lunch. Somewhere around two, I suppose.'

'Any witnesses?'

'The neighbours might have heard us arguing in the street when I first got there.'

'OK.' Win made some notes. 'Good. And after the assault. What happened then?'

'I drove around for a while. I didn't want to go back home. I was frightened he might be following me. Then I went into Coventry . . .'

'What time?'

'About three.'

Win looked up from her notes, her gaze sharp. 'Three?'

Diane nodded.

'Would anyone have seen you, do you think?'

'I bought some make-up. To hide the bruise. I'm pretty sure the woman who served me would remember. The receipt's probably still in my purse, if that would help.' Diane went to pick up her bag, then remembered she'd had to leave it with the custody sergeant.

'Don't worry. I can get hold of it.' Win grinned. 'Well, that's one of Baker's theories down in flames already. So what did you do after that?'

'I went to the cathedral for a while.' Diane wasn't sure she was following. 'Then I came here. Then I went . . .'

'Here?' Win looked up in surprise. 'As in this police station?'

'I was going to report what he'd done, but I lost my nerve.' Diane gave a tight smile. 'It's ironic, really. If there hadn't been such a long queue at the reception desk . . .'

'Excellent.' Win scribbled down some more notes. 'Then what?'

She fired question after question, establishing Diane's exact movements up until she arrived at Arden Hall.

'OK. I think that covers that side of things. Now, these messages from your brother. You say you knew nothing about them.'

'Have you heard them?' Diane clutched her hand. 'Do you know what he said?'

'Not in detail. They'll be played to you during the interview. In terms of your own involvement, the crucial point is that they'd already been played back. Before the mobile was found by DC Collingwood.'

Diane's head was spinning. 'They couldn't have been. The only other people who've been in the house are my husband and my mother, and if either of them had found my mobile, they'd have said so straight away. It doesn't make sense.'

Win frowned. 'Well, we'll just have to cross that bridge when we come to it.' She paused. 'DC Collingwood also found sleeping tablets in your bag with your sister-in-law's name on them.'

'I picked them up after the party. Angelika had drunk herself into a stupor, which wasn't exactly an unusual occurrence. She'd left the tablets lying on her bedside table. I put them in my bag to stop the children finding them. I mentioned it to my husband at the time.'

'Good.' Win glanced up. 'I wouldn't let Baker sense your animosity towards your sister-in-law, if you can help it.'

'No. Of course. I'm sorry.' Diane's eyes filled suddenly with tears. She'd disliked Angelika from the first time she'd met her; she'd be a hypocrite to claim anything else. Yet she felt a sharp, unexpected swoop of loss; Ian's wife had been such a larger-than-life character that it was almost impossible to imagine her dead. Diane cleared her throat, pushing the thought aside. 'Are the tablets relevant?'

Win's face was grave. 'Mrs Somerford was strangled. It appears Dominica and Marshall were smothered, probably with a pillow. Traces of a narcotic substance were present in glasses of milk found in the kitchen. And in the children's bloodstream. It seems they'd been heavily sedated some time before their death.' She paused. 'As had Thomas, which is why he hadn't woken.'

Which meant that Dominica and Marshall hadn't suffered. That Thomas had slept peacefully through whatever mayhem had preceded Angelika's death. Diane struggled to hang on to those thoughts and to block out the others; that whoever had killed Angelika and the children had planned the whole operation with military precision; had fed drugs to the children in the full knowledge of what was going to happen to them. She put her hand to her mouth as the bile rose in her throat. After a moment, she whispered, 'They really think I did it, don't they?'

Win scanned her face. 'No. In my opinion, the most they think is that you may have aided and abetted your brother in some way, and they're hoping that by slapping a murder charge on you, they'll get you to talk.' She gathered up her papers and got to her feet. 'Right. I think we're as prepared as we can be. Don't lose your temper, don't give them any information they don't ask you for. And above all, just remember, it's yourself you're defending, not your brother.' Win smiled her confident smile. 'That can come later, when we've got you out of here.'

23

The interview room was a small, airless broom cupboard of a place with a battered Formica-covered table on which stood a large, three-decked tape recorder and a tin ash-tray. Four plastic chairs flanked the table, two on each side. It was almost laughably like the interview room in every police drama Diane had ever seen on the television. The only difference was that she wasn't an actress, and if there were lines, she didn't feel she'd had long enough to learn them.

Win Keilly sat next to her on one side of the table. On the other sat Baker and another, younger man whom Diane hadn't seen before. Baker explained the procedures. The tape was turned on. Baker's colleague gave the date and time and introduced himself as DS Colin Butcher.

The butcher, the baker, the candlestick maker . . . Diane looked down at her hands and fought the sudden, hysterical giggle that bubbled up into her throat like a sob.

'OK then, Mrs Middleton,' Baker leant back in his chair when the rest of the formalities had been dealt with and Diane had been cautioned for a second time. 'Let's start by going over some of the information you've given us already. You say you went to Arden Hall yesterday as the result of a phone call from your husband at . . .' he consulted his notes '. . . three minutes past nine.'

Diane nodded.

'Please answer the question, Mrs Middleton.' DS Butcher smiled at her, not unkindly, as he added, 'The tape doesn't pick up nods.'

Diane cleared her throat, feeling foolish. 'Yes.'

'And do you have an equally precise time for your arrival at Arden Hall?' Somehow, Baker managed to make her accuracy sound suspicious

'No, of course I don't.' Diane remembered what Win Keilly had said about never giving more information than was strictly necessary. There had seemed something faintly dishonest about the advice; she'd resented the assumption that she had something to hide, when there was nothing. She was already beginning to realise the validity of the woman's instruction.

'So what time do you think you got there?'

'About twenty past nine.' Diane was about to add that she'd driven quickly, then changed her mind. Baker would probably add speeding to the charge sheet, if she did.

'Twenty past nine,' Baker repeated. 'And how long would you say you'd been inside the house last night before the au pair arrived on the scene?'

'Ten minutes? Fifteen, maybe.'

'So you didn't ring for the police or an ambulance, once you had discovered Mrs Somerford's body?' He consulted his notes. 'Your call to the emergency services was in fact timed at twenty-one forty-three, some twenty-three minutes after you reached the house.'

'My client has already indicated that twenty past nine was no more than an estimate of when she arrived,' Win interjected.

'Thank you, Ms Keilly.' There was a slight but audible emphasis on the 'Ms'. Baker's smile was acid as he went on,

'But in any event, the call was not made until after the arrival of the au pair. Is that correct?'

Diane glanced at Win. 'I tried to ring my husband . . .'

'You'd ascertained Mrs Somerford was dead, had you? Checked her vital signs?'

'No. I . . . I could see from the doorway . . .'

'As far as I'm aware, my client has no medical qualifications,' Win Keilly observed.

Baker ignored her. 'You didn't enter the room?'

Diane shook her head; tried to blot out the sudden intensity of the memory.

'Yes or no, Mrs Middleton?'

'No.'

'So for all you knew, Mrs Somerford could still have been alive at that point. Yet instead of calling an ambulance, you say you were trying to ring your husband? Why? Because he already suspected Mr Somerford might have harmed the family in some way?'

'My client can't answer for what her husband might or might not have been thinking,' Win intercepted coolly.

This time, Baker inclined his head in acknowledgement. He turned his attention back to Diane. 'Can you explain how some of Mrs Somerford's sleeping tablets come to be in your handbag?'

Diane was momentarily confused by his sudden change of direction. 'They were on her bedside table. After the party. I was worried the children might find them.'

Win's dark eyes signalled her approval at the restraint of Diane's response. 'My client explained the situation to her husband at the time,' she said.

Baker wrote something down before going on. He paused for a moment, his head on one side. 'I understand that when

DS Phillips interviewed you at the scene, you denied that your brother had made any contact with you after your conversation yesterday morning?'

Diane felt her mouth go dry. 'I told you, I'd forgotten about my mobile. I don't use it very much.' She leant forward. 'Please. Tell me what he said.'

'Are you denying that you listened to the messages, Mrs Middleton?' Butcher asked.

She tried to keep her voice steady. 'Why would I be asking you what Ian said, if I already knew?'

Lovingly, Baker stroked his moustache as he observed her in silence. Backwards and forwards went his thumbnail against the rasping bristles. Backwards and forwards, until Diane felt she was going to scream.

'OK.' He launched himself to his feet with such abruptness that for an instant, Diane thought he was going to come at her, and involuntarily shrank back in her chair, but it was a second tape deck on the small table to one side of the interview room that was his target. 'This is a recording of what we found on your mobile.' He pressed down one of the buttons, his eyes not leaving Diane's face. 'Let's go through this together, shall we? See if it jogs your memory.'

'*You have three saved messages . . .*' The disembodied tone was upper class; slightly patronising. It sounded like one of the early presenters of *Blue Peter*.

The first message was timed at two thirty-five. About the same time Lee Smith had been using her as a punch-bag. Diane closed her eyes as the dear, familiar voice filled the stuffy room.

'I've been trying you on the land-line. Listen . . . Sorry about earlier . . .' Ian sounded distracted. 'I . . . I'll try again later.'

Baker pressed a button and the recording paused. 'Your brother says he'd been trying the land-line. Are you still maintaining you received no messages from him?'

Diane took a shaky sip of water before replying. 'When I got back to the house yesterday afternoon, there were fifteen messages on the answering machine. The first three were from Lee Smith. They weren't pleasant. I thought the rest were from him as well, so I deleted them without listening to them.'

'You knew your brother was on his own. You knew he was upset as a result of the row he'd had with his wife the previous day, yet you're expecting me to believe you deleted your messages without listening to them?'

Diane looked up angrily. 'I'm not expecting you to do anything. I'm just telling you what happened.'

Baker stared at her without responding, and turned the tape back on.

The next call was timed at three fifty-seven. She'd have been in the centre of Coventry then. Diane tried not to think how Ian must have felt when yet again he failed to reach her.

'Listen. She's on her own with them.' It broke Diane's heart to hear the anguish in his voice. 'I need your help, Diane. Ring me.'

Again, Baker paused the tape. 'According to the au pair, she left the house at just before four o'clock yesterday afternoon.'

'She shouldn't have done that. We told her she'd got to stay with Angelika. The children weren't safe . . .' Diane's voice trailed off. None of them had been safe.

'Mrs Somerford apparently insisted on overruling that instruction. The au pair is distraught, as you can imagine. She says she did everything she could. Including ringing your brother as soon as she'd left the house to alert him to the fact that his wife would be on her own with the children for the rest of the day.'

He clicked the tape back on again.

The final message was timed at five nineteen.

'Where the hell are you?' The voice was angry. 'Well, it doesn't matter now. I'm going over there to sort things out myself.' The phone went dead.

Diane rubbed her hand across her face. She tried not to take in the damning implications of Ian's final words, still echoing inside her skull: '*I'm going over there to sort things out myself . . .*'

'So did you help him?' Baker's voice made her jump.

'No.' She tried to concentrate. 'I told you. I didn't even know he'd left me those messages.'

'Someone had listened to them, Mrs Middleton.' It was Butcher who spoke. 'The messages had been saved.'

'My client has already made it abundantly clear that she had no prior knowledge of what was on the tape,' Win Keilly said firmly.

Diane's head was spinning. She made a supreme effort to silence Ian's voice and concentrate. Could Tracey Collingwood have played them? Or Baker himself? Some residual, middle-class respect for the police made it hard for Diane to believe they were deliberately trying to stitch her up. But there was no other possible explanation. Unless . . .

'I told you, Lee Smith was at my house this morning.' She heard and ignored Win's sharp intake of breath. 'He was standing behind me in the kitchen. I thought he'd only just found his way in, but he could have been prowling around upstairs before I caught sight of him.' She nodded emphatically. 'It must have been him.'

'Lee Smith, again.' Baker sighed. 'Is there any particular reason why Mr Smith would want to listen to your voice mail?'

Barely waiting for a reply, he went on, 'A text message was also received on your mobile telephone yesterday from Ian. Timed at twenty-one fifteen.'

Diane held her breath as he read expressionlessly from the sheet of paper he'd taken from the file in front of him. 'Look after Thomas. I'll find a way to keep in touch.' Baker looked up into her face. The message concludes, 'I love you. Ian.'

Diane could feel tears pricking her eyes. She realised just how much she wanted the message to have come from Ian; how much she wanted him still to be alive, no matter what he might have done. Slowly, she shook her head. 'Ian never sends me text messages. He knows I hate them.'

'The message came from his mobile, Mrs Middleton. Same as the rest of them. Are you saying someone else sent it?'

'Ian didn't.'

'So do you have any idea of who else might have sent a message from your brother's mobile to your own?' Baker's voice was heavy with sarcasm.

Diane shook her head.

'The suspect shakes her head,' Butcher murmured into the tape.

'Suspect?' Suddenly, it was all too much. Diane jumped to her feet. 'I haven't done anything! Don't you understand? What the hell's the matter with you? Why are you wasting your time asking me all these stupid, meaningless questions and then not listening to the answers? It's Lee Smith you should be talking to, not . . .'

Win Keilly touched Diane's arm. 'Just try to keep calm.'

'Keep calm?' Diane rounded on her. 'Keep *calm*?'

'Sit down, Mrs Middleton,' Baker ordered.

Diane looked warily at each of them then subsided unwillingly back into her chair, still breathing heavily.

Baker's fingers strayed back to his moustache as he consulted his notes. At last, he looked up. 'Right then. As you seem so keen to bring Mr Smith into this inquiry, let's do just that, shall we?'

Win cleared her throat as she shifted slightly in her chair and shot Diane a warning glance.

'You see, as Mr Smith tells it, it was you who tried to seduce him on the night of his wife's funeral. He claims he was shocked and distressed by your advances, and asked you to leave.'

Diane snorted. 'That's rubbish.'

'He further claims that as a result of that rejection, you have since pestered him, and also made false accusations against him concerning his alleged behaviour towards your brother and, even more distressing for him, towards his own deceased wife.' Baker paused, waiting for a response, then murmured, 'Hell hath no fury . . .'

Win gave him a thin smile. 'Might I remind you we're now in the twenty-first century, Inspector?'

'Convenient, though, to have a ready-made alternative suspect.' Baker's attention was still on Diane as he asked, 'Did you visit Arden House at any other time yesterday?'

There seemed to be no sequence to the man's questioning. Diane was frustrated at how quickly he seemed to have lost interest in the subject of Lee Smith.

'Mrs Middleton?' DS Butcher prompted.

'No.'

'You're quite sure about that?' It was Baker who spoke.

Diane wondered what he was getting at. She glanced at Win Keilly before answering in the affirmative.

'Can you describe to us how you spent the day?'

'I spent the morning at home with my husband. He went out at about two. To play golf.'

'And what did you do then?'

'I went round to see Lee Smith.' Diane was irritated to feel the beginning of a blush as she glanced at the tape recorder.

Baker looked at Butcher and grinned. 'There must be a joke in there somewhere. Playing around while your husband plays a round.'

They were deliberately trying to humiliate her. '*It wasn't like that,*' she wanted to shout at them.

'If you wish to put a question to my client, perhaps you'd be good enough to phrase it in such a way that she can answer it,' Win Keilly intervened acerbically.

'Certainly.' Baker gave her a cool smile then said with exaggerated politeness, 'Mrs Middleton, could you please tell me the reason for your visit to Mr Smith?'

'I went there to confront him. About the letters, and the banners he'd strung up outside Arden Hall.'

Almost imperceptibly, Win shook her head.

'And do you still maintain that your facial injuries came about as the result of an alleged altercation with Mr Smith?'

'Yes.' Diane forced herself to stick to the simple monosyllable.

Butcher leant back in his chair and folded his arms. 'Yet you made no effort to report him.'

'I did, as a matter of fact. I came here yesterday afternoon. To the front desk.'

'You haven't mentioned that before.' Baker gave a small, complacent smile. 'Still, there's a CCTV circuit to the front desk, so we'll be able to check that out.'

If he'd expected to rattle Diane, he was disappointed.

'I know there is,' she snapped. 'I saw it.'

'So you came to the front desk,' Butcher took over again. 'Who did you speak to?'

'There was a young woman . . .'

'You do realise we can check all this out?'

'Yes, of course. I . . .' Diane was beginning to wish she hadn't brought the subject up; it was just going to make her seem crazier than ever. 'By the time I'd got to the front of the queue, I'd changed my mind.'

'Let's be absolutely clear about this, Mrs Middleton,' Butcher leant forward. 'Did you speak to anyone at this police station yesterday afternoon, or didn't you?'

'I . . .' Diane looked away from the man's keen gaze. 'I just asked her for some directions.'

Butcher raised an eyebrow. 'Directions?'

'I was confused.' Diane shifted in her seat. How could she hope to make them believe her, when she sounded so utterly implausible she barely believed herself? 'I didn't know what to . . .'

Baker didn't even bother to let her finish the sentence. 'You see, Mr Smith denies seeing you at any time yesterday.'

Diane was stung by the barely concealed derision in his voice. 'Well he would, wouldn't he?' she snapped.

'What would you say if I were to tell you that Mr Smith's grandfather has given a statement to the effect that Mr Smith spent the entire day with him yesterday, fishing?'

'I'd say he's lying.'

'Who's lying? Mr Smith? His grandfather? Or are you saying they're both conspiring against you? Come on, Diane.' Baker's voice was hectoring. He leant across the table so that his face was close enough for her to smell the stale tobacco on his breath. 'Let's just drop this charade, shall we? Lee Smith had nothing to do with those bruises, and you know it.' He jabbed a stubby finger at her. 'Mrs Somerford's face was bruised too. As if she might have been in some sort of a fight with someone.'

'You are intimidating my client, Inspector.'

Baker sat back in his chair. 'I'm merely attempting to establish the truth, Ms Keilly.'

'As are we all,' Win said pleasantly. 'But before you pursue this line of questioning any further I should tell you that my client has watertight evidence to prove that her injuries are entirely irrelevant to this inquiry.'

For a split second, Baker looked nonplussed. Then he said coldly, 'Perhaps you'd care to elaborate.'

Win smiled. 'Certainly, Inspector.' She passed a sheet of paper over the desk. 'My client was in the centre of Coventry yesterday afternoon. A shop assistant, whom Mrs Middleton is confident will be able to confirm the presence of facial bruising, served her with make-up. I've noted down the details for you.' With another smile, she handed over the credit card receipt. 'As you can see, it's dated and timed. You have already stated that Mrs Somerford's au pair did not leave Arden House until nearly four o'clock, at which time Mrs Somerford and the children were fine. As my client was in Coventry city centre at five past three yesterday afternoon, already bruised, the manner in which she sustained her injuries can be of no possible significance.' She sat back in her chair with the air of one who has just said, 'Checkmate,' and allowed the information to sink in.

Baker and Butcher looked at one another. For a moment, neither of them spoke. Then Butcher said, 'All right, Mrs Middleton. Given that we can establish your whereabouts at around three, what were your movements subsequent to that?'

'When the shops closed, I spent some time in the cathedral. Then I came here and waited in a queue for about ten minutes. Then I went back to the car at about five. I drove around for a while, and then I went home.'

'You drove around for a while,' Baker repeated. 'Where to, exactly?'

'Not *to* anywhere. Just around.' Diane was aware how feeble it sounded. But to say she'd been on her way to see Ian seemed even more open to question.

Butcher sighed. 'So what time did you get home?'

'Just after six.'

'Any witnesses?'

'No. As I've already told you, my husband was out.'

'So from around five until your husband rang you at just after nine, no one can substantiate your account of your activities.' Baker regarded her in silence for a moment. 'Initial reports suggest Mrs Somerford and her children had been dead for at least three hours before the emergency services arrived on the scene at just before ten o'clock. Which means they were killed some time between four and seven.'

'This is crazy! I've already told you . . .'

'Given that we can corroborate your rather . . . convenient presence in this police station at around five, you would still have had ample time to drive over to Arden Hall and be back at home when your husband rang you at three minutes past nine.'

Convenient. They were twisting everything she said. Were they seriously suggesting she'd come to the police station to supply herself with an alibi? 'I've just remembered.' Diane made a supreme effort to gather her thoughts. 'Malcolm. He rang me earlier, as well. Not long after I got in.'

'He rang you earlier.' It was Butcher who spoke. He sounded less than convinced. 'And why was that?'

'We'd had a bit of an argument before he went out. He rang up to make sure I was all right.'

'An argument.' Baker caressed his moustache. 'So what time exactly was this earlier call?'

'I don't know, *exactly*,' Diane replied, stung by the overt sarcasm of his tone. 'Some time between six fifteen and six thirty.'

'But you didn't think to mention it before.'

'You didn't ask,' Diane snapped.

Butcher looked up, pen poised. 'And what was the subject of your disagreement, Mrs Middleton?'

Too late, Diane realised she'd dug herself another hole; the last thing she wanted to tell Baker was that she and Malcolm had been arguing about Ian and Nicola Smith.

It was Win who answered. 'I can see no reason other than idle curiosity for your question, Sergeant. Is there anything else you wish to ask that is of any actual relevance to your inquiry?'

Butcher glanced at Baker.

Win was already beginning to gather her papers together. 'My client has cooperated fully and has answered all the allegations you've put to her. She has given you full details of her whereabouts, which I'm sure you will be verifying in due course. I suggest you have no possible grounds for detaining her further.'

For a moment, neither man spoke. Then Baker leant forward to the three-deck tape machine. 'Interview terminated at twenty-one fifty-seven.'

'Good.' Win smiled at him. 'I think one fishing trip is more than enough for this evening, don't you? I shall, of course, be checking out Mr Smith Senior's story, as I have no doubt you will too.'

Baker stood up and stalked out of the room without further comment.

'That will be all for now, Mrs Middleton.' Butcher also got to his feet.

Diane glanced at Win, unsure of exactly what was going to

happen next. Her heart sank as Butcher added, 'I'll get someone to take you back to your cell.'

'Standard procedure,' Win murmured. 'I'll be with you very shortly.'

She was as good as her word; the door had barely clanged shut on Diane when it was opened again by the custody sergeant. Win came in, grinning broadly. 'Well, I think that knocked some of the wind out of their sails.'

'I don't understand. Am I still under arrest?'

'Technically, yes. But I'm pretty sure they're done with you for now.'

'For now?' Diane echoed.

'Like I said, standard procedure. My guess is you'll be bailed to come back when they've had time to speak to your husband and check out the rest of your evidence, and then that will be an end to it. And I'd imagine they'll be wanting to have another word with Lee Smith as well.' To Diane's surprise, Win put an arm round her shoulder and gave her a hug. 'Well done. That must have been a horrible ordeal for you. You did brilliantly.'

Diane nodded. She was still trying to grapple with the facts. She supposed she should have been relieved. All she felt was grubby, exhausted and filled suddenly with an even greater dread at the prospect of going than of staying.

It was as if Win read her mind. 'Your husband's waiting for you at the front desk,' she said quietly. 'Apparently, he's been there for some time.'

Diane was released from custody at twenty-two thirty-eight. Her possessions were given back to her, forms were put in front of her to sign, and she was handed a piece of paper instructing her to answer her bail in a week's time. Win Keilly walked back with her across the carpark to the front of the police station.

'I'll be in touch.' Win held out her hand. 'Good luck.'

Malcolm was sitting with his back to the door on one of the row of chairs beside the front desk, his head down, his hands between his knees. He looked utterly out of place, and utterly defeated. A copy of the *Daily Telegraph* lay on the chair beside him, folded to the crossword puzzle. None of the clues had been filled in, Diane noticed. He turned his head as she pushed the door open and stepped inside. She watched the expressions that chased across his face as he got to his feet, and wished that she could read them. Then he held out his arms to her and enveloped her to him.

'Let's get you home,' he murmured into her hair.

She smelt the clean, familiar smell of him; soap and starch and the soft mohair of his suit, and felt as if she was home already.

24

The house had been searched in Diane's absence. Malcolm had put everything back, more neatly than she would have expected, but she kept coming across things in the wrong place. Nothing seemed quite real.

Malcolm was gentle, considerate, cautious in what he said. It was as if they'd acknowledged by unspoken, mutual consent that the wounds were still too raw to examine their extent. He listened attentively as she told him everything that had happened at the police station, nodding, frowning sometimes, but hardly speaking at all.

'You must be exhausted,' he said kindly, when she'd done. 'I'll run you a bath.' It was as if she had just returned from hospital, not the cells; as if she'd been diagnosed with terminal cancer, not arrested for murder.

He brought her hot chocolate in bed. Later, he cautiously got in next to her. They lay side by side, not quite touching. She had no idea whether he'd believed her or not, and she was too afraid to ask.

The sense of unreality persisted. Tracey Collingwood resumed her hovering, unobtrusive presence the following morning. She fielded visitors and phone calls, fed the cat, made endless cups of tea. They were besieged by reporters; every coming or going greeted with a pyrotechnic display of flashbulbs. The phone rang constantly. Flowers and cards arrived from friends and business associates. Win Keilly came, as did George Bonham, full of explanations and apologies for not being able to represent Diane himself. An application had been put in at the Magistrates' Court for them to visit Thomas, he told them. An appointment at the contact centre was to be considered at the next court hearing.

Later in the day, Agnes arrived bearing a fruit cake, and assaulting with her umbrella the cameraman who had the temerity to try to take her photograph as she got out of the taxi.

'You should set the dogs on them,' she shouted over her shoulder as she marched into the house, leaving the taxi driver to bring in her suitcase and ignoring the fact that Diane and Malcolm's only pet was the greedy and indolent cat. 'I threw a bucket of water over the wretches outside my flat.'

All trace of softness had vanished; it was as if her previous conversation with Diane had never taken place. In the frightening, unpredictable place that Diane's world had become, it was almost a relief to have her mother back to her old form.

Tracey Collingwood was the next recipient of Agnes's wrath. Agnes was volubly outraged by Diane's arrest, and bristled with hostility every time the other woman entered the room. She talked loudly and at length about police incompetence, before demanding to hear every detail of what she referred to as Diane's 'interrogation'. Tight-lipped, she shook her head vigorously every time Ian's name was mentioned. The police probably sent the text message themselves in order to frame him, she declared; when they weren't incompetent, they were corrupt. She'd seen a programme about the West Midlands force on the television, and they'd been a worse bunch of crooks than the criminals they were supposed to be catching. Never mind that it was years ago. Leopards never changed their spots. After a brief, heated exchange with her, Malcolm announced that he was needed at work. He didn't return until late into the evening.

The following morning Agnes left again, announcing that she had arranged to stay with Doris from the bridge club. She kissed Diane quickly and told her to be strong. Diane watched her stalk, straight-backed, past the reporters and towards the waiting taxi. She was going to miss the older woman, despite the fact that her presence had transformed the house into a war zone; her belligerence had been a welcome alternative to the stifling politeness that had pervaded the house since Diane's arrest.

The next day, they were informed by Tracey Collingwood that the forensic investigations at the cottage had been completed; it was theirs to visit as soon as they wanted to. Malcolm was worried that it was too soon; that seeing the extent of the damage could do nothing other than upset them both. Diane was anxious to get it over with; if she didn't go straight away, she might lose her nerve and never want to go again. Eventually, reluctantly, Malcolm agreed. He had to go to Little Park Street to give his statement, he said. He'd take her over when he got back, if that was what she was certain she wanted.

The short journey to the cottage was made in silence. Malcolm had come back from the police station full of strained, meaningless reassurances. Ian's name wasn't mentioned; neither was Lee Smith's. There was so much they needed to talk about, but each of the opening gambits Diane tested inside her head seemed clumsy or inadequate. Fear of saying the wrong thing made her say nothing. She suspected Malcolm might be having a similar internal battle. It wasn't until he put his key in the lock that he glanced at her and said, 'You're sure you're ready for this?'

She nodded, not sure at all.

The scene of devastation inside the cottage sprang to life as soon as he pulled open the door. A chair lay upended beside the table. The quarry-tiled floor was scattered with shards of broken crockery. One of the dusty velvet curtains hung lopsidedly from its broken fittings. Only the coating of grey fingerprint dust on every surface suggested anyone had been there at all since Ian had left.

'I thought the police might have . . .' Her words petered off.

Malcolm crunched his way across the floor and righted the chair. 'I'll clean up down here.' His voice was gentle. 'You'd better take a look at the studio.'

Oils had been daubed across the walls and floor. Canvases were strewn everywhere, some torn where Ian had trampled on them. A pile of sketches had been ripped and scattered. A small, rational compartment of Diane's brain wondered how she was going to explain to Sidney Cunningham and the others that their entries for The Show were lost to posterity. But it was her own work that had borne the brunt of the vandalism. Diane's hands shook as she picked up her unfinished portrait of Ian, hacked to shreds.

She didn't attempt to restore any sort of order. She simply stood and stared, then quietly closed the door on the chaos and went back down the stairs. When Malcolm turned to look at her, all she could do was shrug helplessly and shake her head. A week before, the destruction of so many hours of work would have been the end of the world. Now, it seemed an utter irrelevance.

She must have been upstairs longer than she'd realised; Malcolm had already managed to restore some semblance of order to the living area. The broken crockery had been swept into a pile, the furniture righted and put back almost as it should have been.

'I thought we might as well have lunch here, if we were coming,' he said as he handed her a glass of red wine. 'Try to make it feel a bit more like home for you again. I called into the supermarket on my way back from the police station. There's bread and pâté.' He rummaged in a carrier bag, not meeting her eye. 'And some strawberries.'

Diane's favourite fruit. She felt her eyes prickle at the small act of kindness. As she took the glass from him, his fingers rested against hers. Just for a moment.

They sat down across the table from each other and silently began to eat, although each mouthful felt as if it would choke Diane, and Malcolm made little more than a token effort.

After a while, he cleared his throat and put down his knife. Diane felt herself tense, wondering what was coming, but all he said was, 'I suppose you'll have to call the exhibition off.'

'Yes.' It seemed ridiculous even to be thinking about the mundanities of work, but at least it filled the silence. 'Yes, I suppose so.'

'Would you like some more pâté?'

'No. Thank you. But it was very nice,' she added quickly.

It was as if they were strangers, their conversation polite, stilted and utterly meaningless. Suddenly, Diane could bear it no longer. 'It's never happened before, you know,' she said in a low voice. 'And it never will again.'

Malcolm picked up another slice of bread. His attention appeared to be absorbed in the task of spreading pâté.

'If you'll only give me a chance to prove to you . . .'

'Not now, Diane.' He didn't look up.

'Not now, or not ever?' Her voice was barely a whisper. She

watched the steady progress of his knife across the uneven surface of the bread, as careful as a plasterer, and wasn't even sure if he'd heard her.

At last he raised his eyes to meet hers. She read no coldness in his expression. Just a world of pain.

'Not now,' he repeated quietly.

And that, she knew, would have to be enough.

The normal routines of life were suspended. Malcolm spent much of his time at home, only going in to the office when strictly necessary. Apart from the visit to the cottage, Diane didn't go out at all. In an odd way, the enclosed cocoon of their strange existence was soothing. They worked together on the garden, grateful for the high walls that protected them from prying eyes. They watched videos brought in by Tracey Collingwood, who still visited every day; bland stuff, tactfully chosen for an absence of sex or violence. Diane found the other woman's presence less intrusive than she would have expected; sometimes, she almost forgot that Collingwood only came to spy on her. Not that there was anything for her to report; the mobile the police had returned to Diane remained silent.

For a couple of days, Ian was front-page news, the scurrilousness of the reporting in inverse proportion to the size of the paper. All made the connection, discreetly or otherwise, between the murders at Arden Hall and Nicola Smith's death. One of the tabloids carried a scantily-clad photograph of the sulky work-experience girl who had briefly replaced her, under the headline: '*Family Man or Fiend: Samantha Reveals All*'. The accompanying article talked of Ian's 'staring eyes' and 'creepy smile'. The college the girl attended was quoted as saying they were re-examining their placement procedures.

Diane insisted on reading every article, listening to every

bulletin. At first, she was terrified that Lee Smith might come up with some sensational revelations of his own, but, for the moment at least, references to her were factual and relatively low-key. Win had assured her that the police would not release her details unless they decided to charge her, and evidently they hadn't; references were limited to a 'forty-two-year-old local woman'. After the first few days, the story was relegated to small columns on inside pages. One by one, the reporters outside the house drifted off in search of fresher drama.

The only reliable reports of what was happening came via Tracey Collingwood, although Diane was all too aware that she and Malcolm were only being told as much as the police wanted them to know. The American authorities had tracked down Angelika's next of kin: an elderly mother in Detroit who had thrown Angelika out when she became pregnant with Dominica. There was no other family, no record of either Dominica's or Marshall's fathers on their birth certificates. The mother had seemed neither surprised nor particularly upset that Angelika and her children had come to such a violent end. Diane felt a great wave of sadness as she listened to what Collingwood had to say; there seemed to have been very little love in any of their lives. She wished she'd made a greater effort to like them.

As the days went by, various sightings of Ian were reported: in Bournemouth, in London, in Alicante. The first few had Diane in a turmoil of fearful anticipation, but none was confirmed, and she began to see them for what they were: the fertile imaginings of those wanting to get themselves a piece of the action, however small. Ian's credit cards, missing along with his passport, remained unused. It was as if he'd vanished into thin air.

Malcolm drove Diane to Little Park Street the following Monday morning. Win Keilly was there to meet them. She

explained that the police would be wanting to interview Diane
again. Nothing to worry about, she said; a couple of hours
should be ample, if Malcolm was intending to park the car
somewhere and wait.

'Good luck.' Malcolm brushed his lips against Diane's
cheek, then pulled her towards him and held her to him, so
tightly that she could feel the beating of his heart.

'None needed,' Win smiled. 'We'll have her out of here in
no time.'

Despite the reassurances, Diane was uneasy. There was
something uncharacteristically low key, evasive almost, about
Win's manner that was quite in contrast to her ebullience
when they'd spoken before the weekend.

It wasn't until Malcolm had got back into the car and driven
off in search of somewhere to park that Win turned to her and
said, 'You two are OK together, then?'

'Sort of.' Diane gave a small smile. 'It's hard to tell.'

'Have you thought any more about whether you want to
press charges against Lee Smith?'

Diane had thought about it constantly. 'Will it help Ian?'

'This isn't about Ian, Diane. It's about you.'

Diane shook her head. 'God knows, I want him punished
for what he did. But I'm just not sure I can stand the thought of
the whole business being dragged through the courts. Things
between Malcolm and me are still so tense . . .' She scanned
Win's face. 'What would you do? Honestly?'

'I'd nail the bastard, personally. But then I'm not married,
so maybe I'm not the person to ask. It would be messy, that's
for sure.' Win paused, her face grave. 'Listen, this may seem
like a very strange question, Diane, but do you have a birthmark on your left breast?'

'I'm sorry?' Diane gazed at her in utter confusion.

'I didn't want to say anything in front of your husband, but the police found a drawing at Lee Smith's house when they went round to interview him over the weekend.' Win ran her hand through her cropped black curls. 'Paint has been daubed across the woman's face, but the rest of it's pretty . . . explicit, I'm afraid.'

'Oh, God.' Diane's bewilderment turned to horrified comprehension.

'You see what I mean about messy.' Win took her arm and steered her towards the steps. 'The police are only interested in it because if it is you, it proves beyond all doubt that Smith's been lying about not being involved with you. Of course, if you press charges . . .' She lifted her shoulders expressively. 'It's a tough call. If you don't pursue it, what Smith did to you may just go on eating away at you. The term "closure" has become a joke, but there's a lot to be said for it, in my experience.' She gave Diane's arm a small squeeze. 'It's a decision you're just going to have to make for yourself.'

Diane was surprised to see that it was Tracey Collingwood who sat alongside Baker in the interview room. She gave a small smile of encouragement as Diane entered. Marginally less embarrassing than two male officers, Diane supposed, although her cheeks were already burning in anticipation.

To his credit, Baker played the interview absolutely straightfaced. He showed Diane the sketch that had been discovered at Lee Smith's house and asked her if she had any identifying features that could link her to it. It depicted a woman, naked against a backdrop of tangled bedding. Her limbs were heavy, replete; her legs splayed wide, one arm thrown up above her head. Even without the small birthmark on the fold of the left breast, Diane could see at once that it was her. Lee's skilful pencil had captured each incipient wrinkle, each tiny pouch and sag of flesh; not with malice, but with a tenderness and honesty shockingly at odds with the savage daub of red paint that obliterated the woman's face. The sketch might have been destroyed out of anger, but it had been created out of love. Diane was furious to feel the lump that was forming in her throat, the ridiculous wave of sadness that vied with her embarrassment. Swallowing hard, she said firmly, 'It's me.'

Collingwood took her to another room and asked Diane to strip to the waist. She examined the birthmark and, with a murmured apology, took a couple of Polaroid photographs. Diane had never felt so humiliated or so ridiculous in her life.

Baker had at least had the grace to turn the sketch over so that it was lying face downwards on the table, when they returned. He spread his sausage fingers and examined them for a moment before he spoke, as if he, too, might be embarrassed.

Eventually, he looked up and said, 'Smith has been interviewed about the assault on you, which he still denies.'

Diane went to reply, but Win touched her arm and shook her head.

'However,' Baker continued, 'I'm satisfied with your explanation of your facial injuries.'

'It remains, of course, your right to press charges against Smith,' Collingwood added.

Diane met her gaze. 'I would if I thought it might help my brother, but it won't, will it?'

Collingwood glanced towards Baker before answering, as if expecting him to intervene, but his only reaction was a slight but audible sigh. 'We think a prosecution would have a good chance of succeeding. Several of Smith's neighbours witnessed the altercation between the two of you at the time in question, and Smith's grandfather's backed down, now it's been explained to him that perjury's an imprisonable offence.'

'Maybe we should keep to the matter in hand for the time being,' Win said briskly. 'Bearing in mind the fact that my client is still herself under arrest.'

Baker inclined his head. 'We are satisfied with your account of your other movements on the afternoon of the murders, Mrs Middleton, including your visit to this police station. The sales assistant in Marks and Spencer corroborates your statement, and a Mr . . .' he glanced down at his notes '. . . Charles Newbould has verified your husband's claim to have rung you at your home between quarter and half past six in addition to his later call.'

Diane frowned. 'Chas?'

'Mr Newbould has confirmed he was with your husband at the time of the earlier call.' Baker looked at her questioningly. 'You sound surprised.'

'No.' She put her hand to her head. 'No. Of course I'm not. So many things happened that afternoon, it's hard to remember the exact sequence of events, that's all.'

For the first time, Baker gave her a smile that might just have been genuine. 'It's been a very trying time for you and your family, Mrs Middleton. I do appreciate that. As I hope you appreciate that we have to consider every possibility during the course of our investigation.'

'Good.' Win was already gathering her papers together. 'I assume my client is free to go, now?'

'What are you going to do about Lee Smith?' Diane asked, when the interview had been officially brought to a close and the tape machine turned off.

'That depends to some extent on your decision.' It was Collingwood who answered, her smile sympathetic. 'I know it can't be an easy one for you.'

Diane gazed at the sketch, still lying face down on the table between them. She imagined it being passed round a jury, along with the photograph of her birthmark. She imagined Malcolm's face. 'I meant about what happened to his wife,' she said.

Win cleared her throat.

'The investigation into Nicola Smith's death is ongoing.' Baker's words were spoken automatically. 'We shall be speaking to Smith again in due course about the obstruction he's caused to this investigation, so one way or another he's going to end up in court.'

Diane detected a trace of irritation in Collingwood's expression as she said, 'Domestic violence cases are notoriously difficult. Usually because the woman involved takes fright and withdraws the allegations. They can take up a lot of time.' She glanced at Baker. 'Some say they waste a lot of time. But if we can get a case as far as the courts, we stand a fair chance of getting a conviction.'

Win raised her shoulders fractionally and murmured, 'Your call, Diane.'

Collingwood leant across the desk. 'Men like Smith shouldn't be allowed to get away with it.'

Diane tried to imagine for a moment what it must be like for officers like Tracey Collingwood, attempting to defend the woman's corner in such a male environment. 'You're right,' she said, not allowing herself to think of the consequences. It was like plunging from the high diving board with no knowledge of whether there was water in the pool; exhilarating, terrifying and hideously dangerous. But it was a risk she had to take; prove Lee Smith had been lying about assaulting her, and who knew what else she might be able to prove, given time?

'You've done the right thing.' Tracey Collingwood caught up with Diane and Win as, some half an hour later, they walked down the corridor towards the front desk. Diane had made her statement, put her signature on the forms. Set the legal process irrevocably in motion.

Through the mesh-reinforced glass panel, she caught sight of Malcolm sitting waiting for her, his eyes glued to the door through which any minute she'd be returning to the outside world. He was clutching a big bunch of carnations.

'Have I?' she murmured, the exhilaration already beginning to dissipate.

He leapt to his feet as soon as she pushed the door open. 'How did it go? Is everything OK?'

Diane held his gaze. There was no easy way to tell him. 'I've decided to press charges against Lee Smith.'

To her amazement, his only reaction was an impatient shake of his head. 'But you're free?'

'Yes. Did you hear what I said, Malcolm? There'll be a court case. Things are going to come out . . .' She glanced at Win. 'Embarrassing things . . .'

He hugged her to him, crushing the flowers as he cut off the rest of her words. 'It doesn't matter. None of it matters, as long as you're safe. I've been sitting here, trying to imagine how life would be without you. And I can't. I want you back, Diane. I want us to be a couple again.'

She took a step back from him, scanned his face. 'It's not going to be easy, Malcolm.'

She wondered if she'd imagined the flicker of doubt in his

eyes before he looked down at the flowers and murmured, 'We'll manage.'

'I'll leave you to it.' Win smiled at her.

'So Diane's not under suspicion any more?' It was as if Malcolm couldn't trust himself to believe it; Diane realised just how much strain he must have been under.

'Her alibis demolished such case as they had,' Win said briskly. 'It was all pretty thin in the first place.'

'George Bonham's just rung.' Malcolm turned to Diane when Win had left them. 'The court has granted leave for us to maintain contact with Thomas.'

'That's good.' She knew she should sound more enthusiastic, but her head was still full of what had happened inside the station.

'Good?' He took her hand and squeezed it. 'It's more than that. Having Thomas to look after is just what we need. Something . . .' he searched for the right word, 'something positive for us to focus on.'

'I didn't know Chas was with you when you rang.' The words were out of Diane's mouth almost before she'd realised she was going to say them.

Malcolm blinked. 'Sorry?'

'The police said Chas had confirmed the time.'

'So?'

'I was just a bit surprised.' Diane tried to sound casual. 'It wasn't the sort of call I'd have expected you to make in front of someone else.'

For a moment, Malcolm paused. Then he sighed and said, 'OK, so he wasn't actually looking over my shoulder. I rang while I was on my way over to Bedworth.'

'You mean he said it because you asked him to?' Diane said, horrified. She glanced behind her, half expecting to find Baker or Collingwood listening in on them; she was only relieved she hadn't mentioned it in front of Win.

'Look, you were telling the truth, I was telling the truth. Chas simply added a bit of independent back-up, that was all.'

'But why would he do that? He could get into all sorts of trouble. We all could.'

'Because the whole idea of you being arrested was so bloody outrageous that he wanted to help.' A flash of irritation crossed Malcolm's face. 'For God's sake, Diane, what's the problem? It isn't as if we were making the bloody call up!'

'That's hardly the point, is it? What would have happened if they hadn't let me go? Do you think he'd have been prepared to stand up in court and perjure himself for me?'

'Knowing some of Chas's dodgy dealings, it probably wouldn't be the first time.' He gave a feeble half-laugh that didn't convince either of them, then frowned. 'OK, maybe I should have told him to keep out of it. But Baker's like a bloody pit bull terrier. It was obvious he thought I was only backing your story up because I'm your husband. You're innocent. Anyone who knows you could tell them that. At the end of the day, what Chas did doesn't make any difference to anything, does it?'

'No.' She shrugged uneasily. 'No, I suppose not.'

'This whole thing's a nightmare. All I want is for us to be able to start picking up the pieces of our lives, Diane,' he said quietly.

And the last thing she wanted was to cause more friction between them. 'You're right,' she said resolutely. 'So tell me about Thomas. What did George say?'

Instantly, Malcolm's sober expression lightened. 'He's trying to fix up for us to see him later today. Isn't that great?'

'Brilliant.'

'I said we'd get over to his office as soon as you were released, so he can give us the details.'

She forced a smile. 'So what are we waiting for?'

They walked together from the police station. Diane ignored the worry that refused to stop niggling in her head; that told her there was only one reason that Malcolm was being so forgiving. The sun was shining. They were going to see Thomas. The two of them, a couple again. 'It's brilliant,' she repeated, and took his hand.

25

George Bonham was waiting for them, a pot of coffee and three cups already on his desk.

'Win rang me,' he said as he kissed Diane's cheek. What a relief.' He gestured towards the tray. 'I'm sorry I couldn't arrange something more celebratory. Another time, perhaps.'

'All that's happened is that I've been cleared of something I didn't do, George. That doesn't help Angelika and the children, does it? Or Ian.' Diane's voice was sharper than she had intended. She softened the words with a smile. 'But yes, it is a relief.'

'I'm sorry,' George's big face was filled with compassion. 'That was tactless.' There was a small, awkward pause, then he went on cautiously, 'But I do have some news that may make things seem just a little less black.'

Malcolm leant forward. 'You mean we're going to be able to see Thomas?'

'This afternoon, if you both feel up to it.'

'Diane?' Malcolm turned to her. It was the first time she'd seen hope in his expression. His too-easy forgiveness was for Thomas's sake, she was under no illusion about that. But it was a start. She and Malcolm were Thomas's future. Maybe, in time, he could be theirs. She nodded. It was the first time in weeks she'd felt anything approaching hope herself.

'Good. Now, as I explained to you before, the visits will take

235

place at the contact centre for the time being,' George went on. 'An independent guardian has been appointed to oversee Thomas's welfare. Gillian Cooper. Eminently sensible woman. You'll like her. She'll want to speak to you before you see him, just to explain a few things. In due course, she'll report back to the court on your suitability as long-term carers for him. There's nothing to stop Social Services placing him with you while he's still technically in their care, if everything goes well.'

'So we could have him home quite soon?' Malcolm asked eagerly.

'I don't want to build your hopes up too soon, but it's a possibility.'

Diane said nothing. She tried to push from her mind the ease with which they were all eliminating Ian from any discussion of Thomas's welfare.

Malcolm cleared his throat. 'Can we take him a toy? This woman won't think we're just trying to . . .?' His voice trailed off.

'Everyone's on the same side here, Malcolm.' George's smile was full of sympathy. 'Of course you can take him a toy.'

The three hours until the appointment at the contact centre seemed to go on for ever. Diane and Malcolm went to the big Toys 'R 'Us on the outskirts of Coventry and wandered from aisle to toy-laden aisle trying to find exactly the right gift. Something that showed how much they cared, Malcolm said, but nothing so flashy it would look like a bribe. Diane had always known he loved Thomas; she hadn't realised just how much.

He chose a velvety, sweet-faced teddy bear, then put it back. Maybe they should go for something educational, he said;

wouldn't the guardian be looking out to see how much importance they put on Thomas's intellectual development? On another aisle, he found a beautifully made set of wooden shapes to be hammered into a block. But what if Thomas were to hit himself with the hammer? Would that make them seem careless of his safety? The simple task seemed strewn with pitfalls. They settled eventually on a compromise: the teddy, a small wooden jigsaw and a picture book. As they were about to pay, Diane spotted a set of brightly coloured keys. She pressed the button on the fob as the package instructed, her eyes filling abruptly at the tinny strains of *Für Elise* that issued forth. It had been a standing joke between Ian and she; his reluctant party piece during that period of his childhood when Agnes had been confident he would become a concert pianist.

With a quick glance at Malcolm, she put the keys down on the counter with their other purchases.

'What on earth's that?' He looked doubtfully at the cheap plastic toy.

'He'll love it.' Diane's voice was thick with tears. She didn't want to try to explain the importance of the silly, tinny tune that would provide some kind of link between the baby and the father of whom he would have no memory. She wasn't sure Malcolm would have understood, even if she'd tried.

Diane and Malcolm were shown into a small office as soon as they reached the contact centre. Diane glanced hungrily into the playroom opposite, desperate to snatch a glimpse of Thomas, but it was empty.

A plump, untidy woman of about fifty hurried in almost as soon as they'd sat down.

'Please. Don't get up. Gillian Cooper. And you must be Mr and Mrs Middleton.' She held out her hand and her plain face broke into a smile. 'I realise how anxious you must be to see Thomas, so let's get straight down to the formalities.'

Diane found herself warming to the woman as she explained procedures and fixed up a date for a fortnight's time when she could visit them in their own home and begin the process of preparing reports. Her manner was friendly, but brisk and businesslike. She explained firmly and with lucidity the reasons why Thomas had been taken into care, and the on-going need for secrecy as to his whereabouts.

'I appreciate how difficult it must be for you both,' she said, when Malcolm attempted to argue. 'You may be able to provide exactly what Thomas needs. You may not. I've only just met you, so as yet I have no way of telling. But what I can tell you is that neither your personal wishes and feelings, nor those of your wife, are the issue here.' She softened the words with a smile of genuine sympathy. 'That sounds harsh, I know. But Thomas's welfare is my only concern. All I can do is try to ensure the courts get things right for him.'

Diane glanced at Malcolm, whose mouth was clamped shut on whatever response was in his head, and said quietly, 'I don't think anyone could argue with that.'

'Good. Anyway,' Gillian Cooper glanced at her watch, 'you didn't come here to see me, did you? Thomas will be here any moment. I'll show you the play area and you can try to make yourselves at home.'

Another family was already in the room. A heavily-pregnant girl stood in the corner, watching the young man who was squatting down, his back to her, as he attempted to make conversation with a boy of about three. The man looked up with a wan smile as Diane and Malcolm entered; the child was wheeling a battered truck across the floor and studiously ignoring him. The hostility between the two adults was palpable. An estranged father, Diane guessed. She smiled nervously back as she took a seat, and wondered what impression the young couple might be forming of them.

After a couple of minutes, Gillian Cooper stuck her head round the door and smiled encouragingly. 'Thomas is here. I'll bring him in.'

Diane nodded and swallowed hard. Malcolm took her hand and squeezed it. She tried to read his expression, but his eyes were fixed on the door, his face rigid with tension.

After a moment, Gillian Cooper returned, Thomas in her arms. Malcolm's eyes lit up, the anxiety vanishing from his face as he let go of Diane's hand and jumped to his feet. She could see his every instinct was to rush forward and grab Thomas. But, like her, he held himself in check, the effort almost painful to watch.

Gillian Cooper bent down and set Thomas carefully on his feet. He clutched her hand for balance, his attention momentarily taken by the boy and the truck.

'Hello, little one.' Diane heard the catch in Malcolm's voice as he dropped to his knees and held out his arms. The baby gazed at him, wide-eyed and solemn, and tightened his grip on Gillian Cooper's fingers. For a heart-stopping moment, Diane feared he might have forgotten them. Then his chubby face split into a wide grin of recognition and he took a couple of staggering steps forward and collapsed into Malcolm's arms with a squeal of delight.

'Clever boy!' Diane was on her knees next to them, the tears running down her cheeks unchecked.

Gillian Cooper smiled. 'I think those might have been his first unaided steps. I'm so glad you didn't miss them.'

Any initial inhibition quickly disappeared as Diane and

Malcolm showed Thomas his new toys and crawled around the floor playing with him. The keys in particular seemed to delight him, his small fingers straying again and again to the button on the fob.

'Good choice,' Malcolm smiled across at her.

Diane would have thought it impossible that she could feel something so close to happiness.

The visit seemed to be over almost before it had begun. Gillian Cooper was apologetic as she scooped Thomas into her arms and said quietly, 'His foster-mother's waiting outside.' His bottom lip started to tremble as he wriggled and tried to get down. 'It might be better if you stayed in here until they've gone.'

Thomas held his arms out to them as she moved towards the door, his eyes bewildered. His screams could be heard over the clatter of Gillian Cooper's retreating footsteps and the reedy strains of *Für Elise*.

Malcolm sank down into his chair, his eyes fixed on the ground. Diane gazed around the deserted room. The other couple must have left at some time during the last hour; she hadn't even noticed. It felt like the emptiest place on earth.

Gillian Cooper came back after a couple of minutes. 'He's OK now.' She looked from one of them to the other. Malcolm hadn't lifted his head. 'They're pretty easily distracted at that age. I've spoken to his foster-mother and she'd be quite happy to bring him along again tomorrow.'

'No. It's too confusing for him.' Diane met Malcolm's gaze as his head shot up. 'You saw his face just now. I don't think we can keep putting him through all of that. Not every day.'

Malcolm glanced at Gillian Cooper, as if wondering if she might intervene. Then he said heavily, 'No, you're right. The last thing we want to do is to unsettle him.'

Gillian Cooper nodded and held out her hand. Her grasp was warm as she said, 'I'll speak to Thomas's social worker. I think she may be in touch with you before the next court hearing.'

Diane felt as if they had just been set some sort of test. And had passed.

Malcolm took her hand as they walked back to the car. 'She was impressed, wasn't she?'

Diane nodded.

'George said that if Social Services thought we were right for him, they might let us look after him even while he's still officially in care. I reckon that was what she was hinting at, don't you?'

'Maybe.'

Malcolm stopped. 'What's the matter? You don't exactly sound over the moon.'

She'd promised herself she wouldn't ask the question; wouldn't risk damaging the fragile equilibrium that they seemed to have found, but the words came blurting out anyway. 'What if Ian comes back, Malcolm. What then?'

'He won't.' Malcolm took her face between his hands. 'He's never coming back. You have to accept that, my darling. We all have to accept it, or we shall go mad. And we have to be strong. For Thomas.'

She nodded, trying to ignore the great void where once her heart had been. 'For Thomas,' she repeated.

Agnes rang almost as soon as they got back.

'I was going to call you,' Diane said guiltily. She should have told her where they were going. She steeled herself for a tirade, mentally calculating whether the news of Thomas's first steps might distract her, or make her worse. But Agnes sounded distracted already.

'I've been trying to get you all afternoon,' Agnes cut in. Diane wondered briefly if she'd found out from George Bonham where they'd been, and was sulking.

'I'm sorry, Mum. I was going to tell you before we went . . .'

Agnes wasn't listening. 'Can we meet?' Her voice wasn't sulky, Diane realised. It was excited.

'What's happened?' A hundred different possibilities flooded Diane's head. Her heart thudded painfully against her ribs. 'Mum, has Ian been in touch with you?'

'Ian?' For a second, there was a wistfulness in her mother's voice that answered Diane's question, but then she said briskly, 'Listen to me, Diane. I've found something out. Doris and I went to that wretched gym that Angelika reckoned she was always going to, and . . .'

'You did *what*?'

'Well, the police are clearly incapable of finding out what really happened. They're only interested in seeing what they want to see. I had my suspicions about Angelika all along. I thought I'd try to find out what she was really up to when she went swanning off.'

Diane sighed. 'And?'

'Well, she wasn't doing yoga, that's for sure,' Agnes said triumphantly. 'The young man at the desk checked the records for me, and she hadn't been there in months. So where was she? That's what I want to know.'

'Mum, are you sure this is such a good idea?' Diane said carefully. She felt as if she'd kicked a cripple, but it broke her heart to think of her mother still trying desperately to clutch at straws, when there were none to clutch.

'Can you think of a better one? Now listen to me. What if Angelika was seeing someone behind Ian's back and he found out, and this other man . . .'

Malcolm put his head round the bedroom door. He smiled, his face still soft with the residual pleasure of the visit as he raised an enquiring eyebrow.

'Mum,' Diane mouthed. She could only imagine what his reaction might be if he could hear the conversation.

He pulled a wry face. 'Give her my love,' he murmured as he went out again.

Diane put her ear back to the phone.

Agnes didn't seem to have stopped to draw breath. 'He could have killed them, and then tried to make it look as if . . .'

'Who could?'

'This other man, of course,' Agnes said irritably. 'Have you been listening to me?'

'Look, Mum. Don't you think it might be better to leave things to the police?' Diane said gently. She'd deliberately kept the more damning parts of the evidence to herself; hadn't mentioned Ian's messages on the day of the murders, or the passport he'd taken with him. Once Agnes got started, God knew what she might find out that she'd be better off not knowing.

Agnes snorted. 'I don't understand how you, of all people, can put your faith in that bunch of incompetents. All this talk about Ian having an affair, and nobody's asked . . .'

Diane massaged her temples. The day seemed to have been going on for ever; all she wanted was a bath, and sleep. 'Does it really matter, any more?'

'Of course it matters! Everyone's been assuming Ian was the one who was being unfaithful, but if we can prove that trollop . . .'

'Angelika's been *murdered*, Mum,' Diane snapped. 'Can't you even leave her alone now she's dead?' She regretted the

243

words as soon as they were out of her mouth. 'I'm sorry. I didn't mean . . .'

'I didn't like the woman when she was alive.' Agnes's voice was cold. 'I'm not going to pretend I did now that she's dead. And I'm not prepared to sit back and allow my son to be blamed for something he didn't do. Even if you are.'

'Of course I'm not.' Diane closed her eyes. The headache that had been threatening all day was hammering against her skull. 'I just think you're going the wrong way about it, that's all. Even if you do manage to prove Angelika was having an affair, how's that going to help Ian?'

'At least it might make the police take their blinkers off.'

'Or make them think he had even more of a motive for killing her.'

'So what do you suggest? That I sit on my bottom and play bridge? If his own family aren't prepared to ask questions . . .'

'For God's sake!' Abruptly, Diane's temper snapped. Malcolm was right; this way led to insanity. 'We can't keep on fooling ourselves like this for ever! If Ian's innocent, why isn't he here? That's the only real question, isn't it? You can play at being a private bloody detective all you like, the answer's still going to be the same.'

There was absolute silence on the other end of the phone. After a moment, Agnes said, 'He's my son.' Her voice was muffled, as if she was trying not to cry.

Diane pressed her own hand to her mouth. As if such a simple action could stifle the grief. 'And my brother,' she whispered.

'So we just sit here and wait, then.'

'What else can we do?' Diane said flatly.

244

26

It was a week later, on a bright, sunny June morning, that the waiting came to an end when a farmer who had got up early to shoot squirrels found Ian's body hanging from a tree in dense woodland less than a mile from the cottage at Corley Moor.

Diane knew what Baker and Collingwood had come to tell her as soon as she opened the door to them. Baker looked uneasy; it was Collingwood who asked her if Malcolm was at home, steered them both into the kitchen, told them to sit down.

Diane stared at the grain of the kitchen table as the words flowed over and round her. No formal identification . . . decomposition of the body . . . dental records . . . She tried to shut her mind to the images. He'd been there all along. When they'd driven to the cottage with her mother, when they'd sat on the threadbare sofa eating pâté, when the cuckoo had called and the hawthorn had flowered, Ian had been less than a mile away. Rotting. Her hand clapped to her mouth, she stumbled to the sink and was violently sick.

She felt Malcolm's arm around her shoulders. Without a word, he guided her through to the living-room, sat her on the sofa. Put a cushion behind her head. Collingwood brought her some water. Her mouth was dry and sour with the bitter taste of vomit, but she seemed to lack the coordination to pick up the glass. She gazed at the trembling hands that lay uselessly in her lap. She thought she'd accustomed herself to the fact that Ian was dead. She thought she'd managed to extinguish the small, irrational flicker of hope she'd so pitied in her mother. She'd been wrong.

It was Malcolm who put the glass to her lips, feeding her the water as if she were a child, then sat down next to her. His strong hand enveloped both her own, absorbed the frantic movement of her fingers.

Baker remained standing, as if awkward in his role as comforter. He glanced towards Collingwood before he said, 'We could leave this until another time, if you prefer.'

Diane shook her head. She needed to know everything; every small detail of what they'd found.

'You're sure it's Ian?' The pressure of Malcolm's hand on hers increased as he asked the question.

'We shall have to rely on dental records and DNA to give us a definitive identification,' Collingwood said gently. 'But you must prepare yourselves for the worst.'

'Apart from the similarity in height and the clothing he was described as wearing at the time of his disappearance, Mr Somerford's passport and mobile phone were found on the body,' Baker added.

'Can I see him?' Diane whispered.

Baker cleared his throat. 'Best not.'

For a moment, no one spoke. Then Malcolm said quietly, 'So do you think he'd been there ever since . . .?'

'We'll have to wait for the results of the forensic examinations before we can come to any conclusion about that, sir.'

'You didn't search the area at the time?'

'In view of the location of Mr Somerford's car, it seemed logical to concentrate our resources on the vicinity of Arden Hall.' There was a trace of defensiveness in Baker's tone.

Malcolm had clearly picked it up. 'Maybe if you'd used fewer of your "resources" on falsely accusing my wife, our family could have been spared some of this anguish.'

'They were just doing their job, Malcolm,' Diane said wearily. She frowned, trying to get things straight in her head. 'So if his car was in Stratford, how did he get back . . .?'

Baker sat down opposite her and took out his notebook. He seemed relieved to be getting down to business. 'That's something we're trying to work out, Mrs Middleton. I wondered if either of you might have any ideas on the subject?'

'No.' Diane glanced at Malcolm, who was staring into space, apparently deep in thought.

'Maybe he took a taxi from Arden Hall to the cottage. On the night of the party, I mean,' he said at last. 'Maybe it's as simple as that.'

Baker paused. 'There's some further information that we haven't divulged until now. On the weekend in question, mobile speed cameras were operational along a stretch of the A46 where some roadworks were taking place. Just before the M40 roundabout. They registered Mrs Middleton's car at twenty-one eighteen, travelling at ninety-three miles an hour.'

Malcolm snorted. 'I suppose you're going to charge her with speeding, now. Good God, man, she was in a state of shock!'

'Maybe you'd let me finish, sir. The same camera picked up Mr Somerford's car exceeding the legal speed limit some thirty minutes earlier, travelling in the same direction.'

'The same . . .?' Diane's brain was racing. 'But that means Ian's innocent!' She jumped to her feet. 'Don't you see? You told me yourself. You said Angelika and the children had been dead for at least . . .'

'Sit down, Mrs Middleton.'

She glared at Baker. Was he really so dense that he couldn't work out for himself what she was getting at?

She felt Tracey Collingwood's hand on her shoulder, pushing her gently back down beside Malcolm.

'I'm sorry, Diane. It isn't quite that simple,' she said.

'The camera also registered it earlier; at approximately seventeen fifty,' Baker went on. 'In addition to which, equipment on the opposite side of the road – driving *away* from the direction of Arden Hall – picked him up some thirty-five minutes later. At eighteen twenty-six, to be precise. If we assume five minutes each way to reach Arden Hall from the spot where the cameras were located, that would allow him around twenty-five minutes in the house at the critical time.'

Diane stared at him stupidly. 'Why would he go away and then come back again? I don't understand.'

Baker spread his hands. 'To be frank, I'm not sure we understand either, Mrs Middleton.'

'Let me get this straight.' Malcolm's face was set into a frown of concentration. 'You're saying that Ian drove to Arden Hall, left after half an hour, and then came back . . .'

'An hour and twenty-two minutes later. At ten to nine.'

Malcolm thought about it, then nodded slowly. 'Which could have been when he trashed the cottage.'

'It's possible. There are any number of possibilities.' Baker looked hard at Diane. 'You're absolutely certain you didn't have any contact with him during that period?'

'It's hardly something my wife is likely to have forgotten,' Malcolm snapped. 'Neither is it likely that she would have had a perfectly normal telephone conversation with me at about the time he'd have arrived here, and then calmly put in a couple of hours' work in the garden, before driving over to Stratford.'

Baker ignored him. 'Mrs Middleton?'

'For God's sake!' Malcolm got to his feet. 'You can come and have a look at the bloody bags of laurel clippings if you're not prepared to take her word, or mine either.'

'I don't think losing our tempers is going to help anyone, sir.' Baker's expression softened somewhat. 'If we hadn't been satisfied with your wife's version of events, she wouldn't have been released without charge. I'm merely trying to get to the bottom of things. I'm sure we're all keen to do that.'

'Of course.' Malcolm rubbed his hands across his face. 'I'm sorry. I just . . .' He slumped back onto the sofa. 'I'm sorry.'

'I wish with all my heart he had come here,' Diane whispered. She forced herself to meet Baker's gaze. 'I might at least have been able to stop him taking his own life.'

Baker nodded gravely.

With an effort, she went on, 'But wherever he went, why would he go back to Arden Hall?'

Collingwood gave a small smile. 'People don't always act rationally when they're in shock, Diane.'

'Maybe he went back to check Thomas was all right,' Malcolm murmured. 'Christ, if you imagine what sort of a state he must have been in. Not that any of us can possibly begin to imagine . . .'

Something had been niggling in the corner of Diane's mind; something that made even less sense than the rest of it. She leant forward and said urgently, 'Win Keilly said that traces of Angelika's sleeping tablets had been found in the children's bloodstream. If Ian was only in the house for half an hour or so . . .'

Baker regarded her with something close to admiration. 'It's a good point. And one we've been giving a lot of thought to.' He looked towards each of them in turn and said slowly,

'It's possible Mrs Somerford might have administered the drug herself.'

'Angelika?' Diane stared at him.

Malcolm snorted. 'This is getting more far-fetched by the minute. Why the hell would *Angelika* want to drug her own children?'

'One of the girls who looked after the children in the past has come forward.' Tracey Collingwood's face was troubled. 'She claims that Mrs Somerford frequently sedated the children if she wanted some time to herself. She was so unhappy with the situation, she threatened to go to the authorities.'

'That's rubbish.' Diane shook her head. 'Ian would never . . .'

'Mrs Somerford apparently accused her of stealing a valuable piece of jewellery. The girl was so frightened she'd get into trouble, she left without saying anything, to Mr Somerford or to anyone else.'

Diane put her head between her hands. She could remember the incident; recalled Ian's shock as he'd told her about the ring that had been stolen; the au pair whom he'd thought so trustworthy.

'We're working on the possibility that one of the children was disturbed by whatever took place between Mr and Mrs Somerford, and that Mr Somerford smothered them rather than risk them giving evidence against him. Then in a fit of remorse, took his own life.' For once, Baker looked genuinely moved. Diane remembered the photograph of the two small children in his office. 'It can only be supposition, of course. But that seems the most likely scenario.'

'Marshall used to sleepwalk,' Diane said quietly.

'I'm sorry?'

She took a deep, ragged breath and looked up. 'Marshall

might have come down in his sleep.' Her eyes filled with tears. 'He probably didn't see anything at all. They were killed for nothing.'

'Dear God,' Malcolm gazed at her, his face grey.

For a second, Baker closed his eyes. Then he said soberly, 'We can't know that for sure. Probably best not to go down that road.'

For a while, no one spoke, then Malcolm cleared his throat and said flatly, 'So that's it, then.'

'It would appear so, sir. There's still the question of how Mr Somerford got back from Arden Hall to Corley Moor, of course. That's the real puzzle.' Baker frowned down at his hands, then looked up with a tight smile. 'But unlike on the telly, in real life it's sometimes not possible to tie up all the loose ends.'

'We appreciate your candour, Inspector.' Malcolm took Diane's hand and squeezed it. Not looking at her, he said quietly, 'So what happens next?'

'We'll have to wait for formal proof of identification, of course. Then there will be a post mortem, and inquests on all four of the deceased. But to all intents and purposes the case is closed.' Baker got to his feet; now that the formalities had been dealt with, he seemed anxious to be gone. He looked down at Diane as if wondering what her reaction might be as he added, 'We're not looking for anyone else in connection with any of the deaths. Including that of Nicola Smith.'

'So Lee Smith gets away scot-free.'

Baker's expression was back to neutral. 'Lee Smith isn't a suspect in this investigation.'

'You're wrong.' Diane held his gaze. 'I might never be able to prove it, but I know you're wrong.'

Baker nodded. 'DC Collingwood will be keeping you

informed of developments. And you know how to get in touch should you need anything.'

Collingwood drew Diane to one side as Malcolm showed Baker to the door. 'Smith's been charged with actual bodily harm and indecent assault. He's coming up in front of the bench tomorrow morning. There'll be a separate hearing on the obstruction charge at a later date.'

Diane felt as if she were being offered some kind of consolation prize. 'What will happen to him?' she asked.

'It's only a preliminary hearing. If he pleads not guilty, it could be months before it comes to trial.'

'*Months?*' Diane repeated incredulously. 'So what happens to him in the meantime?'

'Nothing.' Collingwood gave a small, apologetic shrug. 'I know. It's the way the system works, I'm afraid.'

Diane felt an overwhelming wave of despair. Ian had lost everything, including his life, and Lee Smith was free; might remain free, if he hired a good enough solicitor. No wonder Baker had been so lukewarm about her pressing charges.

'What's the point?' she asked flatly.

'Justice?' Collingwood's voice was gentle.

'Is that what you call it?'

'Look, I shall have to go now.' Collingwood nodded towards the door. 'We came in the one car and he'll be waiting for me.'

Diane shrugged. 'Whatever.'

'We can only get offenders as far as the courts, Diane. The rest is out of our hands.'

'Unless they're dead, of course,' Diane said bitterly. 'If they're dead, you can hang anything on them you like, can't you?'

27

'I don't know how we're going to do this, do you?' Diane stared at the regimental ranks of salvia and lobelia that bordered Doris Crombie's small, immaculate front lawn.

They'd driven over to Leamington as soon as Baker and Collingwood had left; the news of Ian's death wasn't something that could be broken over the telephone.

Malcolm reached across and took her hand. 'Do you want me to go in first?'

Diane shook her head. Much as she would like to take the coward's way out, she knew that she had to be the one to tell her mother.

'Come on, then.' Malcolm's face was sober. 'Let's get it over with.'

Agnes listened Diane out in absolute silence. She sat very still, her hands clasped in her lap. Only her deathly pallor suggested that she had taken the news in at all.

Doris Crombie twittered in and out with tea, a small lace handkerchief pressed to her powdered face. Diane suspected that beneath her breathless, unceasing expressions of horror and disbelief, Doris was thoroughly enjoying being part of the drama, and would be on the phone to the rest of the bridge club the moment they left. She was relieved when Malcolm steered the other woman firmly from the room,

saying that Agnes and Diane needed some time alone together.

Agnes picked up a small, pink porcelain figure of a lady in a
crinoline from the side table next to her. Staring sightlessly
into space, she turned it over and over in her hands, as if she
were telling a rosary. *saying the*

Diane said nothing, too numb herself to be able to think of
any words of comfort.

It was only after some moments that Agnes ran her tongue
over her lips and said in a voice as dry as ash, 'So they haven't
positively identified the . . .' A grimace briefly contorted the
mask of her face. Diane watched the Adam's apple jerk
convulsively under the crêpe-like skin. 'They can't be
sure . . .?'

'It's Ian.' Diane reached forward and took the figurine from
her mother's unresisting fingers.

Agnes nodded. She looked down at her hands as if surprised
to find them empty. Then she got to her feet; slowly, as if she
had aged ten years in the half an hour since Diane and
Malcolm had arrived, and went to the telephone on the fussy
little writing desk by the window.

'What are you doing?' Diane asked anxiously as she picked
up the receiver and began to dial.

'I'm ringing the police.'

'What for?' Diane looked at her, bemused. She wondered
fleetingly if the shock had turned her mother's mind.

'To tell them about Angelika.'

'Not now, Mum.' Diane went over to her. 'They don't need
to know right now.' She tried to take the receiver from her, but
Agnes's grip was strong.

'Of course they need to know,' she said. Her eyes, as she
turned to Diane, were filled with panic, like a child left alone in

the dark. 'How else are they going to find out who killed Angelika and the children?'

'We can't just allow her to go on fooling herself like this.' Malcolm flexed his shoulders wearily.

It had only been with reluctance that Agnes had been persuaded to delay making the phone call until the following day; and with even greater reluctance that she had agreed to come back to Coventry with them. David Fawcett had called in, but had failed in his attempt to administer a further sedative injection. Eventually, Agnes had been talked into a single mild sleeping tablet and had retired to her room, saying that she needed to be up early in the morning. Her face had been flushed, her eyes too bright. She hadn't shed a single tear. Denial, David Fawcett had called it, in what had seemed an oddly American expression for such a down-to-earth GP.

Diane glanced across the kitchen table at Malcolm. He had been gentle with Agnes; had taken the news of her amateur investigations with greater tolerance than she would have expected, and she was grateful for it. So it was with caution that she said, 'So you don't think we should tell the police what she's found out about Angelika?'

They'd been circling the subject ever since Agnes had gone to bed, and there was the slightest edge of exasperation to Malcolm's voice as he answered, 'I just don't see the point. What difference can it make now? Apart from giving the press even more scandal than they already have.'

Lee Smith's name hung unspoken between them. Diane swallowed, knowing how much better it would be to let the subject drop, at least for tonight. They were both exhausted; probably both still in shock. Any minute now, they'd be saying things they didn't mean. Or worse, things they did mean.

'There just seem to be so many inconsistencies . . .'

'Don't you think the police have probably had enough of you trying to do their job for them, without your mother joining in?'

She picked at a loose strand of cotton on the tablecloth, willing herself to stay silent, but the words came out anyway. 'They're missing something. I know they are. Ian's car, for one thing. What was he doing, driving backwards and forwards? Someone must know how he got back to Arden Hall. And another thing. Ian knew Marshall walked in his sleep. He would never have . . .'

Malcolm closed his eyes. 'For God's sake, Diane. Just let it go.'

Their truce was still so fragile; the last thing she wanted to do was to break it. But she was desperate to make him understand. 'He was my brother, Malcolm. And there's something that isn't right.'

'There are a lot of things that aren't right.' Malcolm got to his feet and picked up their coffee mugs.

'I know.' She caught his hand. 'Don't you think I know that? It's just that . . .'

'It's just that your first priority is Ian. The same as it always has been.' Malcolm put the mugs down carefully on the draining board. 'The same as it always will be, even now he's dead,' he said quietly, and left the kitchen, not waiting for her to reply.

There was no further conversation that night. Malcolm came out of the bathroom and got into bed without looking at her. He turned onto his side and switched out his bedside light.

Diane tried to think of something to say that wouldn't make things worse, but she was simply too exhausted. She climbed into the bed next to him, registering his slight movement towards the edge of the bed as her leg came accidentally into contact with one of his. She longed for the warmth of his arm around her, for the reassurance of conversation. She stared into the darkness, knowing that if only she'd listened to what her brain had told her and had kept her mouth shut, that comfort might have been hers.

She was cravenly relieved, the following morning, to discover that Agnes had a raging temperature, and wasn't well enough to get out of bed; at least it postponed her inevitable contribution to the discussion.

David Fawcett returned. 'It could be 'flu. Or it could be a reaction to the shock,' he said when he came back downstairs from Agnes's bedroom. 'Either way, she needs to rest. She's in good shape for her age, but after everything that's happened . . .' He glanced at Malcolm. 'She's pretty agitated about some phone call she reckons she's got to make. She seems convinced you're going to try to prevent her, for some reason. It may just be a function of the high temperature, of course.'

Malcolm's mouth tightened. Breakfast had been an uncomfortable affair, their terse conversation and long silences filled with a simmering resentment that Diane felt unequal to addressing. 'It isn't,' he said shortly.

'Oh?' David Fawcett looked queryingly at both of them. When neither responded, he said, 'Well, I'd try to avoid upsetting her, if I were you. She's not going to be talking to anyone for a day or so, whatever she thinks, so maybe your difference of opinion can be put on hold.'

Malcolm nodded.

'Thanks for coming out,' Diane murmured.

'No trouble.' Fawcett took her hand. 'Is there anything I can do to help you, while I'm here? Something to help you sleep, maybe?'

Malcolm made a small derisive noise in his throat.

'No.' Diane forced a smile. 'Really. I'm OK. I'll see you out.'

'Something to open her eyes might be more useful,' she heard Malcolm mutter under his breath as she left the kitchen.

He was in the study when Diane came back in. After a while, she heard his footsteps creaking across the floor of their bedroom, and the sound of the shower. When he came down, he was wearing his work suit.

'I've got to go into the office,' he said as he straightened his tie.

Diane stopped stirring the eggs she was scrambling for Agnes's breakfast. 'Now? For God's sake, Malcolm! Don't you think there are more important things we should be doing?'

He didn't look at her. 'I'm not sure what time I'll be back. There's a planning meeting tonight. I'd said I'd be there, before all this happened. I may as well go straight there from work.'

'This is stupid, Malcolm.' She tried to keep her voice even. 'Look, we need to talk.'

'No.' He turned as he got to the door, his face expressionless. 'Actually, I think that's the last thing we need to do right now.'

28

Agnes didn't touch the scrambled eggs. After one feeble attempt to get out of bed, she lay back on the pillows, her eyes closed as if to shut out the world. When Diane tried to prop her up and feed her some tea, she turned her head away and mumbled that she wanted to be left alone. She sank into a feverish, disturbed sleep. Within the hour, her breathing had become laboured, her chest rattling with every wheezing inhalation. Diane was alarmed at the speed with which her condition seemed to be deteriorating. She rang the surgery. Dr Fawcett would call in again later, she was promised.

The morning seemed to drag on interminably. Diane checked on Agnes frequently, sponging her forehead, trying to straighten the tangled bedclothes as her mother tossed and turned. The rest of the time she spent wandering from room to room, picking things up, putting them down again.

Steeling herself, she went for the first time since his disappearance into the room that had been Ian's. It was the largest of the five bedrooms; a light, airy room with a French door leading to a small balcony that looked over the front garden. Malcolm had suggested they make it their bedroom, when they'd first taken the house over; it was the obvious choice. Diane had found it difficult to explain her reluctance; it wasn't as if Ian were going to need it again. A room at the back would be quieter, she'd argued, although they were too far from the road for traffic to disturb them. Malcolm hadn't said anything, and they'd put an en suite in what had been Agnes's room and moved in there, instead. At the time, she'd assumed he wasn't that bothered.

The room was much as Ian had left it; Angelika had had her own ideas on interior design, and the masculine browns and coffees of the curtains, the heavy oak wardrobes, had not fitted in with her frilly Laura Ashley chintzes. Somehow, Diane had never got round to redecorating. She'd sit there sometimes, in the brown leather swivel chair that had been their father's, and remember the earnest, rambling conversations she and Ian had had when they were teenagers; filled with the certainty that they could put the world to rights. The confidences they'd shared. The hopes and dreams. It was in this room that they'd agonised over whether Ian should give up his hopes of studying music to follow their father into the business. Here that she'd told him that Malcolm had asked her to marry him, and watched the split second of jealousy that had flashed into his brown eyes, so identical to her own, before he'd hugged her and offered her his congratulations. Here where she'd heard of his intention to marry Angelika, some thirteen years later, and had experienced her own sharp, irrational pang of jealousy.

Had they been too attached to one another? Had the seeds of what was to follow been planted in the closeness that had always seemed as natural as breathing?

She opened the wardrobe. It was still half-full of clothes Ian had never got round to taking with him: some shirts, a couple of suits that Angelika had decreed beyond the pale of fashion, a baggy, threadbare gardening sweater that had been his favourite. Briefly, Diane buried her face in its musty, familiar warmth. Then with the tears streaming down her face unchecked, she pulled everything from the hangers and into a heap on the floor. Curtains and bedding were bundled into the bin-liners she fetched from the kitchen. Energised by her grief, she began to rip up the carpet she and Ian had chosen together. She'd paint the walls a bright, sunny yellow, choose a border print with nursery characters. Or cats. Thomas loved cats. Malcolm could fix a lock to the French door.

It was only when the doorbell rang that she paused for breath.

'Sorry if it's an inconvenient time.' Tracey Collingwood's gaze took in Diane's swollen eyes, her dishevelled hair, the smear of dust across her sweating forehead. 'I just thought you might like to know what happened in court.'

She had forgotten all about it, Diane realised. She wiped her arm across her face and stepped aside to let the other woman in. 'Spring cleaning,' she explained with a tight smile. Tracey Collingwood nodded but made no comment. Diane liked that about her; if there was nothing to be said, she didn't try to say it. 'So how did it go?'

'No plea yet, which is much as we expected. His solicitor will need to take instructions. Smith's been bailed to reappear in a fortnight. The good news is that the magistrates have made it a condition of his bail that he doesn't have any contact with you in the meantime.'

'He's not likely to, is he?' Diane asked as she led the way through into the kitchen and filled the kettle; it had become an almost Pavlovian response to make tea when Collingwood appeared.

Collingwood shrugged. 'Witness intimidation. It's not un-common, especially in cases where it boils down to one person's word against another. A lot of domestic violence cases fall apart because the woman's been got at.' She must have read Diane's expression, because she smiled and said, 'Most of them are on their own, of course, so it's a bit different.'

Diane leant against the sink. 'I'm not sure how long it's going to stay different.' She could feel fresh tears pricking the back of her eyes as she turned round and attempted a shaky smile of her own. 'I'm not sure of anything, any more.'

Collingwood took the kettle from her and guided her to a chair.

'I'm sorry.' Diane searched her pocket for a tissue. 'You're busy.'

'Meaning I'm a police officer.' Collingwood pulled out a chair and sat down opposite. 'I'm also a human being, you know. If it makes things any easier, I'm not even on duty at the moment. I just thought I'd call round on my way home to let you know what was going on with Lee Smith.' She pushed a haphazard strand of red hair behind her ear and regarded Diane with concern. 'You're not going to back out, are you?'

Diane looked down at the soggy ball of her tissue. 'There just doesn't seem much point, any more.'

'What about the next woman he thumps?' Collingwood leant forward and said earnestly, 'Don't let us down, Diane. Don't let yourself down.'

Diane looked into the other woman's plain, friendly face. 'This is really important to you, isn't it?' she asked. 'I mean, more important than just your job.'

'Oh dear.' Collingwood pulled a wry face. 'It's not supposed to show.' She hesitated. 'Let's just say I've had personal experience of being on the other end of a man's fists. My husband, as a matter of fact.' A small smile. 'My ex-husband, I should say. It took me far too long to realise that I wasn't the one who was to blame.'

Diane had a brief, vivid mental image of Tracey Colling-wood's hinterland. It explained a lot, not only about the other woman's hesitant manner, but also about the determination and strength that emerged from beneath the self-effacing exterior, once one got to know her.

'Can I tell you something?' she said suddenly. 'Not as a policewoman, just as you?'

She ended up telling much more than she had intended: about Agnes's utter refusal to accept what Ian had done; about her own guilt that she hadn't done more to stop him; about the row she'd had with Malcolm and the tension between them that she feared would never go away. It was a huge relief to share it all; like the bursting of an abscess. It wasn't that she didn't have anyone else to talk to; it was that they all wanted her to say something different.

Tracey Collingwood let her run on, simply nodding now and then, but making no effort to interrupt or to jump in with an opinion of her own. At last, Diane fell silent. It wasn't until Collingwood had made a fresh pot of tea, poured out two cups and placed one of them in front of Diane that she spoke.

'Firstly,' she said, 'stop blaming yourself for everything that's happened. You made one daft mistake and you've more than paid the price for it. You're not to blame for anything else. Your brother was a grown man, Diane. He made his own choices.'

'But . . .'

'Secondly, OK it would probably be healthier for your mum to face up to reality, but if she won't, you can't make her. She won't be the first parent to live out the rest of her life on a lost crusade. It might be the only way she can cope. As for this stuff about Angelika,' she went on, as Diane started to speak. 'It's material to the investigation, and as such I think it should be made known. In fact, wearing my police hat, I'm obliged to make it known, now that I'm aware of it. As to whether it'll turn out to be of any real significance . . .' she raised her shoulders. 'I doubt it, frankly. I'd say it just reinforces the fact that it was a pretty unsuccessful marriage all round. But I'll pass it on anyway.' She grinned suddenly. 'Although I suspect Baker will appreciate a latter-day Miss Marple on the case about as much as he appreciates a feminist DC.'

'I sensed the two of you weren't that keen on each other.' Diane smiled despite herself. She had the feeling that under any other circumstances, she and Tracey Collingwood could have been friends.

The other woman shrugged. 'He thought I came on a bit too strong with you about pressing charges against Lee Smith. He's a good detective, but like a lot of men, he thinks women who try to stand up for their rights are a pain in the backside.' She grinned again. 'He probably reckons I'm a lesbian. Which I'll assure you I'm not, by the way, before I give you this.' She pulled a card from her bag, scribbled on it and handed it over. 'That's my home number and my mobile number.' Her face became serious. 'If you need someone to talk to, or to scream at, or whatever, I'm only at the other end of the phone.'

'Who were you speaking to?' Agnes dragged herself up in the bed as Diane, bearing a tray, pushed the door open. Her voice was little more than a raspy whisper. Her cheeks, sunken without the scaffolding of her false teeth had a deep, unhealthy flush.

Diane put down the tray and laid her hand against her mother's forehead. 'You're burning up. I'm going to ring the doctor.'

Agnes gripped Diane's wrist, her breathing laboured. 'Was it Ian?'

'It was the policewoman.' Diane's heart sank. She forced a smile as she pushed back a strand of damp hair from her mother's forehead. 'The one you gave such a hard time when you were here before.'

Agnes looked at her blankly.

'Tracey Collingwood. You remember.' Diane reached into her pocket. 'She left her card. See? I told her what you'd found out about Angelika,' she added. 'She's going to make sure it's looked into.'

She'd hoped to placate her mother, but the words didn't even seem to have registered.

'Where's Ian?' Agnes's gaze remained fixed on her face.

'You just lie still, Mum. I'll get the doctor.'

She ran through to her own bedroom, gripped with anxiety. Not Mum; not Mum as well, she prayed to any nameless deity who might be listening. They'd spent most of their lives with swords crossed; it had only been in the last weeks that they'd begun to get to know each other. Her fingers were trembling as she punched in the number.

Her urgency must have conveyed itself to the receptionist, because it was less than half an hour before David Fawcett arrived.

'I'm sorry to bother you again,' she said. 'It's just . . .'

'Don't apologise.' He smiled as he followed her up the stairs. 'I was on my way to some damned Area Health Committee meeting. You've done me a favour.'

His smile became more fixed as he checked Agnes's pulse and listened to her chest. He drew Diane out onto the landing and said quietly, 'She's got quite a nasty chest infection. I think I should ring Walsgrave and see if there's a bed.'

'Can't you treat her here?' The last time they'd been to Walsgrave, it had been to see Ian, the day Nicola Smith's body had been found. 'She absolutely hates hospitals. You can see how confused she is already,' Diane pleaded. 'She was asking if Ian was here a few minutes ago.'

'She is quite poorly. On the other hand, with the beds situation the way it is . . .' he frowned. 'I could try her on some strong antibiotics and see how she goes for twenty-four hours, if you like. But are you sure you're going to be able to cope, with everything else that's going on?'

Diane nodded, more relieved than she could have begun to explain.

David Fawcett scribbled a prescription. 'Is Malcolm around? It would be better if she wasn't left here on her own.'

'He's at work.'

'Oh.' There was a hint of surprise in the doctor's expression. 'Well, in that case I'll run over to the pharmacy at Cannon Park and pick them up myself.' He waved aside Diane's thanks and took a strip of tablets from his case. 'I'll give her a couple now to get her started, and something to bring her temperature down. The sooner we can hit the infection, the better.'

Diane tried the office while he'd gone, half dreading the prospect of talking to Malcolm. She needn't have worried; he was in a meeting, she was told.

'But I'm sure he'll take the call when he knows it's you,' his secretary Val's voice was hushed with sympathy.

'No. Don't disturb him.' What did she expect him to do, in any case? Just the sound of his voice would have been enough until a couple of weeks ago, Diane thought with sadness.

'We were all ever so sorry to hear about your . . .'

'Just ask him to ring me when he's free, will you?' Diane said quickly.

She wondered whether to ring Tracey Collingwood. She'd been surprised at just how good it had felt to unburden herself on such an undemanding listener. But there seemed something faintly ridiculous in calling the other woman just to say her mother wasn't well.

By the time David Fawcett arrived back, Agnes was asleep. The painkillers that he'd given her to reduce her temperature seemed to have had some effect; her papery skin was a little cooler to Diane's touch.

'That's what she needs as much as anything,' Fawcett murmured as he and Diane stepped quietly out of the room. 'I'll call in again before surgery in the morning, but if you're worried about her, you can call me at any time. You've got my home number.'

Everyone was being so kind, Diane thought as she shut the front door behind him. Why was it she felt so entirely alone?

Malcolm didn't ring until after five. Agnes continued to sleep. Diane spent much of the afternoon sitting beside the bed and staring at a novel. Her earlier energy had deserted her; she'd done nothing more to Ian's room than to pile the bin-liners onto the bed and shut the door on the mess. When she heard the phone, she closed her book without bothering to mark the page; she hadn't taken in a single word.

'I was told you'd rung.' Malcolm's voice was distant.

'Mum's got a chest infection.' It sounded such a feeble reason to have called him that she added, 'David Fawcett wanted her to go into hospital, but I managed to talk him out of it. I was just a bit worried, that's all. The fever's made her a bit . . .' she tried not to sound melodramatic '. . . a bit muddled.'

'Why on earth didn't you get Val to call me out of the meeting?' The coolness had instantly disappeared. 'Look, I'm just leaving. Is there anything you want me to pick up on the way home?'

'I thought you were going to the planning meeting.' She hadn't meant it to come out as a recrimination, but that was the way it sounded.

There was a small pause on the other end of the phone. Then Malcolm said quietly, 'I'm sorry for what I said last night.'

'She actually seems a bit better than she did earlier.' She didn't want him to think she was trying to make him feel guilty. 'I'm not even sure why I rang, to be honest. I suppose I just wanted to let you know.'

'We were both at the end of our tethers. But I shouldn't have lashed out at you like that. It was unforgivable.'

She cleared her throat. 'I've started to sort out Ian's room.'

Another pause. 'You don't need to. Not unless it's what you want.'

It was as if they were feeling their way tentatively towards each other across a flimsy rope bridge; one sudden move, one step out of place, and they'd both fall.

'It is.' She took a deep breath. 'I've been thinking a lot about what you said.'

'I had no right . . .'

'You did, Malcolm. You had every right. If we're going to find a way to get through this, we have to look to the future, not the past.' She hesitated. 'But that means both of us. I hurt you terribly, I know that, and I regret it with all my heart. But I can't go on apologising for it for the rest of my life.'

For a moment he said nothing. She wondered if she'd overplayed her hand. Then he said tentatively, 'Fresh start?'

She gripped the receiver. 'Fresh start.'

It was so easy to say. But maybe if they spoke the words with sufficient conviction, they might convince each other.

29

Malcolm arrived home some half an hour later bearing a box of Complan.

'For your mum.' He smiled hesitantly as he handed it over. 'I'm not sure what it is, but the woman in the shop thought it might do her good. How is she?'

'Sleeping. More peacefully now, thank God.' Diane returned the smile as she took the box from him. 'That was kind. Thank you.'

Malcolm looked pleased. 'It's the least I could do.' He sniffed the air appreciatively. 'Something smells nice.'

'I defrosted a couple of steaks. I thought it was time I got round to cooking a proper meal.' They'd been living for weeks on whatever tins she could find in the pantry.

'Great. I'm starving. I'll open some wine, shall I?'

They were both trying far too hard. Diane's cheeks ached with the effort of smiling as she finished preparing the meal. She wondered if they would ever get back to the casual, amicable relationship she'd taken so utterly for granted for more than fifteen years. Malcolm's hand touched hers as he handed her a glass of wine and she felt the brief warmth of his fingers. How could she ever have risked losing him?

They had just sat down to eat when the phone rang.

'I'll get it.' Diane was up first. 'Don't let your dinner go cold.'

She went out into the hall and picked up the receiver.

'There's been a break-in.' The muffled voice was heavily accented; it reminded Diane of Peter Sellers when he'd played an Indian doctor in a film she'd seen once. 'At Somerford's. The alarm's going off.'

'Who's calling?'

The phone went dead.

'Who was it?' Malcolm asked as she went back into the dining-room.

She frowned. 'I don't know. Some man, reckoning there'd been a break-in at the office. He sounded really odd, as if he was trying to disguise his voice.'

'Maybe it was just kids playing around.'

'It didn't sound like kids.' Diane hovered by the door. 'Do you think I should ring the police?'

'You can imagine what a production they'll turn it into.' Malcolm put down his knife and fork with a sigh and got to his feet. 'I'd better go and check, I suppose.'

'But your dinner. . . .'

He gave her a wry smile. 'Here we are, pussyfooting around each other as if we're on a first date, and some bugger decides to start making hoax calls. Sod's law, I think it's called.'

She grinned. It was such a relief to have him back, however fleetingly. 'Why don't I put it all in the oven, and we'll try again when you get back?'

'Why not?' He bent and put his lips to hers for the first time in weeks, the kiss deepening as he held her to him. It was some moments before he stepped back from her and murmured, 'Or alternatively, you could give the cat a treat, and we'll go straight on to dessert.'

He was whistling softly to himself as he walked back towards the car.

Diane was trying to persuade Agnes to take some of the Complan when the phone rang again.

'That might be Malcolm.' She guided Agnes's hands around the mug. 'Just try a bit, while I'm gone. I shan't be a minute.'

She hurried across the landing to take the call. 'Hello?'

Silence.

'Is that you, Malcolm?'

The faint sound of breathing was the only reply.

'Who's there?'

She heard the click of a receiver being replaced and the line went dead. For a moment she stood quite still in the darkening bedroom, then checked the windows and drew the curtains, trying to quell her unease before going back through to her mother.

'Wrong number,' she said brightly, before Agnes could ask. She took the untouched mug of Complan from her mother's unresisting fingers and put it down on the bedside table. Tracey Collingwood's card lay where it had been left earlier. Diane went to pick it up, then, telling herself to get a grip, concentrated on plumping up Agnes's pillows instead.

She went downstairs and emptied the Complan down the sink. With dismay, she noticed that Malcolm's mobile was plugged into the spare socket next to the cooker, where he'd put it to charge when he came home from work. She put some coffee on to brew and went into the living-room to draw the curtains. She glanced at her watch, still feeling edgy. Malcolm had been gone for almost ten minutes. She tried to calculate how long it would take him to check the building and get back again; no more than half an hour or so if everything was in order.

She went through to the dining-room. A wind had sprung up, and the trees outside the window were dancing wildly in the gathering dusk. With a slight shiver, she put on the overhead light and pulled down the blinds. The house was too quiet, the ticking of the grandfather clock in the hall magnified by the silence. The regular metallic thud that she normally barely noticed seemed menacing; ominous.

Diane told herself not to be ridiculous. She went back into the living-room and pulled open the drawer of the cabinet, searching for the remote control for the television. She'd put on something mindless; anything to fill the house with sound. She slammed the drawer shut. Where the hell was the bloody remote? Turning the television on had become a mission, now. Squatting down, she opened the flap on the front of the set and peered at the confusing array of buttons on the control panel, trying to remember how to turn the thing on manually. As she did so, she heard a faint tapping. She straightened up, her ears straining. The tapping was coming from behind the curtain. It could have been the cat, except that the creature was already stretched out on the sofa, full of steak. A tree, then. A branch, blowing against the window in the gale. Except there was no tree that close to the house.

The tapping came again, louder this time. Diane's scalp prickled. Someone was rapping against the glass of the patio door. She moved stealthily towards the hall, then raced up the stairs and into her mother's bedroom.

Agnes's eyes snapped open. 'Has Ian come home?'

Diane gazed down at her mother's wizened face, telling herself not to allow the thought into her head. Not even for a second. Ian was dead. His body might not have been positively identified, but the clothes, his passport . . .

Could have been planted, replied the small, insane spark of hope inside her brain.

Agnes was trying to pull herself up in the bed. 'I knew he'd come.'

'Stay here.' Diane pushed her back down into the pillows and grabbed Tracey Collingwood's card. 'Don't move. Or you'll frighten him away,' she added wildly as she went back out onto the landing and pulled the door to.

What was she saying?

All was quiet when she returned to the living-room. She stood in the doorway, her ears straining for any sound over the thud of her own heartbeat.

Nothing.

She moved into the room, her eyes fixed on the curtains that covered the patio door. Someone was out there; every fibre of her being told her that. She could feel the tingling of the fine hairs on the back of her neck. Someone who was as aware of her presence as she was of his. She pressed her palms against her eyes. Then, before reason could intervene, she strode across the room and pulled the curtain aside.

No one. Just the wildly tossing silhouettes of trees and plants.

She flicked a switch, and the outside light cut a swathe of yellow through the gloom. She thought she spotted a sudden movement in one of the big hydrangea bushes by the path. But there was movement everywhere. She slipped the catch, slid the window open and stepped onto the patio.

'Ian?'

The wind tore the whispered word from her mouth, whipped her hair in front of her eyes. She stumbled, temporarily blinded as she took another step. A strong hand caught her arm as she fell.

'Ian?' she half sobbed, but even before she turned, she knew it wasn't him. She had time for only one small scream of terror before a hand was clamped across her mouth.

'Don't be frightened.' Lee Smith pulled her towards him as she tried to struggle free. 'I just want to talk to you.'

30

As soon as they were back in the living-room, Lee Smith released his grip. His fingers brushed against Diane's cheek as he took his hand away from her mouth.

'I'm not going to hurt you,' he said softly. His face was sickly in the harsh overhead light, his hair wild.

Diane stood absolutely still. He'd planned it out, she realised. Made the phone call to lure Malcolm away from the house. He knew she was alone. Her eyes flicked towards the door. Except she wasn't alone. Agnes was upstairs, sick and utterly vulnerable.

'What do you want?' she said, trying to keep her voice calm.

'To see you.' His eyes searched her face. 'To talk to you. To say I'm sorry.'

Above them, Diane could hear the faint creak of floorboards. She forced herself not to look up. Don't let her come downstairs, she prayed.

Lee had heard it too. His head cocked. 'What was that?'

'What was what?'

Another creak.

'Is there someone up there?' There was an edge of panic in his voice. And panic could only make him more unpredictable.

Her only hope was to keep him calm. Keep him talking until Malcolm got back.

She made herself hold his gaze. 'You know there isn't.'

He nodded. The tiniest of smiles appeared at the corners of his mouth. 'Did you guess it was me?' He assumed the ridiculous Indian accent she'd heard earlier. 'There's been a break-in.'

She cursed her own stupidity. Why hadn't she realised? 'I . . .' She swallowed. 'I wasn't sure.' Desperately, she tried to read his reaction. 'I suppose I thought it might have been.'

It seemed to be enough. He nodded again. 'I knew you'd want to see me, whatever they said. I never meant to hurt you, Diane. You know that, don't you?'

She dipped her head in nervous assent. Was that what it was about? Was he trying to talk her into dropping the case?

'I never meant to hurt you. I just freaked out. But I've had time to think, now. We've both had time.'

Another creak. 'We could talk about it, if you like,' she said quickly.

A flicker of annoyance crossed his face. 'It's not about what I'd like.'

'No. I'm sorry.' How long could she keep him talking? She pressed her sweating palms together, hoping he wouldn't notice how much they were trembling. She tried to focus, to stop herself wondering what he might do to her, when he'd nothing left to say. 'Tell me then. I want you to.'

'It was special, what we had.' He was frowning, as if trying to find the words. 'Even before we got it together it was special. Wasn't it?'

She heard the faint click of a door being opened somewhere above them. Surely he must have heard it too? But his eyes hadn't left her face.

'Yes, it was special.' The words clogged her dry mouth.

'You see stuff in me no one else can see. You make me feel . . .' He shook his head, his mouth tightening. 'Nicki made

276

me feel like I was nothing. A piece of shit. She thought it was just a joke, me wanting to paint. Everyone did. You were the only one who ever told me I was any good.' His eyes narrowed suddenly. 'You weren't just saying it?'

'No.' She cleared her throat. 'You're very good. You know you are.'

'And the sex.' He ran his tongue over his lips. His eyes travelled her; stripped her naked. 'That was good too, wasn't it? The best.'

She nodded dumbly, wondering what might be coming next.

Abruptly, he sank down onto a chair. 'When you told me all that shit about your brother, it was like you were throwing it all back in my face, saying it had meant nothing to you.' He ran his hand through his tangled hair. 'D'you get what I'm saying?'

Diane glanced towards the patio door. It was still open, the half-drawn curtain bellying out into the room. Could she make a dash for it? Get past him before he grabbed her? But what good would that do, with Agnes still upstairs? Please God, she was still upstairs.

'That time I came round before.' Lee's eyes were still on her face. 'I was just so fucked up in my head, thinking you'd made a fool of me. I didn't know what had happened. What he'd done. I'd never have said all that stuff if . . .' He broke off and shook his head slowly. 'Jesus, how could he have done that? Killed those little kiddies?' He jumped up so suddenly that Diane let out a stifled scream. She shrank back from him as he grabbed her by the shoulders and pulled her towards him so that his face was only inches from her.

'It wasn't me sent those letters.' His eyes burned into hers. 'I'll put my hands up to hitting you. I'll plead guilty, if that's what you want me to do. I deserve everything I get for treating you the way I did. But I swear I never sent those letters.' He shook her, his fingers biting into her flesh. 'You've got to tell me you believe me.'

'Yes! I believe you.' She was breathless with terror.

'You mean that?'

'Yes!'

His grip tightened. 'The first time we were together I knew it didn't matter any more. Whatever Nicki and me had finished years ago. Why would I have gone after him, when the only thing that mattered was you?'

She thought she made out the sound of a car, slowing to turn into the long drive, but she knew it was just the howling wind playing tricks. She tried to force her brain into action; to make the mental calculation. Forty, maybe forty-five minutes for Malcolm to drive to the office and back again. Add on some for him to check things out. Take away the time since he'd left . . . The figures slithered away from her. All she knew was that it would be too late.

As abruptly as he'd seized her, Lee let her go. His hand went to the inside pocket of his jacket.

For a crazy moment, Diane wondered if he might be about to pull out a gun or a knife. She half turned, her hands flying up to protect her face.

'Here.' The rolled sheet of paper Lee was holding towards her was such an anticlimax that she almost laughed, until she saw the ferocious intensity in his eyes.

It was a head-and-shoulders sketch of her. The face was partly concealed by a curtain of hair, the lips parted and curving into the beginnings of a smile, the wide dark eyes slightly startled. The fingers of one hand fluttered tentatively against the bare, white collarbone.

'That's how you looked after the first time we made love.' Lee's voice was soft. 'Take a good look and tell me I never meant anything to you.'

Diane's fingers flew up in unconscious imitation of the pose. It was a drawing that spoke of infinite tenderness. Of love. Nothing could have been more at odds with the violence meted out to her by the same hands that had wrought it.

'It's beautiful.' She couldn't prevent the whispered words. Her emotions were in turmoil; anger and revulsion warring with an almost overwhelming sense of sadness for the person Lee Smith might have been.

'It's you that's beautiful.' He reached out and touched her cheek. 'The most beautiful thing that ever happened to me. And I was a stupid enough bastard to let myself blow it.'

She turned her head away. As she did so, she caught a movement outside, and let out a small, involuntary gasp of shock. A uniformed police officer was standing by the patio door, his finger held to his lips in belated warning.

For an instant, Lee froze. Then he spun round, the colour draining from his face.

'Police. Stay where you are,' the man shouted as he threw himself into the room.

Lee's gaze swung back to Diane, his expression unfathomable. Then, shoving her aside, he made a dash for the hall.

'Stay here.' The policeman pushed past her.

Diane ignored him.

'What's happening?' Agnes was clinging to the banister at the top of the stairs, her eyes wide with fright.

The policeman made a dive at Lee as he threw open the front door, cursing as, younger and more agile, Lee swerved away from his tackle.

'It's OK,' Diane shouted after the man. 'He didn't . . .' But her words were hurled away on the wind as he sprinted off after Lee into the darkness.

'Diane?' Agnes called querulously. 'Are you all right?'

Diane hesitated; turned back towards her. As she did so, she heard the roar of a motorbike followed almost at once by the revving of a car engine.

'Go back to bed, Mum,' she shouted over her shoulder as she ran out of the house. 'Quickly, before you . . .'

There was a sudden screech of brakes. A split second later came a deafening, splintering crash. The moment of utter silence that followed it seemed to go on for ever. Her hand pressed to her mouth, Diane raced down the drive towards the road.

The police car was slewed half in the drive, half on the pavement, the driver's door hanging open. Lee's motorbike was on its side in the hedge, its engine still running.

A second policeman was on his knees, bending over Lee. He looked up, his face grey and impossibly young in the orange glow of the streetlight as Diane reached them. 'I was just trying to cut him off. Stop him getting away. The stupid bastard didn't even brake.'

Lee's arms were flung wide, one of his legs bent under him at an impossible angle. His dark hair fanned out across the kerb. Except there seemed to be too much of it. It seemed too long. It took Diane a moment to realise that the spreading stain was blood. She looked down into his wide, sightless eyes and felt a sob gathering in her chest.

The officer who had given chase was speaking rapidly into his mobile. After a while, the younger man pulled himself to his feet. 'Go back into the house,' he said, his voice still unsteady.

Diane didn't move. A gust of wind lifted a stray strand of

Lee's fringe and it danced back from his forehead, shocking against the utter stillness of his face.

'Are you OK?' The voice seemed to be coming from a distance.

She nodded. It felt as if her chest was being crushed. She concentrated on sucking the cool night air into her lungs. In, out. In, out.

'You're safe now.' She felt the man's hand on her shoulder.

The trees cast weird shadows across Lee's body. Like prison bars. He would have spotted the imagery in that.

'Safe,' she repeated, and began to shake.

Malcolm got back as the ambulance was pulling up. A second police car had already arrived at the scene; the younger officer was sitting in the back of it, his head in his hands.

'What's happened?' Malcolm ran towards Diane. 'Is it your . . .?' The question died on his lips. He gazed down at Lee Smith's body. 'Jesus Christ! What the hell's going on?'

'Let's have some room here, please.' The ambulancemen pushed him to one side and knelt down on the kerb.

The older officer established Malcolm's identity, and explained briefly what had happened. 'Fortunately, the lady's mother had the good sense to ring the police when she heard screams . . .'

'Oh my God.' Malcolm gripped Diane's hands, his face frantic. 'Are you all right?'

'Yes.' Diane closed her eyes as a wave of nausea swept over her, and knew she wasn't.

'It might be better if you took your wife back into the house, sir. Someone will be along shortly to take statements.'

Diane felt Malcolm's strong arm around her waist. Leaning against him, she allowed him to take her weight as he led her away, grateful for his support; knowing that without it, she would have fallen. She glanced back once as they neared the front door. Lee's face had already been covered with a blanket.

Another officer was attempting to deal with Agnes. She was at the bottom of the stairs, clutching the handrail and refusing to go anywhere until she had satisfied herself that Diane was safe. 'I heard you scream.' She stumbled forward into Diane's arms, her teeth chattering. 'I didn't know what to . . .'

'I'm fine.' Absently, Diane patted her mother's shoulder as she mumbled the meaningless words. 'Everything's fine.'

'You did absolutely the right thing, Agnes.' Malcolm prised her arms gently from Diane's neck and murmured under his breath, 'Will you be OK for a minute, while I help him get her back into bed?'

Diane nodded. Even such a simple movement took an enormous effort of will.

The policeman looked relieved. 'SOCO will be along in a while, so don't touch anything, please.' He took Agnes's arm. 'Come on then, ducks. Let's get you back upstairs.'

'Get your hands off me.' Agnes jerked herself free.

With a supreme effort, Diane steadied herself against the door frame.

'He's here to help, Mum. Malcolm will go up with you. You're going to catch your death of cold down here. I'll go and make you a hot . . .' She took a step into the hall, then clutched Malcolm's arm as the floor tilted up to meet her.

He put his hand under her elbow to steady her. 'Are you sure you're all right?'

'Yes.' She forced a shaky smile. 'I'll be fine. You see to Mum.'

She stood quite still in the middle of the hall until they had disappeared onto the landing. Then she made her way slowly into the living-room, her hand against the wall for balance. Lee's drawing lay on the carpet where he'd dropped it, one corner lifting and falling in the draught from the still-open patio door, as if it had a life of its own. Carefully, she bent down and picked it up. Above her, she could hear Malcolm's gentle murmurs as he coaxed Agnes back into her bed. She gazed into her own wide, astonished eyes and ran her fingers over the paper, tracing the deft pencil strokes that had so tenderly captured that freeze-framed moment in time. Then, clenching her jaw so hard it ached, she tore the sketch into tiny pieces and, stepping out into the darkness of the garden, scattered them to the wind.

31

Baker turned up first thing the following morning. Diane was still in bed. The nausea of the previous evening had barely receded during the sleepless night.

'Can't this wait?' She heard Malcolm's irritable voice in the hall below as he opened the front door. 'We didn't get to bed until nearly midnight.'

She couldn't catch Baker's reply. She heard him come in, and the front door closing. There was a muted exchange between the two of them, cut off as they moved into the kitchen. Wearily, she got out of bed and pulled on a dressing-gown. She went through to the bathroom and splashed some water onto her face in an effort to dispel the fog that seemed to fill her brain. She glanced at herself in the mirror and hardly recognised the gaunt, grey-skinned face that gazed back. She put her head round her mother's door before she went down-stairs. Agnes was sleeping peacefully, her breathing less noisy, her skin a more healthy colour. Her forehead, when Diane touched it, was cool.

Baker stood up as Diane came into the kitchen; an unusual act of courtesy that alarmed her.

Malcolm fussed around her, pulling out a chair for her and pouring coffee. 'I was just going to come up and get you.' He shot Baker a look. 'I said you were resting, but apparently it's important.'

284

Baker resumed his seat. 'I apologise for disturbing you, Mrs Middleton, but I'm afraid this couldn't wait.'

Malcolm exhaled sharply. 'The officers who were here last night took down every conceivable detail. The bloody living-room's covered in fingerprint dust. I can't see why you have to . . .'

'This isn't about last night. Not directly.' Baker's face was grave as he looked at Diane. 'I'm afraid you should prepare yourself for a shock.'

Malcolm let out a short bark of laughter. 'Christ Almighty! How many more shocks can there be?'

Baker's attention was still on Diane. 'The forensic reports have confirmed that the body found at Corley Moor was that of your brother.'

'I see.' Diane swallowed. It was the moment she'd been dreading. She was surprised it didn't hurt more. In a way, it was almost a relief.

Malcolm came and stood behind her, his hand on her shoulder. There was still a trace of irritation in his voice as he said, 'I don't think there was ever much doubt, was there?'

'Please let me finish, Mr Middleton. The examination further revealed that Mr Somerford hadn't committed sui-cide.' Baker paused to allow the words to sink in. 'He was murdered.'

Diane felt strangely calm. Of course Ian had been mur-dered. He was innocent. How could she ever have thought otherwise?

'Murdered?' Malcolm had slumped down onto a chair, his face ashen. 'I don't understand.'

'Without going into too much medical detail, it seems that the pressure on Mr Somerford's neck could not have been self-inflicted. He was apparently strangled manually, in much the same way as Mrs Somerford. His body was then suspended from the tree at a later time – the pathologist's findings suggest within an hour or so of his death – in an effort to make it appear that he had taken his own life.'

'How long . . .?' Malcolm cleared his throat. 'When did it happen?'

Baker fingered his moustache as if to check it was still there. 'It's impossible to pinpoint the exact time of death, but I think it's logical to assume Mr Somerford's death was part of the same attack as the other murders.'

Diane gazed at him as she tried to absorb the detail of what he was saying. 'But you told us he'd been caught on camera . . .'

'I told you his car had been caught. It's the registration the speed cameras pick up, not the driver.' Baker looked slightly uncomfortable as he added, 'Naturally, this new evidence puts matters into an entirely different perspective.'

'Oh, Jesus.' Malcolm put his hands over his face. 'I just . . .' he shook his head. 'I'm sorry. I can't take any of this in.'

'I realise this has come as an enormous shock to you both, sir.' Baker allowed a respectful pause and then went on, 'Clearly, we shall have to review the entire investigation. We need to try to establish if there's anyone who might have a possible motive.' He looked at Diane, as if expecting her to speak. When she remained silent, he said, 'I see from the statement you made last night that Smith made mention of your brother's death.'

She recalled the urgency in Lee's face the previous night, his insistence that he hadn't been behind the hate campaign against Ian. Could that be the reason why he'd risked breaking his bail conditions to come and see her? Had his apparent sincerity been no more than an act? She'd been prepared to believe he'd played a part in his own wife's death. But Ian? Angelika? She recalled the horror in his face as he'd talked about the children's murders. Could he really have been so cynical? So good an actor? Unconsciously, she shook her head. It didn't begin to make any sort of sense.

She realised that Malcolm was gazing at her. For a second, their eyes met. 'Only to say he'd had nothing to do with it,' she murmured.

'And you believed him?'

She ran her hands down her face, tried to think. All she could see was Lee's pleading eyes. 'I don't know.'

'The man had just forced his way into our house, Inspector. My wife was hardly in any state to be making rational judgements.'

'Indeed.'

Malcolm frowned. 'Let me get this straight. Are you saying you think Lee Smith could have . . .?'

'I'm not saying anything, Mr Middleton. Just exploring every avenue.' Baker flicked through his notebook before looking up and asking, 'Do you happen to know if your brother-in-law had any enemies? Business rivals, possibly?'

Malcolm looked startled. 'What are you talking about?'

'Such things have happened in the past.'

Malcolm gave an incredulous half-laugh. 'This isn't the East End of London.'

Diane still felt as if her brain had been replaced by some nebulous substance that refused to coalesce. She forced herself to concentrate. 'There's the information my mother picked up from Angelika's gym. I don't know how relevant . . .'

'DC Collingwood made out a report, which will be followed up in due course.' Baker gave the ghost of a smile as he added,

'Although I'd be grateful if you could persuade your mother to leave the police work to us, in future.'

'She was closer to the mark than any of us.' Diane's flicker of anger was short-lived; she'd been hardly less dismissive herself of Agnes's dogged efforts to prove Ian's innocence. Her voice wavered as she added, 'At least she never accepted the evidence at face value.'

Malcolm put his hand over hers. 'My mother-in-law is ill.' His tone was cool. 'Hopefully, by the time she's sufficiently back on her feet to get in your way, you and your colleagues will have some idea of just what the hell is going on. Because at the moment it seems to me you're doing nothing more than shooting in the dark.'

'I'm sorry to hear she's unwell, sir.' Baker snapped his notebook shut. 'I don't think there's anything else I need trouble you with for the time being. So unless you have any questions . . .?'

'Where's Tracey Collingwood?' Diane asked. She was surprised, now she thought about it, that Baker had come alone to break the news. Sensitivity wasn't exactly his forte.

'DC Collingwood is no longer part of the investigation team.' Baker's face was closed.

Malcolm frowned. 'Why?'

'I don't think that need be any of your concern, sir.'

Diane was stung by the man's bland dismissiveness. 'She's practically lived here for the last few weeks. She's become more than just a police officer to us. She's become a friend.' She realised, as she spoke the words, how much she meant them.

Baker gave her a small, patronising smile. 'That's precisely the problem, I'm afraid.'

'Meaning what, exactly?' Malcolm demanded sharply.

'I understand a card with her home phone number was recovered from the scene last night.'

'She'd left it when she called round earlier in the day.' Diane wondered what he was getting at. 'She said if I was worried about anything . . .'

Baker shook his head, his gingery eyebrows drawn into a frown. 'It's lucky your mother had the good sense to ring the emergency services. Which you would have been much better advised to do in the first place, instead of relying on the support of one individual officer.'

'It's easy to say that with hindsight,' Malcolm snapped. 'I think that in similar circumstances, most of us might be tempted to try to get through to someone we knew, with the emergency services as unreliable as they are frequently reported to be in the local papers.'

Baker didn't rise to the bait. 'It's felt that DC Collingwood has become too personally involved in the inquiry.'

'Maybe she just thought a family liaison officer's job extended beyond office hours,' Malcolm retorted, but Diane could see he was wasting his breath.

'The matter's out of my hands, I'm afraid.' Baker got to his feet. It was clear from his tone that the subject had gone as far as it was going. 'Please contact the incident room if anything occurs to you.' He gave Malcolm a frosty smile. 'I can assure you we'll keep you informed of any developments. And there may be a few more questions about last night's incident. There'll be an internal inquiry into the circumstances of Smith's death.'

Malcolm looked as if he would have liked to say more, but, after a fractional hesitation, he shook the hand Baker had extended to him.

What were they doing, sniping at each other, bickering

about who was on the case and who wasn't, when somewhere out there, Ian's killer, walked free? It was only as Malcolm was seeing Baker out into the hall that the reality of the situation hit Diane full force.

'Would he have suffered?' she blurted out.

Malcolm swung round.

'Ian,' she said, but not before she'd caught the flash of resentment in his face, and realised he thought she'd been talking about Lee Smith. 'Would he have felt any pain?'

Baker's sharp expression told her that he'd caught it too. His gaze travelled speculatively from one of them to the other before he said quietly, 'I'm sorry, Mrs Middleton, I'm not a pathologist. I'm just a copper.'

Once the facts of Ian's death were made public, life for Diane and Malcolm became a repeat performance of the days following the murders at Arden Hall. The press took up residence again, intrigued both by the unexpected twist in what had been deemed a straightforward scenario, and the discovery that the motorcyclist killed on the Kenilworth Road in a police pursuit was none other than Nicola Smith's young widower. Every sort of speculation appeared in the papers over the following days, the flames of prurient curiosity fanned by the additional news of Lee Smith's court appearance on the day of his death. The tabloids were having a field-day. The phone rang non-stop again. After a few hours, Malcolm unplugged it at the wall; there was no call to wait for, this time, and no Tracey Collingwood to answer it. A replacement Family Liaison Officer had called round; a softly spoken, pleasant enough young DS. But as both Diane and Malcolm had made it clear that they didn't want another stranger in the house, he hadn't stayed long, and hadn't reappeared.

Another wave of cards and flowers arrived, including a massive bouquet of roses from Chas and Lorraine Newbould. The attached card invited Malcolm and Diane to get away from it all by spending a week with them in their villa in Lanzarote. As if the simple act of getting on a plane could put the nightmare behind them. Diane found their insensitivity astounding. She couldn't think of any couple she would less like to spend a week with, but for the sake of the company she knew she had to be polite. She was grateful that she could use Agnes as a legitimate excuse when she sent a brief note to refuse the offer.

As the days passed, Agnes started gradually to return to health, although the chest infection had left her weak and easily tired, so that she spent most of her time in bed. She'd taken the news of Ian's murder with fortitude; but then it was only what she'd known all along. She wanted to know what the police were doing, but as no one had been in touch apart from the would-be replacement Family Liaison Officer, there wasn't much to tell.

As Agnes grew stronger, so Diane seemed to become weaker. The mere act of getting out of bed was a mammoth task for which she had to summon up every available ounce of determination. Nausea made eating impossible. Malcolm brought her strawberries, smoked salmon, all her favourite foods, but just the smell was enough to make her stomach heave. She tried to conceal the fact, attempted to carry on as normal, but she felt utterly exhausted, as if her limbs were made of lead. All she wanted to do was to sleep. It was her body's way of dealing with stress, David Fawcett reassured them both, when Malcolm insisted on her having a check-up. There were only so many shocks the mind could take.

'Leave that.' Malcolm came back into the kitchen when he'd

shown Fawcett out. He took from Diane's hand the potato peeler she'd just picked up. 'You heard what the man said. Sit down. I'll see to dinner.'

'I'm OK. Really.' His kindness touched her, but it also filled her with a growing sense of claustrophobia. 'I've got to do something, or I'll go mad.' She tempered the sharpness of her voice with a half-laugh, but she could see it didn't fool him for a minute.

'I've been thinking. Why don't you get in touch with Tracey Collingwood?'

'What for?' Diane looked at him in surprise. 'She's not even on the case any more.'

'That doesn't stop her talking to you, does it?'

'It was because of me she was dropped. I should think I'd be the last person she'd want to talk to.'

'You don't know that.' He bent down to take some potatoes from the vegetable rack, his back to her. 'You always seemed to get on pretty well together.'

Diane nodded. The idea of Tracey Collingwood's un-demanding company was appealing. She'd spoken to no one other than Malcolm and her mother for days, and there were so many dangerous subjects; so many paths best left untrodden.

'We should at least see how she's getting on.' He looked round at her. 'Didn't you put her home number into your phone? Why don't you give her a ring?'

He was trying to sound casual, but it was plain he was anxious to get things in motion before Diane changed her mind. It made her realise just how much her lethargy must be worrying him.

The phone was answered so quickly that Diane wondered if Tracey Collingwood had been waiting for another call, but she sounded pleased when she realised who it was.

'I've been wondering how you were getting on,' she said. 'I heard what had happened with Lee Smith. Jesus. Are you OK?'

'Not too bad.' Diane tried to inject some life into her voice. 'Mum's a lot better, thank God.' She looked back over her shoulder into the kitchen, where Malcolm was inexpertly chopping carrots. 'And Malcolm's being brilliant.'

He turned towards her and smiled.

'Good.' Collingwood sounded as if she meant it.

'Inspector Baker told us you'd been taken off the case.' Diane wasn't sure whether she should mention it. 'I'm so sorry.'

'Ah, well.' Collingwood sounded philosophical. There was a pause, and then she added, 'So you were right. About your brother, I mean. I feel we all owe you an apology.'

Diane felt a wave of warmth towards the other woman; she couldn't imagine Baker admitting a mistake. 'We were wondering if you might like to come round for a drink this evening.'

There was another, longer pause before Tracey Collingwood answered, 'Yes, why not? That would be good.'

'Are you sure that's OK? I don't want to put you in a difficult position, or anything.'

'Difficult positions are my bread and butter.' Diane could hear the smile in Tracey Collingwood's voice. 'I wouldn't be in the bloody job I'm in, if they weren't.'

Diane was relieved that Doris Crombie had already arranged to come over to visit Agnes that evening; she wouldn't have wanted to hurt her mother's feelings, but neither would she have relished the prospect of Agnes bombarding Tracey Collingwood with questions the policewoman was no longer in any position to answer.

Malcolm was very quiet during dinner. Diane pushed her food round her plate and was grateful that for once he didn't seem to have noticed how little she'd eaten. It wasn't until Doris Crombie had arrived and the two women had been settled upstairs in Agnes's room with a tray of coffee and cakes and the portable television that he said tentatively, 'There are a couple of ideas I thought I might bounce off Tracey Colling-wood, while she's here.'

There was something uncharacteristically evasive in his expression. Diane put down her coffee cup and gave him her full attention. 'What sort of ideas?' she asked warily.

Malcolm hesitated. 'That stuff your mother found out. About Angelika . . .'

She'd half expected him to bring it up after Baker's visit. She tried not to sound defensive as she said, 'Look, I know you thought it was irrelevant at the time, but as things have turned out . . .'

'No. You don't understand. I think it might be extremely relevant. It's just that I'm not sure Baker's going to trust my motivation.' His eyes slid from hers. 'And I'm not sure you will, either. Which is why I thought it might be a good idea to run it past someone neutral, as it were, before I say anything to him.' He picked up his cup and replaced it on its saucer in exactly the same position it had been before. 'I just don't want you getting upset.'

Diane stared at him in alarm. 'What are you talking about?'

He got to his feet and poured himself a glass of wine. 'Do you want one?'

She shook her head. 'What do you mean, you don't want to upset me? You don't have to treat me as if I'm a child.'

'No.' He sighed. 'No, of course not.' He sat down again and took a deep swig of the wine before he went on. 'Those files

Val sent over from the office yesterday afternoon. They were old personnel records.'

'And?'

'Did you know Lee Smith worked at Somerford's for a while?'

She could feel her cheeks reddening; it was the first time either of them had mentioned his name since Baker's visit. 'Yes, I think he mentioned it once,' she said as casually as she could. 'Why?'

Malcolm put the glass down and took her hand, his expression earnest. 'I don't want the police to think I'm just trying to be vindictive, and God knows, that's how it's going to sound. But I've gone over and over it in my head, and everything seems to fit. Well, not everything exactly, but enough to make me wonder . . .' He broke off, chewing his lip as if uncertain whether he should continue.

'Go on.' Diane didn't have the first idea what he was talking about, but she could see it was something important to him.

He was gazing down at his hand, still encasing her own. 'This might sound like complete insanity, but . . .' The door-bell rang. 'Damn.' His expression suggested an entirely opposite sentiment as he got hastily to his feet. 'That'll be her, I expect.'

Diane caught his sleeve. 'She can wait. Just tell me what all this is about.'

Malcolm's hand hovered over the door handle; she'd never seen him look so indecisive.

When at last he spoke, the words came out in a rush. He didn't meet her eyes as he blurted out, 'I think it could have been Lee Smith who was Angelika's lover. And if I'm right, I think he could have been her killer too.'

32

Diane could hardly keep her impatience in check. Malcolm had dropped his bombshell and shot out of the room, to return a couple of minutes later with Tracey Collingwood. Without making herself look a complete lunatic, she knew she had at least to wait until they'd gone through the pleasantries before she asked him what the hell he'd been talking about.

'I'm not even sure what we should call you, as you're not here in a professional capacity,' Malcolm said as he handed the woman a glass of wine. 'DC Collingwood sounds a bit formal.' He'd switched into jovial host mode as soon as she'd arrived. It was almost convincing, apart from the small tic beneath his eye.

'Tracey's fine by me.' Tracey Collingwood pointed to the top of her head and pulled a wry face. 'See? No flashing blue light, tonight.' Her expression became more serious as she turned towards Diane. 'How are you doing?'

She didn't say Diane looked terrible; she didn't need to. Her face said it for her.

'Fine,' Diane answered tersely, wondering how long Malcolm was intending to allow the excruciating social foreplay to continue.

'The last few weeks have been a huge ordeal.' He put his arm around her shoulder. 'Which is why we wanted to thank you for all your support while you were here.'

'Thanks.' Tracey looked mildly surprised.

'Take a seat.' Diane moved away from him, and sat down herself. The weight of his arm had been slight, the gesture meant only to reassure, she knew, but in her present agitated state it had seemed restrictive; oppressive, almost.

'Any idea whether Baker's team is making any progress?' Malcolm rubbed the side of his face and the tic disappeared behind his hand.

'For God's sake, Malcolm. Just get on with it.' Diane's voice was sharper than she'd intended. Her own hand was shaking as she picked up the glass of mineral water he'd put on the side table for her and took a sip.

Tracey looked at them warily. 'What?'

Malcolm looked embarrassed. There was reproach in the glance he shot Diane as he sat down and said, 'I wasn't intending to bring the matter up quite so soon in the conversation. And I know you're not really the right person to be talking to . . .'

Tracey gave a small frown. 'Listen, if this has anything to do with the case, then no, I'm not.'

'No, no I realise that. And the last thing I want to do is put you in a compromising position.' Malcolm cleared his throat. 'It's only a hypothesis at this stage, anyway.'

'Sorry. I'm not with you.'

'Malcolm seems to think Lee Smith and Angelika were having an affair,' Diane said tightly.

Tracey wasn't as good as her boss at being inscrutable; an expression Diane couldn't quite read flashed across her eyes before she said neutrally, 'If you've got any information, it's Bill Baker you should be giving it to.'

'I know. It's just that I can't help thinking he would simply write it off.' Malcolm leant forward in his chair. 'All I want you to do is hear me out. Tell me whether you think I'm being completely off the wall.'

Tracey hesitated for a moment, then shrugged. 'I can't stop you talking, I suppose. But don't expect me to be able to do anything, because I can't.'

'No, I appreciate that.'

'So what makes you think they were having an affair?'

'OK.' Malcolm ran his hand over his face again. 'Well, Lee Smith worked for the firm for a while a couple of years ago. You probably know that already, from your investigations into his wife's death. We wouldn't usually keep records of casual labourers, but Smith apparently had a set-to with one of the foremen.'

'Figures,' Tracey murmured.

'Yes, I suppose it does, with a temper like his.' Malcolm glanced anxiously at Diane. 'Anyway, he was sacked on the spot. There's a report on the file.'

'So what's any of this got to do with Angelika?'

'He was working on the conversion at Arden Hall at the time. Angelika supervised every last brick that was laid on that project, you know that as well as I do; she nearly drove everyone mad. She and Smith would have been bound to come across each other. Yet to my knowledge she never mentioned the fact. Don't you think that's a bit odd?'

'Why didn't you say any of this before?' Diane's heart felt as if it was beating too quickly in her chest. Lee had never mentioned it either. Which was odder. She recalled how he'd made a point of telling her how he'd had to go through Nicola's address book to find out where Ian lived.

'I only found out myself yesterday. And you've seemed so distracted, lately . . .'

'The fact that he'd met her doesn't mean he killed her.' Tracey Collingwood; the cool voice of reason.

'I realise that.' Malcolm hesitated, then went on quickly, 'But if it was him, it would explain why Ian's car was being driven backwards and forwards on the night of the murders, wouldn't it? Smith could hardly have got Ian's body from Arden Hall to Corley on the back of his motorbike.'

'Why Corley?' Tracey glanced at Diane, as if weighing her next words carefully. 'Did Smith have any links with the place that you know of?' she asked at last. 'Would he have known you had a place over there?'

Diane could feel herself colouring. She heard Malcolm's sharp intake of breath as she murmured, 'He could have done.' She forced herself to look at him. 'He never went there, to my knowledge, but he knew of its existence. But I don't see why he'd want to take Ian's body there.'

Malcolm's jaw had tightened. 'I'm not trying to make out I've got all the answers,' he said stiffly. He turned back to Tracey Collingwood. 'I realise it all sounds a bit tenuous. It's just that there are lots of bits that start to fit, when you look at them together. There's all that stuff about him being with his grandfather all day. Everyone assumed he tried to set that up so he could deny he'd been with Diane. But what if he was trying to provide himself with an alibi for something else altogether?'

'It doesn't make sense.' Diane wished she could just agree with Malcolm's theory, instead of challenging it. But she couldn't. She could feel the flush spreading across her face again as she added, 'Why get involved with me at all, when all it was going to do was to draw attention to him?'

Malcolm had clearly already given the subject some thought. 'What if he was manipulating you from the start?

You were with Ian when he called at the house on the morning after Nicola Smith's death, right?'

'Yes,' she said uneasily. 'You know I was.'

'So he must have seen your car. Yet when you gave him a lift home in it a couple of weeks later he reckoned he didn't know who you were.' There was a glint of triumph in Malcolm's eyes. 'Does *that* make sense?'

'It's a VW Polo, for God's sake, not an Aston Martin!' Sheer logic forced her to play devil's advocate, although she knew it would only annoy him further. 'There must be thousands of the damned things. Do you really imagine . . .?'

'Yes, I do. I think he knew exactly what he was doing when he asked you in that first time. He deliberately set out to get close to you so that he could find out whether Ian suspected anything. It seems pretty obvious to me.' An angry red flush was beginning to spread up from Malcolm's collar. 'I can't see why you're so keen to defend him all of a sudden.'

So that was what it was all about. Intermingled with her compassion for Malcolm, for his need to find an excuse for her infidelity, Diane felt an irrational stab of irritation that after everything that had happened, he was still jealous.

'I'm not defending him. I'm just trying to be rational.' She looked away from him, to Tracey Collingwood, half expecting her to tell him, in her usual diplomatic way, that he was talking nonsense. But Tracey was studying him intently, her head on one side, her eyes narrowed in concentration.

'You say you've got documentary proof Smith was employed at Arden Hall?'

'Yes.' Malcolm half rose. 'It's in the study. I can get it, if you . . .'

She shook her head. 'Talk to Bill Baker about it.'

Diane was unnerved by the other woman's reaction. 'You really think it makes any sort of sense?'

Tracey looked faintly embarrassed. 'What I think doesn't matter. I'm not on the case.'

'You don't think he's going to find it all a bit . . . flimsy?' Diane pressed. She glanced at Malcolm and added with a half-laugh aimed to take the sting from the words, 'We didn't exactly part on the best of terms, last time he was here. I got the impression he wasn't that keen on other people doing his job for him.'

'Maybe he should be the judge of that.' Tracey gave her a thin smile. 'I know his bedside manner can leave a bit to be desired, but he's a pretty good copper. He's not one to let personal feelings get in the way of the facts.'

'Maybe I'll give him a ring in the morning.' There was more than a hint of resentment in Malcolm's voice as he caught Diane's eye and added, 'As long as you don't think I shall be making a complete fool of myself.'

Tracey glanced at each of them and said cautiously, 'Let's just say there's some . . . convergence between your thought processes and his own. I can't tell you anything else, it's more than my job's worth. But talk to him.' She got to her feet. 'Look, maybe I should be off.' She hadn't touched the wine.

'I'm sorry.' Malcolm stood up too. 'I've put you in a difficult position. And now I feel I've hijacked your friendship with Diane. I don't want you to think that was why we invited you over. At least finish your drink.'

'Well . . .' Tracey looked undecided.

Diane's head was pounding. It was obvious from what the other woman had intimated that Malcolm's hypothesis wasn't as crazy, or as biased, as it had seemed to her. Was it really possible that Lee Smith could be behind all the murders? Had he been fooling her all along, as he must have been fooling so many others? 'Please don't go yet,' she murmured.

'OK.' Tracey looked up at Malcolm as she sat down again. 'A coffee would be good, if you're making one.'

It was so graceful a dismissal that, without being rude, he had no option but to comply.

'A lot for you to take in,' she said quietly when he'd left the room.

Diane watched the bubbles spiral lazily up to the surface of her glass of mineral water and said in a low voice, 'You really think Lee did it, then?'

'You know I can't answer that.'

'I'm not asking you as a police officer.'

Tracey regarded her in silence, then stood up and closed the door Malcolm had left open. 'I think it's possible,' she said quietly. 'He was a pretty violent character. You of all people know that.'

'Violent enough to commit murder?'

'Someone killed them, Diane.'

'I know. It's just . . .' Diane shook her head. 'First everything was pinned on Ian. Now it's Lee. It just seems too . . . easy.'

Tracey had picked up the implied recrimination. 'Even you have to admit Ian was the obvious suspect. Everyone, me included, thought it was an open and shut case, even if there were a few question marks over some of the details. He'd made a run for it, possibly with your help, or he'd committed suicide – either way, we weren't looking for anyone else, until the forensic came through. Then it was back to square one.'

'So now you go for someone else who's dead and can't defend himself.'

'That isn't the way it works, and you know it.' Tracey sighed. 'Look, I shouldn't be telling you any of this. Colin Butcher – I think he sat in on one of your interviews?'

Diane nodded.

'Well, Colin and I are good mates. In fact, he was fairly pissed off when Baker dropped me from the case. So he's kept me up to speed with what's going on. Now obviously, the fact that Ian had been murdered put everything on its head. All the evidence has been gone through again with a fine-tooth comb.' She paused, then said quickly, 'It now seems certain that Angelika was seeing someone, and it also seems more than likely it was her, not Ian, who was paying off Nicola Smith. If . . .'

Diane cut her short. She'd picked up immediately on the other woman's choice of words. 'Paying off?'

'Look, I've said more than I should already. Can we change the subject?' Tracey picked up her glass and took a sip of her wine. 'Have you seen Thomas again yet?'

Diane was still trying to read the other woman's face for clues; trying to get her head round the implications of what Tracey had let out. Paying Nicola off for what? Could she have found out about the affair? Or had Nicola and Lee been in it together; targeting a rich, bored housewife with the specific aim of blackmailing her? Diane's imagination plunged ahead. If so, had he pushed Nicola from the balcony because something had gone wrong? She felt a cold prickle in the nape of her neck. Was it possible he'd come on to her the night of Nicola's funeral because she was his next victim? The next dissatisfied, over-privileged target on his hit list?

'Diane?' Tracey reached out and touched her arm.

'Sorry?' She shook her head, trying to control the jumble of half-answered questions that were skittering around her brain like rats in a maze.

'It doesn't matter.' Tracey's face was full of concern. 'Look, tell me to mind my own business if you want to, but Lee Smith tried to get round you when he came here that last time, didn't he?'

Diane's eyes slid away from her. 'What do you mean?'

'It's what they do.' Tracey's voice was gentle. 'Make out they're sorry. Tell you it'll never happen again.' Her expression hardened. Diane knew it wasn't Lee she was thinking of as she added harshly, 'Try to worm their way back in so that it can happen all over again.'

'It wasn't like that.' Diane looked away from the bitterness in the other woman's face. Maybe that was exactly what it was like.

Tracey touched her arm. 'I don't know for sure what else Lee Smith was tied up with. Not yet. But don't even start to feel sorry for him. Don't turn him into some kind of romantic hero just because he's dead.'

Diane could think of nothing to say. She wasn't even sure there was anything she wanted to say.

From the kitchen came the sound of cupboards being opened. An unnecessary clatter of plates signalled Malcolm's irritation at being excluded from the conversation.

'Malcolm seems like a nice guy. And take it from one who knows, nice guys are pretty thin on the ground.' Tracey flashed her a small, wry smile. 'Like I say, it's none of my business, but just don't let a bastard like Lee Smith get between you.'

'He's already between us, isn't he?' Diane said flatly. And knew with absolute, despairing certainty that whatever either of them did, he always would be.

33

The next morning, George Bonham came round to see Diane and Malcolm with the news that a case conference was to be held at the end of the week to discuss Thomas's future.

'Gillian Cooper has made the recommendation that he be placed in your care as soon as possible,' George explained. 'Someone from Social Services will want to check out your accommodation and so forth, as he's still technically in their care, but my understanding is that if everything goes smoothly, the application for a care order will be withdrawn. Then, in due course, we can begin the adoption process. Angelika's mother has made it abundantly clear that she wants nothing to do with him.' George shook his head sadly. 'The wretched woman's only interest is in how much she's likely to inherit, which will be nothing, I'm glad to say, as Angelika predeceased Ian. That's something else we shall need to discuss at some stage, by the way.'

Malcolm shook his head impatiently. 'For God's sake, George. Not now. It's hardly the appropriate time to be thinking about probate.'

'No.' George pushed his glasses up on his nose. 'No, of course.' He turned towards one then the other. 'Gillian Cooper's keen for you to resume contact with Thomas as soon as possible. And now that there's no danger of his safety being compromised by his coming here . . .'

'You mean now there's no chance of Ian appearing out of thin air to snatch him.' Malcolm's voice was cool; he seemed less pleased by the prospect of having Thomas back in their care than Diane would have expected. He'd been distant ever since Tracey Collingwood had left; disinclined to continue the conversation he'd seemed so keen to air. Diane knew she'd angered him with what he saw as her defence of Lee Smith. Were things becoming so bad between the two of them again that he no longer wanted the tie of a child to bind them together?

George cleared his throat. 'Thomas's foster-mother is happy for you to have him for a couple of hours this morning, if you want to. I thought it might do you both good. Cheer Agnes up too.' Again, his glance travelled between them. 'If you all feel up to it, of course. No one wants to rush things.'

Malcolm's eyes were fixed on the steeple he'd made of his fingers. He pressed each pad in turn against its opposite number, as if making a mental tally. Then he said slowly, 'It'll have to be this afternoon, George. I've got an appointment with DI Baker at eleven.' His eyes darted to Diane's face. 'I was rather hoping you might come with me.'

It felt like some sort of an ultimatum; a test of her loyalty. Diane experienced a flash of angry resentment. Was that how it was going to be? Was Thomas to be used as a bargaining tool? Acquiesce to Lee Smith's guilt, and she would be allowed to play happy families?

Unfair, she rebuked herself. How could she expect Malcolm to bring up Ian's child as his own, if she appeared to be harbouring sympathy for the ex-lover who could in time turn out to be the killer of that child's father? She asked herself how she would be reacting, had their roles been reversed; tried and failed to imagine Malcolm betraying her as she had so horribly betrayed him. Would she have been prepared to forgive him, been willing to make a fresh start? It wasn't a question she cared to ask herself.

Malcolm was still watching her.

She gave him a tentative smile before she said quietly, 'There's something important we need to sort out first, George.'

They were taken straight up to Baker's office when they arrived at Little Park Street. Diane looked round at the files, the books, the tables of figures Blu-Tacked to the walls. The photograph of the children had been replaced by two new ones: each child in a bright blue sweatshirt bearing the legend *Allesley Hall Primary School*. She visualised Baker on his day off, mowing a pocket-handkerchief of geranium-edged lawn outside one of the neat semis in the rabbit-warren that made up the hilly, sprawling estate of Allesley Park. Out there with all the other teachers and office workers and small business owners, cleaning his car, taking the kids for a ride on their bicycles in the park that gave the area its name. She thought of him going home after work, wondering what his wife was cooking for his tea as he negotiated the ring road, the Butts, the Allesley Old Road, the steep hill of Winsford Avenue. She might have overtaken him as she drove to one of her art classes. Just another bloke on his way home from work. She held on to the thought as Baker gestured them both to sit down, pulled a file from the drawer of his already cluttered desk and sat, arms folded, as he waited for Malcolm to start talking.

Malcolm repeated what he had said the day before, pro-duced the report of the incident that had led to Lee Smith's dismissal.

Baker's expression remained unchanged, but his hand

strayed up to caress his moustache in a gesture that Diane had come to recognise as a sign that what was being said was of interest. Now and then, he nodded. A couple of times, his pale eyes shifted their gaze from Malcolm's face to hers, as if he were gauging her reaction. 'Thank you, Mr Middleton,' he said at last. 'That's very helpful.'

For a moment, Diane thought he was going to blank them out. The annoyance on Malcolm's face told her he thought so too.

'Anything you want to add to what your husband's told me?'

Baker's question startled her; her attention had been on Malcolm. She saw his mouth tighten slightly, but he didn't turn his face to look at her. She cleared her throat, giving herself a moment to gather her thoughts. 'No. I don't think so. Only that it seems to make sense.'

Baker looked at them both, his fingers spread out in front of him as if he were trying to come to some sort of decision. 'OK,' he said at last. 'You've laid your cards on the table, I'll do the same. The evidence we've gathered now leads us to believe that Nicola Smith was receiving money from Angelika, rather than Ian, as we initially suspected.'

Diane hadn't repeated what Tracey had told her the previous evening. She could see the disclosure had come as a shock to Malcolm, even though it only served to flesh out his theory; the tic had started up again beneath his eye. 'What evidence is that?' he demanded.

'Some of the cash points where the withdrawals were made were covered by CCTV cameras. Angelika was caught on one of them. In addition, the final withdrawal was paid back into a building society night safe the day after Nicola's death. The paying-in slip bears Angelika's signature.'

'It never occurred to you to check any of that out when Ian was the prime suspect?' Diane said sharply. She found herself irrationally riled by Baker's sudden willingness to be open with them, as if he'd finally decided they were to be trusted.

Baker looked down for an instant before he met her angry stare. 'The information would have come out in time, I can assure you. At the early stages of the inquiry, we were more concerned with establishing your brother's whereabouts.'

Malcolm rubbed his hand across his chin, his face twisting into a frown of concentration. 'But if the money was paid in so soon . . .' he said slowly.

Baker nodded. 'How would she have known Nicola was dead? It's a good question. One to which we're unlikely to receive an answer, seeing as both she and Lee Smith are also dead.'

Malcolm glanced at Diane before asking, 'So you're sure Smith and Angelika were in this together?'

'It seems pretty certain they were colluding in trying to shift the blame onto Ian.' Baker picked up a biro and tapped it against the desk to mark off each point as he spoke. 'Smith turns up on the doorstep the morning following Nicola's death, and makes the scene at the crematorium. Angelika sets up the letters to herself and to the Chief Constable, and rigs the display at Mrs Somerford Senior's birthday party . . .'

Diane stared at him in disbelief. '*Angelika?*'

'Her fingerprints were found on both the letters and on banners recovered from one of the rubbish bins at Arden Hall.'

Malcolm's hand had moved up to his mouth as the colour drained from his cheeks. 'Jesus. She had the whole thing planned? All that stuff at the party . . . Making out she was going back to the States . . .' Slowly, he shook his head from side to side, as if someone had just punched him, hard, in the face. 'That was just an *act*? Dear God, she always made out she'd had a screen test at one of the Hollywood studios, but none of us ever took her seriously.'

'But she was dead drunk, an hour or so later.' Diane remembered the way Angelika had looked, lying across the bed. The snores, the fart, the snail's trail of saliva dribbling from her open mouth. The best actress in the world couldn't have simulated that.

Baker lifted his shoulders. 'Maybe she was a loose cannon. Maybe that's why Smith decided to get rid of her, as well. As you know, we suspected all along that Angelika was expecting a visitor on the day of her death, which is why she'd given the au pair the day off, and administered drugs to the children. One theory is that she and Smith argued. Maybe she wanted the money back she'd given to Nicola. Maybe she wanted to break off with him, go back to the States as she'd threatened. Maybe Smith had the whole thing planned out in advance and had already decided she was too much of a risk. Whatever, it seems likely that Ian arrived on the scene – we know from his telephone message he was intending to go over there – and caught Smith in the act. So Smith killed him too, and then disposed of the body in such a way that everyone would assume he'd committed suicide.' Baker's face was grim. 'It's a hell of a lot of "maybes", I know. All we've got at the moment is a hell of a lot of circumstantial and not a shred of hard evidence, unfortunately.'

'How about the text message to Diane?' Malcolm asked.

'We're assuming Smith sent it at some time after Ian's death, in order to cover his tracks. But again, we can't prove it.'

'I knew it hadn't come from Ian.' Diane glared at Baker. 'I said that all along.'

Baker didn't reply. Instead, he unclipped a small sheet of

paper, heavily creased where it had been folded into quarters, from the file in front of him and pushed it across the desk. 'We found this in Smith's wallet.'

Diane knew what it was without looking. She swallowed hard, feeling her stomach begin to churn. It was the page she'd torn from her diary the day of the party. She'd still been glowing with postcoital satisfaction as she'd written down the directions. The words 'Can't wait' and the row of kisses beneath them were wavering and lopsided where she'd rested the diary against Lee's naked hip.

Malcolm picked up the paper and read it. He didn't look at Diane as he replaced it carefully on the table, face down.

'I've told you. We never went there,' she murmured. As if that made any difference.

Baker clipped the page back into the file. 'So you can confirm it was you who gave these instructions to Smith?'

'Yes,' Diane said curtly. There didn't seem any good reason to have produced it at all, other than to humiliate her.

It was as if he'd read her mind. 'Pity. We were hoping it might have come from Angelika.'

'No.' Diane looked down at her hands. Why blame Baker for her humiliation, when there was no one to blame but herself? 'I've got the diary at home. I can show you, if you want.'

'That would be useful.' Baker's tone was brisk; if he realised the embarrassment he'd caused, he didn't show it. Or, more probably, he simply didn't care.

'So the bottom line is that you think Lee Smith is the murderer, but you can't prove it?' It was Malcolm who spoke, his voice strained.

'Like I say, there's a wealth of circumstantial against Smith, but precious little else.' Baker was twirling the biro between his thumb and forefinger. When he spoke again, it was with uncharacteristic hesitancy. 'The one thing that's puzzling us more than anything else is why he would kill the rest of them but leave Thomas unharmed. Any ideas why he might have done that?'

'He said he wanted children,' Diane murmured. 'Maybe he couldn't bring himself to . . .'

Baker leant across the desk, his expression alert. 'He actually told you that?'

'He told me Nicola wouldn't let him have any.' But then he'd told her all sorts of lies. Had it just been a cheap way to gain her sympathy? Had her own desperate need for a child been so transparent?

'I recall one of your theories was that Dominica or Marshall might have witnessed the attack on Angelika.' Malcolm said. 'Maybe that was why Smith killed them. There'd have been no need to harm Thomas, would there? He was too young to have seen anything.'

Baker nodded. 'Or to say anything, at least. That's one theory.' It was clear he still had something on his mind. He put the biro down and placed both his hands flat on the table. 'Another possibility is that Smith had some kind of special affection for Thomas,' he said carefully.

Diane stared at him, bemused. 'What do you mean?'

He didn't answer the question. Instead, he turned his attention to Malcolm and asked, 'The report relating to Smith's dismissal is dated January 2002. When would Smith have started working at Arden Hall, Mr Middleton?'

'The project started in the September or October. Angelika was pushing to get it finished before Christmas.' Malcolm gave a wry smile. 'It didn't happen, of course, but . . .'

'And you think it's possible Smith and Angelika came across each other during that time?' Baker interrupted him.

'I think it's almost impossible that they didn't.'

'So there's at least a good chance that they could first have become . . . intimate at around the same time.' Baker's fingers strayed back to his moustache. It was several moments before he asked quietly, 'How old is Thomas, exactly?'

A wave of nausea swept over Diane. She could feel perspiration prickling at her hairline. 'No.' Her voice came out as no more than a whisper. She gripped the sides of her chair and tried again. 'No. Thomas is Ian's son. I know he is.'

She turned to Malcolm, watched the slow dawning of realisation before he closed his eyes.

'You see, another puzzle is why Lee Smith persisted in his attempts to see you, Mrs Middleton,' Baker pressed on. 'Even to the point of breaking his bail conditions. You said yourself he didn't threaten you, didn't attack you. Didn't even ask you to drop the charges against him.' He looked at her keenly. 'I keep asking myself, what was his motive?'

'I don't know.' Diane stared at him, thrown by the change of direction. 'He . . . he just said he wanted to say sorry.'

'He wanted to say sorry,' Baker repeated. 'That was a bit of a change of heart, wasn't it? Why do you think that was? Because he was trying to re-establish the relationship, maybe?'

Diane concentrated on her hands. She would not allow herself to believe what Baker was trying to make her believe. 'No.'

'He could hardly come forward and claim his paternity, could he? He'd have realised that as Thomas's closest surviving relative you'd be involved in his future welfare. Maybe he saw the affair with you as his only hope of keeping in touch with the little lad.'

She shook her head, close to tears. 'That's absolute rubbish.'

Baker paused. Then he said slowly, 'Of course, if Thomas's

DNA was tested, we'd be able to say once and for all whether it was rubbish.'

So that was why he'd been so keen to take them into his confidence. Diane felt another wave of nausea, so strong that she had to put her hand over her mouth to stop herself from vomiting.

For a moment, there was absolute silence. Then Malcolm's hand came down on the desk, so hard that a stack of files fell to the ground with a crash. 'That is the most obscene suggestion I've ever heard,' he said, his voice quiet with controlled rage.

Baker eyed the files but made no move to pick them up. 'It could also be the only way to establish an irrefutable link between Smith and Angelika. Which I assume you're as keen to do as we are.'

'Not if it means branding a little boy a murderer's son for the rest of his life.'

'You're planning to bring this child up as your own, aren't you?' Baker looked at Malcolm hard. 'Are you sure you're going to be able to live with that doubt? Don't you want to know?'

'No. I don't.' Malcolm's whole body was shaking. 'And you should be bloody ashamed to so much as suggest it.'

It could have been the perfect get-out for him; a more plausible means of explaining away her affair to himself than anything he'd managed to come up with, a reason for not taking Thomas on, if he was having second thoughts. And yet Malcolm's only focus was Thomas's welfare. Diane loved him more in that moment than she had ever loved him before. Tentatively, she rested her hand on his clenched fist. She felt the muscles relax. After a moment, he turned his hand palm up to hers and their fingers entwined.

'He's been part of our family for almost a year. We both held him the day he was born.' Malcolm's voice cracked and he was forced to pause as he struggled for composure. 'We love him for who he is.'

'If Thomas isn't Ian's child, we'll lose him,' Diane said, her own voice unsteady. 'We'll have no claim to him, even though we're the only family he's ever known. Please don't do this to him. Don't do it to us.'

'If it was felt to be in the public interest, we could go for a court order.' Baker's eyes strayed fleetingly to the photographs on the filing cabinet.

'What good would it do?' Diane sensed he was less comfortable with the suggestion than he was trying to make out. 'At the end of the day, what difference is it going to make to one single thing? It won't bring Ian or Angelika or the children back to life, will it? Or Nicola Smith?' She looked down at her fingers, intertwined with Malcolm's, and steeled herself to add, 'And not Lee Smith, either. He's dead, for God's sake. There's nothing more you can do to him, however much evidence you've got.'

'Diane's right.' Malcolm leant across the desk. 'What public interest would be served by ruining our lives? You can't bring a prosecution against a corpse.'

'No.' Baker's mouth twisted in anger. 'Not seeing as some clueless numpty of a uniform saw fit to run him over.'

'As far as I'm concerned, the man who ran Lee Smith down deserves a bloody medal,' Malcolm said in a low voice. 'The bastard got what was coming to him.'

'We'd have preferred to have stuck to the due process of the law.'

'Yes, well you've got your performance targets to meet, haven't you?' Malcolm jabbed his finger at the row of charts.

'I'm trying to establish the truth, Mr Middleton,' Baker replied with what sounded like an attempt at genuine apology. 'No more and no less than that.'

'We already know the truth. The only part of it that matters. Lee Smith was a murderer, and now he's dead. End of story.'

Baker sighed. 'I wish life was that simple.'

'From where I'm standing, it's just that. The bottom line is that you're never going to know exactly what happened, are you? And no amount of DNA testing is going to tell you.'

Briefly, Baker shut his eyes. He didn't disagree.

For a moment, no one spoke, then Diane said hesitantly, 'So what happens now?'

Baker bent down and began laboriously to pick up the scattered files. 'The coroner will almost certainly bring in verdicts of unlawful killing by person or persons unknown. There isn't much else he can do.'

'And that will be an end to it?' She wasn't sure whether relief or dismay was uppermost as she spoke the words.

'The case will remain officially open. The evidence will be reviewed from time to time. But the incident room will be closed, and we'll all move on to the next case.' Baker straightened up and dumped the last of the files on the desk, then leant back in his chair and pinched the bridge of his nose in a gesture of weary resignation. 'So yes, basically, that will be the end of it.'

Malcolm let out a long sigh and said quietly, 'At least this way Lee Smith won't be coming out after a few years with the rest of his life ahead of him.'

'There is that.' Baker rubbed his hands across his face. As he stood up, he gave them both a small, reluctant smile that for once reached above the moustache to touch his pale blue eyes.

'It won't have done my chances of Chief Inspector a whole lot of good. But yes, there is that to it, I suppose.'

For the first time in nearly a week, Agnes was up and dressed when Diane and Malcolm got back. She was sitting in the living-room watching morning television wearing a neat jersey suit, her make-up intact, hair as good as she could get it. Apart from the fact that her false teeth looked a little too big for her, it was hard to see there had been anything wrong with her at all. The sight of her touched Diane more than she could say; the effort was all for Thomas, she knew.

Between them, Malcolm and Diane recounted their visit to the police station, leaving out, as if by mutual consent, any reference to the suggestion of DNA testing for Thomas. Angelika's part in the crime was met with no more than pursed lips and a knowing 'I told you so' nod. Lee Smith's involvement evidently came as more of a surprise.

She looked hard at Diane. 'You mean the man who broke in here last week? The one who you . . .?'

'Yes,' Diane said quickly.

Agnes nodded and said with a small smile of self-satisfaction, 'I knew it wasn't the sort of thing you'd have done unless someone had inveigled you into it.'

Malcolm looked down. Diane clamped her lips together to prevent herself from replying. What would she say? That even if Lee Smith had had the entire thing planned, she'd gone along with it with an enthusiasm that would have shocked her mother to the core? She imagined Agnes all those years before, blaming their father's infidelity on the machinations of his mistress. '*If there were no bad women, there'd be no bad men*' – for as far back as she could remember, it had been one of Agnes's many catch-phrases. Maybe she was right.

Malcolm cleared his throat. 'No one will actually be named, unfortunately. There isn't enough hard evidence for that.'

Agnes looked at him sharply. 'But the police are certain this man was the murderer?'

'Absolutely sure.' It was Diane who answered.

Agnes looked down at her gnarled hands, clasped hard together in her lap. Diane saw that her mouth was working and that she was trying hard to fight back tears, and knew that her mother was feeling what she was feeling: nothing. A void where there should have been relief. A curious flatness where there should have been elation. Maybe it was the lack of a trial, with its formal ritual of retribution. Or maybe it was simply that Ian and all the others were just as dead, whoever had killed them.

After a moment, Agnes looked up, her face set into a bright, determined smile. 'So what time is Thomas coming? We should get some treats in for his tea.'

Diane's eyes met Malcolm's over the top of her mother's head, and she knew they were thinking the same thought: that refusing the DNA test had been the only possible decision.

34

The visit went well. The sight of Thomas toddling round the garden, squealing with delight as he chased the long-suffering cat and rediscovered the toys that had always been kept at the house ready for his infrequent visits, was enough to temporarily lift Diane from the haze of exhaustion that had dogged her for so long.

A social worker accompanied Thomas; an earnest young man with pebble glasses and a clipboard. Diane and Malcolm showed him round the house as if he were a prospective buyer, pointing out the flatness of the spacious lawn, the proximity of excellent schooling. They took him upstairs and described the plans they had for the nursery.

'It will be completely redecorated, of course. And the French window will be locked at all times,' Malcolm added quickly as the man looked dubiously at the rickety balustrade surrounding the balcony. 'As an executive with a construction company, I'm more than aware of the safety issues.'

The social worker looked impressed.

They talked about smoke alarms and stairgates, safety catches and fridge locks. Diane suspected the young man's knowledge of children was purely theoretical – an expression almost comically close to alarm came into his face every time Thomas approached him – but she was happy to help Malcolm go down the lengthy checklist with him and nod her head in all the appropriate places, if that was what it took to get Thomas back.

A couple of times during the visit, Diane found herself studying the little boy's face; now and again she looked up to see that Malcolm was doing so too. But when, towards the end of the visit, the social worker asked if they felt ready to take Thomas for a trial placement, neither of them hesitated for a second in saying yes. It was all agreed on the spot; the recommendation would be put before the case conference. Thomas could be with them before the weekend. And if everything went well, that's where he would stay.

That night, Malcolm opened one of his most expensive bottles of wine. He held up his glass and said quietly, 'To the future.'

Agnes looked down at the table for a second, then straightened her shoulders and said firmly, 'To the future.'

Diane could do no more than put her lips to her glass. It seemed all wrong to be celebrating; there were too many ghosts sitting round the table with them; too much grieving left to be done. But there was real warmth in Malcolm's eyes, real hope in her mother's, as they looked at her.

'To the future,' she murmured.

The following days were spent in a flurry of activity as they prepared for Thomas's arrival. Diane and her mother chose paint and nursery furniture. Malcolm organised a gang of decorators and spent all the time he wasn't at work supervising their every brushstroke. Soon the entire house was steeped in the smell of fresh paint. It made Diane feel queasy, but she was also filled with a growing sense of hope as the muted browns and beiges of Ian's old room were brightened by a new coat of clean, sunny yellow.

By unspoken mutual consent, everything was to be new. None of them suggested going over to Arden Hall to fetch Thomas's cot or his clothes or any of his toys; no one could bear the thought of entering the place. Not yet. Maybe not ever.

On the morning they were going to collect Thomas, Baker rang to ask if Diane had found her diary.

The routines of her life had been so overturned in recent weeks that she hadn't given a thought to the small, leather-bound book without which she would usually have been lost. 'I'm sorry,' she said guiltily. 'I'd completely forgotten to look. We've been busy getting ready for Thomas. He's coming in a couple of hours.' She felt the excitement bubbling up in her as she said the words. She glanced through the open living-room door to where her mother was happily putting the finishing touches to a pair of bright, animal-print curtains.

'It isn't that urgent. We're just dotting the "i's" to get the paperwork up to date.' Baker sounded regretful. He paused, then said, 'How is the little lad?'

She cursed herself for having let down her guard. She should have known the diary was a pretty flimsy reason for Baker to ring. 'We're not going to change our minds, Inspector,' she said sharply.

'That wasn't why I asked.' He paused again, then said quietly, 'Look, I'm not the enemy, Mrs Middleton, whatever you might think to the contrary. I've only ever done what I considered best for the investigation. I asked because I was genuinely interested in how he's getting on, and I know a lot of the other lads on the case are too. We don't get many murders involving kids, thank God, but when we do, it cuts everybody up.'

'He's fine.' Diane felt vaguely uncomfortable; Baker as a human being wasn't a concept she was used to. 'Thriving,' she added in a less hostile tone.

'Good. I'm glad.' Baker sounded as if he meant it. 'Right, well I'll let you get on with the preparations. No hurry for that diary. Maybe you could drop it in next time you're passing.'

She set about looking for it straight away; once Thomas arrived, she suspected it would be once more banished to some distant corner of her memory. She tipped out several handbags, searched in drawers, before eventually finding it in her car. She hadn't used it since the day of the party, she realised. She leant against the side of the car as recollection came flooding back. It hadn't really fitted into the little embroidered purse; she remembered how she'd slung it carelessly into the glove compartment as, through the driving mirror, she'd watched Lee smile his slow, heart-stopping smile as he'd waved her off.

Had he known, even then, what was to come?

She forced herself to turn to the torn-out page; Saturday the thirty-first of May, the day of Agnes's party. And adjacent to the ragged margin, the page for Sunday. The first day of June, and the last of Ian's, Angelika's and the children's lives. How few pages it was from there back to the day of Nicola's death; the day the nightmare had begun. She leafed back, past the day of the funeral, past the inquest the previous week, until she got to Friday the ninth of May.

'*Chas and Lorraine's silver wedding. 7.30 for 8,*' she'd scrawled. Had Angelika known what else was to happen that night? Had she and Lee planned things so well between them that she'd deliberately robbed Ian of an alibi by making up the yoga class and leaving him to look after the children?

Her eyes travelled to the adjacent page. *See Ian re Mum's*

party. And below it, a small asterisk. She stared at it stupidly as her heart began to pound and her knees turned to jelly. Her hands were shaking as she turned the pages back until she found the similar marks against the eighth of April; the sixth of March. Despite the heat of the midsummer sun, her skin felt cold and clammy as desperately she flicked the pages forwards again until she came to today's date: Wednesday the twenty-fifth of June. Her legs were trembling so uncontrollably that she had to lean against the car to stop herself falling. How the hell could she have been stupid enough not to realise?

'Are you all right?' Malcolm was standing on the balcony, looking down at her.

She shoved the diary into her pocket and shielded her eyes against the sun as she forced herself to look up at him. 'Fine. The smell of the paint . . .'

'Who was on the phone?'

'Baker.'

Malcolm frowned. 'What did he want?'

'Nothing.' She felt the diary, hard against her hip, and a wave of panic crashed over her like a tidal wave. 'Just to wish us well with Thomas.'

'He didn't say any more about the DNA?'

She shook her head, and saw the relief on Malcolm's face. He looked at his watch. 'I've put the curtains up, so that's everything.' He smiled down at her. 'Ready to go?'

She looked at Thomas's brand-new baby seat, already strapped into the back of the car, a big teddy bear sitting next to it, waiting.

'Ready,' she said faintly.

The rest of the day passed in a blur. Diane tried to focus on what was happening – the moment when they brought Tho-

mas into what was to be his new home, the first family meal
with him strapped into his new highchair, the first afternoon
walk in the Memorial Park, the first bathtime; all milestones
that she'd longed for and should be treasuring. But her mind
was numbed by the cold certainty that none of it was going to
last. She registered Malcolm's happy face, her mother's smile,
Thomas's small sigh of contentment as he clambered up onto
her lap for his bedtime bottle, and was filled with dread when
she thought of what she was about to do.

'What a day!' Malcolm blew out his cheeks as, finally, they
got into bed. 'I don't know about you, but I feel worn out! How
in God's name do people manage twins?'

All she could manage was a nod.

'Is everything all right?'

'Not really.'

His grin faded. 'What's the matter? You're not having
second thoughts?'

'About Thomas?' She could feel the hot tears behind her
eyes. 'Of course not.'

'It's something to do with that bloody phone call, isn't it?'
Malcolm was looking at her closely. 'You haven't seemed right
all day. What did Baker really want?'

'Do you remember what you said?' She couldn't meet his
gaze. 'About how we couldn't brand Thomas a . . .' Her voice
wavered. She had to swallow hard before she was able to finish
the sentence. '. . . A murderer's son?'

'I knew it.' Malcolm's voice was angry. 'He was trying to get
at you again, wasn't he? What is it with that bastard? Why
can't he just leave us alone to . . .?'

'It's nothing to do with Baker,' she said slowly. 'Or
Thomas.'

'Then what . . .?'

She turned so that she was facing him; forced herself to look into his eyes. She felt the words sticking like sharp glass in her throat; the words she'd waited fifteen years to say.

'I'm pregnant,' she whispered, and began to cry.

35

Diane would never forget the expressions that flashed through Malcolm's eyes: the split second of utter astonishment, the slower moment of realisation as the implications sank in, the hardness that had already begun to settle as he turned away from her. How often over the years she'd visualised the moment when she'd give him this news; visualised his reaction.

'It's his, I take it,' he said flatly.

'I don't know.' The times she'd slept with Lee had been right on the very edge of her cycle. Four days after the optimum dates circled in the diary when she and Malcolm had made love, as they did every month; as they'd done every month for the last fifteen years, without her becoming pregnant.

He got out of bed without a word, and began to pull on his clothes.

She watched him fearfully. 'Where are you going?'

'Does it matter?' He kept his back to her as he picked up his car keys.

'Don't go. Not tonight.'

He gave a hollow laugh. 'You mean things will be different in the morning?'

'I'll have an abortion, if it's what you want.' Beneath the bedclothes, her hand slid instinctively to her still-flat stomach.

'What *I* want?' He turned to her, his eyes blazing, his voice quiet with controlled fury. 'It's a bit bloody late to start thinking about that, isn't it?'

'I'm sorry.' She felt as if all the air were being crushed from her lungs. 'I'm so, so sorry.'

He looked down at her, his face expressionless. 'So am I,' he said and left the room.

She lay stock-still for a moment, staring at the ceiling as she listened to the quiet click of the front door closing.

A small whimper came across the baby monitor beside her, as if Thomas had heard it too.

She got out of bed and went through to the nursery. He stirred, his pursed pink mouth sucking at his remembered bedtime bottle as the brightly coloured elephants and croco-diles sprang briefly to life in the swathe of Malcolm's head-lights. Diane heard the crunch of gravel as the car was swung round and the room returned to the dimness of the night-light. Thomas whimpered again, a small frown puckering his face.

'I'm here, baby. Aunty Di's here.' She bent over the side of the cot and stroked his cheek until he burrowed down into his duvet with a sigh and his breathing deepened.

After a few moments, she heard the creak of floorboards and Agnes's head appeared round the door. 'Everything all right?' she whispered, her eyes on the cot. 'I thought I heard . . .'

Diane swallowed. 'Malcolm went to get some gripe-water from the all-night chemist.' She forced a smile. 'Just in case.'

Agnes seemed satisfied by the feeble explanation. She patted Diane's arm. 'It'll get easier as you get more used to it.'

'Yes.' Her heart felt like a stone inside her chest. 'You go back to bed. Everything's fine.'

She looked through the bars at her nephew's sleeping face; the curve of his cheek, the sweep of his long lashes, the small, perfect nose. She could see nothing of Lee there, but then she could see nothing of Ian either. Thomas was Thomas. She put her fingers through the bars and touched his soft blond curls. Would she love him less if Lee was imprinted on his features? Even if they'd agreed to the test, even if it had been proved beyond doubt that he carried the genetic inheritance of her brother's murderer, could she have turned her back on him? And what of the small speck of humanity inside her? She'd longed for so many years to have a child. Could she bring herself to extinguish that life, if Malcolm asked her to?

She sat down on the floor beside the cot, content to watch the gentle rise and fall of Thomas's chest, feel the warmth of his small body as her own limbs grew stiff and her skin chilled with the passing hours. She was suspended in time, not knowing how long she had been there, not wanting to look forwards or backwards, not daring to consider the decisions the morning would bring. She wished the long night might never end.

The birds had already begun to fill the air with song, and sunlight was seeping through the curtains when she heard the car pull back into the drive. A minute later, she heard Malcolm's key in the lock.

She should get up; go down and face him, but she felt unable to move.

She heard his footsteps on the stairs, the silence as he paused by their bedroom and saw she wasn't there. At last, the nursery door was pushed slowly open.

'What are you doing?'

She didn't reply.

'You'll wake Thomas.' He held out his hand. 'Come back to bed.'

Still she didn't move. To get up from that spot, to leave the safe, enclosed capsule of the nursery was to face the real world, and she wanted none of it. She wanted to stay here for ever, with the crocodiles and the elephants.

'Diane, we need to talk.'

'I know.'

It was only in fairy stories that you could shut your eyes and the monsters would go away. Reluctantly, she pulled herself to her feet. Her legs were numb from being in one position; they felt as if they belonged to someone else. She had to take Malcolm's hand to prevent herself from crashing into the cot and disturbing Thomas. His skin felt warm against her icy fingers.

He shut the door when they got back to their bedroom and said in a low voice, 'I've been driving around all night, thinking.'

She started to speak, but he cut across her. 'No. It's my turn. I want you to hear me out before you say anything.'

She nodded, then sat abruptly on the edge of the bed as the nausea she'd been stupid enough to put down to stress engulfed her once more. How much the life inside her was already taking over her body, as it battled for its own survival. She tried to visualise the tiny, prawn-shaped creature she'd seen so many times in books. Had its heart begun to beat already? The buds of fingers and toes begun to form?

Malcolm remained standing. 'I've tried to forget what you did, but I can't. I'm not sure I ever will.'

She nodded dully. 'Why should you?'

'Please. Just let me finish.' He took a deep breath, as if he'd been rehearsing what he was going to say. 'Pretending it didn't happen isn't going to work. You can't just wave a magic wand and make it go away, and that's what an abortion would add up to. Plus the fact that I don't think I could live with the chance, however small, that it could be mine. So it seems to me we've got two choices.'

His voice was brisk, as if he were in a planning meeting, summing up the options. Only the slight tremor of his hands, the tic beneath his eye, gave him away.

'Either we can walk away from each other, and throw away fifteen years of marriage and the chance of giving Thomas the future he deserves, or we can see things through as a couple and make the best of it. This baby might be mine or it might not. The same as Thomas might not be Ian's. I didn't want to know with him and I don't want to know with this one either. And that's not sticking my head in the sand, it's refusing to allow Lee Smith to reach out from the grave and take from me what he hasn't already taken. If that sounds melodramatic, well I'm sorry, but that's how it is.' The words had come out in a rush. Malcolm stopped, as if suddenly embarrassed by his own vehemence, then said more quietly, 'We've always wanted a family, and now we've got one.' At last, he met her eye. 'There, that's my piece done with. Now you can have your say.'

Diane wanted to tell him that she loved him; that she'd be grateful to him for the rest of her life for not forcing her to choose. But now wasn't the time. She had to be sure, before she could allow herself to relax. 'Are you certain you've thought this through?' She scanned his face. 'It going to be difficult.'

'Either way, it isn't going to be easy,' he said soberly. 'We both know that. But in my opinion, it's the best we can do.'

She told Agnes the next morning, both of them sitting in their dressing-gowns at the kitchen table. Thomas had been up since six, but there didn't seem to have been time to get dressed. Malcolm had left earlier for a site meeting, grey with fatigue. Thomas was sitting in his highchair, happily throwing toast at the cat.

Diane watched the emotions warring in her mother's face.

'My goodness, you're going to have your work cut out.' Agnes scrubbed at Thomas's hands with a cloth. She bent down to pick up a discarded finger of toast, then straightened up, her eyes meeting Diane's for a split second before she bustled over to throw it in the bin. 'What does Malcolm think?'

'He's pleased,' Diane answered steadily.

The pause was only fractional. 'Then I'm pleased too.' Agnes came round the table and took Diane in her arms. 'In fact, I'm delighted.'

And that, Diane knew, was the closest the two of them would come to discussing the new baby's parentage. Agnes had spent a lifetime hearing what she wanted to hear. Or putting up the pretence of doing so, at least.

Diane made an appointment later the same morning with David Fawcett, who confirmed the pregnancy and worked out from her dates that the baby would be due at the end of the following February.

'Great GP I turned out to be. I can't believe I missed the signs!' Fawcett's long, serious face broke into an embarrassed grin as he helped Diane down from the examination table. 'I'm absolutely delighted for you both. After all these years. You must both be over the moon.'

Inevitably, the news got out far more quickly than they'd planned. Agnes told Doris Crombie who, sworn to secrecy, told only a couple of people, who just mentioned it in passing to a couple more. By the end of the week, a fresh batch of letters and cards began to arrive, as their friends grasped at the news of a new life in the midst of so much death.

Despite her misgivings, Diane couldn't prevent herself from taking pleasure in the messages of congratulations that made such a welcome change from the condolences of the past weeks. There was so much sadness still ahead of them; the inquests, the funerals, the decisions about what was to be done with Arden Hall and its contents. She watched the strain gradually disappearing from Malcolm's face as he, too, fielded phone calls and opened letters. It was as if their friends' delight were contagious.

The inquests on Ian and his family took place in the middle of July, a couple of weeks after Thomas's first birthday. The verdicts on all four of them were as Baker had predicted: unlawful killing by person or persons unknown. Diane and Malcolm bumped into him outside the courtroom at the end of the proceedings. The case would remain open, he assured them, but they all knew nothing further would come to light. They shook hands, and Baker wished them well for the future. If he'd noticed the slight swell of Diane's stomach, he made no comment on it.

The funerals took place on a sweltering day in August. As a mark of the Somerford family's links with the city, the service was held at the cathedral. Hundreds turned up: friends, colleagues, reporters, the simply curious. No one from America made the journey.

Diane had been dreading the day, but when it arrived, she felt curiously detached; the crowds, the mountains of flowers, the flashguns of the attendant press, lent the occasion an air of almost theatrical unreality. It was only when the four coffins were carried in that she fainted. The same edition of the

Coventry Evening Telegraph that covered the funeral in a double-page spread reported, in a smaller article alongside, the verdict of accidental death on Lee Smith.

As the weeks of her pregnancy stretched into months, Diane's nausea subsided, although the effort of caring for a boisterous toddler left her permanently exhausted. A new rhythm of life developed. She handed in her notice with the local authority. She'd been on sick leave from her evening classes since the murders, and was relieved to be rid of them and their attendant memories. Some of her students wrote to express thanks and regret. She received an invitation to the exhibition, postponed until the following term. She wrote back to thank the new tutor, but she knew she wouldn't attend; that part of her life was behind her for ever. Sometimes, she felt it had never existed. The cottage at Corley Moor was put on the market; she hadn't the time to use it, even if she'd wanted to.

She went out infrequently, partly because of the demands Thomas put upon her time, partly because she felt unequal to the business of getting back into a world of ordinary people going about their daily lives. There were a few people whose company she missed: Tracey Collingwood, George Bonham. But they were amongst the very few people to be aware that the pregnancy wasn't the simple cause for joy that most thought it to be, and out of respect for Malcolm she distanced herself from the others. She missed Ian terribly. She dreamt about him often. Not nightmares, or anything portentous; she had no sense of him trying to speak to her from the grave. Just snatches of ordinary bits of their life together, so vividly realistic in their mundanity that she woke up breathless with loss.

Agnes moved back to the Leamington flat, although she

spent most of her time at the Kenilworth Road house, fussing over Diane and spoiling Thomas. Diane suspected that, despite her mother's undiminished grief for Ian, she was in some ways more content than she'd been in years, now that she was back at the centre of the family.

Malcolm returned to the daily business of the office, but spent as much time at home as he could, calling in during the day, coming home for lunch, as if he couldn't bear to be away from them for more than a few hours. There was talk of a merger with Chas Newbould's development firm. It seemed to Diane that the terms weren't as generous as they should have been, but she knew Malcolm's heart wasn't in the business as Ian's had been. Even Agnes agreed that it made sense, once she'd established that the Somerford name would be maintained.

As the weeks passed, the distance between Diane and Malcolm seemed to diminish. Thomas was no longer the single, fragile link that held them both together; their carefully cultivated politeness and mutual consideration began to relax into something more approaching their previous relationship. His courteous concern for her welfare transformed into real interest, excitement even, as the unborn baby developed and grew. He'd put his hand on her stomach to feel the strengthening kicks and seemed genuinely moved by the miraculousness of what was happening inside her. For hours, then days at a time, Diane could make herself believe that one day they might be an ordinary family, like any other family.

Apart from a few of Ian's personal possessions, the entire contents of Arden Hall had been sold at auction. In the first week in December, the sale of the property itself went through, the new owner being keen to be in by Christmas. On the day before the contracts were signed, Diane forced herself to drive over to Stratford and take one last look at Ian's home. She drove past the estate agent's board with its 'Sold' sign and turned the car into the long, winding drive, remembering all the other times she'd made the same journey. She glanced up at the trees that had borne the poisonous banners Angelika had strung from them and felt a great wave of anger, quickly subdued. Whatever Angelika had done, she'd paid her own price for it.

She parked in front of the house and sat quite still. She didn't get out; now that she was here, there seemed no point. In the car seat behind her, Thomas babbled happily as he played with his toy steering wheel. She'd wondered whether to leave him with Agnes, rather than risk upsetting him, but it was clear that he had no recollection of the place that had been his home for the first ten months of his life. She was filled with sadness to think that Ian would never be more than a name, a figure in a photograph, to the little boy he'd loved so much.

'Right then, our Thomas.' She twisted round and smiled brightly at him. 'Let's go back home.'

She glanced one final time at the heavy oak door that would never again open to reveal Ian's welcoming face. Then she turned the car round and headed back up the drive. It felt as if some final link with the past had been severed.

All that was left for her to deal with now was the future.

36

Diane and Malcolm received dozens of invitations as Christmas approached. Agnes was only too willing to volunteer her services as baby-sitter, but Diane found she was reluctant to accept any of them. Christmas was a time for happiness, and she wasn't quite ready for that, yet. She was grateful that Malcolm didn't try to pressure her. At seven months pregnant, she was entitled to hibernate if that's what she felt like doing, he asserted as he turned down one well-meant offer of hospitality after another. He seemed no more inclined to take part in the festivities than she did herself. She suspected he felt the same as she did; that inside the four walls of their own house, they were safe from the intrusive questions of friends, the tactless comments of strangers, the constant reminders that they were still set apart from their acquaintances by the tragedies and scandals of the past year.

She was puzzled, but greatly relieved, that no invitation had arrived from Chas and Lorraine Newbould to their Boxing Day party. The flashy, open-house buffet that they threw for all their clients and customers at their huge, mock-Georgian manor house in the Cotswolds had become something of a tradition; attendance was obligatory. She found it hard to believe that any delicacy of feeling was responsible for their omission from the guest list, and as negotiations for the merger were apparently going smoothly, there was no reason to think they'd fallen out of favour, as had happened in spectacular fashion with so many of Chas's other associates in the past.

She mentioned it to Malcolm one evening as he was giving Thomas his bath, a task he'd taken over in recent weeks as she became too big and unwieldy to bend over the tub.

'Lorraine's apparently been feeling a bit low, so Chas thought they'd give it a miss this year.' Malcolm went back to dive-bombing Thomas with a plastic duck.

'Doesn't sound like Lorraine.' Diane realised, with a sense of mild guilt, how long it was since she'd spoken to the other woman. 'Did he say what was wrong?'

Thomas kicked his legs and, roaring with laughter, sent a tidal wave over the side of the bath.

'Hormones, he reckons.' Malcolm grinned up at her as he reached for a towel. 'You know what Chas is like. It's the only diagnosis he's ever got, when it comes to women.'

It was almost like old times; the two of them sharing a joke; having a simple conversation that had no uncomfortable subtext, no hidden minefields to be avoided.

'I'll give her a ring.' Diane smiled back at him.

'Come on, trouble. Out you get.' Malcolm bent over the bath and hoisted the dripping Thomas high above his head. Diane felt a warm surge of genuine contentment as the little boy squealed in delighted terror. No one looking in on the scene from outside would guess that they weren't father and son.

Inevitably, Diane didn't get round to ringing Lorraine as she had intended. As Christmas approached, there barely seemed enough hours in the day to keep up with the essentials. Her bulk, and the fact that she had Thomas in tow, meant that even the smallest task took twice as long as it had the previous year.

Shopping was a nightmare, trying to barge the pushchair through crowded stores, fighting for places in lifts where before she would have run up the stairs. The frantic urge to spend, the relentless pursuit of seasonal cheer, she found depressing; she wished she could pull a rug over her head and not re-emerge until the festive season was over. But she was determined to make the effort for Thomas's first Christmas with them.

Returning frazzled and exhausted from yet another trip into the city centre, and in desperate need of a pee, she was dismayed to see Lorraine's silver BMW ZX3 parked in the drive, and Lorraine herself peering through the letterbox. The other woman turned and waved as she heard Diane's car. She didn't appear at all fazed to have been caught snooping.

'Lorraine! What a lovely surprise!' Diane called mendaciously as she got out of the car.

Lorraine teetered across the gravel in stiletto-heeled boots. 'I won't try to kiss you.' She raised a carefully shaped eyebrow and regarded Diane's bump. 'I don't think I could get close enough.'

Diane felt hot and sweaty. Her hair badly needed a trim and she hadn't had time to put on any make-up before she'd left home. She unlocked the front door and pushed it open. 'Go on through. I'll just fetch Thomas.'

He was asleep in the car seat, and gave a tetchy wail that developed into a full-blown roar of protest as she lifted him out into the damp, chilly air. The pressure in Diane's bladder was reaching crisis point, not helped by Thomas's protesting kicks against her stomach as she slammed the car door shut with her hip and carried him, struggling, into the house.

Lorraine was standing in the living-room, examining with evident distaste the gaudy display of dancing reindeer that had so taken Thomas's fancy in the supermarket the previous week.

'Keep an eye on him, will you?' Diane dumped him at the other woman's expensively shod feet and dashed for the cloakroom.

She sat on the loo, the exquisite relief of relaxing her bladder muscles tempered with annoyance. She was well aware that within a couple of days, Lorraine would have put round the word of how poor Diane had let herself go; how hard she was finding it to cope. She wondered if she had time to run upstairs and slap on some lipstick, but she could hear Thomas, still bellowing his disapproval at being woken from his nap, and Lorraine's high-pitched, slightly panicky voice as she attempted to pacify him. Instead, she hurried through to the kitchen to get him a beaker of milk and a biscuit.

'Sorry about that,' she said, when she'd settled him in the middle of a heap of toys. 'Can I get you a coffee?'

'No thanks.' Lorraine eyed Thomas warily. 'I've just had one.'

'So how are you?' Diane tried to ignore the snail-trail of snot across the hem of Lorraine's black cashmere coat. 'Chas mentioned to Malcolm that you hadn't been feeling too good.'

'Did he, now?'

Lorraine's voice had a strange wobble to it; Diane was alarmed to realise that tears were brimming through the thicket of the other woman's mascara. Maybe it wasn't hormones; maybe there really was something wrong with her. She glanced at the stick-like calves protruding from Lorraine's expensive leather boots and asked anxiously, 'What is it, Lorraine? Are you sick?'

'Sick of bloody men, that's for sure.' Lorraine looked up at her and said venomously, 'I've found out Chas has been seeing another woman.'

'What?' Diane stared at her, astounded; she might not like Chas Newbould, but he was the last person on earth she'd have put down as a womaniser.

'You didn't know, did you?' Lorraine's face was suddenly vulnerable, the heavy foundation cream and powder not quite hiding the incipient crow's-feet. 'You haven't all been laughing about me behind my back?'

'No, of course not.' Diane lowered herself clumsily down next to the other woman and put an awkward arm around her shoulder. 'But are you sure? I mean, what makes you think . . .?'

Lorraine gave a bitter laugh. 'Oh, I'm quite sure. I've had a private investigator checking him out.'

'Dear God.' Behind the bickering and sniping, Chas and Lorraine had seemed utterly suited to each other; two halves of the same flashy coin. Diane shook her head, genuinely shocked. 'So how long . . .?'

Lorraine shrugged her thin shoulders. 'Who knows?' She sniffed loudly. 'I'm fairly sure there's been more than one. Could have been going on for years, for all I know.' Her mouth twisted. 'No wonder he's always bleating on about how much money I spend. Probably wanted it all for his floozies. I feel such a bloody fool, having everyone to the house to celebrate our silver wedding, when all the time . . .' She gazed down at the chunky diamond eternity ring that had been Chas's anniversary present to her, and began to cry again.

Diane didn't know what to say. 'Well, if it's any consolation, I'd no idea. And I'm sure Malcolm hasn't either.'

Lorraine took a small lace handkerchief from her handbag and blew her nose. 'I only got suspicious when I found a credit card receipt for some poxy little hotel in Kenilworth.'

'But that could have been business, or anything . . .'

'Wasn't the sort of place he'd have taken a client.' Lorraine's face twisted into a sour smile. 'Bastard must be as tight-arsed with his tarts as he is with me. Anyway, I got the PI to check it out. He slipped the receptionist fifty quid and got a list of dates when "Mr and Mrs Bateman" had stayed there before. Except it seems there was more than one Mrs Bateman.' Tears welled up into her eyes again. 'He even used my maiden name as his cover, the sod.' She delved into her bag and pulled out a folded sheet of paper. 'I'm not stupid, Diane. I keep my eye on him. He'd never have managed to fool me for so long without getting some of his cronies on board.' She blew her nose again, more fiercely. 'I wouldn't be so sure about your Malc not knowing anything about it. They're all the same, men. All selfish bastards at heart.'

Diane withdrew her arm. 'Look, I'm really sorry about all this, Lorraine, but I don't see . . .'

'I'm going to take Chas to the cleaners for this.'

'You're going to divorce him?' Diane tried and failed to imagine Lorraine managing on her own.

'Divorce him?' Lorraine hooted with laughter. 'What planet are you on? No, I'm going to hit the cheating slimeball where it'll hurt him most – in the wallet. But before I confront him, I'm going to make sure the evidence against him is absolutely watertight.' Her mouth twisted into a sneer. 'I know that slippery bugger. He'll think if he throws enough weight around at that hotel, he'll talk them into losing all record of him. But I've got him stitched up. I guessed he'd have got his mates to cover for him and I was right. Golf matches, business meetings – I've blown a hole in half his alibis already, by asking around.' She opened up the piece of paper. Diane could see that the list of dates was already scrawled across and heavily asterisked. 'Look at that. Right through from the beginning of the year, except for a bit round your mum's party. Angelika's scene must have given the randy old sod one hell of a fright when he realised how easily it could have been him in the firing line.' Lorraine seemed utterly oblivious to the tactlessness of the remark. She tapped an improbably long nail extension against the last couple of dates. 'Obviously didn't teach him enough of a lesson, though, because he's at it again.'

Diane shifted uncomfortably in her seat. 'I'm not really sure why you're telling me all this.'

'Chas doesn't keep a diary. Reckons he can keep everything in his head.' Lorraine snorted. 'Frightened I'd find it, more like. A couple of the other golf-club wives have gone through theirs to see if their old men reckoned they were out with him while he was up to his tricks. I'm just asking you to look through the dates that are left and see if Malcolm was covering for him as well.'

Diane glanced longingly at the clock. Malcolm would be back for lunch any time. He'd know far better than she how to handle the woman. 'Are you sure this isn't just some kind of misunderstanding?' she said weakly.

'Grow up, love. Just because you and Malcolm are Mr and Mrs Perfect.' Lorraine's mouth tightened to a hard, scarlet gash. 'Chas is going to wish he'd never been born by the time I finish with him.'

Mr and Mrs Perfect. Diane looked down at her hands, for fear her face might give her away.

'I'll leave it with you.' Lorraine slapped the list down on the coffee table, apparently cheered by the thought of the revenge she was going to wreak on Chas's bank balance. She leant forward and patted Diane's hand. 'Anyway, enough about me. How are you keeping? We've all been so worried about you.'

Diane knew the 'we' in question would be the other golf-club wives. Neither she nor Malcolm had been near the place since Ian's death; they were probably all beside themselves with curiosity.

'I'm fine,' she said crisply.

'Of course you are.' Lorraine nodded, knowingly. She paused for a moment, then added in the same treacly voice, 'We all think you're so brave, coping the way you have.'

Diane didn't respond. She suspected that Lorraine's visit had been prompted as much by curiosity as by any sudden need to unburden herself, but if she thought she was going to leave with any more gossip than she'd have already picked up from the golf club, she could think again.

Lorraine shook her head and continued with relish, 'It must be torture for you, them never finding out who did it. And then all that terrible business with that other woman's husband.' She arranged her features into an expression of sympathetic concern as she cut to the chase. 'That must have been a real nightmare for you.'

A more sensitive soul might have been put off by Diane's expression, but not Lorraine. She leant forward and asked confidentially, 'The reports were all a bit vague. What happened, exactly?'

Diane breathed in sharply. 'I'd rather not talk about it, if you don't mind.'

Lorraine regarded her in silence for a moment, her head on one side, then said brightly, 'Tell you what. I will have a coffee, after all. Just to keep you company.'

Diane's heart sank, but short of downright rudeness, there wasn't much she could do. 'I'll go and put the kettle on,' she said reluctantly.

'No, no. You stay there with Thomas.' Lorraine got to her

feet with a bright smile. 'I'll get it. I'm sure I shall be able to find everything.'

Diane glanced towards him, but he was rolling a car across the carpet, in a contented world of his own. 'It's OK. He'll be fine for a couple of minutes. I'll see to it.' The last thing she needed was Lorraine poking about in the kitchen cupboards, telling everyone how poor Diane had let not only herself go, but the house as well.

Lorraine followed her out into the kitchen anyway. 'Mind you,' she drawled as she ran a skinny finger across the dust on the percolator Diane hadn't used for months, 'if you were going to get indecently assaulted by anyone, you could have done a lot worse, couldn't you?'

'I'm sorry, I don't follow,' Diane said icily.

'Well, he was rather gorgeous, wasn't he?'

Diane gripped the edge of the sink. Lorraine was just fishing. She must blank the woman out, not rise to the bait.

'I recognised him as soon as I saw his picture in the papers. Of course, he didn't have his hard hat on then, but you wouldn't forget those sultry dark eyes in a hurry, would you?'

Diane knew she was getting sucked into a conversation she didn't want to have, but she couldn't prevent herself from asking sharply, 'What do you mean?'

'Didn't you know?' Lorraine looked pleased with herself. 'He used to work for Somerford's.'

'Yes, I'm aware of that.' Diane cleared her throat and said in as casual a voice as she could manage, 'I understand he was employed for a while at Arden Hall.' She regretted the words as soon as they were out of her mouth; the last thing she'd meant to do was to give Lorraine something else to chew over.

'Was he, now?' The other woman's eyes were sharp with curiosity; Diane could almost hear her brain ticking. But then she shook her head and said, 'No, he couldn't have been. Well, not weekends, at any rate. Arden Hall was being done the same time the extension went up on the nursing home Chas's mother's in. I remember, because Chas got arsey about Ian wanting all the experienced blokes over at Stratford and putting a load of casuals in at the home to try to get it done before all the old biddies got dumped there for the Christmas holidays. Not that I was complaining. All that beefcake stripped off to the waist. Better than the usual set of hairy builders' bums, eh?' She laughed raucously. 'I don't think the old bat knew what had hit her, I was over there that much. Specially weekends, when your bloke was there.'

'He wasn't *my* bloke, as you call him,' Diane said tightly. 'And he wasn't at the nursing home, he was . . .'

The rest of the sentence was cut off by a reverberating crash, followed almost immediately by a sharp squeal of panic.

'Thomas!' She pushed past Lorraine and ran back into the living-room. The small Christmas tree that had stood on a table in front of the patio doors lay on the floor, baubles and lights scattered everywhere. Thomas stood in front of it, his eyes wide with fright, his chubby fingers still clutching the bag of chocolate pennies that Diane thought she'd hung out of his reach. He dropped them as she came into the room, his face crumpling.

'It's all right, darling. It doesn't matter.' She gathered him up into her arms, and held him to her. 'Don't be frightened.'

'Oh dear.' Lorraine stood in the doorway, making no move to help. 'Honestly, Diane, I don't know how you stand all of this. It's no wonder you've let yourself get into such a state.'

'Perhaps you'd better go,' Diane snapped. She kissed the top of Thomas's head as his sobs subsided to a snuffling grizzle. 'He's tired. I need to put him down for a nap.'

345

'Oh.' Lorraine blinked. 'Well, if I'm getting in your way . . .'

Diane couldn't be bothered to keep up the pretence of politeness a moment longer; the sooner the prying bitch was out of the house, the better. 'Yes, you are, to be frank.'

'Right, then.' Lorraine snatched up her bag. 'I'll find my own way out.' She paused at the door, an angry flush clashing unbecomingly with her blusher. 'No wonder Malcolm doesn't want to be seen out with you any more.'

Diane pressed Thomas to her. 'And what's that supposed to mean?'

'Try taking a look in the mirror, luv, and you might find out.' Lorraine turned on her stiletto heel and flounced out, slamming the door behind her.

37

Diane put Thomas down for his nap, then went back into the living-room and sat down wearily on the sofa. Lorraine's perfume still hung heavily in the air, making her feel sick. She put her ear to the baby monitor. Thomas was still snuffling and grizzling. She glanced at the clock; it was probably too close to lunchtime for him to sleep. Malcolm would be home any minute; she should be getting something ready.

She tried to put from her mind the rubbish Lorraine New-bould had been spouting about Lee Smith working on the nursing home in Solihull, but she couldn't stop herself from feeling unsettled. In a lot of ways it made sense; Ian had been so fussy about every last detail at Arden Hall that she could well imagine him diverting all the experienced teams onto the project. But if Lee had been working in Solihull, there was no reason to suppose he'd known Angelika. And if he hadn't known Angelika . . . No, it was nonsense, Diane told herself sharply. Typical Lorraine, trying to make out she'd recognised him, just so she could try to put herself as close as she could to the centre of the scandal.

Diane shook her head dismissively as she bent forward and picked up the sheet of paper still lying on the coffee table. Who else but Lorraine would not only drive round publicising her husband's affair, but also produce a checklist for all their associates?

There were some twenty dates on the list, ranging back to the beginning of the year, about half already asterisked and scrawled over in Lorraine's spiky hand. Diane noted the names of several of Malcolm's acquaintances who, if Lorraine were to be believed, had been willing to provide the philandering Chas with an alibi. A couple of them surprised her. But then Chas was a powerful and persuasive player; a hard man to refuse. She tried not to ask herself if Malcolm's arm could have been similarly twisted.

She went to screw the paper up, but she couldn't stop herself running her eye down the remaining dates first. There were a couple in February, and one in March when she knew she and Malcolm had been away for the weekend. The next was in May – just the night before Chas and Lorraine's silver wedding party. She felt a sudden, unexpected twinge of sympathy for the woman. Who wouldn't get bitter and twisted, married to such a bastard?

Her eyes moved down to the next date, and she froze, hardly able to believe her eyes. But it was there, in black and white. Sunday, the first of June. The day of the murders. The day when Malcolm and Chas had been playing golf and visiting a potential site in Bedworth.

Her hand travelled to her throat as she tried to grapple with the implications. There must be a mistake. The receptionist must have got the dates wrong. Frantically, she scanned the other dates, but they meant nothing to her. The next wasn't until the beginning of November, leaving a gap of some five months. Had Lorraine been right? Had Angelika's outburst frightened Chas off? She felt a shiver of dread, like an icy trickle of water down her spine. Or was it conceivable that there was an altogether more sinister explanation? She tried to bring her careering thoughts under control as a thousand pieces of the jigsaw rearranged themselves inside her head, and made no more sense than they had before. Angelika had been having an affair. Chas had been having an affair. Lee hadn't been at Arden Hall, but at some nursing home in Solihull . . .

A loud wail from the baby monitor announced that Thomas wasn't going to settle. Diane folded the paper, shoved it into her pocket and hauled herself to her feet. Her head was spinning. There had to be a logical explanation. There must be. It was just that she couldn't think of one.

She was changing Thomas's nappy when she heard the front door open. Although she'd been expecting Malcolm, the sound of his voice still made her jump.

'Anyone home?' he shouted, and Thomas's eyes lit up as he twisted his head round towards the sound.

'In the nursery.' Diane's heart was beating uncomfortably fast in her chest as she heard his footsteps bounding up the stairs.

'Hello, there.' His head came round the door and disappeared again in their daily ritual of peek-a-boo.

Thomas shrieked with laughter.

An ordinary, happy domestic scene. Why couldn't she just leave it that way?

Malcolm pecked her on the cheek as she pulled up Thomas's dungarees with shaking hands.

'What sort of a morning have you had?' He swooped the little boy up from the changing mat and held him high in the air, laughing at Thomas's laughter, not listening to her answer.

'Lorraine Newbould called round.' She was amazed at how normal her voice sounded.

'Yes?' His eyes were still on Thomas. 'How did she seem?'

'Angry, actually.' Her heart was hammering. She could feel the sweat prickling on the back of her neck.

Slowly, Malcolm lowered Thomas from above his head and said, 'What about?' His voice didn't sound as surprised as it should have done.

She'd meant to bring the subject up more gradually, work her way round to it. But the question came hurtling out, bald and accusing. 'Have you been covering for Chas while he's been seeing his mistress?'

If she hadn't been looking out for the fractional pause before Malcolm responded, she might not have noticed it. But she had, and it answered the question for her.

He gave a small half-laugh. 'What a ridiculous thing to suggest. I told you, Chas reckons Lorraine must be . . .'

'She's been using a private investigator to follow him. She's got a list of dates.' Diane swallowed. 'One of them is the first of June.' She watched the colour drain from Malcolm's face. She'd prayed he hadn't realised; that he hadn't known where Chas had been. But he had. The logic she'd been trying to ignore told her that he must have done. 'You knew, didn't you?'

Malcolm had recovered himself quickly. 'I haven't the faintest idea what you're talking about.' He shook his head. 'I don't know what rubbish that woman's been filling your head with, but she's clearly having some kind of nervous . . .'

She wanted so much to believe him. 'You knew he'd been seeing Angelika, and you said nothing.'

'This is nonsense!' The tic had set up beneath Malcolm's eye. 'Look, you're overwrought.' He shifted Thomas's weight and put a hand on her arm. 'Why don't you go and have a lie-down, and I'll . . .'

'I'm not an invalid.' She tried to shake herself free. 'And I'm not stupid, either, so don't try to lie to me.'

'Calm down.' His expression hardened. 'You're becoming hysterical.'

'My God,' she said slowly, only just beginning to comprehend the full horror of it. 'You've known it was him all along, haven't you? That's why you rang me, sent me over there to find the bodies. Christ, no wonder he was so keen to back you up about the timing of those phone calls. It wasn't me he was letting off the hook, it was himself.'

Malcolm's voice was dangerously quiet. 'Shut up. You're frightening Thomas.'

'Was it you who forged that report, or him?'

'I don't know what you're talking about.' Beads of sweat stood out on Malcolm's forehead, giving the lie to his derisive laugh.

'Lee Smith didn't work at Arden Hall at all, did he? You just stitched him up between you because he was dead and couldn't defend himself.'

'Oh, I see! That's what all this crap is about.' His mouth twisted into a sneer as he let his eyes travel down to her swollen belly. 'Still can't take the fact you're carrying a murderer's bastard?'

She was stunned by the naked hatred in his face. How could he have been harbouring all that venom, and have kept it from her? She lashed out at him in the most damaging way she could, despising herself even before the vicious words left her mouth. 'Right now, you're most likely the one doing that, you fool,' she spat. 'Why else do you think Chas Newbould didn't kill him too?'

Tears of self-disgust were already running down her face as Thomas whimpered and put his arms out to her, as if he'd understood. He was an innocent baby. Whoever had fathered him, none of this nightmare was his fault.

Malcolm let go of her arm and cradled Thomas to him, as if trying, too late, to protect him from her poisonous words.

'I'm sorry, little one. I didn't mean . . .' She tried to take him, but Malcolm turned, physically shielding the baby from her with his body.

'Don't you touch him,' he hissed. He stood Thomas in the cot, and bent to kiss the top of the silky blond head.

'For Christ's sake, Malcolm!' She grabbed his arm, tried to drag him away. 'What's the matter with you? How can you even bear to have him look at you, when you've been protecting the man who murdered his family!'

He jerked free of her, his gaze still on Thomas. 'We're his family.'

The little boy clung onto the bars, looking at them, his eyes wide with bewilderment.

'Dear God, was that the deal?' Diane took a step backwards. Her mouth was dry, her heart pounding so that she felt it might burst at any minute. 'You keep your mouth shut and we get the baby? Is that how he talked you into . . .?'

He spun round, his eyes blazing. 'You just don't get it, do you? But then you wouldn't. A ruthless bastard like Chas Newbould. A lout like Lee Smith. But not Malcolm. He'd never have the guts. Not good old Malcolm.'

'What do you mean?' she whispered, but cold certainty was already beginning to settle on her like a stone.

'Chas Newbould didn't talk me into anything.' Malcolm gave a mirthless laugh. 'Quite the contrary, in fact. He nearly bloody wet himself when he thought he was going to have his cover blown. As far as he's concerned, I was just getting my end away with some tart that Sunday, the same as he was. Oh, don't look so bloody shocked. You were always so busy mooning over your temperature charts and ovulation kits, I could have been screwing half of the West Midlands, for all you cared.'

She put her hands over her ears to block him out. It wasn't happening. It couldn't be happening.

'No you don't. Not this time.' He grabbed her wrists, forcing her arms down. 'For once, you're going to listen to me.' His face was suffused with rage. 'For fifteen years I've played second fiddle to you and your bloody family. Do you think I ever wanted to work in the business, licking your brother's boots? Did you think I wanted to give up the home I'd provided for you so that we could move into this bloody mausoleum? Did you even stop for one second to wonder? No, of course you didn't. Good old Malcolm would do as he was told, just like he'd always done. Get his cock out once a month when you decreed the time was right, then disappear back into the woodwork.' He gave a savage laugh. 'Ironic, when you think of it. The only time in fifteen years you fuck someone for the hell of it, and that's when you get pregnant.'

She tried to struggle free, but his fingers dug into her wrists all the harder as he pushed his face close to hers. 'I can't begin to tell you how much pleasure it gave me to screw Ian's wife, to watch him with Thomas and know it was my son he was doting on.'

'He isn't. He's . . .' The bile rose in Diane's throat, cutting off her words.

'Look at him. You're the bloody artist. Can't you see the resemblance?' He forced her round so she was facing the cot. 'No, of course you can't. Because you don't want to know the truth, any more than Ian wanted to know the truth.'

She searched the little boy's face, but she could see no more of Malcolm in him than she'd been able to see of Lee Smith.

Or Ian, however hard she tried. He was simply, uniquely Thomas.

'He must have had his doubts. Christ, he must surely have known he'd never be enough to satisfy a woman like Angelika. But then, even if he did realise she was playing away, he'd never suspect good old Malc. That was the beauty of it! He hadn't got the first idea. Even when the stupid bastard turned up at Arden Hall and found me standing over her body, he still never had a bloody clue!'

When was it that this man she'd imagined she loved, thought she knew so well, had gone mad without her noticing? Diane swallowed down the bitter liquid, overwhelmed by sudden fury. 'So you murdered the mother of your child? You're proud of that? You can stand there and *boast* about it?' Her voice was trembling with rage. 'Tell me, Malcolm. What kind of monster does it take to be able to do something like that?'

There had been nothing calculated in her words. They were born of no more than the deepest revulsion; an instinctive, dangerous reaction that, even as she uttered them, she realised could cost her her life. But it seemed they had hit their mark. Malcolm let go of her, his hands dropping to his sides as his eyes strayed back to Thomas, the brief moment of his triumph already spent.

'I never meant that to happen.' He shook his head and gave a small, incredulous laugh as if he himself could barely believe what he'd done. 'It was just an affair, for Christ's sake! If only that greedy little cow hadn't found out and started black-mailing us . . .' He was staring at the cot, as if speaking directly to Thomas. 'I'd have been happy to just pay her off, but Angelika wasn't having any of it. She couldn't bear the thought of anyone getting one over on her. Don't you understand?' His gaze swivelled abruptly to Diane's face, as if hoping for benediction. 'I didn't know that's what the mad bitch was going to do, did I? She just said she wanted to make the final payment herself. Christ, the woman was going away anyway. Why throw her out of a bloody window?'

'*Angelika* killed Nicola Smith?' Diane breathed.

'She might have got away with it, too, if she'd left it there. But no, she just had to try to stitch Ian up, instead of leaving well alone. The letters, the banners, that stupid scene at the party . . .' Malcolm shook his head, his expression almost impatient. 'It was all so bloody unnecessary.'

'Unnecessary?' Diane felt the fury boiling over again. 'You strangle her, you smother two innocent children. When Ian arrives and realises what you've done, you murder him too. And you call it *unnecessary*?'

'We had a row. Christ, you know what Angelika's temper was like. I was just trying to shut her up, stop her waking the children.' A spasm of what could have been genuine remorse crossed his features. 'I didn't realise she'd drugged them already. I thought Marshall had seen me. How the hell was I supposed to know he walked in his sleep? Any more than I knew that silly bitch of an au pair had rung Ian and panicked him into coming over. It didn't need to happen. None of it needed to happen.'

Diane gazed at him, dumb. This man with whom she'd shared almost half a lifetime was insane. He'd actually convinced himself that the appalling crimes he'd committed were no more than the inevitable consequence of a chain of unfortunate mishaps.

And now he was going to kill her, too. What other option did he have?

He took a step towards her and she shrank back, pressing

355

her hands to her mouth to prevent herself from screaming, her eyes darting frantically round the room as she searched for a means of escape. He was between her and the door to the landing. Her back was against the French door that led onto the balcony. She could feel the key digging into her. But even if she could reach behind her, turn it in the lock without Malcolm realising what she was doing, the only way from the balcony was the long drop onto the concrete path below.

He put his hand up and she flinched, tensing for a blow, but instead he reached out and stroked her hair. 'We can still be a family, Diane,' he whispered. 'You, me and Thomas. And the baby.' His hand moved down so that it was resting on her stomach and she felt the child inside her shift, as if it, too, was shrinking from his murderous touch. 'We've both done things we regret. But we can forgive each other, can't we? Make a fresh start, like we promised?'

Her fingers closed around the key and she arched her back slightly so that she had room to manoeuvre it in the lock. Maybe if she could get out there, and screamed for help, she could attract the attention of a passer-by. In the cot, Thomas had begun to cry, not used to being so ignored. The noise concealed the click as the key turned. But even as she pulled down the handle and felt the door give, she knew how hopeless the plan was; the house was set too far back from the road. Who would hear her?

She forced herself to meet Malcolm's gaze, forced her teeth to stop chattering as she said steadily, 'Maybe we should go downstairs and talk about it. Thomas is hungry. We don't want to upset him. He needs his lunch.'

Malcolm's face hardened. He withdrew his hand. 'How do I know I can trust you? What's to stop you calling the police the minute my back's turned?'

'What good would that do me?' Her brain was racing. The baby shifted again, urging her to fight for their survival. She forced herself to take his hand and press it back against her stomach. 'What's done is done. Neither of us can put the clocks back.'

She saw disbelief seep into his eyes and knew she'd over-played it. He might be insane, but he wasn't stupid; he knew she'd never forgive Ian's murderer so easily. 'I'll lose every-thing if you go to prison. Do you think I'd be allowed to keep Thomas once it's known I'm not related to him?'

Malcolm's expression wavered. For an instant, he glanced back towards the cot. She tried to judge the distance to the door. But his gaze was back on her too soon.

'He'd go back into care,' she ploughed on desperately. 'Be brought up thinking his father was a criminal. Do you suppose I can bear the thought of that any more than you can?'

Slowly, he shook his head, his eyes still doubtful.

'We could move away. Abroad, if you like. Somewhere near the sea.' She ran her tongue over her dry lips. 'The children would like that.'

'The children,' he repeated with a tiny smile.

Thomas's sobs were reaching a crescendo as he rattled the bars of the cot in his own effort to escape.

Malcolm turned towards him again. 'Don't cry. Daddy's here. Everything's going to be . . .'

Diane seized her chance. Pushing Malcolm away from her with all her strength, she made a frantic dash for the landing. Her fingers closed round the handle and she pulled the door open with a sob. Glimpsed the stairs that led to safety, the telephone waiting for her call to the police, before the door was slammed shut and Malcolm dragged her back into the room.

'You bitch.' He yanked her arm up behind her back, so that it felt as if it were being torn from its socket.

The sweat poured down her face. She clenched her teeth against the pain that seared through her shoulder. 'Do you think the police are going to buy another death in this family?'

'You're depressed.' He was forcing her back towards the French window. Vainly, one-handedly, she made a grab for the chest of drawers to anchor herself. 'Baker's going to understand what a strain you've been under. Especially when he knows you were carrying the baby of the man who murdered Ian.' He was panting with effort as he dragged her, struggling, across the room. 'Who could blame you for wanting to end it all?'

'You'll never get away with it,' she gasped, but she knew he would. She'd hardly been out of the house for months; no one would question his story that she'd been getting more depressed, less able to cope with every day that passed; Lorraine Newbould would be only too eager to testify to that. Chas was the only one who might suspect, and he was far too deeply implicated himself to rock Malcolm's boat.

She tried to cling onto the cot, but Malcolm dragged her away with another agonising jerk to her arm. Thomas's screams were becoming more and more frantic. The struggle was terrifying him. But in a day, a week, a month, it would be gone, as all recollection of Arden Hall was gone. The only witness to her murder was too young to retain any memory that she had ever lived.

She was becoming exhausted with the effort of fighting. Dizzy with the struggle of sucking air into her constricted lungs, she knew she was close to blacking out. Maybe it would be better just to let go. Maybe Ian had been guiding her hand when she'd unlocked the door onto the balcony, as if in readiness. Maybe he was waiting for her somewhere, willing her to hurtle into oblivion and join him.

The baby kicked fiercely inside her, a life extinguished before it had started if she didn't fight for its existence.

Sobbing for breath, she made one last, desperate effort to free herself. But Malcolm's grip was too strong. He too was fighting for his survival, and he had much greater physical strength on his side. Grunting with effort, he pinioned her to him and threw himself against the French window.

It gave easily under his weight.

Far more easily than he had expected.

Diane glimpsed the startled expression on his face as the unlocked door flew open; heard his small cry of surprise as he loosened his grip on her arm and flailed at the handrail in an effort to regain his balance.

She hadn't the energy left to push him very hard.

She watched the split second of horror in his eyes as he fell backwards, the terror of realisation as the flimsy wooden spindles of the balcony gave way beneath his weight. She felt the frantic scrabble of his fingers as he reached out and tried to grab her arm. To save himself? To take her with him? With the last vestiges of her strength, she pushed him away from her.

The thin scream seemed to last for ever until he hit the path below. She didn't look down; she didn't need to. The sickening thud of hair and flesh and bone on concrete told her all she needed to know. For what seemed an eternity, she leant against the door frame, her eyes closed, her hands cradling her belly as the baby heaved and settled itself. Then she turned back towards the nursery and Thomas, and whispered soothingly, 'Don't worry, little one. Aunty Di's here.'

38

She has never felt so utterly spent. Every muscle of her body aches with exhaustion. But there's exhilaration too; the knowledge that they've travelled a painful, dangerous journey together and have survived it, safe and unscathed. A voice floats down to her from a long way off, telling her to relax, but she's too tired to listen to it for long. She nods, her eyes already closing. It's over. At last she can sleep.

She dreams of Ian. They're children again, chasing each other through trees. Ian has a balloon. His legs are shorter, but they're faster, too. He's getting further and further away from her, the balloon held above his head in triumph. And suddenly it isn't a game any more. She wants the balloon; wants it with all her heart. Further and further he runs into the trees, until she can barely see him, and still she runs, every sinew straining to catch him as she stumbles over roots and snags her hair on overhanging branches. The carpet of leaves seems to suck her feet downwards, so that every step is maddeningly slow. Somewhere in the back of her mind, she knows it is just a dream.

She comes to an opening in the trees, but Ian is nowhere to be seen. She looks around, calling his name, and suddenly he's there in front of her, so close she can reach out and touch him.

She looks at him and smiles. 'I thought you'd gone.'

His face is sad. 'Take it.' He holds the balloon out to her.

But the string slips through her fingers. The balloon sails up into the sky. Frantic, she jumps up to catch it. Her fingertips close round the trailing string as it floats out of reach, and she pulls it back down towards her.

'It's safe. I've saved it for you.' Laughing, she turns back to Ian. But he has vanished.

'Wake up, Mrs Middleton.'

Gradually, the bobbing balloon translates itself into David Fawcett's smiling face. 'Thomas would like to meet his new sister, if you feel up to it,' he beams.

Diane goes home the following morning; she's been away from Thomas too long already. The next day, a photographer comes from the *Evening Telegraph*. The evening after that, the headline trumpets from the front page: '*Tragic Widow's Moment of Joy.*'

Diane doesn't want to read it, but she knows she must. She'll get a scrapbook to put it in; their own private history book. The article tells the story of the unsolved murders at Arden Hall. The tragic fall that's robbed baby Thomas of his beloved uncle. Diane finds some nail scissors and carefully cuts it out of the paper, ready to put in her scrapbook.

The photograph shows a beaming Thomas, his arm round Diane's neck as she cradles the baby in her arms.

Agnes bustles in with flowers: a vast bunch of pink roses from the Newboulds. She puts them on the dressing-table next to the flowers that have already come. From Win Keilly. From George Bonham. From the staff at Somerford and Newbould. There's a teddy bear from Baker and the boys at the station, a card from Tracey Collingwood. Everyone's so pleased to know something good has happened, at last.

Diane looks down at the newspaper cutting. A million times

in the weeks since Malcolm's death, she's asked herself if she should have told the truth. There are so many ghosts whose deaths have gone unavenged.

Thomas appears round the door, his face smeared with chocolate. She smiles at him.

Agnes hoists him up so that he can gaze down at the puckered, sleeping face in the cot. It's so wonderful, the way he's taken to his baby sister. It reminds Diane of how she was with Ian. She watches her children and her throat constricts with tears, but she mustn't cry. It isn't going to be a household of tears. She leans over and lifts Ina from the crib. There's too much to smile about for tears.

Agnes studies Ina's sleeping face, the mop of dark curls so heartbreakingly like her father's.

'Malcolm would be so proud,' she says. 'She's the spit of her daddy.' She pulls Thomas onto her lap and gives him a fierce squeeze. 'Just like you're the spit of your daddy, my darling.'

Diane smiles as she looks at them fondly, these three people who are all she has left in the world.

Her mother, who sees what she wants to see; hears what she wants to hear.

Her children, for whom she will carry the truth with her to her own grave. Sometimes, she's afraid the burden will be too great. But who is there to share it?

She'll love her daughter as much as she'll love her adopted son, for the individuals they are, for the people they will become. She hopes it will be enough for them.

That, and the blessing of the fathers they will never know.